P9-EMR-593

MYSTERIES OF COVE

Other Books by J. Scott Savage

Mysteries of Cove series

Fires of Invention

Farworld series

Water Keep

Land Keep

Air Keep

Fire Keep

Case File #13 series

Zombie Kid

Making the Team

Evil Twins

Curse of the Mummy's Uncle

J. SCOTT SAVAGE

Visit us at ShadowMountain.com

All characters in this book are fictitious, and any resemblance to actual persons, living or dead, is purely coincidental.

Library of Congress Cataloging-in-Publication Data

Names: Savage, J. Scott (Jeffrey Scott), 1963– author. | Savage, J. Scott (Jeffrey Scott), 1963–. Mysteries of Cove ; bk. 2.

Title: Gears of revolution / J. Scott Savage.

Description: Salt Lake City, Utah : Shadow Mountain, [2016] | Series: Mysteries of Cove ; book 2 | Summary: Trenton and Kallista travel to a steampunk version of Seattle hoping to find Kallista's missing father, but instead find themselves in the middle of a war between the Order of the Beast, who worships dragons, and the Whipjacks, who are building weapons to destroy the animals.

Identifiers: LCCN 2016013360 | ISBN 9781629722238 (hardbound : alk. paper)

Subjects: | CYAC: War—Fiction. | Seattle (Wash.)—Fiction. | Dragons—Fiction. | Technology—Fiction. | LCGFT: Steampunk fiction. | Fantasy fiction. | Action and adventure fiction.

Classification: LCC PZ7.S25897 Ge 2016 | DDC [Fic]—dc23

LC record available at https://lccn.loc.gov/2016013360

Printed in the United States of America

Edwards Brothers Malloy, Ann Arbor, MI

10 9 8 7 6 5 4 3 2 1

When I was growing up, librarians were my superheroes.
This is for the wonderful women and men of books
who change the world every day.

"It does not do to leave a live dragon out of your calculations, if you live near him."

—The Hobbit *by J.R.R. Tolkien*

1

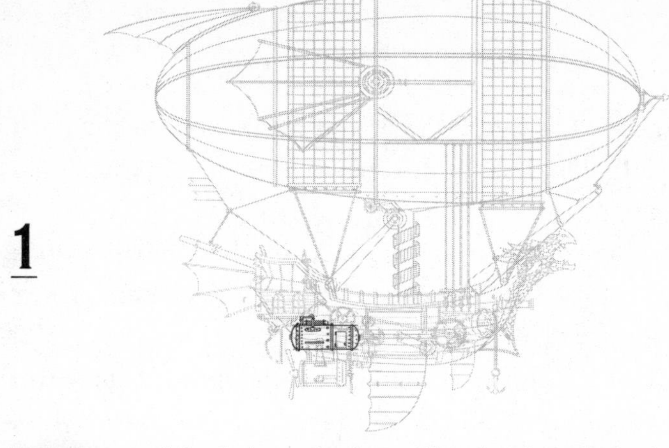

Trenton lifted the side flap of his leather flight helmet, and a blast of mountain air instantly made his exposed ear go numb. He bent his head over the side of Ladon, the flying mechanical dragon he and Kallista had built, trying to locate the source of the sound he was almost sure he'd heard a moment earlier.

Kallista, seated in front of him, scanned the air behind them, her eyes wide and shoulders hunched.

"It's not a dragon," Trenton said, anticipating her worry. During their first week outside the mountain, they'd spotted two or three of the monsters every day. Fortunately, all of the sightings had been from a distance, and they'd been able to dive into the cover of trees before they were spotted.

Since then, they'd discovered the creatures were most active from noon to evening. By only flying at night and in the mornings, they were able to avoid them for the most part. Still, the sun had been up for several hours, and it was probably time to find a safe place to hide until nightfall.

Kallista's shoulders relaxed even as her eyes narrowed in the skeptical expression Trenton had grown all too used to. "Still think you're hearing *music*?"

Trenton gripped the control sticks in front of him tightly with his gloved hands. "I didn't say it was *music*." The truth was, he didn't know what the sound was or if there had really been any sound at all. He thought he'd heard a kind of tinkling. Like glass, or metal, or—

"Maybe there's a group of musicians hiding in the woods playing a waltz." Kallista lifted the earflap of her helmet and grinned. "Oh, yes, I can hear it too. Isn't that a flute?"

"Turn around and look where you're flying," Trenton snapped, trying to pretend her words didn't sting. The two of them got along much better now than when they had first met, but there were still times when they grated on each other like the connecting rods of an unoiled crankshaft.

Kallista yanked her helmet down, the smile disappearing from her lips. "I *was* looking where I was going. You were the one who was staring down into the trees looking for imaginary musicians. You should be watching for dragons or looking for signs of my father."

She thought she was the boss just because her father had designed the dragon. Maybe she'd forgotten that if it wasn't for Trenton, they would never have discovered the turbine engines and never have gotten off the ground.

"Keep an eye on the pressure gauge," Kallista shouted at him without turning around.

Keep an eye on your own gauges, Trenton thought but didn't say.

Leo Babbage had intentionally designed the dragon so that it took two people to fly it. Trenton controlled elevation, the tail, fireballs, and most things relating to the engine and boiler. Kallista handled steering and the dragon's legs, head, and neck.

Just because she steered didn't mean she was in charge, though. They were supposed to be a team.

He glared at the back of her head before checking the

pressure gauge that monitored the buildup of steam inside Ladon's boiler.

It actually *was* a little high. The needle had moved several lines into the red. Instead of coal, they were burning wood that they'd collected from the forest floor.

Wood was much easier to find than coal, but the burn rate varied greatly from one chunk to the next. In just a few minutes, the pressure in the boiler could jump from safe to highly dangerous. If it got too high . . . Well, that wasn't something he wanted to think about.

Focused on opening the release valve, he barely noticed a flash of light out of the corner of his eye. Sunlight reflecting off something to the south glinted once, twice, then disappeared. It seemed to have come from a clearing a mile or two away, but despite studying the rocks and trees, he couldn't find it again. "Did you see that?"

"See what?"

Trenton opened his mouth to ask Kallista to circle around for a closer look, then thought better of it. What was the point? It was probably just water or a shiny chunk of rock.

Besides, she'd probably reply with another snide remark. *Maybe it was your band again. A trumpet reflecting the sun.* After eight hours in the air, he didn't need any more of that.

As he turned away from the clearing, a shadow dropped over his shoulder. He looked up, expecting to see a cloud. Instead, he found himself staring straight into the gold eyes of a deadly red dragon no more than one hundred yards above them. Sunlight glittered off the beast's crimson scales as it cut through the air toward them.

"Watch out!" he screamed to Kallista.

Drawing back its sinewy neck, the dragon roared and dove toward them.

Ramming the lever on his right as far forward as it would go, Trenton sent Ladon plunging toward the ground, the red dragon following closely behind.

Kallista's head snapped left, and her eyes went wide. Surprised as she was, though, her reflexes were as sharp as a blade. At the same time the dragon opened its huge, fang-filled mouth, Kallista yanked the flight controls hard to the right.

Trenton ducked his head, expecting a ball of flames. Instead a thick yellow cloud spewed from between the dragon's jaws. Kallista's maneuver meant they'd avoided almost all of the cloud, but a few droplets beaded on the sleeve of Trenton's jacket. Everywhere the liquid touched, the leather bubbled and foamed.

Yelping, Trenton wiped his sleeve on Ladon's metal skin. The yellow drops fizzed, marking the metal, before disappearing.

"What is that?" Kallista shouted.

"Some kind of acid," Trenton yelled back.

Correcting its course, the red dragon closed in on them again. Less than twenty feet above the forest, Trenton searched for an opening to fly into, but the treetops were too dense to break through.

Behind them, the monster roared and shot another stream of yellow acid.

Almost as if they were a machine themselves, Trenton pulled back on his controls at the same time Kallista turned hard left. Cutting up and around, they circled toward the beast. For just a moment, the red dragon was in their sights. Kallista turned Ladon's head, and Trenton mashed the fire button with his fist.

A ball of flame blasted from Ladon's mouth. It hit the red dragon, and the acid cloud around its head exploded in an inferno, fire shooting everywhere.

"The yellow stuff burns!" Trenton whooped. He hit the fire button again, but the dragon changed course, avoiding his shot.

Kallista pushed up her goggles and twisted around to get a better view. "Banking left," she called, pulling the controls.

Understanding what she had in mind, Trenton dropped Ladon a little before pulling up sharply.

The red dragon reacted to their maneuver, but not quickly enough.

Rising under its exposed belly, Trenton pounded the fire button three times in quick succession. A volley of flames scorched the beast between its front legs. Screaming in anger and—Trenton hoped—pain, the dragon banked away.

Watching the way it turned, Trenton realized something. "It can't maneuver as quickly as the green dragon."

"It's not as nimble," Kallista agreed.

The green dragon they had killed in the attack on Cove had been more flexible than Ladon. It had responded to their attacks so quickly they'd been unable to gain an advantage until the very end. But the red dragon needed more room to turn and reacted less quickly.

"It's faster, though," Trenton warned as the dragon sped toward them.

Kallista yanked her goggles back over her eyes and gave a wicked grin. "Let's use that against it," she called, pointing upward.

Trenton pulled back on the flight stick, and they climbed swiftly into the air. As the dragon rose after them, Kallista steered left and right, bobbing about like a loose wheel. Close behind, the dragon screamed, spitting one cloud of acid after another. Puffs of steaming liquid filled the air around them, but Trenton and Kallista easily avoided the clouds.

Still, the red dragon was closing in. They'd flown so high

that Ladon's wings strained to climb in the thin air. "We have to drop!" Trenton shouted.

Kallista watched the red dragon point its scaled snout toward them. "Not yet."

Trenton clutched the controls, staring backward in terror as the beast opened its huge jaws. Tendrils of yellow smoke trailed from its nostrils.

"Hold on," Kallista ordered. "Wait . . . Wait . . ."

Eyes bright, the dragon howled and shot a stream of acid directly at them.

"Now!" Kallista shouted.

Trenton pushed the control forward with his right hand, sending them into a neck-snapping dive. At the same time, he began to retract Ladon's wings with his left hand. The result was immediate. Ladon plummeted toward the trees below like a stone.

Screeching in frustration, the dragon tucked in its own broad wings and dove after them.

Rushing wind pressed Trenton's goggles against his face as he searched for an opening in the trees. But the forest below them was a sea of solid green, the clearing he thought he'd seen more than a mile away. Trenton pointed toward the opening. It was far away, but it might be their only chance.

Kallista shook her head, strands of her black hair escaping from her helmet and slapping her face. She pointed toward the rapidly approaching treetops with one gloved finger.

What was she thinking? Trenton stared down at the forest wondering if he'd missed an opening. Nothing. Diving into the trees would rip them to shreds. He reached for the controls to pull them out of their free fall, but Kallista pointed down at the forest again, then up at the dragon closing in.

Following her gesture, Trenton's mouth dropped open. "Are you crazy?"

Kallista's lips rose in a maniacal grin that stretched from ear to ear.

Trenton's gaze bounced from the dragon to the trees, wondering which danger would tear them to bits first. There was no doubt Kallista was impulsive. She'd made that abundantly clear from the first time they'd met. The question was, would he go along with her madness?

Clenching his jaws, he made his decision. Trenton pointed Ladon toward the biggest tree he could find. He swore he heard Kallista cackle as she adjusted their course, aiming them directly toward the tree.

Just as they were about to be crushed between the dragon behind them and the trees below, Trenton spread Ladon's wings and pulled back on the flight stick. Ladon's entire frame groaned.

Slammed into his seat as Ladon fought to break out of the dive, Trenton watched the entire sky disappear behind glittering red scales. Kallista banked hard. Branches snapped all around them. A dark green bough caught Trenton across the side of the head, and for a second he thought he was going to pass out.

The branches tugged and slapped, threatening to yank them out of the air. Then they were out of the trees, nothing ahead of them but clear blue sky.

Behind them, the red dragon let out a howl of fury as it crashed into the trees with a terrific cracking of wood and scales.

"Yes!" Kallista whooped, pumping her fist in the air.

Trenton gawked at the hole in the trees, not quite sure how they hadn't been taken down with the dragon. Sweat soaked the inside of his helmet, and the flight controls chattered in his grip.

Kallista circled toward where the dragon had crashed to get a better look, an elated grin on her face.

"What are you doing?" Trenton yelled. "Let's get out of here."

"I just want to make sure it's dead."

"Are you kidding?" Trenton pounded his fist against the side of the dragon. "The sun's been up for hours. We've got to find cover."

Still grinning, Kallista steered them to the opening where Trenton thought he'd seen the flash of light earlier. With practiced ease, they glided to the rocky ground and came to a running stop under cover of several large trees. As soon as Ladon's legs had stopped moving, Kallista yanked off her goggles and threw her helmet into the air.

"Did you see that? Rust! That old dragon smashed through the trees like a rod through an overheated engine."

"We nearly got smashed too," Trenton said, trying to catch his breath.

Kallista went on like she hadn't even heard him. "It was amazing! We should do it again. Let's go back and see if it's still alive. We can fly through the trees, open Ladon's talons, and—"

"What are you talking about?" Trenton yelled. "We are *not* going back."

Kallista stared at him as if she couldn't believe what she was hearing.

"Don't you know how close we came to dying back there?" Trenton asked.

Kallista snorted. She tugged her gloves off and set them beside her on the seat. "Coward," she muttered.

Trenton leaned forward. "What did you call me?"

Before Kallista could answer, Ladon began to shake. Just below Trenton's left leg, a crack appeared and steam hissed out. He looked down at the pressure gauge and saw the needle had risen all the way to the end of the dial. He reached for the release valve, but it was too late. Below them, bolts popped like buttons on the front of an overstretched shirt.

The steam tanks screeched as the metal twisted, and Trenton knew what was about to happen. "Jump!" he screamed, grabbing Kallista's hand.

Together the two of them leaped from the dragon just as the boiler exploded behind them.

2

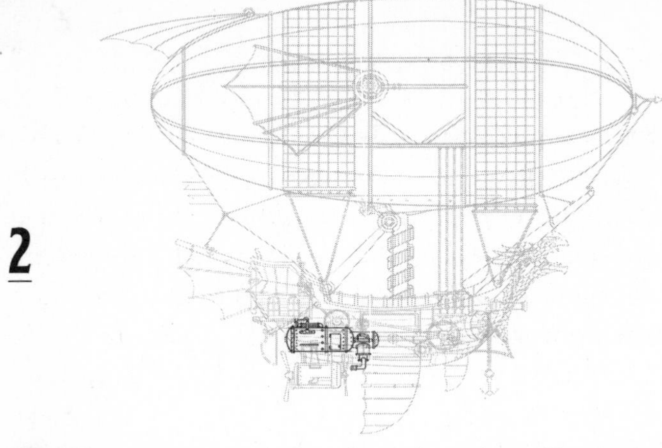

Balancing on one of Ladon's front legs, Trenton grabbed for the wrench. "Let me take care of that."

Kallista refused to release the tool. "I can do it quicker," she said without turning around from loosening the pipe she was working on. She spun off the fitting and pulled away a section of metal that looked like it had been twisted by a giant's hands. With a grunt, she tossed the pipe to the ground.

Her eyes were narrow slits, and a deep line etched the middle of her forehead. Trenton's throat tightened as he looked at the growing pile of broken and bent pieces. Back at the factory, they could have had Ladon back in shape in no time. But here in the woods, with only the most basic tools . . . He shook his head.

"It's my fault," he said. "All the more reason to let me fix it."

Kallista set the wrench down and wiped a greasy hand across her cheek. "No. It's not."

"Of course it is." Trenton's voice rose. He kicked the metal framework, the thud unnaturally loud in the quiet of the deep woods. "I broke it. I'll repair it."

Kallista blew out a long, slow breath and faced him. "It's *not* your fault."

"I . . ." Trenton began, ready to argue, before realizing what she had just said. "What do you mean? Of course it's my fault."

Kallista ran her fingers over the dragon's buckled metal

skin. "There was no way you could have monitored the pressure gauge *and* fought off the dragon at the same time. If anything, it was my fault for pushing the engine too far. I could have found another way to escape. I was . . ." She pushed a lock of hair out of her face and blinked. "I was showing off." Her eyes glistened.

Trenton leaned forward, looking at her more closely. Were those tears? Was what he'd taken for anger actually sadness? He'd seen Kallista show many emotions, but never anything quite like this. He wasn't sure how to react.

Gently he touched her arm. "I'm sure we can find a way to fix things."

Kallista gave a strangled laugh, and Trenton was more confused than ever.

"Of course we can fix it," she said, rubbing her eyes with the back of one hand. "My father was the best inventor of all time. He knew this kind of thing might happen, so he designed the boiler to come apart if the pressure got too high."

Trenton scratched his neck. Were all girls this hard to figure out? He hadn't been very good at understanding Simoni either back when the two of them had been working together. He wished his friend Clyde were there to translate. Clyde seemed to understand girls.

"So . . . you're not mad at me?" he ventured.

She shrugged. "No more than usual."

"And you aren't worried about fixing the dragon?"

"No."

Okay, at least that was something. "But you *are* upset. Right?"

Kallista rolled her eyes. "And I thought my father was bad with people." She squeezed the bridge of her nose between her fingers, squinting up at the sky. "Yes. I am upset. And sad. And frustrated. Anything else you want to know? My blood type or maybe my favorite food?"

"Cheese," Trenton said instantly.

Kallista looked at him and blinked.

"Whenever we were working on the dragon, you gobbled up any fresh cheese I brought from the food production level," Trenton explained.

Kallista snorted.

At least it brought the hint of a smile to her face. He wondered if he should leave her alone for a while and see if she felt better when he returned. Sometimes when he got stuck working on a machine, he'd step away for a while and see if things looked different with fresh eyes when he came back.

Instead, he balled his gloved hands and asked, "If you're not mad at me, what are you mad at?"

"Myself," Kallista said, the line appearing in her forehead again. "We've been searching for ten days, and we haven't found a single sign of my father."

Trenton relaxed, glad it wasn't his fault. Then he felt guilty for having thought that. Kallista's father meant everything to her. He was the reason the two of them had started following the clues that led them to build the dragon in the first place.

"Don't blame yourself," he said. "The problem is that we have no idea what we're looking for." He pulled off his goggles and fiddled with the lenses. "Maybe he didn't leave any clues behind. Maybe he just, you know, started exploring."

"He wouldn't do that," Kallista said at once. "He wants me to find him. That's the whole reason he left the letters. He knew we'd build the dragon and come after him once we saved the city."

That seemed like a pretty big stretch, even for a man as smart as Leo Babbage, but Trenton knew better than to mention it. "We've searched all around the mountain. If he left some kind of clue, we'd have found it by now."

"That's not the way the game works," Kallista said. "The clues aren't always obvious. Sometimes you can look right at them without even realizing they're there. I should have found it by now, though. I'm not trying hard enough."

When Kallista was little, she and her father had played a game. He'd leave clues for her to follow. When she solved them, she'd find a prize. She'd told Trenton all about it when they'd been searching for the pieces of the dragon.

The thing was, life wasn't a game. Trenton just wasn't sure Kallista understood that. He hesitated to say what he was thinking, but at some point they needed to face the facts.

"Maybe your father *couldn't* leave you any clues," he said, worried he'd upset her even more. He glanced back to where the red dragon had crashed into the woods. "Maybe something happened to him once he left the city."

Kallista picked up the wrench and slapped it against the palm of her hand. "That's what I'm afraid of."

• • •

An hour later, Kallista was still working on Ladon. She leaned inside the boiler so far only her feet and lower legs were visible.

Trenton kicked at a small patch of ice tucked beneath the roots of a tree. While the mountains were still white, here in the valley the snow was almost completely gone. One of the things he already missed about Cove—or, rather, Discovery; it would take some time to get used to the new name—was how consistent the temperature was. Outside it could go from warm sun to icy rain in minutes.

"Okay. So I guess I'll go for a walk or something? Do some exploring?" Trenton looked up at Kallista, but she didn't show any sign she'd heard him. "Maybe I'll track down a bear and wrestle its fur off. You know, for a blanket?"

Still no response.

Sighing, he tucked his gloves into his coat pockets and headed off into the trees. He understood that Kallista needed her space. She'd spent so much time by herself or with only her socially awkward father for company that she wasn't used to being around other people for long periods. She started to get cranky when she didn't get enough alone time.

Trenton totally understood that. He felt the same way more often than he wanted to admit. He was much more at home around machines than people. When he was tightening and adjusting things, he felt more like himself. Give him a sputtering engine and he could break it down and figure out what was wrong with it in no time. If only emotions could be adjusted as easily as gears and springs.

Once again, he wished Clyde were there to give him advice.

"I realize working on machinery helps her unwind," he said, pretending his friend was walking beside him. "The thing is, it helps me too. I don't see why we can't both work on the dragon."

Trenton kicked a pinecone down a small hill, sending it bounding into the shadows, while imaginary Clyde stuffed a roll into his mouth and nodded sagely.

"She doesn't want to admit it, but if we don't find some sign of her father soon, we'll probably have to go back to the mountain."

Clyde rubbed his chin as though weighing that option.

Trying not to slip on the carpet of thick brown needles, Trenton made his way down the hill. The exercise warmed him up, and he unbuttoned his coat and tied it around his waist. He scratched a bug bite on the back of his arm and winced at the pain that shot across his red skin. "One thing I didn't expect about being outside is that the sun actually burns your skin if you leave it exposed too long."

Clyde, who had somehow found a plate of cheese, chewed a square of cheddar and raised his eyebrows in surprised wonder.

"Just between you and me," Trenton said, lowering his voice, "being outside kind of scares me. At first you're like, 'Wow, look at the sun and the sky.' It's sort of exciting knowing you can go anywhere you want. Then you start to realize there are no walls, no protection. Sure, you can go anywhere, but you have no idea where you're going or how far away it is.

"Even worse, anything can come at you from any direction. Bugs, animals, *dragons*! And you don't even want to hear about the weather. Water falls from the sky, but sometimes it's frozen. With no warning."

Something crashed in the distance, and he stopped quickly, remembering the red dragon.

Imaginary Clyde vanished with a frown.

The dragon was probably dead after that fall. But what if it wasn't? What if it was only wounded? And what if it smelled him and Kallista and was tracking them even now?

"Maybe we should go back." Trenton's voice sounded much too loud in the stillness. He glanced around, wondering exactly how far he'd walked. "I'm going back," he whispered, trying to keep his voice from trembling. "To check on Kallista."

As Trenton turned to climb up the hill, he spotted a flash of light through an opening in the trees. Standing perfectly still, he let his gaze wander through the forest until he could pinpoint the source of the light. It was coming from a ridge just beyond the edge of the tree line.

He glanced at the sky. It was well after noon. The dragons would be out hunting. He should get back to camp—now. Still, the glinting light tugged at his curiosity like a string attached directly to the center of his brain.

Maybe for a minute. Only until he saw what was making the light.

Sticking close to the trees until he had reached the edge of the woods, he studied the side of the mountain. The light was definitely coming from the ridge. It flashed and moved like someone holding a mirror. But he didn't see anyone.

"Hello!" he yelled. "Is someone there?"

The only response was his own voice bouncing off the side of the mountain. *Get back to Kallista,* he chided himself. *It's probably just a smooth piece of granite or a chunk of crystal. It's not worth risking your life.*

Only, if it was light reflecting off rock, why was it moving? It had to be the same light he'd seen flashing earlier. But how could he have seen it from the air so far to the north and also from down here?

After checking the sky to make sure no dragons were in sight, he took a deep breath and dashed out into the open. Rocks tumbled down the slope behind him as he scrambled toward the ridge. He was afraid to take his eyes off the reflection for fear he'd lose the spot, but he knew he had to watch for dragons, too. He was far enough from the cover of the trees that he'd never make it back if one of the keen-eyed monsters spotted him.

At last he pulled himself onto the outcropping and sighed.

It was nothing.

A pool of water collected in a natural basin reflected the sunlight onto an especially smooth wall of rock. What a waste of time. He could only imagine what Kallista would say if she discovered what he'd done.

He kicked a rock into the basin, then paused as the stone

sank to the bottom. There was something odd about the pool. It was almost perfectly circular. Looking closer, he saw areas along the edge where the rock appeared to have been cut, shaped. And the water seemed to reflect the light more than it should.

He dropped to his knees, reached into the pool, and pulled out a handful of bits of crystal. Mica, he thought it was called. There were hundreds of the shiny rocks spread evenly over the bottom of the pool. What were the odds of that happening naturally?

Sunlight bounced off the water and danced on the wall of rock above it. Trenton's heart danced with it. He ran his wet hand along the wall behind the pool, noticing how smooth it was. Not just smooth, *polished.* A perfect mirror reflecting the light of the water. Light flashed and swayed as the wind blew across the surface of the pool.

The basin and the rock wall were clearly a natural occurrence, but the rest of it? That wasn't a coincidence or a simple oddity of nature. Someone had intentionally created a signal that, when the sun was right, could be seen for miles. But who? And why?

3

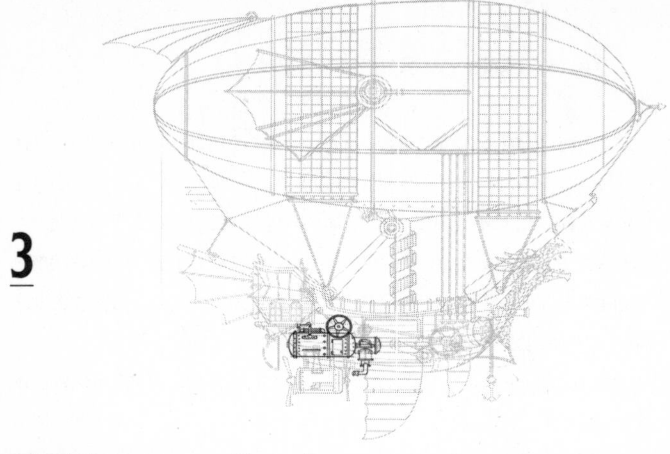

Kallista was still working on Ladon when Trenton returned to camp. As soon as he told her about the pool, though, she demanded that he take her there.

The wind wailed in the trees, and Trenton checked the sky. There were a handful of black shadows flying in a lazy circle in the distance. "Maybe we should wait until this evening."

"You might not be able to find it in the dark." Kallista pushed past Trenton.

"You don't even know where you're going," Trenton said, following her.

She whirled to face him, a wrench still in her hand, her cheeks flushed. "Then show me. It's a clue from my father. I know it is. This is exactly the kind of thing we've been looking for."

Trenton wasn't so sure. He'd searched the pool and the rocks around it for any kind of sign or message without any luck. But she was already heading toward the mountain, and he had to hurry to catch up. "For all we know, someone else could have made it."

"Have you seen a single person since we left Discovery?" Kallista asked.

She was right. They'd spotted deer, squirrels, even a fox, and, of course, plenty of dragons. But no other people. Unfortunately, he was pretty sure the abundance of dragons and the lack of people were directly related.

Keeping one eye on the flying shadows in the distance, he led Kallista back to the ridge. She knelt by the side of the pool and stretched her hand over the water, watching as the sunlight cast the shadow of her fingers on the wall. A small spring trickled water into the basin, keeping it constantly full. Long-legged bugs skittered over the blue surface.

"This was cut recently," she said, pointing to the same lighter rocks around the edges that Trenton had noted. "It appears that the spring was here all along. But he shaped it and filled it with the crystals to reflect the light better." She turned and looked out over the valley. "This is the perfect spot to create a signal. I'm surprised we didn't notice it from the air."

Trenton decided not to mention that he actually *had* noticed it. "What's the point, though? Why bring us here?"

"No idea," Kallista said. "But I'm going to find out." She ran her fingers through the rocks at the bottom of the pool, stirring them around. When nothing came of that, she moved to the polished wall, muttering, "What's the next clue? Where did you hide it?"

Somewhere deeper in the woods an animal screamed, and Trenton stared at the shadows in the sky, shading his eyes with one hand. Dragons were meat eaters. He and Kallista had seen plenty of them carrying the local wildlife clutched in their talons. If a dragon was hunting nearby, it could rise out of the trees at any minute and spot the two of them standing unprotected on the side of the mountain.

He listened intently, straining to determine where the scream had come from. The wind picked up, whistling through the branches of the pines below them, and he heard something. It wasn't a dragon, though; it was a sound he'd heard several times before while they were flying over the woods. A faint tinkling, like a chime, or bells, or . . .

"No," he muttered. He was not going to tell Kallista he was hearing music again.

The wind grew stronger, and with it, the sound increased.

Kallista stopped searching and turned. "What is that?"

"*You* hear it too?" Trenton asked.

Kallista tilted her head. "It sounds like *music.*" Before Trenton could enjoy the satisfaction of an "I told you so," she darted down the side of the mountain. "This way," she called, racing into the woods.

It was hard to track down exactly where the music was coming from. The sound seemed to carry on the wind, bounding from tree to tree like a bird in flight. Every time the wind stopped, Trenton and Kallista paused, heads cocked as they waited for the music to begin again.

"What do you think it is?" Trenton whispered.

"I feel like I should know. But . . ." Kallista pressed her fist against her forehead, concentrating.

After nearly an hour of searching, the tinkling was so close Trenton felt like it had to be right in front of them. Maddeningly, the wind stopped just as he was sure they were about to find whatever was making the sound.

Kallista shifted from one foot to another as though she could force the wind to blow by sheer determination, but the woods remained still.

Trenton tilted his head back. Maybe the air was moving higher up. His eyes traced the trunk of the nearest tree, following it up and up, until . . .

He paused, scanning up and down. Something moved in the shadows.

"Kallista," he whispered.

She glanced toward him, obviously irritated by the interruption. Then her eyes followed his upward gaze. Her mouth dropped open.

Hanging from a thick branch roughly as big around as his forearm were pieces of metal dangling on an almost invisible wire. Not just any metal either. He recognized the gold shine at once. It was the same metal they'd built Ladon from. The same gold alloy Leo Babbage had discovered.

• • •

Trenton barely breathed as Kallista slithered out onto the branch. She was close to twenty feet in the air with nothing between her and the ground if she slipped. "Be careful," he called.

"I told you I've got this," Kallista snapped, worming her way toward the thin metal cable. Trenton had offered to go up. As if that had even been a possibility. Kallista was determined to solve her father's puzzle herself. Even if she had to break a few bones to do it.

Watching from below, Trenton tried to position himself directly beneath her. He wasn't sure how much good he could do if she fell, but at least he felt like he was helping in some way.

Ankles locked around the branch, Kallista stretched out her arm until the fingers of her right hand touched the wire. The branch swayed under her weight, causing the metal pieces to chime as they clattered against each other—the *music* he'd been hearing for days.

Clearly Leo Babbage had counted on either the sound or the flashing light—or both—to lead them here. Although Trenton had no idea how the man had managed to get the wire up there in the first place.

Kallista grunted. "Almost have it. I just have to untwist the wire."

Higher in the tree, a bird chirped out a warning *cuckee-cuckee*, and the wind moaned through the branches.

Kallista inched forward. "Almost . . ."

Without any warning, the wire came loose and the pieces fell.

"Ahh!" Kallista screamed, slipping on the branch. Bits of bark showered down as she scrambled to hold on.

"I've got you!" Trenton yelled, throwing out his arms.

Hands clasped firmly around the branch above her head, Kallista hung in the air, her feet dangling. Trenton braced himself to catch her, but she only glared down at him. "Forget about me. Are the pieces all right?"

Trenton looked at his hands, realizing he must have grabbed the metal chimes when he'd reached out to catch Kallista. "Oh. Yeah, I think so."

"Good," she called down. "Don't do anything until I get there." She swung hand over hand along the branch until she reached the trunk.

Trenton watched her scurry down the tree like a squirrel after a stray nut and shook his head. She really was a maniac.

"Okay, let's see what we've got," Kallista said once she was back on the ground.

Trenton handed her the wire. Eight pieces of metal were tied to it: a gold circle nearly the size of his palm, a threaded ring that looked like it might screw onto the circle, a spindle, something that looked like the hand of a clock, and several other pieces he didn't recognize.

Kallista ran her finger over the smooth alloy. "He must have made them before he left."

Trenton nodded. "It looks like the pieces go together."

The words had barely left his mouth when Kallista charged forward and wrapped him in a bear hug. "Thank you, thank you, thank you," she chanted, spinning him in a circle.

"For what?" He laughed, feeling dizzy.

"For not giving up." Just as quickly, she released him, sending him flying to the ground.

Sitting in the dirt, Trenton gave her an amused half smile. "I've finally figured out why I can't read your emotions."

"Um-hmm," she said, focused on the metal pieces she'd taken from him.

"It's because you change from one to the next so quickly."

Kallista turned the metal circle over in her hands, examining it closely. "Look at this."

Trenton got up, brushed pine needles from the seat of his pants, and stood close to Kallista. One side of the circle was marked with a series of small lines around its entire outer edge. Every ten marks there was a number, starting at zero and going up to 350. He'd noticed them before but didn't know what they meant.

"See here," Kallista said, pointing at an elaborate letter *N* just below the zero. "It stands for north." She touched the three other letters marked on the circle: an *S* at the bottom of the circle, with a *W* and *E* on either side. "North and south, west and east—like the sections of Discovery."

Together they assembled the pieces, first screwing the ring onto the circle. They fitted the spindle into the center of the circle and tightened it in place. It took them a moment to figure out what to do with the clock hand, but then Trenton realized it fit onto the top of the spindle, allowing the needle to spin freely.

When they got done putting the mechanism together, it looked a little like a clock with a lid that opened on the top. But Trenton couldn't see how it would keep time since it had no gears or springs and only one hand.

"I recognize this," Kallista said. "My father made one for me a long time ago."

"How do you wind it?"

"You don't. It's not a clock; it shows you directions." Slowly Kallista turned the circle until the arrow pointed to the *N*. She peeked through a slit in the cover. "That way is north."

"Only because you turned it that way," Trenton scoffed. He took the contraption out of her hands and turned it so the *N* faced the opposite direction. "Now that's north."

"No, look at the arrow. No matter which way you turn the circle, the tip of the arrow always points north."

That was the silliest thing Trenton had ever heard. He turned the circle so the arrow would point another direction. The clock hand bobbed a little when he moved it, but it swung back to point in the same direction every time. He looked under the circular plate to see how it was done, but the little clock hand was moving all by itself.

"It's called a compass," Kallista said, taking it back from him. "It shows you which way you're facing."

Trenton shrugged. "What's the point? I know which way I'm facing." He pointed in front of him. "That way."

"Ha. Ha." Kallista gave a fake laugh at his joke. She hid the compass behind her back. "Which way is east?"

"It's . . ." Trenton paused, then lowered his hand. In the city it was easy to know which direction you were facing by checking the buildings around you. But here in the woods the trees all looked the same.

"How about southwest?" Kallista asked.

Trenton shook his head.

"Let's go back to the camp," she said. "I want to show you something."

4

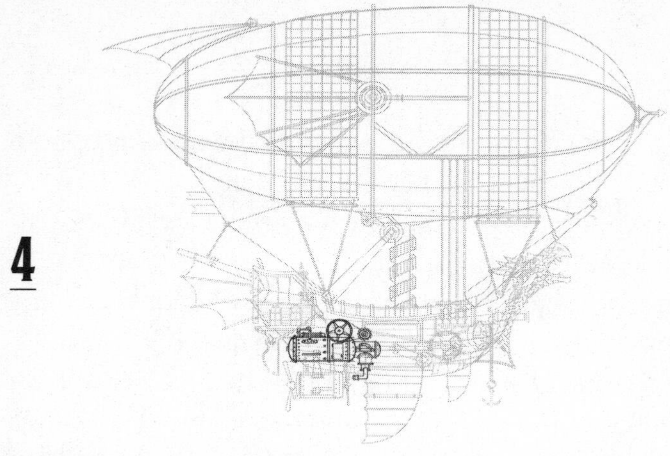

Before leaving the area, they searched around the rest of the tree, digging in the dirt at the base of the trunk and examining the bark for loose pieces or hidden messages, but there were no other clues.

As soon as they returned to camp, Kallista said, "Wait here," and climbed up Ladon. She opened the compartment where they kept all of their food, water, and belongings and came back with a leather satchel.

She flipped through the papers inside, then pulled out an old-looking sheet covered with curved lines and scribbles. "My father collected maps," Kallista said. "This one is of the outside world around our mountain." She turned the map until the *N* on the top matched the direction the compass needle pointed. She tapped a picture of a mountain near the bottom of the page. "This is Discovery."

Trenton studied the paper. It was beautiful. The blue areas must be water—rivers and lakes; the green area, forests. Triangles marked mountains. Lines snaked every which way. Trying to follow one to the end made his eyes water.

He knew the old leaders of Cove had done everything they could to keep people from even thinking about leaving the mountain where they'd sealed themselves up for protection.

Including getting rid of anything that might cause people to consider exploring the world beyond, like a map.

How much information had the leaders of Cove destroyed? How much knowledge had been lost?

"Things could have changed over the last hundred and fifty years," he warned, tapping his finger on the lines of the map.

"Some," Kallista agreed. "But mountains and rivers don't change quickly—if at all. Look," she said, pointing to a large blue area on the far left side of the map. "That's the ocean."

"The ocean," Trenton murmured. He'd learned about it in school. A body of water so vast you could travel for weeks and never reach the other side. Of course he'd also been told it was a stinking mess of pollution and disease. Just like he'd been told the air outside was unbreathable.

He now suspected it was another of the many lies the people of Cove had been fed by the old leaders. What would it be like to fly Ladon to the ocean and see it for themselves?

"What are these?" he asked, pointing at several strange words printed in various places on the map.

Kallista ran her tongue across her cracked lips. "Cities." She and Trenton stared at one another.

One thing Trenton had learned in his history classes that did seem to be true was that before the citizens of Discovery had sealed themselves inside the mountain, people had lived in cities spread around the globe. According to Trenton's teachers, the cities had been destroyed by technology and creativity. Now he knew the truth: the world had been attacked by a plague of dragons.

"Do you think any of the cities are still standing?" he asked.

"My father thought it was possible."

Trenton looked from the compass to the map. What if there were more cities like Discovery, places where people had found a way to survive? "Do you think that's where your father went? To one of these cities?"

Kallista frowned. "Maybe. But which one?"

That was the question.

"We have to be missing something," Kallista said, hurling a rock into the trees.

Trenton sat down and leaned against Ladon's leg. "We could fly to the nearest city and see if anyone has survived. Maybe that's what your father wants us to do."

"My father wouldn't have left things to chance. He left the compass because he wanted us to follow him wherever he's gone. He does everything—"

"For a reason," Trenton finished. How many times had he heard that?

Kallista scowled, clearly frustrated, and not just by Trenton's interruption.

He studied the compass. "How does this work?" There didn't seem to be any moving parts besides the clock hand that spun.

"It's called magnetism. The needle is a magnet, and the Earth is a magnet. The north pole of the Earth attracts the north end of the needle."

Trenton didn't understand half of what she'd said, but it intrigued him anyway. He lifted the lid and examined the little opening. "What does this do?"

"It's called a sight," Kallista said. "The numbers around the outside are degrees. If you know where you are on a map, you can use the sight and the degrees to figure out how to get from one place to another."

Trenton held the compass up to his eye and peered through the sight. As he lowered it, he noticed something inside the lid. "What's this?" he asked, flipping the compass upside down to see better.

Kallista sat down next to him. There were tiny letters engraved inside the rim of the compass lid. Squinting, Trenton was able to make them out.

The hour is the key.

"What does that mean?" he asked.

"It means I was right." Kallista took the compass. Hands trembling, she studied it from every angle for more clues. "My father's waiting for me. I'm going to study this until I figure out where he is." She pulled her satchel closer and took out more of her father's papers.

Trenton nodded. It *was* kind of like a game. He couldn't wait to find out what was next. "How can I help?"

Barely glancing up from the compass, Kallista said, "You can fix the dragon. Since you were the one who broke him."

• • •

By the end of the day, Trenton was more convinced than ever that Leo Babbage was a genius. What had looked like a total disaster when the boiler first blew now seemed manageable. The key pieces of the dragon—all made of alloy—had barely been touched by the explosion due to the boiler's construction. The pieces which *had* been damaged could either be hammered straight or replaced fairly easily.

As the sun began to set, he wiped his greasy hands on a rag and examined his work. He hadn't tried to fire the boiler up, but he already knew that with a few more hours of work, Ladon would be safe to fly.

It was as if Kallista's father had *expected* the boiler to blow. No, it wasn't "as if." There was no question the boiler had been designed with the expectation that at some point it would overheat. Had Leo calculated that after the dragon was built, it would be modified to burn wood and taken outside? Trenton was positive he had. And if he'd anticipated that, what else might he have planned for?

He glanced down at Kallista, who had spent the afternoon poring over Leo's maps and papers, pointing the compass in different directions and muttering to herself. She was obviously smart and a very talented mechanic, but she didn't think things through the way her father did. She was far more likely to make decisions on the spur of the moment than to calculate the kind of long-term plans Leo obviously had.

Trenton rooted through the food-storage compartment until he found cheese, bread, and a couple of apples and climbed down the dragon.

"Ready to eat?" he asked, taking hold of a metal rung and swinging himself to the ground.

Kallista held the map up to the last rays of light, stared into the distance, and grunted.

Trenton set the food on a nearby rock. "Everything okay?"

"No. Nothing's okay." She rolled up the map, shoved it and the compass into the satchel, and rubbed her eyes.

"I take it you haven't figured out the clue yet."

Kallista glared at him, her face strained and deep circles under her eyes. "I've studied all his notes, looked through his books. I was hoping the hour he mentioned had something to do with sunset. Maybe the compass or the map would have markings you could only see when the sun is going down. But it didn't work. None of it works."

"My mom always says you think more clearly when you've had something to eat."

She flopped to the ground. "I'm not hungry."

Instead of arguing with her, Trenton dug a hole in the soft forest floor, surrounded it with rocks, and, using flint and steel, started a small fire. When Kallista was in this kind of mood, talking to her didn't help. He'd learned to let her get out of her funk by herself.

Considering the depth of the hole and the ring of rocks, the fire would be unlikely to attract any dragons that might be out at night, but the flames would provide enough heat to stay warm and to cook over. When the fire was burning steadily, he stuck a couple of pieces of bread onto the tines of a forked branch, sprinkled bits of cheese over the top, and held the stick just above the flames. Soon the smell of toasting bread and melting cheese drifted through the evening air.

Kallista sniffed. She looked at the bread, then glanced across the fire at him. "That smells good."

"It probably tastes terrible." Trenton waited until the cheese was bubbling, its aroma making his mouth water, before removing the bread from the heat. "I'll let you know after I eat it." He thought he might have caught the faintest hint of a smile on her lips.

She scooted closer. "Think I could talk you into sharing?"

Trenton feigned surprise. "Share? I thought you weren't hungry."

She narrowed her eyes.

He sliced an apple while the cheese cooled enough to eat it.

"Fine. I *am* hungry. Can I have a piece?"

He tapped his fingers, and she clenched her fists.

"Please."

"Sure," he said, offering her the stick. "All you had to do was ask."

For the next few minutes, the only sound either of them made was munching and swallowing. "Another?" Trenton asked after swallowing the last bite of his toasted cheese sandwich.

"Yes, please," Kallista said around a mouthful of food.

5

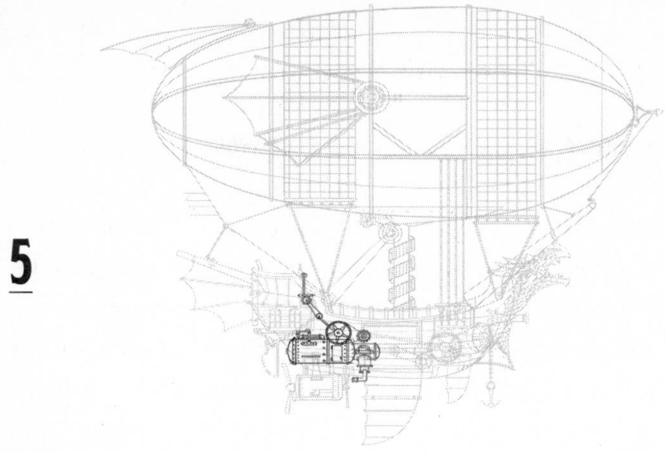

By the time they finished their meal, the sky had turned to black velvet studded with glittering diamonds that sparkled above them. Stretching out on the ground to get more comfortable, Trenton poked a twig into the fire. "What was it like having such a smart father?"

Kallista toyed with a bit of apple peel, rolling and unrolling it between her fingers. "I don't know. He taught me things I never would have learned in school. I wouldn't be half the mechanic I am if it wasn't for him." Her eyes flitted toward the leather bag with the compass in it. "Only . . ."

"What?" Trenton tapped the twig on a rock, making sparks fly, and yawned.

"Did you ever feel like you were letting your mother down?" she asked. Her eyes were hard to read in the flickering light of the flames. "Because you wanted to be a mechanic, and she . . ."

Kallista didn't finish the thought. She didn't need to.

Trenton's mother had been injured in a mining accident. He'd always viewed it as a failure of the safety equipment, even more so now that he knew there had been technology available that could have prevented the shaft walls from collapsing.

But his mother looked at it completely opposite. She blamed her crippled legs on technology. If it wasn't for machines, they wouldn't have needed to mine the coal to power the city. She believed machines were evil, and she had done everything she could to stop her son from working on them.

"I think about it all the time," he admitted. "When I was working in food production, she was so happy. I can only imagine how much it hurt her to find out I'd been working on the biggest machine of all the whole time. I love her, and the last thing I want to do is cause her more pain than she's already in."

He realized the twig had burned almost to his fingers and quickly dropped it into the fire. Thinking about his mom had a way of distracting him. "Things are different with you. Your father wanted you to become a mechanic, and you did. He wanted you to build a dragon, and you did. You haven't done anything to disappoint him."

"It's not what you think," Kallista said. "He didn't only want me to be a mechanic. He wanted me to be a *great* mechanic, like he was."

"You are," Trenton said, but she cut him off.

"No. I'm good—but I'm nowhere near the mechanic he is. I was never good enough. When we played games, I'd think three moves ahead while he thought thirty. When I couldn't solve his games, I could tell he was disappointed. When I did solve them, it wasn't fast enough. I wasn't as good at math as he wanted me to be. I didn't remember enough of what I read. All I've ever been is a disappointment to him." She rubbed a hand across her upper lip and tried to smile. "Honestly, sometimes I think he wished I'd been a machine instead of me."

Trenton didn't know what to say. No matter what his mother thought of him being a mechanic, he'd always known she loved him. Looking up at Ladon, he searched for a way to change the subject.

"I think your father knew we'd bring the dragon out here. And that we'd modify it to burn wood."

"Of course he did," Kallista said. "I told you. He was always thinking thirty moves ahead." She started to say something else, then paused.

"What's wrong?" Trenton asked.

Kallista rubbed her palms on her pant legs. "He thought ahead."

"Right. So?"

Her eyes got a faraway look, and Trenton could tell she wasn't listening to him anymore. "Far ahead," she whispered. "So far ahead. He'd want to make sure that if anyone besides us found the compass, they wouldn't understand what the message inside meant. What if the clue didn't refer to something out here but to something he knew we already had?"

She began flipping through her father's papers, stopping suddenly on one. Her eyes lit up. "Here," she said, pulling out a page.

Trenton scooted around the edge of the fire until he was at her side. The paper was one of the letters her father had left for her inside the box where he'd hidden the truth about the dragons. He read it again, remembering the shock and terror he'd felt the first time he'd seen it.

> *It is now the eleventh hour. You have seen what I have gathered and know what I know. Understand that I am sure everything in these documents is true. I have been traveling outside secretly. The air is clean and fresh. But on three occasions I have seen real dragons for myself.*
>
> *More than thirty years ago, when Discovery was built by our founders, no one expected it to last this long or grow to such degrees. Huge piles of dirt and rock have built up outside to the point they are impossible to miss. Smoke plumes like a beacon. No doubt they both draw the dragons*

to our location. I have seen the beasts circling our mountain as though called here. I do not know whether they smell our scent, see our debris, and hunt us, or if killing is simply a part of their nature.

Whichever is the case, I can tell you that they will discover us shortly. The great beasts come closer with every passing month. They will discover our city soon, and they will not stop until they get inside.

"This is it," Kallista said, tapping the first sentence with one finger. "'It is now the eleventh *hour*.' That's what the clue in the compass is talking about. 'The *hour* is the key.'"

Trenton's heart began to race. She might be right. "Okay. It's the eleventh hour, and the hour is the key. What are we supposed to do next?"

Kallista studied the letter and laughed out loud. Trenton hadn't seen her this excited since the day they left the mountain. "It's the easiest puzzle he's given us so far." She grabbed the stump of the twig Trenton had burned.

"The key is eleven," she said. Tapping one finger on the page, she began counting, starting with "It," until she came to the eleventh word on the page.

"I," she said, using the blackened end of the twig to underline the word. Quickly, she counted eleven more words. "Am."

Trenton realized there was a hidden message within the letter. Something no one would ever find unless they had both the letter and the clue inside the compass. The key was to count every eleven words.

"Traveling!" he shouted, finding the next word. "I am traveling."

They kept counting and underlining until they reached the

end of the letter. By the time they were done, fifteen words had been underlined.

Trenton read the words out loud. "'I am traveling three thirty degrees to a location called see a tell. Come soon.'" He turned to Kallista. "See a tell? Does that mean anything to you?"

Kallista's forehead scrunched up as she studied the page. "Get me the map and the compass."

Trenton pulled the items out of the bag and set them on the ground near the fire.

"'Three thirty degrees' obviously refers to the markings on the compass," she said, tapping the notch on the rim of the compass marked 330. "We have to assume he was starting from Discovery."

Carefully she placed the compass at the spot on the map marking the mountain city where they had built Ladon. Turning the map so the *N* on the compass and the *N* on the page lined up, she traced her finger up and to the left until she came to the name of a city. She and Trenton saw it at the same time.

"That's it!" Trenton yelped. He traced his finger from the ocean on the left side of the map along a blue line that came inland and down until he touched the letters *SEATTLE*.

"Seattle," Kallista said. "My father is in Seattle."

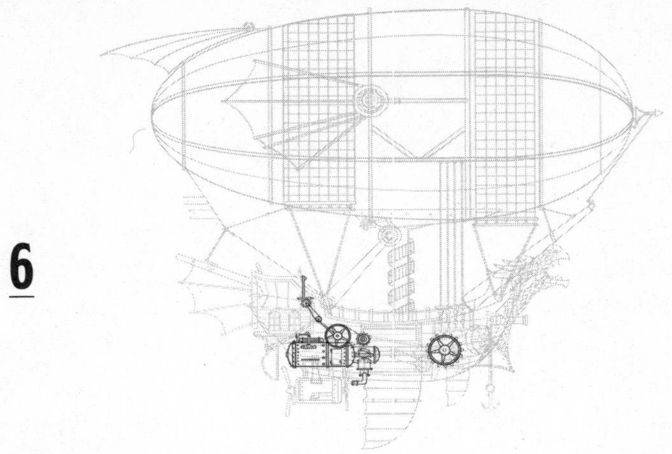

6

Trenton woke to the sound of crashing metal. Sticking his head out from the blankets wrapped around him, he saw the first faint pink hues touching the clouds over the mountains to the west. The sky provided just enough light for him to make out the silhouette of a figure pounding on Ladon with a hammer.

"What are you doing up so early?" he shouted, rubbing the sleep from his eyes and face. Kallista normally slept in her seat on the dragon, while he preferred the softer ground beneath it. Most of the time, he was up an hour or more before she rose. But now she was wrestling pieces into place with an energy she didn't normally attain until the sun was well up in the sky.

Kallista pointed to a pipe with an L-bracket on one end. "Hand me that part over there."

Wrapping his blanket around his shoulders like a cloak, Trenton grabbed the bracket and climbed up beside her.

Kallista took the part and immediately set to work bolting it to a section of the wing frame. "Sorry for waking you, but I couldn't get that piece in without smacking it."

"How long have you been working?" Trenton stifled a yawn and wrapped his blanket more tightly around him. In another few hours, the sun would warm the air. But now, the temperature was cool, and the morning breeze was brisk. "We can't fly until it gets dark."

"Couldn't sleep." Kallista sighted along the pipe, making sure it was straight, tapped it a little, and gave him her sweetest smile. "I made you breakfast. Well, I didn't exactly make it. But I got out fruit and bread."

Trenton frowned, suspicious. Kallista was never this nice unless she was trying to get something from him. "You want to fly during the day."

"We'll stay low," she said. "And duck into the trees at the first sign of danger. I promise."

Trenton stared at her. "We can make it to Seattle in a day or two at most. It's not like we're late."

Despite the cold, drops of sweat beaded on Kallista's forehead as she wrestled another piece into place, pushing it with her shoulder until it clanked into its hole. "It will be easier to see landmarks during the day."

"It will also be easier for dragons to see *us*."

Kallista sighed in exasperation. "My father left the city *two years* ago. Knowing him, he probably expected me to find his clues within days after his disappearance. Trust me—we're late."

"You said yourself he set a timer to make that tube fall into the feeder belt," Trenton said, shuddering at the memory of how close he'd come to being fed into the incinerator the day he found the first of the clues Leo Babbage left for his daughter to discover. "There's no way you could have solved it any faster than you did."

Kallista climbed down from Ladon. She clasped her hands in front of her. "I haven't seen my father for over two years. Most of that time, I thought he was dead. Is it too much to ask that we hurry now that we know where he is?"

There was no reason to take such a big risk and every reason to be cautious. Flying during the day guaranteed they'd be seen.

Especially since they'd be flying slower to make sure they stayed on course.

Only it wasn't just a genius inventor they were looking for. It was Kallista's only living parent—a man she'd thought was dead until a few weeks ago.

Trenton nudged her with his shoulder. "I'll get everything packed up and eat breakfast while you finish here."

"We can eat breakfast in the air," Kallista said. "And I've already packed everything except the tools I'm using and what you were sleeping in." She studied her work. "Ladon will be ready to fly in fifteen minutes if I hurry."

Trenton laughed. "Fine. But before we leave, maybe you could, um . . . wash up a little?" He wrinkled his nose. "You smell like you've been working all morning."

• • •

That evening, according to the map, they had nearly reached the city called Seattle. By hugging the treetops and ducking into cover at the first signs of danger, they'd managed to avoid three separate dragons. He hoped their luck would last. To their left and right, water glinted in the light from the setting sun, and far to the west, he thought he could make out the ocean. The air felt damp and had a distinct salty smell he'd decided he liked.

Kallista checked the map, consulted her father's compass, and nodded. "I think we're almost there."

"What do you think it'll look like?" Trenton asked. He'd tried to picture a city out in the open instead of one tucked safely inside a mountain and realized he couldn't do it.

"Big," Kallista said. "Hundreds of buildings, I bet. Some ten stories tall or more. It could be ten times as big as our city. I'll bet the people even drive automobiles."

Ten times as big as Discovery. Was that even possible? And *automobiles*. When Discovery was still called Cove, the city's leaders had used the invention of automobiles as an example of the kind of technology that had destroyed the outside world. Now that he knew that wasn't true, Trenton was itching to try one out.

Kallista put away the compass. "We should look for big walls. They'd need them to keep out the dragons."

Standing on Ladon's back to get a better view, Trenton searched for some sign of walls or the twinkling metal of a moving automobile. All he saw was more trees. "You're sure it's still there?" he asked, dropping back into his seat. "The pictures from the newspapers . . ."

The pictures Leo Babbage had discovered of the time shortly before Discovery's founders had sealed themselves inside a mountain had been disturbing to say the least. People running for their lives. Buildings on fire. Of course, it couldn't have been that way everywhere, but Ladon had flown over other spots identified as cities on the map: Buckley, Kent, Renton. Maybe those places had existed when the map was made, but there was no sign of them now.

"The people from the other places all gathered in Seattle," Kallista said as surely as if she'd seen it herself. "They built a fortress to protect the people. They are probably fighting the dragons with weapons we can't even imagine."

"How can you be sure?"

Kallista tapped the compass. "If it wasn't still there, my father would have come back to warn us."

Unless something bad has happened to him. But Trenton couldn't say that out loud. He shouldn't have even thought it. Leo Babbage had led them right so far. He told himself there was no reason to believe he wouldn't now.

He leaned over the side of the dragon, hoping to catch a view of the magnificent city. "Let's try to the left."

Kallista turned Ladon's controls until they were nearly over the water. As they reached the shore, something small and gold shot out from the tree line. Trenton barely registered the blur of movement before Kallista shouted, "Incoming dragon!" and yanked them even farther left.

Craning his neck to try to follow the creature's movements, Trenton flew upward to gain some distance. But the small dragon stayed right with them. "It's fast!" he yelled.

That was an understatement. It flitted about like a bird. One second it was on the left of them, the next it was on the right. It was impossible to match the dragon's fast maneuvers, and with Ladon's recent repairs, Trenton worried that a sharp movement might break something loose.

Was it even a dragon at all? It was much smaller than any of the other dragons, about the size of a human, and although it was hard to get a clear view, Trenton was sure he saw two sets of wings flapping so fast they were nothing but a glittering golden haze.

The creature opened its mouth, letting out a roar that was really more like a squeak, and shot a pair of small fireballs in their direction.

"Look out!" He ducked as the tiny flames flew past his head.

Okay, definitely a dragon.

Hand poised above Ladon's fire button, he tried to get a clear view of the beast, but the sun's glare kept blinding him—almost as if the diminutive dragon was intentionally flying between them and the sun.

"Get me a clear shot," he called.

"I'm trying." Kallista turned sharply, attempting to shake

the creature, but it responded too quickly, matching every move they made.

Zipping behind them, the dragon shot another series of fireballs.

Trenton hit the altitude control, diving down fifty feet, but the flames still singed the back of his jacket and flight helmet. He checked the boiler gauge. So far it was holding.

As the dragon flew toward them for another attack, he yelled, "Hold on tight." Waiting until the gold blur was directly behind them, he tilted Ladon's wings nearly horizontal, bringing them to a quick stop. The force of the maneuver threw him forward against his restraints. At the same time, he swung Ladon's massive tail. Metal crunched with a satisfying *chunk*, sending the little dragon spinning out of control.

Instantly, Kallista turned Ladon's head, and Trenton slammed the fire button. Flames blackened the gold dragon's top right wing and sent it spiraling off course. It howled, giving them a dark-eyed glare before disappearing into the trees.

Kallista shook her fist after it. "Go home and tell your mommy you got beat up by the big kids."

"Maybe we better get out of sight for a while," Trenton said. "Just in case it really does have a mommy. I'd hate to fight a bigger version of that." He looked at Ladon's tail and rear legs to see if they'd taken any damage.

"We should be almost . . ." Kallista's words died away, and Trenton turned around to see what was wrong.

Just ahead, near a circle-shaped bay, the trees had all been cleared. Trenton recognized the shape of the waterline from the map. This was where the city of Seattle should be. But if a city had once existed here, it no longer did now.

As Kallista steered toward the opening, Trenton took them lower. Getting a better view, he realized the trees hadn't been cleared away as much as they'd been *burned* away. Everything except a few stunted bushes was charred a deep black, as if the area had been systematically burned to the earth. The ground looked like a giant bed of coal, and the air stank.

The only signs a city had ever existed were the scattered holes filled with broken brick and charred wood. A few blackened plants grew in the holes and climbed over piles of rubble. It was like looking at a gaping wound in the otherwise beautiful green woods that surrounded it. A permanent scar on the land.

"Maybe it's the wrong place," Trenton said. But he knew it wasn't. This was definitely the spot they'd seen on the map.

Kallista shook her head, lips pressed together until they nearly disappeared. "I don't . . . He couldn't . . ." Unable to put her thoughts to words, she continued to circle the area.

Trenton wanted to look away. Thinking about what must have happened to the people here made his stomach churn. But he couldn't stop staring. This wasn't a single attack. The dragons must have come here over and over, attacking the same spot with a fury that made no sense.

And it hadn't happened a hundred and fifty years earlier or the trees would have grown back by now. These attacks were recent.

Staring down at the mangled landscape, he thought he saw something move. "Circle around," he called, pointing toward a patch of stunted bushes near the shore.

Kallista brought them back over the spot while Trenton dropped even lower to get a better look. There was nothing by the bushes but a pile of rocks and a bit of rusted metal. He couldn't have seen anything. Still—

Without any warning, the small bushes moved and the rusted metal tilted, opening a dark hole in the blasted earth. At the exact moment Ladon passed over the hole, something shot up out of the ground. Twisted hooks flew toward them, trailing long lengths of ropes.

Before Trenton or Kallista could react, the hooks looped around Ladon's legs and tail, wrapping the ropes around them.

Kallista tried to turn, but the cords yanked tight.

Trenton pulled the flight stick backward, trying to break free.

The ropes twanged but held.

From below, a mechanism began to reel them in. Kallista slashed with Ladon's talons, and Trenton swung the tail, but it was no use. There were too many ropes, and they were too strong.

"Hang on!" he screamed as they began to drop. They were going down.

7

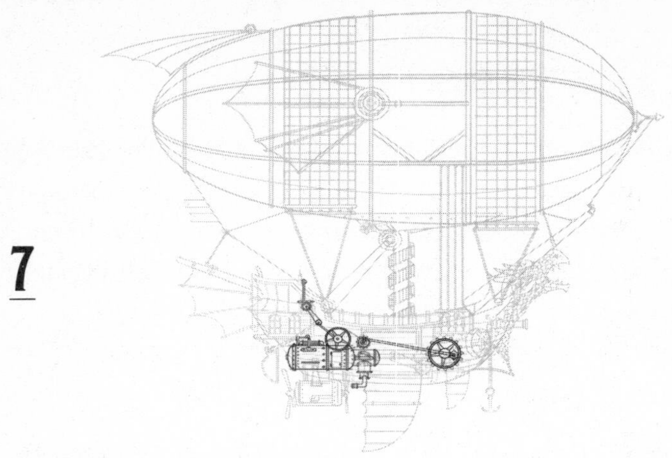

Trenton's head slammed forward into the controls as Ladon bucked and trembled.

"Do something!" Kallista yelled. She swung Ladon's legs, trying to snap the ropes. But whoever or whatever had shot the hooks at them had placed them in such a way that breaking free was impossible.

Clinging to the straps of his harness, Trenton knew he was losing control. Ladon's wings continued to flap, but the ropes were twisting them sideways, making it impossible to get any lift. Another few seconds and they'd tumble helplessly out of the air. He thought he could hear one or more voices shouting excitedly below, but he couldn't make out any words.

His eyes scanned the instruments and stopped on the fire button. If they couldn't cut the ropes, maybe they could *burn* through them. "Get me a clear shot," he yelled, stretching forward to reach the button.

Seeing what he was trying to do, Kallista cranked Ladon's neck around until the dragon seemed to be looking at his own belly.

Unsure if he was about to shoot a rope or themselves, Trenton hit the control. Flames blasted from Ladon's mouth, and something whizzed past Trenton's face. It took him a second to realize it was the end of a burned rope.

Down below, the voices changed from excitement to fear.

"Again," Kallista called.

Trenton hit the button and felt Ladon shift as another rope broke. Immediately the dragon began to right itself, but before they could break free, two more hooks shot out of the hole. One of them narrowly missed hitting Kallista before catching on Ladon's right wing.

Trenton yanked at the rope, trying to tug it loose, but the hook was set.

Pounding the fire button with his left hand, he tried to keep them in the air with his right. Kallista twisted the dragon's head for a better angle while using Ladon's front and back talons to claw at the cords.

It was no good. There were too many ropes. Every time they broke one, two more shot up at them. They were going down. The question was would they do it falling or flying? Glancing toward the ground, Trenton estimated they were at least a hundred feet in the air. A fall would probably kill them.

The hole below had grown impossibly large, and he could make out a pair of faces peering up at him.

"Take us down," he called to Kallista, tilting the wings.

Eyes wide behind her dusty goggles, Kallista nodded. Tethered to the ropes like a kite, she sent Ladon into a tight spiral. For a split second, the cords loosened slightly, and Trenton aimed them toward the opening.

Kallista pointed Ladon's head at the hole and gave Trenton a grim smile. He knew exactly what she had in mind. They might be going down, but whoever had caught them was going to regret it.

"Careful what you wish for," Trenton whispered as he held his palm over the fire button. It was a saying his mother had repeated to him so many times when he'd talked about being a mechanic.

A stream of orange and red destruction shot from Ladon's jaws into the open hole. The voices howled in fear as the faces disappeared from sight.

Tightening his harness straps, Trenton rushed down into the opening and braced himself for the crash.

• • •

Dust and debris floated around Trenton, and the smoke-filled air burned his throat. Something sticky made it hard for him to open his right eye. He reached up to clear his vision, and a bolt of a pain shot through his temple.

"What'd we bring down?" said a boy's voice from below and to his left. "That'd be no dragon."

Trenton looked around, trying to figure out who was speaking.

"Ain't no beast," agreed a second voice; this one sounded like a girl. Footsteps echoed below, accompanied by a weird mechanical *click-sproing*, *click-sproing* sound, as if a clock had come to life.

Something banged against Ladon's metal body, and a sharp whistle spilt the air. "Worth more bits than the crew ever seen, I'd wager," said the girl.

Shifting in his seat, Trenton tried to figure out where he was and how badly he was hurt. His harness had held him in place, and Ladon seemed to be upright. Stretching his arms and legs, he groaned in pain, but he didn't think he'd broken any bones.

He sat upright and saw that the front seat was empty, the harness straps hanging loosely to either side. "Kallista," he tried to shout, but his voice came out in a muted croak.

More clanging came from below, again accompanied by the strange clicking sound. Someone was climbing the ladder. He tried to open his harness, but the straps had twisted in the fall, and he couldn't get the clasps to release.

The clicking grew closer.

Panicked, he tried to slide out of his seat, but the straps were too tight.

A *sproing* came from right beside him, and a pair of strangely twisted hands gripped the edge of the dragon. A second later, two brown eyes peeked over. Trenton jerked away.

At the same time, Kallista leaped from where she'd been clinging to the other side of the dragon. Wielding a heavy wrench above her head, she scrambled across Trenton's seat to place herself between him and the intruder.

"Move another inch and I'll bash your head in, I swear it."

"Rust!" the girl yelped and ducked out of sight.

"What's the hubbub?" the boy called from below.

Footsteps clanged down the ladder. "Couple o' pigeons in the roost."

"What? On top of the dragon?"

"Told ya—ain't no dragon. It's made of metal."

Who were the people down there and why were they speaking so strangely?

The voices quieted, and Kallista pulled her knife from her belt. She cut Trenton loose from the straps. "Are you okay?"

"Fine," Trenton said. Machinery rumbled overhead, and a set of large wooden gears began rotating, sliding the wood-and-metal ceiling shut.

Trenton climbed out of his seat, and Kallista handed him the blade, keeping the wrench for herself. He peeked over the side of the dragon, but it was hard to make out anything in the darkness. "Who are they?"

"I don't know. But I'm pretty sure there's only two of them—a boy and a girl. Something's wrong with the girl. Her arms and hands are scarred, and she's got some kind of machine hooked up to her legs. I saw her winding it right after we crashed."

A weapon, maybe? Trenton turned the knife in his hand. He noticed blood seeping through Kallista's right pant leg. As he leaned over to get a better look, the room started to spin.

Kallista pushed him back in his seat. "I'm fine. It's just a cut. But you've lost a lot of blood. Can you see from that eye?"

Trenton squinted, wincing at the pain. "A little. Where are we?"

"Underground room of some kind. Hard to tell without more light, but I think we smashed up whatever they were using to shoot at us."

Trenton reached for Ladon's controls. "Can we get out?"

Kallista's brow wrinkled. "Coal feeder's jammed up, and it sounds like the turbine is completely ruined. I was taking a look to see if we could fight our way out when the girl climbed up. We aren't going anywhere without repairs."

With the ceiling finally closed, the space around them disappeared into nearly complete darkness.

"You—on the dragon," the girl's voice called up. "Won't hurt ya none if ya come down without a fight."

"'At's right," said the boy. "Ain't gonna tuck ya into bed, are we?"

"*You're* the ones who are going to get hurt," Kallista yelled back.

"Why do they talk so weird?" Trenton whispered.

Kallista shrugged. "Maybe that's the way everyone in the outside world talks. Cove was isolated for a long time." She rested her wrench on her shoulder. "Do you think you can climb down?"

Whether it was his head clearing or his eyes adjusting to

the light, Trenton found he could see a little better. "I think so. What's your plan?"

Kallista snorted. "Get down without getting 'tucked into bed,' whatever that means, and figure it out from there."

Trenton shrugged. "Works for me."

As quietly as they could, they slipped over the back right side of the dragon. The ladder was on the front left side, where the people below were most likely waiting for them. Using the ropes still attached to the dragon, they slipped under the damaged wings and moved to the rear legs.

Halfway to the ground, Kallista froze. "Look at that," she whispered.

Trenton rubbed his eye and stared in the direction she was pointing.

For a second, he thought it was another dragon. Then he realized it was a wooden vessel with the head of a dragon. Hanging from a set of beams on the far side of the room, the craft was nearly a hundred feet long. Two large fans were attached to the back, large wings or fins extended out from the sides, and a spiral staircase wrapped around a heavy mast in the center of the deck. Above the vessel was a large silver oval at least as long as the ship. Every forty feet or so, a wooden hoop encircled the oval shape, creating a framework.

"What is it?" he whispered.

Kallista shook her head. "No idea."

Trenton leaned forward, trying to get a better view. Was it some kind of massive automobile? If so, where were the wheels? Or maybe it was a boat. The oval shape above it could be a sail.

Kallista tugged at his arm. "Come on. We have to get down before they notice we're gone."

Together they grabbed the ropes and shimmied down the dragon, then dropped silently to the ground. The floor felt odd under Trenton's feet. Kneeling, he ran a hand across it. "Wood," he murmured. "The whole floor is made of it." In Discovery, wood was a luxury. Yet here it seemed to be every place he looked.

Pressing against Ladon's back right leg, they peered toward the front of the dragon. Two figures stood looking up at Ladon and whispering. The boy was tall and bulky, his arms and legs a series of sharp angles. The girl was small, with a strangely bent body. Trenton could see the leg machine Kallista had mentioned, but not exactly what it was.

Broken beams, ropes, and hooks were strewn across the floor, the remains of what these people had used to shoot them down. A few of the pieces were still smoldering from Ladon's flames.

What kind of place was this, with wooden floors, giant vessels hanging from the ceiling, and strange people who shot visitors out of the sky?

Before he could puzzle it out, he heard the sound of running feet coming from a nearby passage. Lights flickered on the walls as a half dozen figures raced through a doorway. Torchlight flooded the room, illuminating the oddest group of people Trenton had ever seen.

8

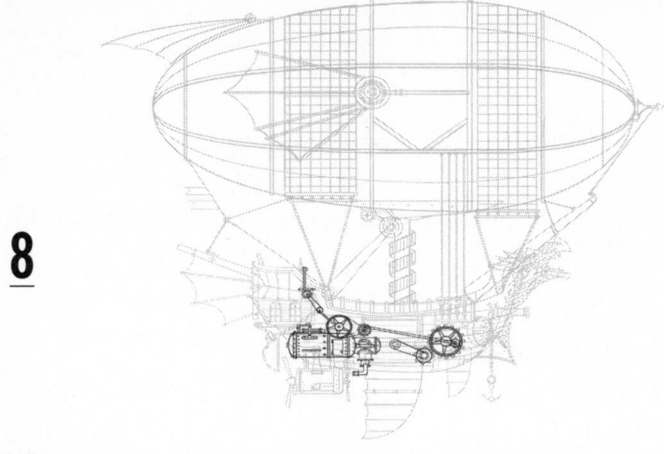

Standing just inside the entrance to the large room was a group of men and women dressed in long red robes that nearly touched the floor. Each person wore a three-sided black cap with a pointed top.

For a moment, Trenton thought their hats were somehow floating high above their heads. Then he realized they'd done something to make their hair stand straight up; their hats were balanced on top.

A man with a square black beard stepped forward. The others flanked him, drawing swords from black leather scabbards at their waists.

Soldiers, Trenton thought. But that wasn't quite right. Something about the way they walked—smoothly and deliberately, their robes barely moving with each step—gave him a sense these weren't fighters.

"What's going on here?" the man demanded, his voice ringing with authority.

Trenton opened his mouth to answer before realizing the group was looking past him and Kallista at the boy and girl who had shot them down.

Holding her hands out to her sides, the girl stepped forward with a strange sort of hop. Each step she took was accompanied by a click, a soft *sproing*—like a spring unwinding—and a metallic clang.

As she drew nearer to the torches, Trenton could see she had been injured in some way. Her neck and face were a smooth walnut brown, but her arms and hands were twisted and pink, and part of her scalp was wrinkled and hairless.

Both of her legs were encased in metal from her ankles nearly to her hips. For a moment, Trenton thought it had to be armor or a weapon of some kind. But as he looked closer, he realized they were mechanical braces that helped her walk. When she leaned forward, the brace ratcheted down, compressing from nearly straight into a V-shaped angle. The bending caused the clicking sound.

With the brace angled, she appeared to press a trigger with the ball of her foot. A large spring on the side of the brace unwound with a *sproing*, a key on the side rotated, and a series of gears and levers snapped the device open, hopping her forward like a clockwork frog.

Had her legs been injured by whatever had scarred her arms? If so, where had the braces come from? They'd obviously been built from mismatched scraps. He could see gears that looked like they'd been scavenged from an engine and metal brackets with uneven sides and rough edges. There appeared to be a gauge to measure when the spring needed to be rewound.

Kallista elbowed him, and he realized he'd been edging toward the group to get a better look at the girl's braces.

"Ain't what you think, Martin," said the girl, shifting from one foot to the other with a clinking noise.

"Whipjacks. I should have known." The man stared down at her, and even from where Trenton was standing, he could feel the cold in the man's gaze. "You have attacked the sacred dragons. You will pay for this." Unlike the others, his words were clear and crisp, as though each had been cut with a sharp knife.

"Rust, no!" the girl cried, her eyes going wide. She waved at her companion. "Tell 'em, Weasel."

The tough-looking boy with ropy muscles shuffled forward, looking like he wanted to be anywhere but there. "Plucky ain't gammoning you. She's telling the truth." He tugged at a bolt stuck through his earlobe.

The man glared at him, and Weasel took a step backward. "That is, I mean, it ain't no *dragon*, Martin. Sir." The boy pointed at Ladon. "See for yerself."

Kallista pulled Trenton back into the shadows as the group turned in their direction.

Holding the torch above his head, Martin stared up at Ladon. "What is this . . . this abomination?"

"A machine," Plucky said, rubbing her hands together. "Bagged it meself, didn't I?" Beside her, Weasel coughed, and she shrugged. "That is, me and Weasel shot it down." She banged the dragon's leg with a piece of wood. "All metal. Worth a healthy lot of bits, yeah, yeah?"

A red-robed boy, his cap balanced on top of a mass of blond hair, stepped forward and glared at the two of them with cold blue eyes. "Weasel and Plucky were hunting the holy ones. Look—their weapons are in flames. They've been planning this for weeks."

"We never did!" Plucky cried.

"Let's get out of here," Kallista whispered.

There didn't appear to be any way out of the large room except for the main door. As Trenton and Kallista eased toward the opening, more footsteps pounded outside the room, and another half dozen burly men and women charged through the doorway.

These were definitely guards, dirty-faced and dressed in hardened leather armor with round wooden shields on their backs. Each of them carried a short, wide sword or a metal-tipped spear that looked well used.

Trenton and Kallista were caught between the two groups with no way to escape.

Weasel looked from the guards to the robed figures and held up his hands. "Plucky's telling ya true, sirs. We was only here working on the catapult, right? Protecting the city. Wasn't even thinking 'bout no dragons when we hears this hubbub coming from above. Thought maybe we was under attack. Opened the doors and seen two figures riding this great—"

He turned, gesturing to Ladon, and spotted Trenton and Kallista trying to hide against the wall. "There they is now. They're the ones you want."

Trenton froze as all eyes in the room turned to him and Kallista.

"Guards, grab the intruders!" Martin shouted.

A swarm of people rushed toward him, and Trenton got one last look at Kallista before he was spun around, a spear jabbing him in the back.

• • •

Trenton stumbled down a winding corridor lined with age-darkened wooden beams. A spear point jabbed him whenever he slowed to less than a run. At the end of the passage, a tunnel sloped upward and to the right. He started that way, but the spear poked painfully into his rib cage.

"Down."

Descending the crumbling brick staircase to his left, he

risked a glance over his shoulder at the woman who'd been rushing him through a warren of dimly lit passages for the last ten minutes. It was hard to see her clearly in the bouncing light of the metal lantern she carried. All he could make out was a stern face—all planes and lines.

She jabbed him again. "Keep your eyes straight ahead."

At the bottom of the stairs, a long hallway with stone walls and a dirt floor worn smooth by long usage turned first right, then left. Several doors opened to either side of him, but there was no time to see what might be behind them.

Trenton stopped as the passage seemed to dead end at a wall of brick and stone. Had he taken a wrong turn somewhere? He opened his mouth to ask what he was supposed to do, when the woman grabbed him by back of his hair, forcing his head down until he was looking at a slimy metal culvert sticking out of the wall. The pipe was between two and three feet high. A trickle of greenish-brown water dripped from the end.

"I can't," he gasped, realizing what the woman wanted him to do. He wasn't claustrophobic exactly—how could he be when he'd lived his whole life inside a sealed mountain?—but the thought of squeezing into the small pipe made him feel like retching.

"You *can*," the woman said, holding the spear point to the side of his throat. "And you will. Or I'll spill your guts right here." She pushed him down to the pipe, then yanked his head backward until her face was beside his. Fetid breath washed past her brown teeth as she spoke. "Don't be thinking about trying to take a run neither." Her green eyes sparkled. "Folks get lost down here, and there are much worse things than me crawling about. Things just waiting for a sweet morsel like you."

Unsure which was worse, the stink of the guard's breath or the stench coming from the pipe, Trenton climbed into the opening, the guard following close behind him. With the only light coming from behind him, he had no idea where he was headed or what he was crawling through until his hands touched it.

Where were they taking him? And what had they done with Kallista? The last he'd seen, a guard had been marching her down a different tunnel, his spear pressed against the back of her neck.

Leo Babbage couldn't have had any idea what was going on or he would never have led them here. If the outside world was all like this, Trenton would be happy to spend the rest of his life inside the safety of his mountain.

"What are you going to do with us?" he asked, his voice echoing inside the pipe.

"Might spend your days rotting in prison. Though my guess is the Red Robes have something better in mind."

Groping forward, his right hand found only empty space. Before he could catch himself, he fell three or four feet and dropped face-first on the hard ground. His teeth slammed shut on his tongue, and the taste of blood filled his mouth.

Before he could cry out, the woman was pushing him into a small, unlit room with brick walls. A metal grate slammed closed behind him.

"Wait," he yelled, gripping the bars. "You don't have to do this. We weren't doing anything wrong." But it was too late. The woman clicked a heavy padlock into place, then turned and ducked back toward the pipe.

"Make yourself comfy." She laughed as she disappeared into the opening. "Sweet dreams." Then she was back in the pipe, and with her, the light from the lantern disappeared.

9

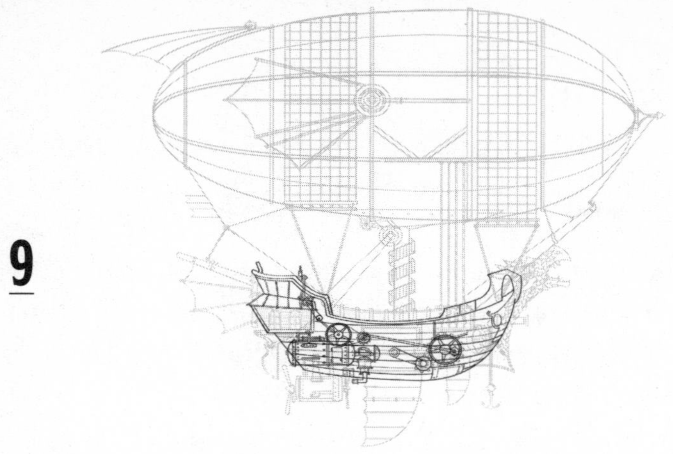

Alone in the dark and the cold, Trenton explored his cell. Reaching out with his hands, he found that the walls were no more than four or five feet apart. Enough room to sit, but not enough to stretch out. Not that he wanted to stretch out. The floor was damp and seemed to be made from the same crumbling red brick he'd seen in the tunnels. There was no bedding or furniture of any kind.

"Hello?" he called, wondering if Kallista had been locked in another cell nearby. No answer. He held his breath, straining to make out any sound, but for all he could tell, he might have been the only person alive, buried thousands of feet underground.

At the thought, the room around him seemed to take on an additional weight. He knew he couldn't be any more than a few hundred feet below the surface at most, but it was hard to shake the feeling that the whole stinking, run-down place might collapse on him at any moment.

Trying to calm himself, he leaned his back against the wall. Locked in a damp cell with no idea of when or how he would get out, the last thing he wanted to do was sleep. But as the adrenaline of the battle wore off, the exhaustion of flying all day caught up with him, and slowly his eyes slipped shut.

Sometime later he jerked awake to the sound of rustling

in the darkness. Freezing, he tilted his head to listen. His neck was stiff and his muscles ached. He must have been asleep for a while.

For a moment he heard nothing and thought he must have imagined the sound. Then it came again. A quiet, shuffling noise as if something were creeping stealthily toward him. It seemed to be coming from above his head.

He stood and raised his arms. As small as the cell was, he expected to touch the ceiling easily, but even with his hands stretched as far as he could reach and standing on tiptoe, he couldn't touch it.

The sound came again—a quick shuffling, followed by a clicking he recognized at once. "Hello?" he called.

The sound stopped.

"Hello," he called again. "Can you hear me?"

There was no answer, but he knew who it was. "You're the girl who shot down our dragon, aren't you? Plucky. That's your name, isn't it?"

Still no response.

Where was she? If she could get in, that meant there had to be a way out.

He tried again. "I won't hurt you, if that's what you're afraid of."

"Ain't scared," the girl's voice whispered. "Least not of you." The clicking came again from what sounded like a few feet above his head. "Make sure the guard is gone."

"Of course she's gone," Trenton said. "That's why it's dark as a mine in here."

"Look through the bars," Plucky hissed. "She could be hiding."

Trenton pressed his face to the cell door, although he knew

no one was there. His eyes had adjusted enough to the darkness that he could see the empty corridor outside.

"Fine. I looked. She's gone."

"Can't be too careful, right?" Plucky said. "Ain't in no hurry to ride the three-legged stool, yeah, yeah?"

"What's the three-legged stool?" Trenton asked.

"Ain't never heard of the three-legged stool?" She sounded shocked. "It's a necktie party."

Trenton shook his head. It was hard to understand what the girl was saying. Not just because of the strange words she used, but also the way she talked. She had an odd, nasally accent, stretching out her consonants and clipping the ends of her words like flowers off a stem. "Three-legged stool, necktie party? What do those mean?"

"Where are you from?" Plucky snorted. "I'm talking about giving you the rope necklace. Your feet dangling in the air."

Finally Trenton understood. He wished he didn't. Skeletal fingers danced along the length of his spine. "They're going to hang me? Why? What did I do?"

"Trespassing's a hanging crime, ain't it?"

Trenton clenched his fists. "We weren't trespassing, and you know it. You shot us down."

The girl shifted above him, and a puff of grit fell into Trenton's eyes. "'Course, if the Order gets you, no telling what they'd do."

"Slow down," Trenton said. "You aren't making any sense. Or if you are, I don't understand it." It was like he had plunged into a different world. Now that he thought about it, that was exactly what he'd done.

"Red Robes hates nuffin worse than someone messing with the beasts," Plucky said.

"What beasts?" Trenton asked, wiping the dirt from his face. "You mean the dragons? Why would they care?"

Plucky blew through her lips as though she'd just stepped into the cold and shuddered.

Trenton stepped back so quickly his head banged against the wall. "Can you help me get out of here?" he asked.

"Rust and corrosion, do I look like a gudgeon now?" Plucky said. "If I was to help you escape, it'd be me own head in the necklace. Only thing the guards hates more'n a trespasser is a traitor. Course us Whipjacks tries to avoid the guards and the Red Robes both, right?"

Trenton slapped his palm against the wall. "I don't understand half of what you're saying. What's a Whipjack?"

A slow *click-click-click* came from above, and Trenton thought Plucky might be winding her leg machine.

"Not what—*who*," she said. "Whipjacks is me crew."

Trenton thought he was beginning to understand at least a little. The people in the red robes and strange black hats were something called the Order, and they were possibly worse than the guards, who wanted to hang him. Plucky and Weasel were Whipjacks, but he had no idea what they wanted.

"If you're not here to help me escape, why are you here?"

"Where ya from?" Plucky asked. "And what ya doing here?"

"None of your business," Trenton said. Why would he possibly trust the girl who had attacked him?

She was silent so long he could practically hear the wheels spinning in her head. "Tell me about your machine," she whispered.

So *that's* why she'd come. He folded his arms across his chest. "You want to know about our dragon?"

"Said so, didn't I now?" Plucky puffed, sounding irritated.

"What do you want to know?" Trenton asked. "How to

make it fly? How to make it breathe fire? It can melt metal, you know."

"Yeah, yeah?" Plucky murmured, obviously fascinated. "Tell me then, right."

Trenton grinned in the dark. He might be able to negotiate his way out of this cell after all. Once he was free, he could find Kallista. "Well, the first thing you need is the key. You know, to get it started."

Plucky moved again, and Trenton grimaced as more dust fell into his face. "Where is it, then? This key."

"I've got it. Guess they didn't think to search me before they locked me up. Good thing, too, because without the key, the dragon's just a big pile of junk."

"You telling me a clanker?" she demanded. "I ain't falling for no stories."

Assuming a *clanker* was a lie, then, yes, Trenton was telling one. Ladon didn't need a key; pushing the ignition button started it. But she didn't know that. He patted his pocket. "I have it right here. Come on down if you don't believe me. Or get me out."

"Flash it," she said. "Hold it up where I can see."

"I don't think so. You want the key. You get me out of this cell."

"Told ya, I can't spring ya," Plucky said. "What I *will* do is make ya a deal."

Trenton squinted into the darkness. "What kind of a deal?"

"Well now, cully, that's more like it," Plucky's voice changed, and Trenton knew he couldn't trust her any further than he could throw her. "You gives me all rights and considerations to your metal dragon, and when I piece it out, I give you thirty percent of the bits."

It took Trenton a moment to figure out what she had said.

When he did, he nearly choked. "You want me to give you the dragon so you can tear it apart and sell it? Why would I do that?"

"Told you—I'll split the swag with ya. Seventy-thirty. Straight to the mark. Good piece'a bits for both'a us."

Trenton shook his head. "First of all, it's not mine to give. And second of all, what good are 'bits' going to do me if I'm dead?"

"Dragon ain't gonna do you no good once you're dangling from the three-legged stool neither," Plucky said. "I was only trying to—"

Her words cut off, and Trenton realized he could hear footsteps approaching from outside his cell. "I wasn't never here," Plucky whispered.

A moment later a light shined through Trenton's cell door, and the guard who had locked him up appeared. "The Order wants to see you."

"What do they want with me?" Trenton asked, squinting at the bright light. "My friend and I—we didn't do anything wrong."

The guard swung open the grate and laughed. It wasn't a happy sound. She approached Trenton, holding out a sack made of black cloth. "Tell it to the patriarch."

Just before the sack dropped over his head, Trenton looked up and spotted a pair of gleaming eyes watching him through a crack in the wooden ceiling.

10

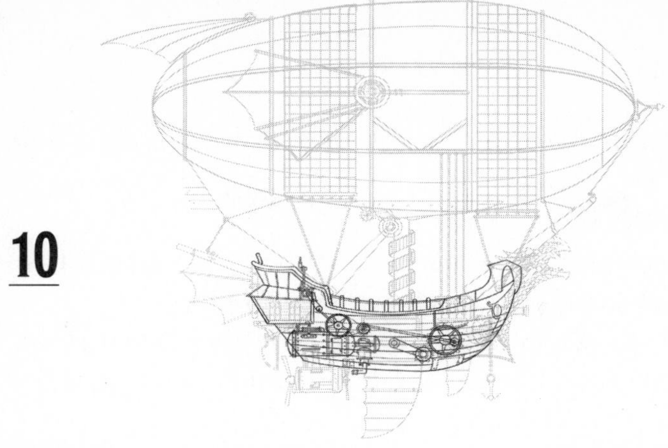

Trenton had no idea how long he was forced up and down stairways, through twisting passages, and in and out of pipes. Behind him, the guard gripped his shoulders, steering him left and right—pinching painfully whenever he even thought about trying to escape.

Several times he heard what sounded like the steady thrum of pistons and the clanging of steam-powered machinery. At one point a rushing sound echoed around him and the bag over his head slipped enough for him to see a wooden bridge with foaming white water roaring beneath it.

How big was this place? From overhead he'd seen nothing but blasted land and charred trees. Yet the more he traveled through the underground tunnels, the bigger he realized the labyrinth was. Why go through so much trouble to hide?

The dragon attacks. While the founders of Discovery had protected their city by sealing themselves safely inside a mountain, these people had camouflaged themselves beneath a false exterior of decay and ruin. It was actually quite brilliant.

He heard the sound of raised voices before he could make out who was speaking or what they were saying. The hands on his shoulders tightened and pushed him forward more quickly. They rounded a corner, and all at once the words became clear.

"Put down the club," said a male voice somewhere to Trenton's left.

"Try and take it from me."

Under his sack, Trenton grinned. It was Kallista, and from the sound of it, she wasn't taking captivity well.

"I told you yellow-bellies to hang on to her," said the male voice, sounding both amused and exasperated. "How hard is it to bring a girl from her cell?"

Footsteps echoed and someone called, "Come on, now. Hand over the club, and we'll—"

A heavy *thunk* was followed by a yowl of pain.

"Get off me," a voice howled.

"Grab her or I'll flog you all!"

Trenton tried to twist away from the guard holding him. Strong fingers dug into his neck, but he managed to shake the bag loose in time to see half a dozen guards charge toward Kallista, who had apparently broken free from her guard and was a wielding a piece of wood nearly three feet long.

Kallista swung the club, catching a dirty-faced woman in the ribs, but the others quickly grabbed Kallista, pinning her down and wrestling the board from her hands.

"Leave her alone!" Trenton yelled. He stomped on the foot of the guard holding him, picked up a loose brick, and charged toward the group. Before he could get to Kallista, though, a long silver blade brushed the front of his neck. A hand gripped his elbow.

"You and the girl stand down. Now."

Unable to turn with a blade at his throat, Trenton flicked his eyes to the right. It was the blond boy in the red robe he'd seen earlier. Trenton dropped the brick and slowly raised his hands.

"Much better," the boy said. He shoved Trenton toward a

group of guards. "See if you can do a better job of hanging on to this one."

As the blond boy turned away, sliding the sword back into the scabbard hanging from his waist, Trenton noticed the pommel atop the weapon's hilt was a dragon's head.

"Get over here," growled a guard with a sizeable gut and bloodshot eyes. He yanked Trenton backward, pulling his arms roughly up behind him and tying his wrists together.

"Are you all right?" Trenton whispered to Kallista once the two of them were pushed together.

"Fine." Kallista glowered at the guards, twisting the ropes tied around her hands.

Trenton noticed that several of the uniformed men and women, including the dirty-faced guard, were keeping a safe distance from her. Remembering the first time he'd met Kallista and how she'd attacked him, he didn't blame them.

He looked around and saw that they were standing in the center of a sort of town square. To the left, right, and behind them were narrow streets lined with smooth stones. Shops and buildings made of brick, stone, and wood crowded together like tired children waiting for the school bell to ring so they could all go home.

All around, the streets were beginning to fill with men, women, and children. Dressed in everything from rags to fur and leather, most had a hungry look to them—their faces pinched and their eyes sunken. While none of them looked exactly friendly, they appeared more curious about what was going on rather than threatening.

In front of them, a gray fountain that might once have been white gushed water sporadically from the mouth of an angel with a missing right arm. Beyond the fountain was an impressive-looking building with heavy metal-bound double doors. Unlike the fountain, the marble stairs leading up to the doors were polished a gleaming white.

And instead of being lit by torches or lanterns, the streets were illuminated by thousands of lightbulbs hanging from a web of wires that stretched overhead from one building to another. The lights brightened and dimmed in unison, and Trenton thought he could make out the drone of a generator somewhere in the distance.

Craning his neck, he studied the bulbs and wires. While most of the city looked old and run-down—everything was covered in years of grit and dirt—the bulbs and wires appeared to be more recent. Probably added in the last couple of years.

He leaned close to Kallista. "What do you think they're going to do with us?"

"No idea," she whispered. "But I really don't like the look of those people in the robes."

Trenton followed her gaze. The people gathering at the top of the stairs were dressed in red robes and odd black hats. They glared down at Trenton and Kallista with expressions ranging from suspicion to outright hate.

What could they possibly be so angry about? Was it because Trenton and Kallista had discovered their city? Because they had flown Ladon there?

As the last few robed men and women made their way to the double doors, Trenton noticed how the people gathered in the streets moved clear as if they feared them too.

Once the last person had climbed the stairs, a bell rang from inside the building, and the doors swung open.

"Move," a guard said, pushing Trenton and Kallista past the fountain, up the stairs, and toward the doors of the building. Trenton glanced at the ornately carved sign above the entryway: The Order of the Beast. The letters O and *B* were painted red with the head of a dragon on either side. The dragon looked to be the same as the one he'd seen on the blond boy's sword.

Inside, the building was filled with benches made of dark, polished wood. The walls were lined with tapestries hanging from floor to ceiling. Trenton noticed a recurring trend in the woven images.

"Pretty clear they know about dragons here," Trenton whispered. In Cove, no one had ever even heard of the creatures until the green dragon had attacked the town square.

Here, not only were there dragons on the tapestries, but every bench had a dragon carved into the back, and the pattern of the tiles on the floor gave the distinct impression of orange flames on a black background.

Kallista shrugged. "What do you expect? They must be attacked by them almost daily."

That was probably true. It was a wonder the city had managed to survive at all. Still, something seemed off, and he couldn't quite put his finger on it.

When they reached the front of the room, the guards pushed them against a wooden railing that faced a raised platform. It appeared this was the place where they were to be judged—and sentenced.

Trenton eyed the robed men and women who were taking their places behind a table on the platform. City leaders of some kind—like the council back home? Or security? Although they were armed with swords and bossed the guards around, they carried themselves with an odd solemnity.

"Let's be careful exactly what we say. At least until we know what's going on," Trenton said.

Kallista barely seemed to hear him. "Let me do the talking," she said, glaring at the men and women around the room.

"I'm not sure that's such a good idea," he said. Kallista didn't have great people skills.

Slowly the benches behind them filled. Those wearing robes sat in the front, and everyone else was in the back. Trenton's legs felt weak, and he wished he could sit down, but no chairs or benches had been provided for them. When the room was full, the double doors swung shut, and another bell sounded.

Martin stepped from behind a blood-red curtain at the front of the room. Trenton recognized him by his square black beard. Martin walked to the center of the platform, raised his hands to his mouth and called out, "All rise for the patriarch of the Order, Wilhelm the Divine."

Everyone in the room stood as the curtains swished aside and an elderly man stepped forward. He wore a red robe, but unlike the others, no hat. Instead, his gray hair was cut so close to his head that he looked nearly bald.

After all the buildup, Trenton expected a formal ceremony. Instead, the man tugged at the shoulders of his robe, coughed into his fist, and took a seat behind the table.

Around the room, everyone else sat as well.

Covering a yawn with his hand, Wilhelm the Divine shuffled quickly through a stack of papers on the table. He rubbed his forehead with the side of one hand and shot a disinterested look at Trenton and Kallista.

"You have been charged with trespassing, a capital offense. What say you?"

Trenton opened his mouth, but Kallista spoke first. "I've got this." Scowling at the gray-haired man, she said, "We didn't trespass. We came here looking for my father. One of your citizens shot us down. If anyone should be punished, it's you, for attacking us."

Trenton wished she'd tone things down, maybe take a less

argumentative approach. Even *she* admitted she wasn't good with people, which was why she had a hard time making friends.

"What she means," Trenton said quickly, "is that we came looking for your city. But not to enter it without your permission. The only reason we entered was because someone pulled us out of the sky with ropes and hooks."

The patriarch's tangled eyebrows arched, and he leaned forward. "Out of the sky, you say?"

"That's right," Kallista continued. "We flew here on a metal dragon we built ourselves. And thanks to you, it's damaged. I have no idea what it's going to take to fix it, but I expect you to provide us with whatever we need."

"Clearly a lie," Martin said. "You could never have come here through the air. The dragons that secure our city would never have allowed it."

Secure? Trenton looked at the tapestries lining the walls, and a terrible thought ran through his mind. He tried to raise his hands before remembering they were tied behind his back. "It's clear you don't want us here, and I think it was a mistake for us to come. If you let us fix our machine, we'll fly away and never come back."

The patriarch listened closely. "You say you *flew* here. Did you not encounter the beasts of the air?"

Kallista scoffed. "Lots! We fought a gold dragon right outside your city. And before that, a red dragon—"

"Let's focus on getting us home," Trenton said, cutting her off. Couldn't she see the way the people in the room were reacting? They weren't impressed that the two of them had fought dragons. If anything they looked shocked and disbelieving, even angry.

The people in the benches leaned toward one another, whispering.

The old man's eyes narrowed. His hands squeezed tightly together, and the veins on the sides of his neck bulged. "*Fought?* You *fought* the golden dragon?"

"Blasphemy," spat Martin. "Dragons are immortal. They cannot be opposed by humans."

"Really?" Kallista smirked, clearly amused.

But no one else was amused. The people in the red robes looked furious; everyone else seemed terrified.

Trenton jabbed an elbow into Kallista's ribs, trying to get her to stop, but it was too late.

Leaning against the railing, completely unaware of what was happening around her, she grinned. "We've not only *fought* your immortal dragons, we've killed one. Maybe two."

Instantly the room went silent. Then, in unison, the robed men and women stood and drew their swords.

Trenton shook his head. "Bad idea."

11

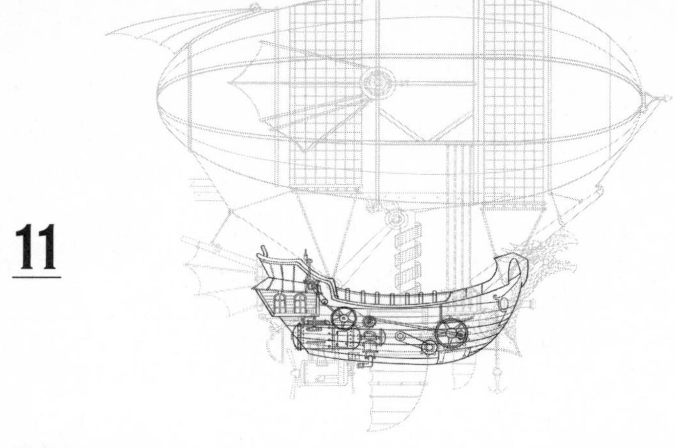

Kallista might have gotten a little c-carried away," Trenton stammered, trying to salvage the situation. "We really didn't *fight* the gold dragon. It attacked us, and we kind of scared it away. We *did* fight a red dragon, but we don't know for sure that it died. As for . . ."

His words died away as the patriarch rose from his chair. "You defile the Order of the Beast with every word that spews from your lips."

"The Order of the . . ." Trenton edged back from the railing, bumping into the guard standing behind him. He didn't know what he'd said wrong, but clearly things had gone from bad to much, much worse. He glanced toward Kallista. For once, she didn't have anything to say.

"Look," he tried, starting again, "let's forget all about the dragon stuff." To his left, a woman gasped, and he realized he was making things worse. "I mean, we obviously made a mistake coming here. So, if you could just let us go—" Several pairs of hands grabbed his arms and shoulders. Trenton looked back, expecting to see the guards, but he was surrounded by a sea of red robes.

Martin turned to the patriarch. "Clearly these children are liars who blaspheme the name of the holy beasts. The fact that they claim to have fought—to have *killed*—immortal beings proves their words are false. They mock the Order, and they mock the beasts. What do you wish to be done with them?"

"Imprisonment," the patriarch said, his face twisted with rage. "For life."

"No!" Trenton screamed as robed men and women dragged him and Kallista down the aisle. "Say something!" he yelled at her. "Tell them this is a mistake."

But Kallista only stared at him, her eyes wide and dark against her pale white skin.

Kicking his feet against the floorboards, Trenton tried to twist away, but it was no use. Silver blades flashed around him, and dozens of hands pinched and punched him as he and Kallista were pulled toward the back of the room.

Seconds before they were yanked outside, though, the double doors flew open, and eight people stormed into the room.

The group included both men and women, although it was hard to tell who was who. Several of the men had hair past their shoulders, and at least one woman was bald.

They looked like they were dressed up for some kind of costume party. Shirts, pants, and scarves so brightly colored they nearly hurt your eyes to look at were mixed with leather boots, vests, and gauntlets.

Draped over, around, and under the clothes were sparkly metal necklaces, hoops, pins, and bracelets. Many had pieces of metal piercing their noses and ears. All wore boots that came up to their knees, and each person was armed with a wooden shield and either a spear or a long knife.

A heavily muscled man with a wispy red beard stepped in front of the people holding Trenton and Kallista. He wore a dark leather vest and a red-and-yellow scarf tied around his neck. Bits of metal glittered from his arms, and it took Trenton a second to realize it wasn't armor but rings and pins inserted through the skin of the man's forearms and biceps.

Resting the butt of his spear casually on the toe of one boot, he grinned. "Right kind of ya to deliver these two pigeons to us."

Everyone froze for a moment, then the blond-haired boy charged forward, his sword held up in front of him. "Get out of the way. Patriarch Wilhelm the Divine has sentenced these prisoners to life imprisonment for blasphemy against the holy dragons."

Although the tip of the boy's sword was less than an inch from the man's bare chest, the man simply scratched the back of his neck. He grinned at Kallista. "Ain't nobody telled ya to leave the dragons alone?" His eyes slipped from Kallista to the blond boy. "No doubt Renato'll be crabbed by these cullies' bad behavior. What's say you give 'em to me and we find out? Yeah?"

Martin charged through the crowd, hands clenched. "What's going on here?"

"These thugs are trying to take the prisoners," the boy said.

Martin turned to the man in the vest. "What are you doing, Slash? These are our prisoners."

Slash pinched his nostrils between his fingers, then wiped his hand on his green-and-gold pants. As scared as he was, Trenton couldn't help noticing the way the man jingled with every movement.

"Right, Martin. But see, the thing is, these two ain't exactly yours."

"What are you talking about?" Martin demanded.

"They was nabbed by Whipjacks, wasn't they?" Slash jerked his thumb behind him, and Weasel and Plucky came forward. "Took the cullies in, didn't ya now?"

"Right that," Plucky said, pounding her chest with her fist. "Shot their flying machine ourselves, yeah, yeah."

Weasel glanced at the swords now pointed in his direction. He tugged at the bolt in his ear and nodded uncomfortably. "Bagged it all right."

Slash grinned. "Which makes 'em ours."

Martin scowled. "Cochrane can't have them. They've been sentenced by the patriarch."

"*Dimber Damber* Cochrane wants them down to the wharf." He emphasized his words deliberately, making Trenton think *Dimber Damber* must be some sort of title. "So tells your Red Robes to hands 'em over. Now."

Trenton glanced between Slash and Martin, not sure he wanted to end up with either one.

Martin shook his head. "That's not going to happen. Tell your leader, the dimber damber, he can't have them."

Slash lifted his spear from his boot, and both groups tensed. "Gingerly now, mates. Would be a shame should the lights go out of kilter." As though he controlled them by the sound of his voice, the lightbulbs both inside the building and out in the streets dimmed briefly. When they came back up, Slash was pointing his spear at Martin's midsection.

"Or . . ." Slash continued, waggling the tip of his spear toward the robed commander, "should the water pumps go feets-up." Outside, a coughing sound came from the fountain, and the water stopped flowing from the angel's mouth.

It appeared the Whipjacks controlled the machinery that ran the city, and Trenton couldn't help wondering who the man behind the machines was, and how everything worked.

Martin grimaced, clearly struggling with what to do. He turned toward the front of the room, but Wilhelm the Divine was no longer at the table.

Raising his sword, the blond boy stepped between his commander and Slash. "They aren't going anywhere," he said. With a flick of his wrist, he knocked Slash's spear aside.

Slash shrugged. "Guess we'll just have ta tell Cochrane we failed. You can keep the prisoners." Lifting his free hand, he snapped his fingers.

Instantly the lights went out.

Trenton heard a grunt, then someone grabbed him around the waist and hefted him over a shoulder.

"Hang on, pidge," whispered a good-natured voice. "This'll be quite a ride."

• • •

Sometime later, Trenton was carried out of a tunnel and dropped in the middle of a brightly lit room.

"Get your hands off me," Kallista growled as the bald woman carried her through the door.

"My pleasure," the woman said, dumping her on the ground like a sack of bolts. She turned to another Whipjack. "Thinks she's too good for us, that one. Rather be carrying about a bleating sheep."

Despite their situation, Trenton couldn't help grinning. Kallista had complained the whole time the woman was carrying her.

The woman crouched down and cut through the ropes binding Kallista's hands. Then she turned and freed Trenton. "Don't makes me regret this, right?"

Keeping an eye on the Whipjacks, Trenton helped Kallista to her feet.

Unlike the randomly placed bulbs in the city, which cycled from bright to dim, the light here was steady and spread evenly around the room. It was cleaner here, too. Instead of dirty stones or old wood, the floor was covered with highly-polished tiles. The bricks on the walls were bright red and looked recently scrubbed.

Still, the air felt more humid here and had a briny smell that reminded him of working with the plankton tanks back home. Did that mean they were closer to the ocean?

What caught his attention the most were the rows of interesting equipment along the walls.

Unable to stifle his curiosity, Trenton approached a circular machine with a feeder belt, several mechanical arms, and what looked like a nozzle. He leaned in for a closer look. Stacked on the feeder belt was a series of small metal rods. On the front of the machine was a gleaming brass button. Trenton wondered what would happen if he pushed it.

"Admiring my work?" asked a voice from across the room.

Trenton turned to see a man sprawled across a chair so large and ornate it was nearly a throne. Blue eyes peered curiously out from a narrow face so perfectly proportioned it looked like it had been carved from stone. Long dark hair framed his face and hung past his shoulders.

A carefully trimmed beard and mustache covered most of his chiseled jaw, and his mouth quirked in a crooked smile.

Like the other Whipjacks, he wore a combination of leather, colorful cloth, and fur, but the quality seemed to be a step above anyone else's in the room, and his shirt was covered with polished metal circles that looked like badges of some kind.

Even though he appeared to be in his midtwenties, it was clear by the way the others looked at him that he was their leader. The one Slash had called Dimber Damber Cochrane.

A sharp-looking dagger with a leather-wrapped handle appeared in Cochrane's right hand. "Take another step toward the door, girl, and I puts this"—he flipped the dagger so he was holding it by the blade, ready to throw—"in yer vitals."

Trenton turned to see Kallista edging toward the door. Eying the dagger, she slunk back to the center of the room.

Smiling, Cochrane slid his dagger inside his vest and sat up. "'At's more like it." He pointed to the machine Trenton had been admiring. "Want a go at it?"

Trenton looked from the man to the machine, wondering if he was serious.

Cochrane nodded. "Go ahead."

Trenton pushed the button. Inside the machine, an engine started up. A moment later there was a puff of smoke, and the belt began to turn. As the first rod neared the end of the feeder belt, a set of metal claws picked it up.

Kallista edged over for a closer look, and the two of them watched as the claws bent the rod into an O shape. As the second rod neared the edge of the belt, another set of claws fitted it through the O, then bent it as well, forming connected links. At the same time, a puff of fire shot from the nozzle, welding the first link closed.

Soon a third link was connected. Then a fourth. Trenton released the button, fascinated by what he'd seen. "It makes chains!"

Cochrane waved his hands in an "aw shucks" gesture. "Ain't nothing, really."

Kallista grabbed a rag from the side of the machine and lifted the hot chain from the tray. She eyed the finished product carefully. "The links don't line up. This one on the end isn't even completely closed."

Cochrane's eyes narrowed, and his face went faintly red.

Trenton stared at her. Was she *trying* to get them killed?

Then the leader of the Whipjacks shook his head and

laughed. "Told you it were nothing." He leaned across the side of his chair and pulled a lever. With a clanking of gears, the seat, which had been partially reclined, straightened and turned toward Trenton and Kallista. He pulled another lever, and a pair of metal clamps closed around his feet and slid his boots off. Then the entire chair began to vibrate.

Cochrane leaned back and sighed with pleasure.

Trenton got the feeling the man was trying to impress them. If so, it was working. "Did you make that yourself?" he gushed.

Cochrane pushed the lever back, but nothing happened. Grimacing, he tried again. This time the vibrating stopped. He eyed the two of them with obvious interest. "Done a'bit of tinkering. Few things to make the city better."

"A *few* things?" hooted Slash. "You've turned Seattle upside down."

Cochrane gave him a sharp look, and Slash quieted at once.

"As I was saying," the dimber damber said, "I cobbled together a thing or two here and there. But nothing like the kind of work you two done with that dragon of yours. It's . . ." He brushed his hair over one shoulder and tugged at his beard. "It really flies, then?"

"It *did*," Kallista said. "Until your stooges shot us down."

Trenton kicked her with the side of his foot, but Cochrane only laughed. "Got a lot of spunk, you do. I could use a couple of mechanics like you two. What say you come work for me?"

Trenton could barely believe the turn of events. One minute they were about to be locked in prison for life, and now this intriguing man was offering them a job as mechanics. Before he could say a word, though, Kallista shook her head. "Not interested."

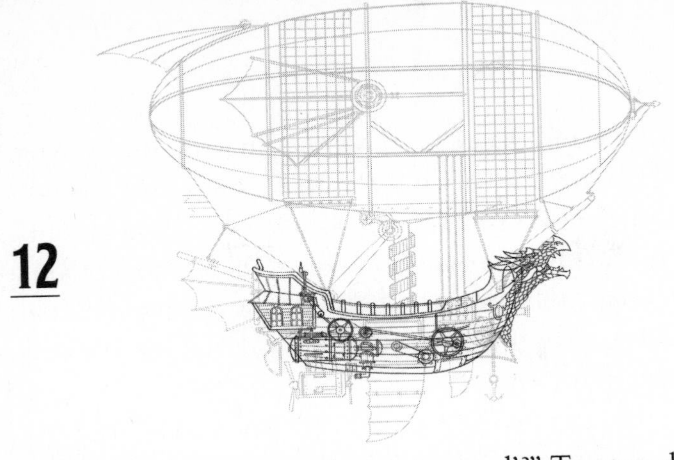

12

What do you mean 'not interested'?" Trenton demanded, nearly shaking with anger. It was one thing to not be friendly toward other people, but this was going too far.

Kallista folded her arms. "We came here to find my father, not to build chain machines or, or"—she waved her hand at the vibrating chair—"whatever *that's* supposed to be. Since he's obviously not here, I'll fix my dragon and keep looking for him."

"It's not just *your* dragon," Trenton said. "I helped build it. I get some say in this decision."

Cochrane watched the two of them with equal parts amusement and irritation. "Didn't say I wanted ya fixing chains, now did I?"

"I don't care what you want us to fix," Kallista said. Trenton would have gladly pushed a pillow over her face to keep her from talking. Not that it would have done any good. She wasn't listening to anyone. "I didn't come here to work for you or your Whipjacks. I'm not staying any longer than I have to. I know my father came looking for your city. He probably saw how pathetic it was and kept going. I'm doing the same."

She turned and started for the door. Immediately the Whipjacks, who had been watching quietly, started forward.

Cochrane rose from his chair, running his fingers across the handle of the long knife sticking out from his belt. At the same time, the rest of his crew surrounded Trenton and Kallista.

"Here's how it is," Cochrane said, the amusement gone from his voice. "Walk out now, the only decision you make is how you croak. If the Red Robes find you, they lock you up until you starve to death. The guards find you, they sends you on a one-way passage to the three-legged stool for trespassing. That's assuming none of the fine folks in our fair city tap you along the way and steal the clothes off your back."

"Tell us what you need us to do," Trenton said at once.

Cochrane turned to Kallista. "You plummy with that?"

Kallista stared at Trenton as though he'd betrayed her. Trenton shrugged. What did she want him to do—go along with her and get themselves killed?

"I'm listening," she said.

"Good decision," Cochrane said. "Now that we got that out'a the way, why don't you two tell me your names."

"I'm Trenton, and this is Kallista," Trenton answered for both of them, figuring the less Kallista said right now the better. For a split second, he thought he saw a change in the man's expression.

"I am Renato Cochrane, dimber damber of this motley crew known as the Whipjacks," Cochrane said, making a deep bow. "How dost do, my buffs?"

"How dost do?" repeated the rest of the men and women in the room.

Unsure of what to do, Trenton bowed back. "All right, I guess. Considering everything. How are you?"

Several of the men and women in the room snickered. Kallista rolled her eyes. But the answer seemed to please the Whipjack leader. He nodded and returned to his chair, crossing his legs and leaning back. "Plummy. You said you came here to our humble home looking for something—or someone?"

Trenton glanced toward Kallista before continuing. "We

came here looking for Kallista's father, Leo Babbage. He left our city about two years ago, and we think he was headed here."

"What city might you be from?" Cochrane asked slowly.

Kallista shook her head slightly, but the result of not answering questions appeared to be death, death, and more death. Still, it would be good to be careful. "It's in the mountains," he said. "Miles and miles from here."

"The mountains?" Cochrane's eyebrows arched.

"Came on a great metal dragon, they did," Weasel said, tugging the bolt in his ear. "Plucky and me shot it down with the catapult you—"

Faster than a spinning crankshaft, Cochrane reached inside his vest, pulled out his dagger, and sent it flying across the room in a blur of silver.

Squawking in terror, the boy lunged backward. The knife sliced through the sleeve of his shirt. Blood dripped as he cupped his arm to his chest.

"Did I ask ya to come here and flap yer gums?" Cochrane growled.

"Sorry, Dimber Damber," Weasel hissed between clenched teeth. "Didn't mean no offense."

Cochrane nodded to his dagger, which was embedded in a wooden beam on the far wall, and one of the Whipjacks hurried to fetch it. "Now then," he said, wiping the blood from the blade on his pant leg, "tell me about this city o'yours. And don't try telling no clankers. I can spot a lie a mile away."

Trenton understood the man well enough: Tell the truth or suffer the consequences. Besides, it wasn't like it mattered if the Whipjacks knew about Discovery since they had no way of getting there. He tried to keep the details to a minimum, but by the time he was done, Cochrane's eyes were gleaming. He twisted the ends of his mustache. "You say this city of yours is powered by steam and coal?"

Trenton nodded.

"Dig it from the mines, do you?"

"Where else would it come from?" Kallista said, rolling her eyes.

Trenton wanted to tell her now was a bad time for sarcasm.

Cochrane ignored her jibe. "Grows your own food, too, I suppose. You have people working the fields?"

Around the room, the rest of the Whipjacks listened intently.

"Yes," Trenton said cautiously.

Cochrane whispered something under his breath that sounded like *It's true*. Then he leaned back in his chair and put his hands behind his head. "And the two of you are mechanics?"

Kallista snorted. "One of us is. The other one is a farmer." She jerked her thumb at Trenton.

"We *both* built the dragon," he shot back, feeling his cheeks burn with embarrassment.

"Aye, and a fine thing it is, I wager." Cochrane closed his eyes as though deep in thought. Trenton wondered if they'd said something wrong again. After a moment, the dimber damber opened his eyes and leaned forward, pointing to a group of Whipjacks. "Four of you get in the hallways and make sure no one is lurking about." Then he motioned Trenton and Kallista to come closer.

"The Order wants ya planted in the ground. They may say they're locking you up—be more humane and all—but they have a nasty habit of forgetting to feed prisoners. Guards want you dead too. But I can protect ya."

"How?" Trenton asked.

"This part of the city's known as the wharf. No one comes

here without my say so. Besides . . ." He waved up at the lights. "They give me any trouble, an' they lose their electricity."

Kallista sneered. "And what will this *protection* of yours cost us?"

"Been working on some projects," the dimber damber whispered. "Mechanical-like things. I wants you two to help me put 'em right."

"You want us to build things for you?" Trenton said.

Kallista tugged at her shirtsleeves. "And in return we get what?"

Cochrane blinked as though the answer was obvious. "Why your lives, o'course. And food and a roof over yer heads."

Trenton spoke up before Kallista could say anything that might get them killed. "Can you give us a minute to discuss your offer?" He looked around at the Whipjacks and their weapons and swallowed. "Um, in private?"

"Certainly," Cochrane said. "Use the shop." He motioned to a door near the back of the room.

Stepping through the door, Trenton immediately felt at home. Although the quality of tools hanging from the walls was nowhere near as good as what had been in Leo Babbage's shop, the organization was surprisingly similar. Clearly this was the workplace of someone who knew their way around machines.

Before he could finish admiring the tools, Kallista grabbed him by the back of his jacket and spun him around. "What are you doing, trying to make decisions for both us?"

Trenton pulled out of her grasp. "You mean trying to keep us from getting killed? Every word out of your mouth has done nothing but dig us deeper and deeper into trouble."

Kallista ran her hands through her unruly black hair and sighed. "All I want to do is get out of here and find my father."

"I know. I do too. It's just . . ." Trenton held out his hands. "Let's say you're trying to unscrew a bolt, but it's stuck."

Slowly Kallista's lips rose. "You're using a machine analogy on me?"

"What?" Trenton asked, trying to appear innocent. "It's just an example."

"A mechanical example, because you know I'm lousy dealing with people."

Trenton grinned. "Okay, so maybe I thought you'd have an easier time dealing with a bolt than a human. Was I wrong?"

Kallista shook her head. "Go on."

"Both of us are better dealing with machines than people. But sometimes people are like machines."

"'We are all gears and cogs in a magnificent machine,'" Kallista intoned, placing her hand on her chest as if they were back in Cove, standing before Chancellor Lusk. Both of them burst out laughing.

"Stop it," Trenton said, looking toward the door and hoping no one had heard them. When they finally stopped giggling, he continued with his example. "When a bolt's stuck, do you bash it with a hammer?"

"Depends how mad it made you," Kallista said.

Trenton shook his head. "You oil it, tap it, and work on it until eventually it comes loose. That's what we have to do here. We both know the most important thing is finding your father. That's the bolt. But to do that, we first have to find a way to stay alive. Then we have to fix Ladon. *Then* we find a way to escape."

Kallista walked the length of the workbench, sorting through the various tools. "You're saying we loosen the bolt, then we yank it out."

"Exactly."

"Okay. We'll try it your way. But if that doesn't work, we try mine."

"What's that?" Trenton asked.

Kallista lifted a tool from the workbench. "The hammer."

Trenton and Kallista walked back into the room where Cochrane was waiting with an expectant grin.

"All right," Trenton said. "We'll help you."

Cochrane nodded.

"Under one condition," Kallista added. "Not only do you keep us alive, but you also give us the parts and tools we need to fix our dragon."

"I'll help rebuild it, luv," Cochrane said. "Unfortunately, though, it's no longer *yer* dragon."

"What are you talking about?" Trenton blurted.

"Of course it's ours," Kallista said.

Cochrane nodded. "It was. Thing is, you lost it in fair battle. To the victor goes the spoils and all that."

Plucky marched forward, clicking and sproinging with each step. Beside her, Weasel grinned, blood still dripping from his arm as he flexed his muscles. "It's ours now," he said.

13

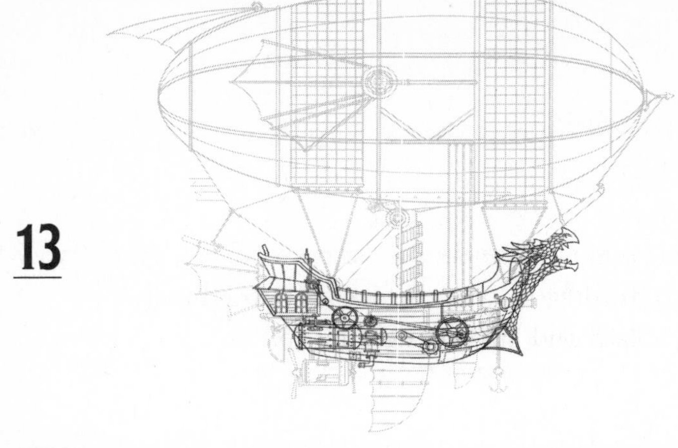

That's not fair!" Kallista shouted. She took a step forward, and Trenton grabbed her by the arm. The situation was bad enough as it was. The last thing they needed was for Kallista to make things worse.

Her whole body shook with anger.

"Hold on," he said, looking from Kallista to Cochrane and thinking quickly. "You said they won the dragon in battle. But they didn't defeat us."

Weasel pushed his chest out and tucked his thumb behind the studded club in his belt. "You calling me a liar? Grabbed you clean out'a the air, we did."

"Right we did," Plucky said.

"What are you saying?" Cochrane asked Trenton. "Someone else made the grab?"

"No." Trenton spoke fast. Kallista's knuckles were white. Weasel looked ready to attack, and the rest of the Whipjacks were getting restless.

"Here's the thing," he said, trying to keep his voice steady. "It's true that they shot us with the catapult. But they didn't pull us all the way down. We dove down on our own. And they did damage our dragon, but we destroyed their catapult. I think that makes it a draw. Neither of us won."

Cochrane scratched his beard.

"Stow that," Weasel grunted. "He's trying to bilk us of our rightful spoils." He wrapped his hand around his club, but Cochrane stopped him with a wave.

"Quit the rumpus," the dimber damber said. "As each of you lays claim to the dragon, only one way to settle things."

"A tilt," Slash said, his eyes lighting up.

"A tilt," echoed the other Whipjacks.

"What's that?" Trenton asked.

Cochrane grinned. "The two of you ride at one another, trading bastes with cudgels."

Bastes and cudgels?

Kallista's arm relaxed a little in Trenton's grip. "You're talking about jousting."

Cochrane nodded. "That's right."

Jousting? Trenton remembered hearing something about that in one of his history classes. Knights on horses tried to knock each other to the ground with long metal lances. But that was an ancient practice. No one did that anymore.

"First one what knocks the other off his mount twice wins," Cochrane said. "Who rides for each side?"

"I do," Weasel said with a dark grin.

Before Trenton could think about what he was saying, he spoke up. "I do."

"Very well," Cochrane said. "We have ourselves a match."

• • •

That night Kallista was still furious. "What gave you the right to volunteer?"

They stood at the base of a steep wooden staircase, waiting to be led outside to where the match would occur. Apparently disputes were settled immediately here.

Trenton grimaced. They'd been over it a hundred times. "I just did. Things were getting bad."

Kallista opened her mouth to reply, but Trenton held up his hand.

He exhaled sharply. "You need to think before you act."

"Big words from someone who just volunteered to get bashed off a horse." Now it was Kallista's turn to frown. "You've never even ridden one."

"Neither have you," Trenton said. "How hard can it be? You steer with one hand and hold the stick thing in your other hand."

"Lance," Kallista said. "It's called a lance. My father had books about jousting. People died from getting hit with lances."

Trenton ran his fingers through his hair. "Well, it's too late now." He turned to a bony Whipjack with a crooked nose. "Why do they hold the tilts at night?" he asked.

"You touched, boy?" the man said, tapping his head. "Night's when they sleep. No one goes outside during the day lest they get swallowed whole."

"He's talking about the dragons," Kallista said.

"I know what he's talking about," Trenton grumbled. He turned back to the Whipjack. "What are the rules?"

The man laced his fingers together and cracked his knuckles. "Ain't no rules 'cept bash the other fellow off his mount twice. Croak him at the first blow and you win outright, yeah?"

Trenton tried not to think about what he'd gotten himself into.

"Here we go," said the man as another Whipjack carried over a large wooden club and held it out to Trenton.

"What's that?" Trenton asked. On the fat end of the club was a square metal head, roughly the size of a brick.

"Yer cudgel," the bony man said, grinning.

"My . . ." Trenton looked at the club, realizing what they wanted him to do with it. "I thought we used lances?"

"Don't know nothing 'bout no lance," the second Whipjack grunted, still holding out the club. "Take yer weapon or don't. Up to you."

Trenton took the club, his arms sagging under the weight. It was like hefting a three-foot sledgehammer. How was he supposed to ride a horse and use this at the same time?

"What's this for?" he asked, squeezing a metal trigger near the base of the handle.

Both men jumped back as the head sprang off the end of the club, smashing into the wall behind them. Chips of brick and mortar exploded from the impact, and Trenton stared at the head of the club now hanging from the end of the handle by a thick metal spring. Great, he was going into battle with a spring-loaded sledgehammer on an animal he'd never seen let alone ridden and the only rule was that if you died first you lost. How could anything possibly be worse?

"Where's my armor?" he asked, remembering the pictures of knights in his history books. They had worn heavy metal suits.

"Armor?" The two men burst into startled laughter. "Who said anything 'bout armor?"

Okay, it was worse.

"See you been testing your cudgel," Renato Cochrane said, walking around the corner. "Let's get you outside and get things started."

With the help of the two Whipjacks, Trenton reattached the metal head to his club and hefted it over his shoulder.

"Want me to carry that for you?" Kallista asked.

Trenton glared at her and started up the stairs.

"Sure you want to do this?" Cochrane asked. "Be a shame if ya croaked. Hate to lose a good mechanic."

"I'm sure," Trenton said.

Cochrane nodded, unsurprised. At the top of the stairs, he pushed open a metal door that squealed on its hinges, then he disappeared into the darkness.

Outside, the air was cold and damp. Trenton stamped his feet, trying to stay warm. The ground was a mixture of sand and gravel, and he thought he could hear the sound of waves washing against the shore.

"Least we have a full moon," one of the Whipjack men said. "Nasty bit'o business when there's no light." He grinned, revealing a gap where his center teeth should have been. "Hard to see the damage."

The men led him to an open area with a long wooden rail running down the middle. The rest of the Whipjacks had already gathered to watch the fun.

Trenton studied the night sky. "You're sure the dragons are asleep?"

"Nothing's sure with dragons," Cochrane said. "Mostly they sleep at night. But should they show up, it's every man for hisself."

As they neared the railing, Trenton frowned. "Where are the horses?" The others gave him quizzical looks, so he added, "You know, to ride?"

Cochrane reached across the railing with an amused grin and took hold of a metal lever Trenton hadn't noticed before. He pulled the lever, and the ground under Trenton's feet began to rumble. "Might want to step back," the dimber damber said.

Squinting into the darkness, Trenton watched the ground split open in front of him. He moved away as quickly as he could with the weight of the club still on his shoulder. Slowly a pair of giant doors slid aside, revealing an ominous black hole.

How many of these doors did they have hidden here? Or was this the same one they'd opened to shoot the catapult?

From inside the hole came the *thump, thump, thump* of a steam engine, followed by steady grinding. The Whipjacks nudged each other, obviously excited.

Trenton leaned as far forward as he dared. Something was rising out of the darkness. At first all he could see were bits of gleaming metal, then a platform appeared out of the ground. In the center of it were two bizarre-looking machines.

"What are they?" Kallista whispered.

Trenton shook his head. As the platform clanked into place, he dropped his club to the ground and approached one of the creations. From the back, it reminded him of a bicycle. It had a large, studded metal tire in the back. In the center of the machine was a leather seat above a small, wood-powered steam engine, and beyond that was a set of handlebars for steering. Up to that point it could have been a steam-powered bicycle.

The front of the machine was where everything went wrong. Instead of a front tire, there were a pair of mechanical legs and a metal horse's head with lamps where the eyes should have been.

Trenton stepped around to take the whole thing in. While part of him was terrified of having to ride the machine into battle, another part of him started analyzing how everything worked. His hands automatically crept to the tool belt he wore everywhere.

Cochrane grinned and patted the steam-powered horsecycle on the head. "What do ya think of my creation?"

14

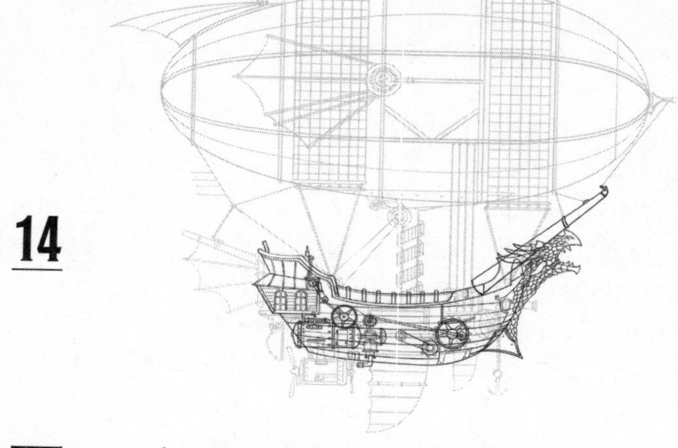

Trenton knelt on the ground, hands and arms covered with grease to the elbows, tools spread out around him. Kallista leaned close, the two of them studying the inner workings of one of the machines. Around them, the Whipjacks laughed and placed bets on whether Trenton would survive the first round.

"I don't get it," he whispered to Kallista, loosening a cable that ran from the handlebars, around a set of pulleys, to a gearbox that drove the feed belt. "Why wouldn't they connect this directly?"

"Move over and give me room to see," Kallista said, elbowing him aside. Inserting a slim screwdriver into the gearbox, she popped off the lid and peered inside. "This makes no sense. It delays the throttle acceleration by a full second at least." Grabbing a pair of pliers, she twisted the box until the entire thing popped out onto the ground.

"What are you doing?" Trenton barked. The last thing he needed was to break the machine just before the match. If he did, the Whipjacks would probably make him forfeit the match and let Weasel hit him with the club anyway.

"Give me those wire cutters," Kallista said. Trenton handed her the tool, and she clipped nearly six inches of the cable, running it directly to the control that fed wood into the miniature boiler. "Try the throttle now."

Trenton climbed onto the seat, started the machine up, and twisted the control on the right handlebar. Instantly the engine roared to life, and the upraised legs churned. If the legs had been in their proper position, he would have shot straight forward and plunged over the side of the opening into the pit below.

"Much better," he said, grinning.

Kallista wiped her hands on a rag and nodded.

Trenton got off and squatted to get a closer look at the mechanics that made it all work. "Why did they build the throttle that way in the first place?"

"Because whoever designed it didn't know what he was doing."

"Other than that, though, it's a pretty ingenious creation," Trenton said. "The legs give you better traction in the sand plus the ability to drive over practically anything, the back wheel is indestructible, and the engine is surprisingly powerful for its size. It almost looks like something your father would build."

Kallista tossed the rag aside. "If my father had built it, it would work properly. He never would have made these kinds of mistakes. It's like that chain machine. A solid idea but bad execution."

"Whoa there now," Cochrane said, walking up behind them. "What are ya doing to my machine, mucking up the works?"

"We're making it run the way it should have in the first place," Kallista said, hands planted on her hips.

The dimber damber picked up the gearbox, turning it over in his hands and peering into the machine's engine. "No one said you could go messing with the ruddy thing. It was fine the way it was."

"You told us yourself there were no rules," Trenton said.

Cochrane tossed the gearbox aside and shrugged. "Suit

yourself. It'll be your soul case the death hunter scrapes off the ground, now won't it?"

"I hope not," Trenton said under his breath.

"Head on over, then," Cochrane said, pointing to one end of the wooden rail. "The match is ready to begin."

As Trenton climbed onto the machine, Kallista handed him his cudgel. "I used a couple of spare parts to make a bracket on the handlebars. Rest the handle of your club on that. Weasel might be strong enough to hold his weapon and drive at the same time, but you're not."

"Thanks for the vote of confidence."

Ignoring his comment, Kallista wiggled the right front leg of the horsecycle and tightened a bolt. "The suspension is terrible. I'm surprised the legs haven't fallen off already. But I modified them a little and—"

"I know," Trenton interrupted her. "I was right there. I'm the one who suggested it. Look, we've done everything we can to improve my chances. Now it's up to me."

Kallista bit her lower lip, then suddenly lunged forward, pulling Trenton into an awkwardly stiff hug. "Don't die." Before Trenton could think to hug her back, she released him and kicked a rusty spring. "I don't want to lose the dragon."

"Right," Trenton said. "The dragon."

Trying to look like he knew what he was doing, Trenton steered his horsecycle to his end of the rail and paused at the starting mark.

Cochrane motioned for him to stop the engine, and Trenton obeyed.

"Ya both know the rules," the dimber damber called. "There are no rules." The other Whipjacks roared at the joke, and Cochrane waved toward the tall Whipjack with bony arms and legs. "Stork will call the start. Fight hard and try not to go feets-up."

Balancing on his machine, Trenton felt cold sweat run down the back of his neck. "Don't crash, don't crash," he whispered over and over to himself. If he lost control in the loose sand and fell, all Weasel would have to do was ride up to him and hit him over the head.

"Combatants, start yer machines," Stork shouted, holding an oily rag above his head.

Trenton pushed the ignition, and the horsecycle roared to life. Across the railing and on the other side of the field, Weasel did the same.

"Hoist yer cudgels."

Trenton lifted his club and rested it on the left side of his handlebars, trying not to notice how easily Weasel hoisted his. To his left, Kallista pumped her fist in the air, but he could see that her body was shaking as badly as his was. He'd taken as many practice runs with the machine as he had time for, but the horsecycle's controls still felt uncomfortable and placed in the wrong positions. He'd hoped it would be similar to controlling Ladon, but it wasn't anything like that.

"Ride!" Stork yelled, dropping the rag. The crowd roared.

Across the field, Weasel sped forward.

Trenton accelerated, but in the excitement of the moment, he twisted the throttle too far, and the horsecycle nearly raced out from under him. Trying to catch his balance, he leaned forward, and the back wheel slipped left in the sand, knocking him against the railing.

"Not so fast!" Kallista screamed.

Trenton released the throttle, and the engine nearly stalled.

"Hulver head!" shouted someone from the stands.

"Cully!" yelled another.

Trenton had no idea what those names meant, but he was pretty sure they weren't compliments.

On the other side of the railing, Weasel was racing toward him.

Trenton tried again, this time accelerating more carefully. The horsecycle's legs churned smoothly, pulling him forward. Trenton twisted the accelerator again, and wind whipped through his hair.

Realizing he'd been looking down at the controls, he raised his eyes. Weasel was nearly on top of him. Trenton lifted the cudgel with his left hand and felt for the trigger. He couldn't find it. The wooden handle slipped in his sweaty palm, and he glanced down. There it was, farther back. He'd gripped the handle too far forward.

Lights flashed in his eyes, and he looked up to see Weasel's club aimed straight at his face. Sliding his left hand down the handle of the club, Trenton accidentally twisted the accelerator all the way back. The horsecycle's legs churned in a blur of sand and metal. His back wheel slid out from under him, and he felt himself falling. Reflexively, he squeezed the trigger.

At the same moment that he felt the spring in his cudgel discharge, something flew above his head.

On the other side of the railing, Weasel grunted in pain and flew backward off his machine.

Trenton hit the ground, getting a mouthful of sand, and rolled to a stop. His horsecycle coughed once and died. Then people were running toward him, laughing and shouting.

"You did it!" Kallista yelled, lifting him up. "You won the first match."

• • •

"That was great," Kallista yelled, patting him on the back.

"I fell off my horsecycle and only managed to hit him with my club by dumb luck," Trenton said.

"Dumb luck is better than no luck," Kallista said. She adjusted something in the engine near the boiler. "Now you know what you did wrong. Next time pull out more slowly and keep your balance. Weasel comes out fast—you can tell he's ridden these before—but he doesn't have much control. Take your time and aim for his chest."

Raising his hands above his head, he twisted painfully left and right. His ribs felt like he'd been hit with a monkey wrench, and his left knee had an odd wobble to it, but other than that he felt okay. He knew he'd gotten off lucky.

"Want me to cut back on the throttle?" Kallista asked.

"No. I think I just got overexcited by the crowd."

"All right, then." She stood up from the horsecycle and punched his shoulder softly. "Just one more win."

"One more," Trenton agreed. Starting up the engine, he rode back to the rail and took his place at the starting mark. With the first-round jitters out of the way, he actually felt pretty good. He had a better feeling for what he was doing, and, really, he couldn't do much worse than he'd done the first time.

"Ready," Stork called, raising his flag.

Trenton started the engine. He eased the throttle forward and felt the horsecycle tug beneath him. He dried his palms on his pants and gripped the club firmly, making sure his finger was on the trigger this time.

Across the field, Weasel fiddled with something on the ground then picked up his weapon.

"Ride!" Stork yelled, dropping the flag.

Trenton twisted the accelerator smoothly, and the horsecycle raced out on to the sand. He turned it farther, and the legs churned instantly. Maybe that was his angle. He had better acceleration than Weasel did. If he waited until the last moment, then sped up and fired his weapon, the surprise might get him the win.

Keeping his left handlebar just outside the railing, he planted his feet and gripped the weapon.

Weasel was racing toward him, back hunched, hair flying.

Everything came down to timing. Three, two—he was almost there—one. He twisted the accelerator handle all the way, and the horsecycle leaped forward.

Trenton lifted his weapon at the same time Weasel did his. With cold air burning his eyes, Trenton reached for his trigger.

At that moment, Weasel released his accelerator, reached into his pocket, and flung something forward.

Bits of rock and grit sprayed Trenton's face, blinding his vision. Unable to see where he was aiming, he squeezed the trigger. The shock of the spring release pushed his arm back, but he knew instantly that he'd missed.

An instant later, a dark square appeared in front of his eyes, and a giant fist slammed into his head.

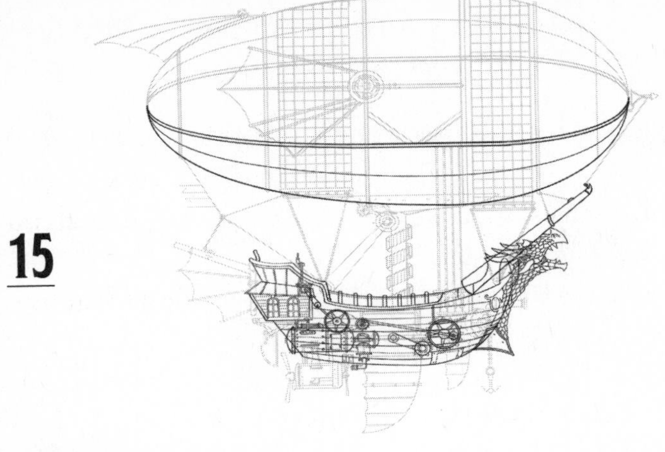

15

Can you hear me?"

Trenton groaned, tried to sit up, and instantly vomited. "Did we crash the dragon?"

"Looks like he's gots'a second nose alongside the first," Slash said, the metal on his arms flashing in the moonlight.

Trenton tried to remember where he was and what he was supposed to be doing. There was somewhere important he had to be. "The dance," he muttered, his words slurring. "I need to take Simoni to the dance."

"Bashed him a good one," said a woman with a scar slicing her right eyebrow.

Trenton looked at the crowd of faces jammed around him and suddenly remembered where he was. "Did I win?" he asked.

Kallista shook her head.

"Give him a lump pie," hooted Weasel.

"Yeah, yeah." Plucky laughed. "Flogged his head, all right."

"You cheated," Kallista snarled. "You threw dirt in his face."

"No rules, dear," Weasel said with a sneer.

"Trenton loses round two," Cochrane said. "If he can't ride a third match, he forfeits—"

"Who says I can't ride?" Trenton tried to get to his feet but fell backward as everything began to spin.

"Sit down," Kallista said, putting her hands under his arms

and easing him next to a large rock. "You aren't in any shape to go anywhere."

"We win!" Plucky shouted, dancing around on her mechanical legs. "The dragon is ours."

"Let's go strip it down," Weasel said. "I can count our swag already."

Trenton dropped his chin to his chest. He'd failed and lost the dragon. Kallista was right. He never should have volunteered to fight.

"Hold on," Kallista said, standing up. "Trenton might not be able to ride, but I can."

"Forget it, girl," Weasel said, a mocking smile on his face. "One rider. Three matches. He can't ride, he forfeits. Them's the rules."

Kallista charged toward him and shoved him in the chest so hard he nearly fell. "You keep saying there *are* no rules, so *I* say I'm riding the third match."

Plucky pulled out her knife and started toward Kallista as Weasel grabbed his cudgel from the ground. Trenton tried to get up from the rock, but the earth tilted at a sudden angle, and he found himself lying on his side.

"Pull up," Cochrane said, stepping between them. "The girl has a point. Rules only say you lose if you croaks or falls twice."

"See," Kallista said. "There's nothing saying I can't ride for Trenton. I'm his . . ." She looked around as if searching for the right word. "His second."

"No," Trenton moaned, using the rock to pull himself back up. Getting the dragon back wasn't worth risking Kallista's life.

"Cunning, that one," said Cochrane, nodding at Kallista.

Weasel scowled.

"Afraid of losing to a girl?" Kallista asked the burly boy.

"Fine!" Weasel growled. "I look forward to silencing your

noisy gob. When I finish pummeling you, your friend'll be planting what's left'a ya."

"Don't do it," Trenton croaked, but no one was listening.

Kallista started up the horsecycle and rode it to the starting mark.

As Stork lifted his rag to start the final match, Trenton noticed a figure moving to his right in the darkness. As he turned his head, the figure darted away, but he was sure it had been the blond-haired boy from the Order of the Beast. What was he doing out here?

Out on the field, Stork shouted, "Ride."

Trenton spun around as Kallista twisted the throttle. But something was wrong. The horsecycle's engine coughed, roared, coughed again, and stalled.

The crowd moaned as Kallista pushed the ignition again.

The engine turned over, belched a puff of smoke from the boiler, and died. The horsecycle must have been damaged in the crash.

"Get out of there!" Trenton shouted. He pushed up from the rock, stumbling toward the field as the ground rolled under his feet.

Kallista dropped her club and leaned over the side of the machine, working frantically on the engine.

Racing toward her, Weasel let out a victory whoop. "I'm coming for ya, luv!"

"Stop the match!" Trenton screamed.

Kallista looked up from the engine, eyes wide. "Don't hit me," she yelled at Weasel, throwing one hand over her face.

Weasel slowed, relishing the moment. "Smile, girl, this one's going straight in yer big gob."

As Weasel lifted his weapon over his head, Kallista suddenly reached down and grabbed her cudgel. Hitting the ignition with her thumb, she started the engine and cranked the throttle in a single motion. The horsecycle lunged forward. Using its momentum, she swung the club up and pulled the trigger.

The head sprang forward, connecting with Weasel's chin. Still holding his club above his shoulder, Weasel was completely unprepared for the blow. His horsecycle continued to race forward, but he fell off the back, hitting the ground. He let out a deep groan.

For a moment the crowd froze, then they all burst into applause.

Trenton stopped where he was. It had been a trick. Kallista had only pretended to stall the engine to draw Weasel in.

Kallista turned off her engine, pushed the horsecycle up on its kickstand, and walked to stand over her dazed opponent. Dropping her club by his side, she knelt down and said, "No rules, luv."

• • •

Trenton woke the next morning to a finger jabbing him in the ribs. Fire raced up his side, and his eyes snapped open. "Stop it, Kallista," he groaned. "I feel like I—"

"Like you fell down a well?" Cochrane nodded sympathetically. "I'd imagine your head'll be thumping for a few days."

Trenton gingerly touched his fingers to the lump on his forehead and winced.

Cochrane kicked the side of the small wooden cot. "Get up."

"Give me a minute." Trenton climbed out from under the threadbare blanket, pulled on his boots, and followed Cochrane into the hallway, where Kallista was already waiting.

Without looking back, the dimber damber led them through a series of twisting passageways.

"Where are we going?" Trenton asked Kallista.

She shook her head and held out her hands, palms up.

Although Seattle and Discovery were both built underground, the two cities couldn't have felt more different. Except for the mines, Discovery was open, with high ceilings, bright lights, and parks. The shops and buildings were tall and almost exclusively metal, built in straight lines to look identical to every other building in the section. Due to the exhaust fans, a slight breeze constantly blew faintly sooty-smelling air through the streets.

Here, even the center of the city had a cramped, almost brooding, feel to it. Buildings and homes tended to be small, made of wood or brick, and tucked protectively into nooks and crannies. The air was damp and dank. In some areas it smelled salty, in others it stank of trash and rot.

There was no sense of order or planning. Some of the passages were wide, with stone or brick-lined streets. Others were narrow and crooked, the walls and floors bare dirt. It was as if the people who designed the city had gone out of their way to make every building and home completely different from the one next to it.

Trenton found the idea both exciting and frightening at the same time.

The people here were different, too. In Discovery, despite the fact that things had always been tightly controlled—or maybe because of it—citizens were generally open and friendly. No one worried about getting enough to eat or having good clothing.

In less than a day, Trenton had noticed how different the people of Seattle were. Part of it was the way they dressed. On the one hand there were the members of the Order of the Beast with their clean red robes and odd black hats. On the other hand, there were the Whipjacks with their fur, leather, and metal body piercings. But even in between, there were people dressed in fine shirts and pants, while others wore mismatched rags that were too big or too small.

As he and Kallista followed the dimber damber, no one waved or called out greetings. Hungry eyes peeked through cracked open doors or watched from the shadows. There was a sense of wildness and unpredictability that made him wonder if the city was like the joust from the night before—no rules except survival. Trenton had the feeling that if they hadn't been with Cochrane, he and Kallista would be in real danger.

Cochrane noticed him eyeing their surroundings and grinned. "Curious history this city has. Back in the late 1800s, there was a big fire. Burned most of the buildings to the ground."

"From the dragons?" Trenton asked.

"No. This was before the beasts showed up. The fire was caused by an industrial accident, if you believe the stories. Destroyed almost all of the downtown. But it did some good—killed all the rats and other vermin." Cochrane grinned.

To their left, something small and dark splashed through a puddle and disappeared through a hole in a wall that was green with moss.

"Looks like it didn't kill *all* the vermin," Kallista said.

The dimber damber chuckled. "We're near the water. This part of the city is known as the wharfs. Before the dragons came, there were docks and warehouses. A bustling port. Now it's mostly just wet—with lots of nasty wharf rats, of both the four- and two-legged varieties."

He looked pointedly back at them as though warning them to be on guard, then continued. "After the fire, folks built their city up again, as they almost always will. But this time they decided to build the new city above the old one. More than twenty feet above it. To keep it from flooding and such.

"Much of the old city remained—turned into basements, filled in with gravel or sealed with brick and stone. This came in quite handy when the dragons attacked. While the upper city burned to the ground again, the survivors took what they could and moved underground."

Kallista glanced at Trenton. "He sounds different," she muttered to him.

"He's not using that strange accent or the weird words," Trenton agreed.

They stopped at a wide canal, the water sluggish and dark, and Cochrane stepped into a small boat. Remembering the rats, Trenton eyed the canal uncertainly. Having never been in a boat before, or in any body of water bigger than the fish tanks back home, Trenton hesitated. When Kallista climbed in, though, he didn't have any choice but to join her.

"All this was under the original city?" Trenton asked as Cochrane untied the boat.

"No." The dimber damber pushed them out into the center of the canal, rowing against the current. "There wasn't much more than a couple dozen rooms and tunnels at first. But over time, the people who survived the first round of attacks added to it. They dug out what they could, bracing the walls and ceilings with scavenged beams, timber, and brick. Couldn't do anything above ground on account of the dragons, so they built the warrens and streets you see here."

That explained that haphazard feel to the city. What would it be like to create a city with no plans or blueprints? Using only your own imagination and what you could scavenge?

As the boat drifted into a tunnel, Cochrane picked up a lantern from the floor of the boat and lit the wick. "The original streets make up our city center and surrounding areas. It tends to stay drier. Fewer rats, less dangerous. It's controlled by the Red Robes and the wealthier folks. The wharfs are home to people living closer to the fringe. Whipjacks make the rules here. Which means I am the law."

Trenton covered his nose and mouth as they passed through a particularly rank-smelling tunnel. Something pale and swollen floated past. "I think you got the bad end of the deal."

Cochrane's eyes narrowed. "Until recently the Order had all the power. That's changing."

"Why are you telling us this?" Kallista asked.

The dimber damber studied her. "I thought you might find it interesting. Being the daughter of an inventor and all."

Kallista jumped up from her seat, and Trenton grabbed the side of the boat as it rocked beneath them. "I never told you my father was an inventor."

"Didn't you?" Cochrane asked, a small smile playing around his lips. "Maybe I just assumed, based on what I've seen of you."

"You've seen him, haven't you? Tell me what you know," Kallista demanded. "Where is he?"

Cochrane held up a finger. "All in good time." Pulling hard on the right oar, he steered them into another, narrower waterway.

"Why are you talking differently now than you were before?" Trenton asked, hoping to change the subject and give Kallista time to calm down. "You're not using all those strange words the other Whipjacks use."

"The *Cant*," Cochrane said. "Long before the great fire, there were two classes of citizens. The respectable folk and the seedier crowd—thieves, beggars, and other persons of ill repute. Immigrants mostly, who were offered only the hardest, lowest-paying jobs. They developed a private language among themselves. A code of brotherhood, if you will. The Whipjacks are descendants of that second group. But since it's just the three of us, I don't really think it's necessary. Do you?"

"No," Trenton said.

"I wasn't always a Whipjack. I was born an ordinary citizen, destined to spend my days grubbing for food, shelter, and a bit extra. Then my mother and father died of fever, and I didn't have even that. I'd likely have died if I hadn't shown a knack for the trade."

Trenton shifted on the hard wooden bench of the boat. "The trade?"

Cochrane rubbed his thumb and forefingers together and grinned. "Purse lifting, shoulder shams, rum dubbing. In short, taking whatever I could without getting caught."

"This is all very interesting," Kallista snapped, "but what does it have to do with my father?"

So much for her calming down.

Cochrane maneuvered the boat up against a small stretch of shore along the far side of the tunnel. At first Trenton couldn't understand why, then he spotted a narrow opening in the wall. It wouldn't look like anything more than a space where a few bricks had fallen out if he hadn't been looking for it.

The dimber damber tied the boat to a small rock outcropping and faced the two of them. "The Whipjacks took me in and kept food in my mouth. That's probably where I would have stayed—nothing more than a blackguard, killing whatever animals I could find for food and stealing whatever I could get away with—if I hadn't met a man a little over two years ago. A man who was searching for the great city of Seattle. Said he'd read about it in books and newspapers. That man opened my eyes to talents I didn't know I had. That man changed my life."

He stepped out of the boat and nodded toward the opening. "Leo Babbage."

16

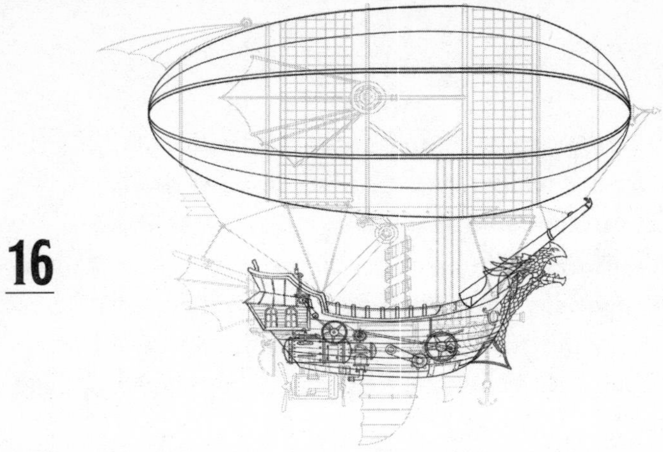

I knew it!" Kallista shouted. "I knew he made it here. Why didn't you tell me before? Where is he?"

"Quiet," Cochrane commanded. He glanced up and down the tunnel, then whispered, "We're close to the center of the city—Red Robe territory. Keep your mouths shut and follow me." Without another word, he and his lantern disappeared into the crack in the wall. Instantly the tunnel went dark, the only light coming from an opening farther downstream.

Trenton studied the entrance as best as he could in the darkness. The wall looked unstable, with bricks poking out at odd angles and piles of loose dirt and scattered rocks here and there. "This looks like a cave-in waiting to happen."

"Who cares? My father's in there," Kallista said before heading into the opening as well.

Trenton approached the crevice and peeked inside. Unlike the other passages in the city, this one was barely wide enough for a single person to fit through. The walls were bare dirt and looked like they had been dug out by hand.

Kallista had been suspicious of Cochrane at first. Rightfully so, considering they had no idea what motives he might have. But as soon as Cochrane mentioned her father, she was willing to follow him anywhere. Someone had to look out for her.

Just before he slipped through the opening, he heard a splash behind him. Spinning around, he looked up and down the tunnel. It was impossible to see more than twenty feet in either direction. He didn't think anyone was there. Maybe it had been a fish. Taking a deep breath, he ducked his head and stepped through the crack.

He expected that Cochrane and Kallista would have waited for him, but when he emerged on the other side, the light of Cochrane's lantern was rapidly disappearing. Running his hands along the rough dirt walls, he hurried to catch up. He came up behind Kallista and the dimber damber, who were deep in conversation. Neither of them appeared to have noticed that Trenton wasn't with them before or that he had caught up now.

"—no idea there was anything here until your father dug it out," Cochrane continued. "Apparently he had a map of the old city with him and was looking for something specific."

"Yes," Kallista said, nearly skipping. "He loves maps. We had hundreds around the house."

Cochrane nodded. "Since the dragons drove humans underground, the people of Seattle have been focused on two things: one, not being eaten by the dragons, and two, finding enough food to stay alive. Unfortunately, those two needs don't always go hand in hand. The best places to hunt are usually the best places to find dragons. Your father, on the other hand, had a thirst for one thing."

"Knowledge," Kallista said at once.

Cochrane paused to look at her. "He used to quote a saying by someone named Benjamin Franklin."

Kallista grinned. "'An investment in knowledge pays the best interest.'"

"That's right. Every time I asked him why we were digging this tunnel, he repeated that phrase to me. There were days I thought I would go crazy if he said it one more time."

"Oh, I know." Kallista nodded emphatically.

"If you knew about him all along, why are you just now telling us?" Trenton asked.

Kallista shot him an impatient look, but Cochrane nodded. "Secrets can be dangerous things in this city. I had to make sure you were who you claimed to be."

A few feet ahead, the tunnel widened, revealing a brick doorway. Cochrane paused outside it, turning to face the two of them. The flickering light of the lantern he held near his waist turned his mouth into a stern scar and his eyes into sockets of darkness. "When Leo Babbage arrived here, he faced the same threats you do. This city doesn't have many rules, but one of them is that strangers are not taken in. We don't have enough food to support the people we have. You saw for yourselves how trespassers are treated."

Trenton shivered, and it wasn't because of the cold air in the passage.

"The other rule, and this one is even more stringently followed than the first, is that dragons are never to be opposed. For a hundred years, the Order of the Beast has worshipped the dragons as divine beings. They offer them food and valuables at the beginning of every month, as well as on certain important holidays. In exchange, the dragons leave our city in peace. That's what gives the Order the power to rule the city."

"It didn't look very peaceful outside," Trenton said, remembering the burned trees.

Cochrane nodded. "Like I said, things are changing. For as long as anyone can remember, the dragons who hunt in these woods have spared us. That's not to say they don't eat anyone they catch wandering outside, but they have left the city itself alone. They were ruled by a great green beast with emerald eyes. Then, a few months ago, the green dragon disappeared."

Trenton and Kallista looked at each other.

"You two know something about its disappearance, don't you?" the dimber damber asked.

They both nodded.

"Did you . . ." Cochrane ran his fingers through his long dark hair, both fear and excitement evident on his face. "Did you *kill* it?"

"It's not like we wanted to," Trenton said.

Cochrane grinned fiercely, his eyes dark shadows above the glow of the lantern. "He said you would, but I didn't believe it. Maybe it comes from spending so much time around the Order, but I really thought they might be immortal."

"We didn't have any choice," Trenton said. "It invaded our city."

"As he said it would." The dimber damber nodded. "And you destroyed it with that machine of yours? That dragon you built?"

"My father left the designs for us," Kallista said. "He was sure it was only a matter of time before the dragons found our city. He would have built it himself, but the government discovered what he was up to, and he had to fake his own death in order to leave the city."

"And he came straight to a city where fighting dragons is not only against the law, it's considered blasphemy, treason."

Kallista's face went white, and Trenton felt his heart sink. "They didn't hurt him, did they?" she asked.

Cochrane put his hand on her shoulder. "They didn't even know he was here. I met him out in the woods while I was hunting. When he told me who he was and why he was here, I realized the danger and kept him hidden."

"Why *did* he come here?" Trenton asked. "Did he know about the Order?"

"No. He had no idea anyone worshipped dragons. I'm not

even sure he believed me at first. He came here for one reason." Cochrane glanced at the doorway. "Let me show you."

Holding the lantern above his head, Cochrane stepped through the opening. Trenton and Kallista looked at each other, then hurried after him. Inside the room, it was hard to make out anything other than a few tables and stacks of what might have been anything from bricks to crates of food.

Cochrane reached behind him to flip a switch, and suddenly dozens of lightbulbs came on. Kallista's mouth dropped open, and Trenton gasped.

"Welcome," Cochrane said, "to what remains of the Seattle Public Library."

• • •

Kallista was the first to recover. "Look at it all," she said, running her hands over what had to be at least a hundred books spread across a long wooden table. Around the room were row after row of shelves filled from floor to ceiling with books, magazines, and even a few newspapers.

Trenton followed behind her, afraid to touch anything. He'd seen books before—in Leo Babbage's workshop, and, of course, in school—but an entire *library*? The thought took his breath away. He'd never imagined there could be this many books in existence. "There must be thousands," he whispered.

"Hundreds of thousands," Cochrane said. "Unfortunately most of them are still buried, and of the ones we dig out, only a few are salvageable. The library burned along with everything else when the dragons showed up. Fortunately, the library had a basement. Your father believed that, when the fires started, the librarians moved as many books and important documents as they could into the basement because many of the books we found were sealed in protective wrappings. But more than a hundred years of weather and soil have done their damage."

"Where is he?" Kallista begged, looking around. "Is he here?"

Cochrane shook his head and sighed. "I'm sorry."

Kallista's sucked in a sharp breath. "He's not—"

"Dead?" Cochrane shook his head. "No. At least not as far as I know." He pointed to several chairs lined up along one of the tables. "Take a seat, and I'll tell you everything. It won't take long."

When Trenton and Kallista were sitting, he took a seat across the table from them, pushing the stacks of books aside. "When I first met your father, the stories he told me were so fantastic I couldn't believe them. A city inside a mountain. Food growing in nothing but water. People living in complete safety. It sounded too good to be true. Obviously, I wanted him to take me there. Who wouldn't?

"But he had a different idea. He said that it was only a matter of time before the dragons, well *a* dragon at the time, discovered his city. He believed that the people who founded your city had once built a secret weapon capable of fighting dragons, but the information they had been working on was long since destroyed."

The dimber damber waved his hands at the shelves of books. "He came here hoping to find information about what that weapon might have been. Although your founders failed in their attempt to fight the dragons the first time, he hoped that by improving upon what they'd built, he might have a chance of defeating the beasts a second time."

"Why hide him, then?" Trenton asked. "Why not tell everyone what was happening and get their help?"

"You forget who runs the city."

"The Order of the Beast," Kallista said.

"Precisely. If they heard even a hint of your father's plan, they would have done whatever it took to stop him." Cochrane steepled his hands in front of his face.

"But what about us?" Trenton asked, realizing what a terrible mistake they'd made. "We walked straight to their highest leaders and told them we'd killed at least one dragon, maybe two."

Kallista stared at the table. "Me and my big mouth again."

"Don't be too hard on yourself," Cochrane said. "You didn't know who you were dealing with, and by the time I found out you were here—and who you were—it was too late to warn you." He paused, studying Kallista. "Your father and I had been working on the catapult Plucky and Weasel used—without my permission, I might add—to bring down your dragon. In their defense, they thought they were attacking a real dragon, but if that had been the case, they'd both be dead." He shifted his intense gaze to Trenton. "When I heard about your mechanical dragon, I realized where you must have come from. I sent Plucky to your cell to learn more about you. She may not get around too quickly, but she knows her way around the city better than anyone."

So that was what she'd been doing there. It hadn't all been about learning how to use the dragon. Then again, as tricky as she was, maybe it had been.

"But now that the Order knows we killed a dragon, it's only a matter of time before they come after us," Trenton said. "I'm almost sure I saw one of them spying on us at the tilt. The boy with the blond hair."

"I'll look into it." Cochrane tugged at the end of his moustache. "Don't worry about the Red Robes. They think you're lying. They're still convinced the dragons can't be killed. If they thought dragons were *not* immortal, it would destroy their entire belief system. Besides, they won't touch you as long as you're under my protection. I carry a lot more clout in the city now than I did when your father first arrived."

He waved his hands, encompassing the entire library. "That's the deal we made. I kept his presence here a secret, and he searched for information on the weapons he believed could be used to defeat the dragons. He also helped me discover my talent for inventing. Together, we brought the city something it had been missing since the dragons attacked—technology."

"The lights," Trenton said, remembering how new the bulbs and wires had looked in the town square.

"And the fountain," Kallista added.

Cochrane nodded. "Electricity and plumbing were fables until he arrived. Stories from a long-lost past. Obviously he couldn't reveal himself, so I had to take credit for the inventions. Now I not only command the Whipjacks, I also have the loyalty of the entire city. The Order wouldn't dare stand against me."

"I understand," Kallista said, drumming her fingers on the table. "But where is my father?"

Cochrane nodded and offered her a small smile. He walked into the stacks of books and returned with a white envelope. As he laid it on the table, Trenton saw Kallista's name written on the front. He recognized the handwriting immediately from the many plans and letters he'd seen written in the same tight script.

It was from Leo Babbage.

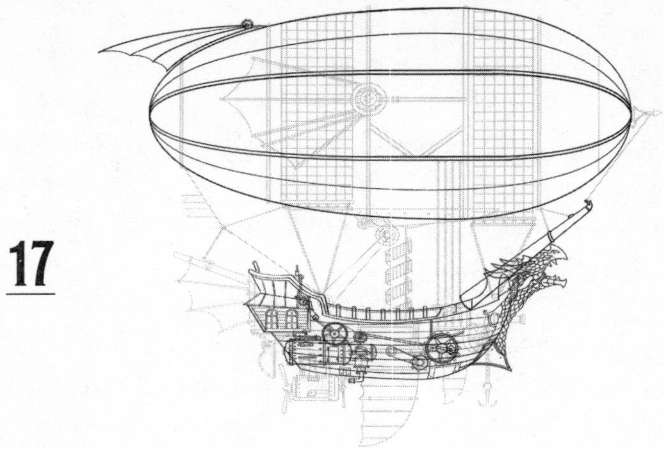

17

Kallista opened the letter with trembling hands. Sitting beside her, Trenton touched her elbow. "Do you want me to read it to you?" Back home, she'd been unable to read her father's letters for fear of what they might say.

She shook her head. "Thanks, but I can do it."

Trenton waited as her eyes scanned the writing. He could see that it was a single page, covered front to back and top to bottom, but he stayed far enough back to give her privacy. She read it over once, twice, then handed it to him.

"Are you sure?" Trenton asked.

Kallista nodded. "It applies as much to you as it does to me."

Smoothing the page flat on the table, he read the words of a father to his daughter. Leo Babbage had never been someone who spent a lot of time with emotion, and this letter was no different. He got straight to the point.

Kallista,

I hope this letter finds you well. And since you are here reading this letter, you *__have__* *found my plans, assembled the mechanical dragon, defeated the beast that will undoubtedly attack the city, and then followed my clues to Seattle. Bravo! I knew you could do it.*

While I would like to wait here for your arrival, I'm afraid that will not be possible. As Renato has undoubtedly told you, I am on the cusp of a rather remarkable discovery. One that may well turn the battle between dragons and humans back in our favor. I am afraid I must leave at once to track down additional clues.

Please know that I am thinking of you always. Do not come looking for me. Stay and help Cochrane build the machines we have designed. Unlike the plans I left for you in Cove, these schematics will provide you everything you need to know.

Your father,
Leo Babbage

Your father. Trenton shook his head. Not even a *love* or *dear*. There was no doubt Leo was a genius, but he was not good with people, not even his own daughter. He handed the letter back to Kallista.

Cochrane watched the two of them closely.

Kallista slid the paper across the table to him. "You can read it. It's not exactly personal."

She could say that again. Would it have killed her father to wait for her?

Cochrane scanned the letter quickly, front and back, nodding here and there. "What does he mean in the last paragraph? This part—'unlike the plans I left for you in Cove'?"

Kallista explained how her father had intentionally left parts of the plans for Ladon blank, knowing that as they discovered how to build the steam turbine and the wings, they would also discover that the government had been intentionally hiding technology.

"Why would they do that?" Cochrane asked. "Especially if the technology was beneficial to them?"

"They didn't want to fight the dragons again, so they blamed technology for destroying the outside world," Trenton said.

"I suppose your father would agree."

Kallista snorted. "No, he wouldn't. My father loves technology. He is an inventor."

Cochrane scratched his beard. "All I know is I once heard him say technology brought the dragons here, and it would take technology to send them back."

"That doesn't make any sense," Kallista said.

But did it? Trenton had never considered what caused the dragons to appear in the first place. The papers he'd read had only reported the appearance of the dragons and the damage they'd done. Not where they came from or how they had arrived in such massive numbers so quickly. Was it possible humans could have been at least partly responsible for the destruction of their own world?

"So," Cochrane said, "this is what I've hired the two of you to help me with."

"Help you do what?" Trenton asked. "It seems like you've got everything under control here. What do you need from us?"

"Wait here," the dimber damber said. He disappeared into the shelves and came back a few minutes later with several large sheets of paper. Trenton immediately recognized them as mechanical schematics.

Cochrane set them on the table and slid them across for Trenton and Kallista to examine.

Kallista and Trenton leaned over the first page. It was a large metal cylinder on wheels. Looking over the plans, Trenton realized it was designed to shoot metal balls ranging from three- to six-inches in diameter.

"It's called a cannon," Cochrane said. "You've heard of them?"

Trenton shook his head and was surprised to see Kallista do the same. He thought her father had told her about everything. Even stuff the school didn't allow.

After the cannon was a fist-sized sphere that exploded after the wick was lit.

"Weapons?" Trenton asked.

Cochrane grunted. "Cannons and explosives. They've been used in wars for hundreds of years, even before the dragons arrived. Leo and I found dozens of mentions of them here in the library. But you've never heard of them before?"

"No," Trenton admitted. "Probably another technology our leaders didn't want us to know about."

"Or it was *the* technology," Cochrane said. "The technology your city's founders used against the dragons."

Kallista studied the plans. "What powers these devices? How do these metal balls get shot of out this cannon?"

The dimber damber tapped his nose. "That is the question. It took us a lot of digging, but we discovered a reference to an explosive substance used in all of these devices. Gunpowder."

"And you have some?" Trenton asked, excited. If they could fling metal balls or exploding spheres at the dragons, they'd be unstoppable.

Cochrane placed his hands flat on the table, eyes glittering. "Not yet. But we're close. That's the discovery your father was talking about. We were getting near when he left."

"And that's what you want us to help you with?" Kallista asked. "Figuring out how to make this explosive substance?"

Cochrane waved his hands. "Leave that to me. It's only a matter of time until I find it. No, I need you for something else."

"I don't understand," Trenton said. "If these weapons have been around for hundreds of years, why don't your people have them now?"

"I'm sure they did once," Cochrane said. "But after the dragons came, the people of this city were beaten down to nothing. Any technology they might once have had was lost in the struggle to scrape up enough food to survive. No doubt they hung on to their weapons for a time. But what good were they once the gunpowder ran out?"

He spread his first two fingers, pointing them at Trenton and Kallista. "It sounds like the city in your mountain managed to retain almost everything they had—even added to it—while on the outside, after a hundred years, people here had been reduced to the basics. Water, fire, and whatever food they could trap, grow, or scavenge. It wasn't until the last fifty years that we started to rebuild. And it's only since Leo Babbage showed up that we even realized how much we'd lost."

Cochrane gestured for Trenton and Kallista to come closer to the table. "I need you two for something much more important than gunpowder or weapons. Cannons and explosives are only useful if the dragons come to you. What we need is a way to take the weapons to *them*." He slid a second set of plans over. "I came up with these on my own."

These designs were much more advanced. There was a steam-powered vehicle with heavy metal wheels, large protective plates, and fitted with both guns and cannons. More horsecycles like the ones Trenton and Kallista had used in the joust, also fitted with weapons to fight the dragons. And finally, there was a huge wooden vessel shaped like a dragon and attached to a giant oval sphere that floated in the air. Each was equipped with the explosive weapons he'd seen earlier.

"You designed these?" Kallista asked, clearly skeptical.

"With your father's help. He recognized my talent and showed me how to use it."

Trenton pointed to the last set of designs. "I saw this back in the room where Plucky and Weasel shot us down."

"I call it an airship," Cochrane said. He spread his arms wide. "With these machines, we can take the battle to the dragons on land *and* air."

Trenton chewed the inside of his lower lip. "We barely managed to keep from getting killed, even with Ladon. This doesn't look nearly as maneuverable. The dragons would shoot you down with one blast of flame."

"They would if they could get close enough," the dimber damber said. "But that's where our weapons will give us the advantage. We can fire on them from any direction long before we get within range of their fireballs." He grinned. "For a hundred and fifty years, we've hidden from the monsters that drove us underground. Now it's our turn to fight back. To turn the tables on them. This is the start of a revolution that could spread across the entire country."

Would it work? The small gold dragon would be hard to hit with a single ball, but maybe if you loaded the cannon with many smaller balls so it created a spray pattern, and lined up several cannons in strategic positions—

"If you have the plans, why haven't you already built them?" Kallista asked, interrupting Trenton's thoughts.

Cochrane shrugged. "We've started. The thing is, as you may have noticed, I don't have the best mechanics. My people don't have the experience. You two, on the other hand, are sharp as nails. You noticed the issues with the chain maker right away. And my chair. The design is flawless, but no one can seem to get it right. With my brains and your know-how, we can get these whipped into shape in no time. Then we find the recipe for gunpowder and, pow, the dragons drop like flies."

"I don't know," Trenton said. "Isn't the Order of the Beast

going to be mad when they discover you're planning on attacking the dragons?"

Cochrane laughed. "That's the beauty of my plan. I don't need to say anything about attacking the dragons. I'll tell the Red Robes the truth: That the two of you flew here from a city with technology much more advanced than ours. They're already frightened of your flying machine. All I need to do is suggest that more of your people might show up on similar machines and that the only way we can defend ourselves from attack is with my weapons."

"Ladon is the only flying dragon we have. And we'd never attack another city," Trenton said.

"They don't need to know that."

Kallista tugged at her lower lip. "If we come from a hostile city, why would we agree to build your weapons?"

It was an excellent question, and one the Order would ask, too.

"You said it yourself," Cochrane answered. "You came looking for your father. He left your city because he didn't believe in attacking others. The two of you feel the same way. That's why you left, and why you've agreed to help us."

It sounded plausible enough that the Order might believe it. Especially if they were as afraid of Ladon as Cochrane claimed.

And staying here wasn't the worst idea. Sure, they'd come looking for Kallista's father, but they never expected to end up in a situation like this. And now that they knew how many dragons were outside, they were going to have to come up with a plan to defend themselves.

"You protect us from the Red Robes, and we join your team to help build these machines?" Kallista asked.

"Not join, *lead*. I'll give the two of you tools, room to work, raw materials, and full control of all the resources at my disposal. That includes a team of Whipjacks to do whatever you need them to."

Trenton had been slouching in his chair, looking over the plans. Now he sat up straight. "You want us to be in charge?"

Cochrane smiled. "Isn't that what I said? I've got people who can handle a wrench and turn a screwdriver. What I need are thinkers, planners, builders. If you're even half as brilliant as Leo is—and I think you are—there's no one who could do a better job. While you lead the team, I'll be figuring out the final ingredients to make gunpowder."

Trenton had always dreamed of working on machines. It was what he'd studied for, what he'd expected to spend his life doing. Then his dreams had come crashing down when he'd been assigned to food production instead. What the dimber damber was suggesting was everything he'd hoped for and more. This wouldn't just be repairing existing machines, it would be building something new, something advanced, in a place where creativity was not only accepted but encouraged. It sounded too good to be true.

He turned to Kallista, expecting her to be as excited as he was. But she shook her head, a deep line creasing her brow. She opened her mouth, and Cochrane held up a hand, stopping her.

"I know you want to look for your father. And, to be honest, I can't blame you. But look at his letter. He told you to stay and help me. He specifically said not to go looking for him."

"That's just his way of protecting me," Kallista said. "He's stubborn."

Trenton coughed into his fist to keep from laughing. Stubbornness was definitely a trait that ran in the family.

Cochrane pressed a finger to his lips, drawing a deep breath. "Here's the thing. First, your dragon is no condition to go anywhere. Second, even if it was ready to fly today, you have no idea where to look for Leo. You help me build my weapons, and I'll not only give you the tools and materials to repair your dragon, but I'll also have my people help with the repairs."

Take the deal, Trenton urged silently. *You agreed before*. Maybe she'd forgotten that it hadn't been so long ago that they'd been sentenced to spend the rest of their lives in prison. If Cochrane really wanted to, he could seize Ladon and force them to work as slaves. This offer was the best option they had. Maybe the only one.

"Will I have access to the library?" Kallista asked.

"Of course. Day or night."

It was more than fair. Still, Trenton was relieved when Kallista nodded.

"All right."

Cochrane leaned back in his chair and grinned. "Wonderful. Let's get to work."

18

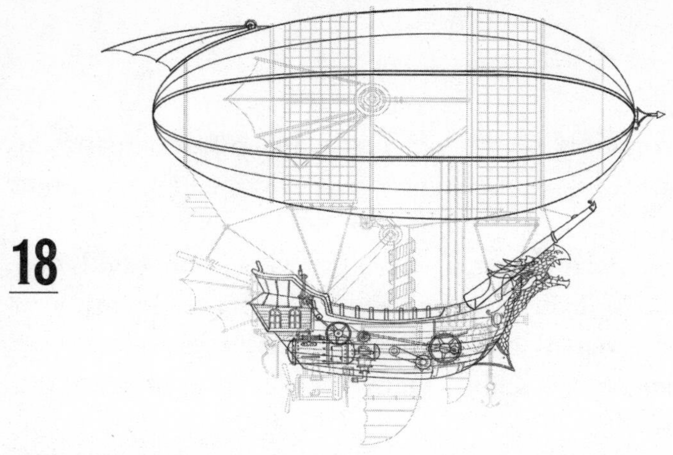

Trenton had to admit that Cochrane moved fast.

Twenty-four hours after they'd agreed to help the dimber damber build his machines, Trenton and Kallista were standing on a platform in the room they called the bay. It was surprisingly large and didn't smell too bad. They'd even managed to string rows of lightbulbs across the ceiling.

Trenton glanced at the walls, which were bare concrete with small metal nubs sticking out every so often, and wondered what this room had originally been.

Standing below them was a group of nearly thirty people. Most were Whipjacks, but there were also several ordinary citizens. What had Cochrane promised them for their efforts?

Not surprisingly, there weren't any members of the Order. That was fine with him. The last thing he needed was for the Red Robes to discover what they were actually building here.

To his left was the airship Trenton had seen hanging from the rafters. To his right was Ladon, a large wooden scaffold raised up along one of his damaged legs. And in the center of the room was a huge junk pile of beams, brackets, old engines, and anything else with enough metal to make it worth cutting, welding, or melting.

"I can't believe they don't have any ore," Trenton said, surveying the room.

"Hmm?" Kallista barely looked up from the stack of books

she had taken from the library. Trenton glared at her, and she finally shut the book, marking her page with one finger. "What did you say?"

"Are you paying attention at all to what's going on here?" Trenton asked. "Ever since we came back from the library, your nose has been buried in one book after another."

"It's interesting," Kallista said. "There are a lot of things I've never heard of."

Trenton thought there was more to it than that. "You're looking for something."

Kallista moved the book slightly behind her back. "No. Just browsing."

Trenton didn't believe her for a second, but the people milling around the room were starting to become restless. They'd all volunteered—or been encouraged by Cochrane—to help build what they'd been told was a project that would defend their city against the invasion of a powerful outside army that might be arriving anytime.

When Cochrane had told them the project would be led by two of the very outsiders they needed to defend themselves against, there'd been some serious complaining. But the dimber damber had explained that Trenton and Kallista were the ones who'd warned them of the coming danger.

He was confident Trenton and Kallista could win them over once the people recognized what skilled mechanics they were. Of course, it would have been nice if he'd been there to show his support.

Trenton sifted through the set of diagrams he had spread out on his makeshift workbench and eyed the woefully inadequate inventory of tools they had to work with. "How do you want to start?"

"Whatever you want," Kallista said, her book open once

more. This was totally unlike her. What happened to the bossy girl who wanted to control everything every minute of every day? He snuck a look at what she was reading, hoping for a clue, but it was only a history book.

"Ho there," Plucky called up, waving her hand. "Think I'll climb up the dragon. Have a bit of a look-see, yeah, yeah?"

Trenton pushed the plans aside. Clearly Kallista wasn't going to be much help.

"Um, hello, everyone?" he called down to the people. A couple of them responded with muttered hellos, but most simply glared at him. So much for winning them over. "I need to make assignments, I guess." Cupping his hands to the sides of his mouth, he called out, "How many of you have ever done any actual mechanic work? You know—building, repairing?"

Ten or so raised their hands.

Great.

"All right, all of you with experience, come up here for the tools. Make sure you each get two screwdrivers—a straight head and a Phillips—an adjustable wrench, a pair of pliers, and, uh, I guess anything else you know how to work with." He looked around the group again. "Anyone worked with cutting and shaping metal?"

Two people tentatively raised their hands.

"Good enough. Let's put you over there. The rest of you start sorting through the metal heap. Iron in one pile, steel in another, copper, brass, and anything else you find in a third."

As the people separated into groups, he nudged Kallista. "Can you give me a hand?"

"Sure," she said, wandering toward the tools. But he noticed she hadn't closed her book.

Hurrying from one group to another, he quickly got people sorted out and working on one project or another. It turned out that Plucky was actually quite a skilled mechanic. He put her in charge of opening up Ladon and removing any broken pieces.

Weasel was either dumb as a post or simply lazy. Trenton didn't want him anywhere near the dragon. Instead he sent him and several other muscular men to carry in a billows, an anvil, hammers, and everything else they'd need to set up a rudimentary blacksmithing shop. They didn't have fancy welding tools or a machine shop, but that didn't mean they couldn't set up their own homemade forge.

Much of the scrap metal was covered in thick layers of grease, dirt, and other unidentifiable crud. "We need to get all of this washed off," he said.

"Got just what you need," Slash said. He pulled up a metal cover set in the floor and unwound a heavy hose. "Pumped straight out'a the river, ain't it? Cold as a sow's nose, but it'll blast the gunk out a'right."

It looked like it would do the trick. "But then we'll have water and dirt all across the bay."

The Whipjack pointed to a grate set in the floor. "Everything goes slick as a whistle down the drain."

Trenton peered through the bars and saw a set of steep, slime-coated stairs. A foul stench floated out of the opening, and he thought he saw a pair of red eyes staring up at him. "What's down there?"

"Sewer," Slash said, wrinkling his nose. "Stinks something awful, don't it?"

That was an understatement.

It turned out that once they cleaned everything off the metal at least half of it was too rusty or corroded. Unusable. "We don't have near the parts were going to need," he muttered to himself.

"I'd focus on getting the airship up and running," said a voice from behind him.

Trenton turned to see a blond boy, slightly taller than he was, wearing patched overalls and a pair of sturdy-looking boots. "Grab a set of tools and . . ."

He blinked in surprise and looked quickly around, wondering if the rest of the Red Robes had come with the blond boy to arrest him or shut down his projects.

"Something wrong?" the boy asked.

"It's just . . ." Trenton swallowed. "I didn't recognize you without your robe. And your hair . . ." He extended his fingers over his head, miming the tall, stiff hair.

"We only wear the robe and wax our hair for formal occasions. You happened to arrive when we were in the middle of a meeting." He held out his hand. "Ander Dorrity."

For a moment, Trenton stared at the outstretched hand. Hesitantly he shook it. "Look, if you've come here to arrest me, Cochrane said—"

"Relax," Ander said. "The dimber damber and Patriarch Wilhelm have apparently worked something out. All members of the Order have been ordered to leave you and your friend alone to build your machines. Speaking of which, where is your friend?"

Trenton glanced around. Sometime while he had been moving from team to team, Kallista had disappeared. He had a pretty good idea where she'd gone. Not that he was going to share anything with the Red Robe who had no doubt come here as a spy. "No offense. But if you didn't come to arrest me, why are you here?"

"I want to help." Ander pulled a pair of work gloves from his back pocket. "I'm pretty good with my hands."

Trenton sniffed. "You want to *help*?"

"Why not? I'm surprised everyone isn't here. After all, we're doing this to defend the city, right?" Ander's cool blue eyes studied Trenton closely.

"Right." Trenton nodded. "Against an outside attack."

"Then I want to do my part. Where do you want me?"

It had to be a trick. But if this was a test, it was a good one. Agreeing to let Ander help was inviting him to spy on everything they did here. But sending him away was all but admitting they were hiding something.

Trenton shoved his hands in his pockets. "Thanks, but we already have enough people."

Ander's eyebrows twitched slightly. He jerked his thumb at the airship hanging from the rafters. "I don't see anyone working on that."

"It's not a priority," Trenton snapped. "At the moment I'm trying to figure out where we're going to get enough raw material to make everything we need."

He hoped Ander would take the hint and leave. Instead, Ander's lips rose in a smile that seemed to say, *I know a lot more than you think*. "I'd focus on the airship, then. Get that working, and you'll have all the metal you need."

Trenton glanced at the huge wooden vessel with the deflated sack hanging above it. "How do you figure that?"

"Grab the plans," Ander called.

Before Trenton could respond, Ander jumped off the platform and headed toward the rope ladder hanging from the bottom of the airship.

"Hold on. That's not—" Trenton started. But it was clear Ander wasn't listening. Trenton searched through the papers on his table. There were actually two sets of plans. One for the airship itself and another labeled ENVELOPE INFLATION METHOD.

Rolling both of them into a tube, he followed Ander, who was already halfway up the ladder.

As Trenton reached the top of the ladder, Ander leaned over the side and grabbed his hand to pull him up. Standing on the deck, Trenton realized they were a lot higher up than he'd expected.

Ander grinned. "Want a tour?"

"You've been up here before?" Trenton asked.

Ander lowered his chin, blond hair hiding his eyes. "I've been a lot of places." He spun on his heel and led Trenton across the polished wood deck. "This part is called the gondola. It's got a railing all the way around it, but you'd still want to stay away from the edges in a storm, I'd imagine."

"Sure," Trenton agreed.

In the center of the deck, a circular, metal staircase led them around a thick wooden mast and down through an opening in the deck. Ander led him one level down and into a small room at the front of the ship.

"This is the captain's cabin." He spun a large, spoked wheel. "This is how you steer the ship. These levers control the propellers, air scoops, and valves."

Trenton scanned the vessel's plans. From what he could see, Ander knew what he was talking about. It was actually quite impressive. If they could build something like this by themselves, what did they need him and Kallista for?

"What's down there?" he asked, peering into the level below.

Ander walked up beside him. "That's the storage area, doors to load and unload cargo, and the winches. The steam engines that power everything are in the back. Come on," he said, heading back up the metal staircase and into the large silver oval above the ship. "The part you need to worry about is up here."

"I'm guessing this is the . . . envelope," Trenton said, unrolling the second set of plans.

"Very good." Ander led him along a narrow walkway inside a large wooden frame covered with silver cloth. Although there was no light inside the envelope, the material was thin enough Trenton could see, at least a little.

Ander pointed to a series of thin wooden hoops and beams. "It's got a semirigid frame, inside and out. When you fill that big bag, up it goes. If you want it to come down, you fill those smaller bags with air from the scoops. If you want to go up, you empty the air from the smaller bags."

"Wait a minute," Trenton said. "If air is in the smaller bags, what's in the big bag?"

"Hydrogen. It's a kind of gas. Unfortunately, no one's been able to make enough of it to fill the envelope. I'm guessing that's where you come in. Figure out how to fill this with hydrogen, and you'll have all the metal you need."

"How will fixing the airship get us metal?"

"Ruins," Ander said, tapping Trenton's chest. "When the first dragons punished the inhabitants of the city for their lack of faith, they burned everything made of wood. But there's still plenty of metal lying around outside. Most of it's rusted, of course, but there's enough that isn't to build whatever you want. Only problem is, there's no quiet way to go out and get it. Unless you float in at night and snatch it up." Ander spread his arms as if presenting the airship as evidence.

It could work. It made sense that there would be ruins. Now all he needed to do was figure out how to create a gas he'd never even heard of until today. No pressure at all.

How did Ander know so much about the ship? Cochrane hadn't mentioned anything about the Red Robes being allowed in the bay. Trenton remembered seeing the boy at the joust and wondered how much time he spent skulking around where he didn't belong. "You seem to know an awful lot about this," he said as they returned to the captain's cabin.

Ander took the wheel and stared out the forward window as though he were guiding the ship through the air. "I've been fascinated with this vessel ever since they began work on it."

"You must really love airships," Trenton said, examining the shining brass control levers.

"I love the idea of flying," Ander said with a deep sigh. "I hope to go up someday, to watch the dragons in flight up close."

"Up close?" Trenton nearly laughed. "Do you have any idea what those monsters would do to you?"

Ander's expression hardened instantly, his features taking on the edge he'd shown the first time Trenton saw him. "Dragons aren't *monsters*. The holy beasts are divine beings of infinite wisdom and power. The unenlightened fear them because they don't understand them. You'd do well to remember that."

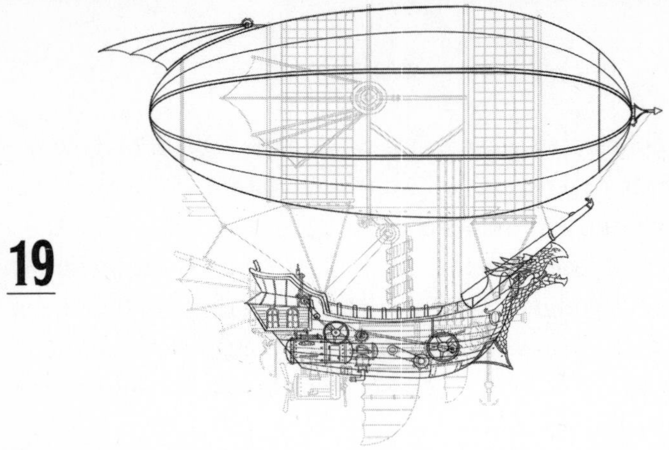

19

The next week passed in a blur of planning and building. The teams working at the forge were making steady progress on sorting the metal and creating the parts Trenton needed. But it was clear most of the workers assembling the machines lacked the necessary experience to keep things running smoothly. He constantly found himself dealing with one issue after another.

Worst of all, though, they were nearly out of scrap, and he hadn't been able to figure out a way to make hydrogen to fill the airship's envelope. If he didn't figure it out soon, everything would come to an abrupt halt.

Then there was the fact that Cochrane's plans appeared to have serious flaws. While the dimber damber might be an excellent inventor, his design skills were less than perfect. Trenton wished he could show them to Kallista and get her input, but she never seemed to be around when he needed her.

He checked her room every morning before going to the bay, but she was always gone. Night was the safest time to gather food and hunt, so most of the city was empty by dinnertime. He usually ate his meager meal of dried meat and wilted greens, or sometimes only a little boiled grain, alone. Kallista hadn't come to dinner once. It was almost like she was avoiding him.

On the morning of the eighth day, he rolled out of bed extra early. He washed quickly, threw on his clothes, and checked

Kallista's room. Once again it was empty, and her bed didn't look like it had been slept in. Didn't she care that they'd made a commitment to Cochrane? Skipping breakfast, he ran back to the bay.

When he got there, he heard a banging sound coming from inside the dragon. Finally! As Trenton climbed the ladder, he forced his jaws to unclench, but he couldn't keep his temples from pounding.

They were supposed to be a team. That meant both of them doing an equal share. Slapping his hands on each rung, he rehearsed in his mind all the things he was going to say to her, how she needed to keep her promise, how they either worked together or not at all.

The hatch at the top of the dragon was open. He swung inside, braced his feet on either side of the steam engine, and stuck his head into the turbine housing.

"Where have you been?" he shouted at the girl bent over a fan shaft.

"Rust!" Plucky screeched. She jumped up, banging her head on the top of the housing, and dropped her wrench. Spinning around, she glared at Trenton. "What you shooting your gob off at me for? Nearly stopped me heart."

"Sorry," Trenton said. "I thought you were Kallista."

"Seen her pop in a hour ago with a load'a books, yeah, yeah. Looked over the plans and scatted out again fast as could be."

Trenton leaned against the side of the hatch. "Books, huh? Should have guessed." He looked over the turbines. Plucky had made quite a bit of progress. And she was the only one here at this time of the morning. "I guess they call you Plucky because of your energy?"

"No." She picked up her wrench and went back to work,

removing a bent fan blade. "It's cause'a me scars. Dragon burned me like a crust when I was a chit. Done for me ma and da, too.

Trenton's mouth dropped open. "A dragon killed your parents?"

"Yeah, yeah. Most thought they'd be putting me to bed with a shovel as well." Plucky shrugged. "Only I cheated death and survived. Folks said I looked like a plucked chicken, so they started calling me Plucky."

How horrible. He'd had no idea. "I'm so sorry."

He glanced down at her legs. Close up, it was clear the braces had been made by hand from whatever materials were available. Some of the metal pieces were rusted, and an entire section of the left brace was held together with bits of twisted wire. And yet there was an elegance to the work. The braces were both light enough for her to get around and powerful enough to propel her forward. In contrast, her bent legs looked like some mechanic's hastily thrown-together project.

"Did you . . . ?"

"Build them?" Plucky smirked. "Weren't like no one else were going to do it for me, yeah, yeah?"

Trenton looked away. "I'm sorry," he said again, knowing he was repeating himself. His face burned, and his tongue felt thick and awkward in his mouth.

Plucky waved her hand. "There's plenty worse off'n me. Speakin'a worse . . ." She glanced back at him. "Notice you been spending a lot of time with that Red Robe. You wanna be careful a' him. He's a peeper, that one. Spies for the patriarch himself. Seen him creeping about when he thinks no one's watching."

That had been Trenton's suspicion as well. It made sense that the Order would be suspicious of what was going on in the bay. What better way to keep an eye on things than sending one of their own? Ander had shown up to work every day. He wouldn't volunteer to help unless he was up to something, would he?

Clearly, he couldn't trust the Red Robe. And yet he'd found himself liking the boy as the two of them worked on the airship. Ander's beliefs about dragons were completely over the top, but his desire to fly seemed sincere. Was he spying or only hoping for a chance to climb into the air like the creatures he was so crazy about?

The problem was, Trenton didn't know who he could trust.

Weasel was trouble, constantly glaring at Trenton and shirking his work whenever he could. There was no doubt the boy was only there because the dimber damber made him. But what about Plucky? Was she really working on the dragon to help him? Or was she trying to figure out how it worked so she could take it for herself?

What he needed was someone to talk with. To compare notes. Someone like Kallista. But she, of course, was never around. The dimber damber might be able to give him some insights, but Cochrane was putting all of his time into figuring out how to make gunpowder.

Trenton nodded. "Thanks for the warning," he said to Plucky. "I'll be careful what I say around him."

He turned to leave, when Plucky asked, "Is it true what they say? That you and the girl done for the great green dragon?"

Trenton looked back slowly. What had she heard?

"Guess I don't believe that truck about them beasts being impossible to kill, now do I?" Plucky said, her expression fierce. "That monster's the one what cooked me ma and da. If you done for it, that's a good thing. No matter what the Red Robes think."

For a moment, Trenton considered telling her the truth.

Didn't she deserve to know after what she'd been through? Only, if word got out that he was claiming to have killed the green dragon, it could get him and Kallista into even worse trouble.

"They're monsters," he said at last and climbed up the ladder before she could ask anything else. Dragons were killers, pure and simple. How could anyone think they should be worshipped?

Heading down Ladon's side, Trenton thought about what Plucky had told him. How much grit would it take to not only survive the death of your parents and the permanent scarring of your arms and legs, but to then create your own mechanical leg braces as well? He wasn't sure he trusted her, but that bent girl might be the toughest person he'd ever met.

On the other side of the bay, he stopped beneath the airship, studying the tank of water he'd rigged up the night before. Ander had been right. In order to lift the ship, the envelope had to be filled with hydrogen—a gas that was lighter than air. According to Cochrane's design notes, the trick to creating hydrogen was running a low-voltage electrical current through water using a pair of metal electrodes.

When he was in school, Trenton had focused most of his energy on math and other mechanic-related classes. He wished now that he'd paid more attention to his chemistry lessons. The concept itself was straightforward enough. Water was composed of hydrogen and oxygen. An electrical current separated the two hydrogen elements from the one water molecule. If done right, oxygen would bubble up from one side of the tank and hydrogen from the other.

Trenton didn't know whether Cochrane had learned this from the books in the library or from Leo Babbage. What he did know was that no one had been able to make the process effective enough to create the gas in high quantity. No matter what they tried, the gas bubbled so slowly it would take months to fill the envelope.

The first thing he'd tried was adding salt to the water. He understood enough about electrical currents to know that salt water was a better electrical conductor than fresh water. That helped. But not enough. Working late into the night, he'd managed to double the amount of electricity put out by the generator. Now he glanced from the plans to the tank, hoping the additional electricity had made a difference.

He'd intentionally come early enough to run his test before the rest of the workers arrived. If he failed, he didn't want a roomful of people to see it. After rechecking the connections, he lowered the wires into the tank. He placed a metal tube above the positive electrode and lit the candle attached to the end of the tube. If everything worked right, the hydrogen bubbles should flow up the tube, hit the flame, and burn brightly.

Of course, that was assuming the tank didn't explode, he didn't electrocute himself, or he didn't light the whole thing on fire. He glanced up at the airship, wondering if he should move the experiment farther away from the wooden vessel. Plus, people would be finishing breakfast and arriving soon.

He hurried over to the generator and gave it a crank. The engine kicked into life, smoke floating out of its grating. Holding his breath and shielding his eyes, Trenton grabbed the switch and pushed it down.

Bubbles began to float out of the water. He watched closely, waiting for them to increase. After a minute or two, he shook his head. The flame was barely flickering as a meager stream of hydrogen trickled up the tube. It wasn't anywhere near enough to fill a container the size of the envelope.

He shut his eyes and slammed his fist on the plans. What was he doing wrong?

"Not what you were hoping for?"

Trenton didn't even need to turn to know who he'd find watching him. There was only one person in the city who managed to slip around so quietly. "What are you doing here, Ander?"

"Thought I'd come in early and see how the new and improved generator works," Ander said with a smile. He was dressed in a pair of overalls and work gloves, just as he was every day. "What can I do to help?"

Trenton could swear the boy was mocking him. He turned off the generator and rolled up the plans. "How about finding someone else to spy on?"

Ander's smile disappeared. "You think that's what I'm doing?"

"You're the only Red—I mean, member of the Order here. Clearly they aren't fans of Kallista or me. What am I supposed to believe?"

"The Whipjacks aren't the only ones concerned with protecting the city." Ander folded his arms across his chest.

Trenton snorted.

"You think I don't know what people on this side of the city think of the Order?" Ander said, locking eyes with Trenton. "You think I don't know the kinds of things they say about the *Red Robes?*" He stared until Trenton was forced to look away.

"Fine," Trenton said at last. "You can help."

"Excellent." Ander slapped him on the shoulder. "Then the first thing I should point out is that your wires are completely corroded."

"What?"

Ander walked to the tank and pulled out the wires. The

metal tips were covered with green and brown gunk. The combination of hydrogen and salt water had completely corroded them, dramatically cutting down on the current that would run through them.

"Want me to clean them off?" Ander asked.

"No," he muttered. If they'd corroded that quickly, it would keep happening. He needed to attach some kind of probe to the end. Some kind of metal that wouldn't be affected by the salt and hydrogen. He scratched his head, looking at the pile of junk. Nothing there would work. "You don't happen to know where we could find some silver, do you?" he asked.

Ander beamed. "Of course. We *spies* know all kinds of things."

20

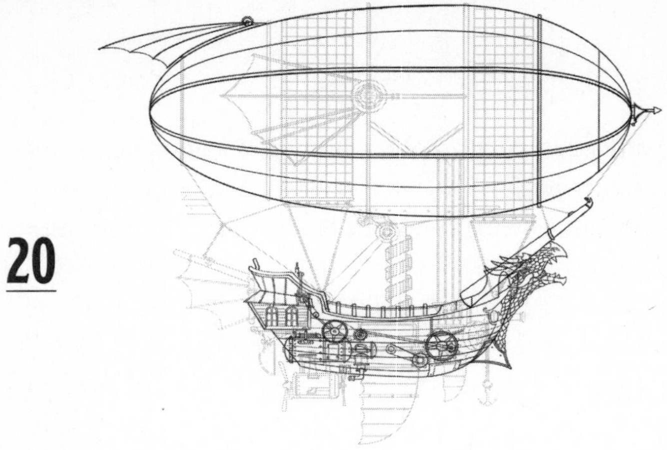

Ander might or might not be a spy, but he definitely knew his way around the city. At least the side ruled by the Order. As Ander led him to someone who could trade silver, Trenton kept a close eye out for any other members of the Order. The dimber damber had assured him he was safe, but he noticed the looks he got from the occasional red-robed figures they passed.

As they walked, he studied the homes and the occasional stands selling clothing, tools, and what little food there was. This area looked much different than the wharf. The buildings dug into the rock and dirt were still small and tucked close together, but the air smelled cleaner, the walls didn't run with water, and he didn't see any signs of the huge rats that scurried everywhere near the canals.

The city of Discovery might have its issues, but at least everyone there had a comfortable home and enough to eat. "It must be nice to live in the good side of town," he said.

Ander looked at him from the corner of his eye. "You think the Whipjacks live in the wharf because they have to?"

Trenton paused midstride. "Obviously they're not there because they want to be."

"As a matter of fact, they are," Ander said. He nodded to Trenton, and the two of them continued through the maze of tunnels and passages. "What do you know about the history of Seattle?"

"Just what Dimber Damber Cochrane told me," Trenton admitted. "There was a fire. The people rebuilt the new city on top of the old one. Then the dragons came and burned everything to the ground."

Ander bobbed his head. "The purging. The sacred beasts destroyed the wicked and cleansed the ground."

Sacred beasts. Well, that was *one* way to look at it. Although he guessed the people who were murdered didn't see it that way. Trenton didn't bother trying to hide his disgust when he spoke. "And after the *purging*, the few people who escaped the dragons hid underground, barely managing to survive, until the Whipjacks introduced technology."

"Is that what Cochrane told you?" Ander frowned. "It wasn't technology that saved the city. It was the Order. Fifty years ago, the first patriarch struck a bargain with the dragons. We would offer them food and valuables every month, and in exchange they would leave the city alone."

"Some deal." Trenton laughed. "You figured that if you keep their bellies full, they won't eat you."

Ander's face tightened, but he refused to give in to Trenton's taunts. "It's more than feeding them. We communicate with each other. It's a meeting of the minds."

"You're not saying you think dragons can talk, are you?" Trenton rolled his eyes.

"Of course they can." Trenton must have made a face, because Ander shook his head. "It's not like you and I talk. But if you listen closely, you can hear their thoughts, understand their needs. And they can understand humans too. There's a bond you build up with them over time."

Trenton could sort of understand where Ander was coming

from. Working in food production, he'd met people who spent so much time with the cows and sheep they seemed to have developed a type of unspoken communication with them. The thing was, dragons weren't cows, and sheep couldn't incinerate you with a single breath.

"You're saying you trained them?" he asked.

Ander laughed out loud. "Heavens, no. There's no training the holy beasts. But you can work with them. Did you know that up until recently they hadn't attacked our city in nearly fifty years?"

Something about that statement felt wrong to Trenton. An idea tugged at the back of his brain like a loose string. But he couldn't think why. "The dimber damber said that was when the city started to rebuild."

"Before then, people were lucky to live into their late twenties," Ander agreed. "Everyone cowered in their holes, savages afraid to sneak outside for more than a minute or two at a time. But thanks to the Order and our relationship with the dragons, peace was established. Our city began to grow."

Trenton couldn't disguise his disbelief. "I saw your city when I first arrived. It doesn't look like the dragons are all that peaceful. We got attacked by two of them on the way here, and your entire forest is burned to the ground."

"That's because something has happened to the green dragon. The other dragons know it, and they're angry. They're looking for him, and more are on their way." Ander's eyes drilled into Trenton's. "They won't stop until they discover what has happened to their brother. Not even the Order may be enough."

Trenton felt the hairs on the backs of his arms prickle. The Order believed the dragons were immortal, but if they discovered that he and Kallista had been telling the truth about killing at least one, he didn't think even the dimber damber would be able to protect them. Quickly, he changed the subject.

"You think that protecting the city from the dragons gives you the right to tell the Whipjacks they have to live in the wharf?"

The anger disappeared from Ander's eyes. "No. I don't. And neither does the Order. The Whipjacks choose to live by the canals because it suits them. They prefer to hide in the dark and damp. It helps them protect their . . . *secrets*."

He was silent, letting that sink in, until they stopped in front of a door. "This is the family I was telling you about. They have some jewelry that has been handed down for generations, including a pair of silver earrings we can melt."

Trenton hefted the bag of food he'd taken from Ladon's storage compartment. It seemed like an awfully small amount to trade for a family heirloom. "Are you sure this is enough?"

Ander gave Trenton the same judgmental look Trenton had given him earlier. "It must be nice to live in a city where having enough to eat can be taken for granted."

• • •

After Trenton had gone to all the effort of finding the silver, melting it, and coating the ends of the wires, the tank still didn't create enough hydrogen for what he needed. As the same slow dribble of bubbles rose from the water, he tried not to notice the way Weasel and some of the other workers eyed him from where they were toiling at the forge. But it was clear to him what they were thinking.

This is the person we're counting on to build our weapons? To defend our city? He can't even get a single ship in the air.

They'd be out of metal in a day, two at the most. Then what? How would he explain to Cochrane that he'd failed at the first real mechanic's job he'd been given? There had to be a way to make it work. He just didn't know what it was. Why hadn't he paid more attention to chemistry in school?

The steady rumble of the generator seemed to mock his efforts, and he turned it off with an irritated snap. Ander, who'd been watching him with an unreadable expression, peered into the tank. "Maybe you could use another set of eyes to look this over. I haven't seen your friend around lately."

The very thought of Kallista made Trenton's mouth curl in frustration. He did need another set of eyes. And the set he needed most was nowhere to be found. No doubt she was off reading her precious books.

Books, he thought, suddenly knowing exactly where he could find her.

"I'll be back in a little while," he told Ander. "There's someone I need to talk to."

Ander arched an eyebrow. "Would you like me to come with you?"

"No. Stay here and keep everyone on task." The last thing he needed was a representative of the Order following him. He wasn't sure if, with all his sneaking about, Ander knew about the library or not. If he didn't, though, it would be better to keep it that way.

After grabbing the plans for the airship, Trenton hurried to the canal, following the same route Cochrane had lead him and Kallista down the morning after the joust. He'd never rowed a boat before, and he circled aimlessly in the water until he figured out how to pull the oars in unison.

Even then, it took him more than twice as long as it had with Cochrane rowing to navigate the tunnel. He'd also forgotten to bring a lantern, but there was enough light to make out another boat tied to the shore.

As soon as he got there, he looped his rope around the rock, jumped from the boat, and felt his way to the opening in the wall. The passage was completely black but so narrow there was no chance of losing his way.

Before long he saw light ahead and hurried to the open door. Just as he'd expected, Kallista was seated at the table, bent over a thick volume.

"Have you been here the whole time?" he shouted, charging into the room.

Kallista's head snapped up.

Before she could answer, he slammed the airship plans on the table, knocking over a stack of books. "You're supposed to be helping me. We're supposed to be fixing the dragon and building the weapons. Instead you're hiding in here with your, your . . . *books*."

It didn't sound nearly as impressive as he'd hoped it would.

Kallista marked the page she was reading with a scrap of paper. "You don't know how to fix Ladon by yourself?"

"Of course I know how," Trenton blustered. "That's not the point."

"Then what is the point?" Kallista shut the book and rested her chin in her hands. "I stopped by this morning, and it looked like everything was fine. You certainly have plenty of help."

Trenton dropped into a chair and groaned. "Why are you the only person who can make me this crazy? Except for my mother."

"It's a talent," Kallista said. "If you'd wanted me there, all you had to do was say so."

"Like you'd have paid any attention." Trenton looked at the mountains of books piled around her. "Have you been down here all week?"

"Mostly." At least she had the decency to look embarrassed.

She pushed her hair out of her face, and Trenton noticed the smudged purple shadows under her eyes.

"Have you eaten or slept at all in the last twenty-four hours?"

"What time is it?" she asked. She ran her fingers through her hair, then looked at her hand and grimaced. "I guess I should probably wash, too."

Trenton shook his head. "What's so important that it's worth skipping eating and sleeping over?"

"I . . ." Kallista shook her head. "I'd rather not say right now."

"What happened to 'All I care about is finding my father'?" Trenton snapped. "If you'd been helping, Ladon would be fixed by now, and we could leave."

She studied him closely. "Is that what you want? To leave?"

Of course it was. It wasn't like he wanted to stay here forever. They'd fix the dragon, figure out a plan, and go looking for Leo Babbage together. Maybe not today. He still had to figure out how to make hydrogen. And the airship needed some adjustments. And he'd had an idea about improving the horsecycles . . .

Kallista nodded as if he'd spoken the words out loud. "This is what you've always wanted. A chance to build things, use your talents. To see what you are really capable of. Without your mother looking over your shoulder."

Trenton balled his fists. "This has nothing to do with my mother." But was that completely true? He had to admit that even when he'd thought he was going to train as a mechanic, part of him had dreaded seeing his mother's reaction to her son working on machines. Here he'd felt a freedom he'd never known at home. Was that so bad?

"There's nothing wrong with enjoying the freedom of being

on your own," Kallista said. "It's part of growing up. I have to admit that I like being able to learn new things without feeling like I'm going to be tested on them or like I'm not living up to my father's expectations. Sitting here studying by myself is . . . liberating."

"So you're going to stop working on the dragon? You're going to give up looking for him?"

"I haven't given up." Kallista ran her fingers across the cover of the book she'd been reading as though eager to get back to it. "There's more than one way to follow his trail, though. He knew I'd follow him here. And he knew that once I did, I feel the pull of the knowledge here as much as he did."

Trenton thought he understood, at least a little. "You're studying the same books he did, aren't you? Following his trail through what he was reading." He looked around the library, realizing that Kallista felt the same way about books that he felt about machines. "Tell me what you've learned."

"I'll tell you as soon as there's anything to tell," she said. "So far I haven't discovered anything important." But she refused to meet his eyes as she spoke, and he was sure she was lying. Why? What happened to working together?

"Forget it," he said, jumping up from his chair. "You'll do what you want when you want without caring about anyone else. You're as bad as your father."

Kallista's jaw snapped shut, and he wished he could take back what he'd said.

As Trenton began to walk away, Kallista said, "You forgot these."

Trenton looked back and realized he'd left the airship plans on the table. "Give them to me," he said. Coming here had been a mistake. She wasn't going to help him, which was fine because he didn't want her help anymore. He didn't need it.

But Kallista was already unrolling the schematics. She glanced briefly at the airship design and moved to the envelope instructions. How did she know that's what he was stuck on? Had she seen his tank? Her eyes pored over the document.

Trenton froze, not knowing if he was more afraid that she'd wouldn't be able to figure out what was wrong or that she would.

Her fingers traced the lines of the schematic, then stopped. "Here," she said, tapping a spot on the page. "Your wires are too thin to run the current you need. Decrease the gauge, and you should be fine."

Trenton stared at her as she gave him back the pages, then he turned and walked away.

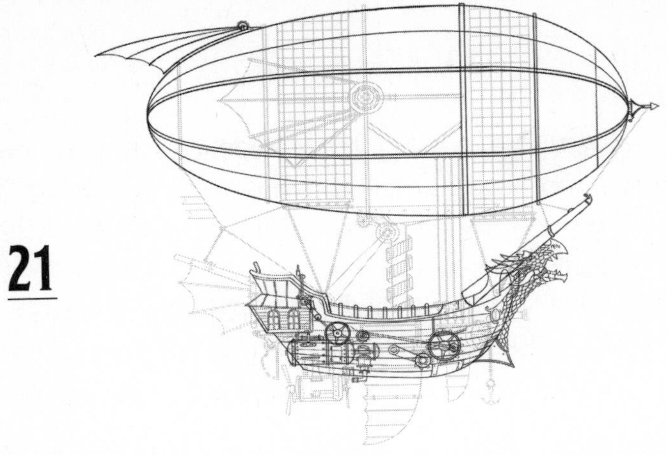

21

Four days later, Trenton stood beneath a fully inflated airship. The envelope was stretched as tight as a full belly, and the vessel tugged at the ropes that were the only thing keeping it from floating to the top of the bay.

"Rum job," Cochrane said, clapping him on the shoulder. Whenever they were in front of other people, he returned to the Whipjack way of talking. Trenton supposed it was to keep the respect of his crew.

No light filtered through the crack in the sliding doors overhead. It was night, and time to take the airship for its maiden voyage. Already the twelve-person crew, all dressed completely in black, faces smeared with ash to stay hidden in the night, were climbing up and down the ladder getting everything ready for takeoff.

"Maybe we should have dyed the envelope black," Trenton murmured.

"Gray is perfect," Cochrane said. "It's nearly invisible in the moonlit sky at night, and it blends in better during the day if we need to go out then."

"Is that why it's shaped like a dragon? For camouflage?"

"Aye." The dimber damber nodded. "She won't fool a dragon close up. But from a distance, it's possible the beasts will take her for one of their own."

Ander, recognizable only by the bits of blond hair peeking through his ash, waved at Trenton from the top of the ladder.

"Are you sure we want to bring a member of the Order with us?" Trenton asked.

Cochrane grinned. "It's the perfect plant, lad. Long as one of them is with us, the Red Robes got no reason to fear we're pulling some kind of sneak." He held a hand out to the ladder. "After you."

Up top everything was ready. The tanks were loaded with fuel, the ballast was tied down, and the ropes and nets they'd use to haul in whatever metal they found were hooked to the lifting winches.

"Square crib?" Cochrane asked as he stepped into the cabin.

"Everything's plummy," said Slash. He was still wearing his leather vest, but every inch of exposed flesh was dark with soot. Even the metal bits in his arms had been blackened.

Cochrane turned to Trenton, holding a hand out to the controls. "Mind if I takes the helm on our first go?"

"Of course," Trenton said. He hadn't considered that anyone else would pilot the craft. It was one thing to know how the airship worked, another thing entirely to be responsible for steering it safely on its first voyage.

"Plummy," Cochrane called. "Prepare for takeoff."

"Prepare for takeoff!" repeated a crew member.

Down below, a rumbling sound started up, and the doors overhead slid open, filling the sky with silvery moonlight.

"Start the engines," Cochrane ordered.

As the steam engines came to life, Trenton felt the deck begin to vibrate under his feet. Watching the crew members scurry about their jobs, he felt a pang of disappointment that Kallista had chosen to stay in the library. After all, if it hadn't been for her, he might never have figured out how to fill the envelope.

He was also sad that Cochrane hadn't allowed Plucky to come, but he said her braces were too noisy for a job that relied on stealth.

Trenton's nerves thrummed like an electrical current was racing through his body. He could sense the same nervous energy in the rest of the crew. They'd rehearsed the necessary steps to get the ship airborne over and over, but nothing could prepare them for the real thing where a single mistake could send them all crashing to the ground.

"Are you sure you know how to do this?" he murmured to Cochrane.

"Not a bit," the dimber damber whispered back with a reckless grin. "Cast off the lines!" he shouted to the crew.

Trenton pressed his hands against the thick glass of the viewport, staring with wonder as the wall of the bay began to lower in front of him. Of course, it wasn't that the room was going down; they were going up.

Beads of sweat formed on Cochrane's face as he used the steering wheel and levers to guide them toward the center of the room. At first the airship moved in fits and starts, the deck wobbling beneath their feet, as the dimber damber got the feel of the controls.

"Easy there, my girl," Cochrane whispered as the edge of the envelope brushed against one wall of the bay.

Trenton held his breath as the cloth above gave a high-pitched squeal. Engines pounded, fans whirred, the gas in the bag above them hissed. Then the walls disappeared completely, and he was looking up into a star-filled night sky.

Cochrane heaved a sigh, and Trenton realized the dimber damber had been holding his breath too. "That's it, luv."

"Amazing," Trenton whispered as they rose higher and higher above the ground. Once they were several hundred feet in the air, Cochrane turned the wheel and increased the speed of the engines guiding them out over the trees.

"Come take a look," Ander said, tugging on Trenton's arm and leading him up the stairs to the main deck of the ship.

Outside, Ander hurried to the side of the gondola and leaned out, letting the cool air ruffle his ash-darkened hair.

Trenton eased up beside him, gripping the rail tightly with both hands. "It's so quiet." Flying Ladon was a constant assault on the senses—the roaring engines, the blasting wind, the flapping wings. He had to watch gauges and twist the controls every minute. But this—floating gently through the sky, the thrum of the engines and the whir of the fans barely loud enough to hear—this was like floating on a cloud.

"It's how the dragons must feel as they glide through the air," Ander said. Closing his eyes, he leaned farther into the damp night air and sighed.

Watching the boy's pure enjoyment, Trenton had to remind himself of his own suspicions and Plucky's warning that Ander was a spy. He certainly didn't look like one right now.

"You're really not scared of them?" Trenton asked.

"Of dragons?" Ander said. "Scared is the wrong word. I'm not afraid of them, but I do respect what they are capable of. You can't take lightly something that powerful. That majestic."

Trenton looked back toward the disappearing underground city of Seattle where the bay doors were sliding shut. In the dim moonlight, it was just possible to make out men and women with bows and spears heading out to hunt. The adults would spend the next few hours searching for deer, rabbits, birds—anything they could cut up and put in a pot—while the children gathered roots, berries, and other edible plants.

"It must be hard to find food at night," Trenton said. He knew that's what they did, but he'd never seen it for himself.

"It's had a huge impact on the city," Ander agreed. "Now that no one can go outside during the day, food supplies are running low."

Trenton noticed a black circular stone pedestal some distance from the city. "What's that?"

"The place of offering," Ander said. "It's where we sound the holy horn to alert the dragon we've left food for it. At least it was until . . ."

Trenton rubbed his arms as a chill ran down his back. Had he and Kallista caused this by killing the green dragon? It wasn't like they'd had any choice. They'd been defending their city. But if what Ander said about the Order was true, maybe there'd been another way. Maybe they could have offered some of their city's food to the dragon instead.

"The thing I don't understand," he said, "is how you kept all of the dragons from attacking. You couldn't have fed them all."

"We didn't need to," Ander said. "The green was the oldest. The rest of the holy beasts respected it. We communicated with the green dragon, and the green dragon warned the rest to leave us alone."

There he went again, acting as if dragons were intelligent. As if they talked to each other. More like the green dragon was the biggest and strongest. Trenton and Kallista had seen faster creatures and nimbler ones, but none that were as big or as strong as the green monster. The only reason the other dragons stayed away from the city was because they were afraid. Honestly, he was surprised the green dragon had bothered to leave its easy food source to explore the mountains at all.

Ander rubbed his chin, accidentally clearing away the soot from his skin. "Where you come from, no one worships the dragons?"

Trenton laughed, then stopped, remembering that, although

the dragons slept at night, any loud noise could wake them. "Until recently, I hadn't even known dragons existed."

"How is that possible?" Ander asked, sounding skeptical.

Apparently Cochrane hadn't shared everything he knew about Discovery with the Order. "Let's just say our city is very well protected. I don't think the dragons knew about us either until a few weeks ago."

Ander tilted his head. "What happened to change that?"

"Well, that was when one of them—" Trenton snapped his mouth shut as he realized how close he'd come to telling Ander about the attack. The Red Robe might seem all right now, but that could change in an instant. Is that what his friendliness had been about? Trying to pump Trenton for information? "Let's just focus on our job," he said.

A few minutes later, the deck shifted under their feet as the ship began to descend.

"That's the factory," Ander said.

"What factory?" Trenton asked. "I thought we were looking for scrap metal."

"We are. The best place to find it is old buildings. We used to bring wagons here to scavenge. But now that we can't go out during the day . . ."

"Right," Trenton said, wishing Ander would stop reminding him of what killing the green dragon had done to their city.

At the top of the stairs, a crew member waved at them to come down. Back inside the cabin, the dimber damber gathered his crew around him for last-minute instructions. "You've all done a bang-up job so far. Let's grab what we need without getting into trouble, right? We're just about to the old factory. I lowers ya down in the nets. Ya finds whatever metal ya can and loads it up. Trenton'll tell ya what's rum and what's clank, won't ya, lad?"

"Sure," Trenton said.

Cochrane patted him on the shoulder. "Most important thing is keep yer lanterns hooded and make no sounds. Snug as a mouse's paw." He tilted his chin toward the ceiling. "Remember that up there is hydrogen. Highly combustible. One flame and there won't be enough of us for the body snatchers to fight over. Anyone sees ary a sign of a dragon, we quit the job at once."

The dimber damber pointed at a rope hanging from the ceiling. "Last thing. This be a horn to signal the crew in case of an emergency. Problem is, if you can hear it, so can the dragons. Don't make me use it, yeah?"

"Yeah, yeah," the crew members all agreed.

Trenton followed the eight Whipjacks who would be scavenging with him down the stairs. They quickly climbed through the door in the floor and into the cargo nets while two of the crew manned the winches that would lower them down.

"Opening the hatches," Cochrane called down.

A moment later, the floor swung away beneath the nets, and Trenton looked down to see nothing but squares of knotted rope between him and a hundred-foot drop to the ground. The winches started up, and they were suddenly hanging in midair.

When Ander had talked about a factory, Trenton had imagined an old run-down building like the one where he and Kallista had built Ladon. What he hadn't taken into account was that it had been a hundred and fifty years since the buildings had been abandoned. In that time, nearly everything had collapsed, trees and bushes growing up to cover them.

Only by squinting could he make out the remains of the factory walls and foundation. A shadow moved swiftly over the clearing, and the crew members looked up to see dark clouds blowing in.

"Looks like a storm's a'coming," Slash said.

Overhead the airship shifted, swinging the nets directly toward a thick tree trunk.

"Look out," Trenton called, pressing against the net as branches slashed at his hands and face. He kicked at the tree. "Don't let the rope tangle."

Together the Whipjacks in the nets pushed off as Cochrane struggled with the airship's controls. When they finally reached the ground, Trenton and Ander shared nervous grins.

"That could have been bad," Ander said.

Trenton agreed. It wouldn't have taken much to snap the ropes or tip them all out. He quickly realized, though, that coming to the factory had been the right choice. There was metal everywhere. Using picks and shovels to clear off the dirt and brush, the Whipjacks brought him loads of metal, and he sorted through the best pieces, keeping the ones solid enough to work with and abandoning the ones too rusted or corroded.

After nearly three hours, they'd salvaged as much scrap as the ship could hold and still remain airborne. It should keep them working for at least a few weeks. After they'd loaded the last piece of metal into the nets, Trenton used the cover of his lantern to flash a signal to the men running the winches.

"Everybody in the nets," he called, and they squeezed themselves in with the scrap.

Overhead, the engines started up, and the nets rose into the air. Trenton kept a close eye on the trees—assuring himself they were well clear of the branches this time—while checking the envelope for any signs that the extra weight was putting too much strain on it.

"Rum work," Slash said, slapping each of the men and women on the back. "When we gets back, I'll personally—"

With a soft *thunk*, the winches cut off, leaving them swinging halfway between the ground and the airship.

"What's going on?" Trenton called up.

There was no answer.

Ander gasped. "Look!"

Trenton glanced into the sky and saw a winged shape drop out of the clouds. It was a dragon, but one bigger than any he'd seen before. He rubbed his eyes, trying to tell himself the moonlight was playing tricks on him. But, no. This monster was at least twice as big as the green dragon had been. Black wings three times the length of Ladon's carried it through the air with a rhythmic *whump-whump-whump* he could hear perfectly although the beast was several miles away.

The creature soared down over the trees, and Slash whispered, "Look at the horns on it."

Clutching the net with ice-cold fingers, Trenton saw them too.

Huge, curving horns like daggers jutted out from either side of the dragon's head. There was something odd about its neck, too. He could make out thick scales or armor extending from the back of its head to the base of its wings.

As if sensing their presence, the dragon turned toward them, and all the workers in the net gasped as one. Two glowing green eyes cut through the dark night like spotlights.

Trenton's stomach lurched—a cold sharp blade slashing his insides. "I thought dragons only came out during the day," he whispered to Ander, his voice high and thin with terror.

"Mostly," Ander said. "But this is a night hunter. And older than any dragon I've seen before."

The beast circled the forest once, twice. It shook the night with an ear-shattering roar, then plummeted into the trees. A second later, a scream ripped through the air.

"Tell me that was an animal," Trenton begged, feeling like he might throw up. But as the black dragon rose into the air, blotting out the stars, the shape hanging from its jaws was clearly human. Someone from the city.

Instantly, the engines started up again.

"Get those hatches shut!" Cochrane yelled down as soon as they were inside. "We're getting out of here."

As the crew climbed out of the net, Ander's hand dug into Trenton's bicep. "I heard his thoughts. He's searching for his green brother," he said, his eyes wide. "He won't stop until he finds him."

22

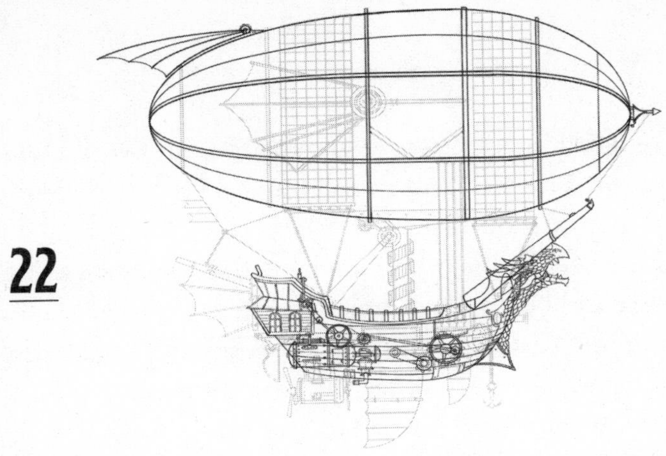

Trenton got very little rest that night. Even when he did sleep, a black demon with glowing green eyes haunted his dreams, stalking him relentlessly as he ran through a burning forest. Morning was no better. The entire city appeared to be in a daze. The victim of the dragon was a father of two young children. Rumors circulated that people were looking for someone to blame, and Trenton had a pretty good idea who that someone would be.

When he arrived at the bay, red-eyed and with a pounding headache, he discovered that three members of his team had not reported for work. Even those who did show up seemed distracted, whispering among themselves.

Sorting through the scrap metal they'd recovered the night before, he kept thinking about Ander's words. Obviously the boy had no way of knowing why the dragon was there. The idea that he could understand the beast was nonsense. Dragons were unthinking monsters that ate and burned everything in their path.

Only that wasn't completely true, was it? Didn't the fact that the Order had managed to arrange a truce with the green dragon prove that they possessed some intelligence? This new black creature was a giant. If it had come looking for the green dragon, how long would it take before it tracked a path back to

Discovery? Could the people there stop the beast if it was determined to attack them? If Trenton and Kallista weren't there to use Ladon to fight the black dragon?

And there were other dragons to think about as well. Dragons with acid breath, and dragons with two sets of wings that were as nimble as a tiny bird. If the beasts could track the dead dragon, maybe by scent or by markings left behind . . .

He shook his head and hurried to check on Plucky's work with Ladon. The sound of tools on metal clanged from inside Ladon's framework as he climbed the ladder.

"How are things going?" he called when he reached the top.

A moment later, Plucky's head popped out of the open hatch. "Plummy!" If she was bothered by the events of the night before, she didn't show it. She held up a piece of twisted metal. "Got the last ramshackled fan blade off, didn't I? Nasty one that was. Now we just needs to start installing the new parts, yeah, yeah?"

"Good work." Trenton climbed through the hatch to survey the progress. They didn't have the metal alloy they'd used for the original turbine blades, but he'd found something else he thought would work. If everything went right, Ladon would be repaired in less than a week.

Then what?

He and Kallista needed to get back to Discovery to warn them about what was happening outside. But would Renato Cochrane let them leave? He was building an army of war machines, after all, and Ladon was the most powerful weapon in the city.

Plucky was right. The bad blades had all been carefully removed. He gave the shaft itself a hard shove, and there was no wobble at all. There were a few nicks and scratches along the inside walls, but there didn't appear to be anything deep enough to cause a leak. It wouldn't take them long to attach the new blades and try it out. He climbed out of the hatch and pulled himself into the front seat.

Plucky followed him out. "Mind the back leg lever. It's a bit wobbly."

"Thanks." Trenton moved the lever forward and back. She was right. It had either worked its way loose or been damaged in the accident. "Wait," he said as Plucky crawled into the seat behind him. "How do you know this controls the back legs?"

An expression of guilt crossed the girl's face, then disappeared so fast it might never have been there. "Read the plans, didn't I?"

Trenton didn't remember showing her the plans except to explain how to access the turbines and remove the damaged blades. But it was more than that. He noticed how comfortable she was sitting in the second driver's seat. "You've been trying it out, haven't you."

Plucky puffed her cheeks. "I never."

"You have," Trenton said. Was that why she'd been coming in so early? To figure out the controls? "You didn't try to start it, did you?" She could wreck the whole engine by starting it up with the turbines open like that.

"Do I look dumb?" she barked. "Ain't cracked, is I?" She smirked. "Noticed there ain't no keyhole on the starter, though."

Trenton blushed. "I might have lied about that." He gave her a considering look. She'd been the hardest worker on his team by far. "Would you like to start it? When it's all repaired?"

Her eyes widened. "Could I?"

"Sure. You've done more to get it running than anyone else. You couldn't actually fly it or anything—that takes a lot of practice." He knew that from personal—and painful—experience.

"But I could let you move the wings. Maybe blow out a fireball of two."

Plucky's face glowed with hope. "Ain't telling me another clanker, is ya?"

Trenton chuckled. "Does I look like the kind of person who would tell a clanker?"

"No," she said with a grin. She ran her fingers lightly across the buttons and levers that controlled the dragon's actions, and Trenton wondered how she'd feel when they flew the dragon away. "Surprised the girl ain't here more."

"Kallista? She's working on something else right now."

"She misses her da, yeah, yeah?" Plucky said.

Trenton nodded. He couldn't blame her for wanting to find her father. He'd only been gone for a few weeks, and as much as he enjoyed the freedom, he was surprised by how much he missed his parents.

He missed his father's calming presence and his wise advice. But he also missed his mother. Yes, they'd argued, but she always asked how his day had gone. When they weren't fighting about technology, they had a lot in common. He knew she'd want to hear all about the mountains, lakes, and forests he'd seen outside.

"I misses me ma and da too," Plucky said.

Trenton looked up. He'd forgotten that both of her parents had died when she was little. "You remember them?"

She nodded. "Even when we was so poor there was hardly no belly timber in the house, Ma made a stew what stuck to your ribs." She licked her lips at the thought. "And Da used to play cards with me for hours."

"I'm sorry," Trenton said. Even with his mother's strong opinions about machines and technology, he'd been lucky to have both of his parents at home. Sometimes he forgot just how lucky. He needed to remember that when he got frustrated with Kallista.

"Are you okay?" he asked. "This newest dragon attack can't be easy. With everything you've been through, I mean."

Plucky looked down at the controls. She opened her mouth, but at that moment, the bells began to clang from the roof of the bay. It sounded like they were coming from the hallway, too.

These weren't the normal bells used to signal the start and end of a workday. They tolled over and over with a clear sense of urgency.

Plucky jumped in her seat, a stricken look on her face. Down below, the workers dropped what they were doing and hurried out the doors.

"What is it?" Trenton asked. "Are the dragons attacking?"

"Order of the Beast's calling an emergency meeting," Plucky said. "We gots to bolt." She grabbed the large metal key on the side of her leg braces and began to wind it.

"Let me help you," Trenton said. He grabbed the key and cranked it around and around until the large drive spring was tightly coiled.

As soon as he finished, Plucky climbed over the side of the dragon and hurried down the ladder. "Move it," she called. "The Order don't like it when you're late."

Trenton followed her down. "What do they want?"

"No idea," Plucky said. As soon as her feet touched the ground, she began her hopping run toward the door. "But it ain't never good."

• • •

By the time Trenton reached the town square, people were streaming into the headquarters of the Order of the Beast. Many of them looked like they'd just rolled out of bed—eyes bleary and hair uncombed. The members of the Order were the exception. Each of them was dressed in the red robes, swords at the waist, black caps balanced on hair that was sticking straight up. Obviously this meeting wasn't a surprise to them.

Following Plucky up the gleaming white stairs, Trenton searched for Kallista. Had she been in her room when the bells started, or was she down in the library where she might not be able to hear them?

"Will the rest of the Whipjacks come?" he asked, remembering that the two sides weren't on the best of terms.

"Whole city comes to emergency meetings," Plucky said, elbowing her way through the crowd. "Don't wants to miss nuffing important, yeah, yeah?"

She was right. By the time they made it through the doors, the entire room was completely packed, with more people squeezing in behind them. They slid onto the end of a bench near the back of the room.

Trenton watched the people come through the door. There was a clear sense of agitation among the bustling crowd. By now everyone must have heard about the black dragon from the night before. Was that what this meeting was about? It almost had to be.

By the time the last few people entered, there were no seats left, and the latecomers had to stand at the back or in the aisles.

Cochrane was near the front, next to the members of the Order, and most of the Whipjacks were crowded together on the right. Trenton looked for Kallista, but she wasn't with them.

Martin stepped to the front of the stage and introduced Wilhelm the Divine. Everyone stood for his entrance, then took their seats.

As the patriarch approached the podium to speak, a hand

tapped Trenton's shoulder. "Slide down," Kallista said as she slipped in beside him.

"Where have you been?" he asked, squishing to his left to make room for her. "Didn't you hear the bells?"

"I heard them. I just didn't know what they meant. I was reading."

The patriarch cleared his throat. "We have gathered here for a matter of vital concern to the city. Last night a new dragon appeared. It killed Mikey Stephenson, who was hunting at the time."

Around the room, people leaned forward, whispering to one another and shaking their heads.

Kallista glanced at Trenton and mouthed, *At night?*

"I saw it last night from the airship," Trenton said quietly. "Twice as big as any of the ones we've seen. With horns. And its eyes glow."

Kallista raised a hand to her mouth. "An alpha."

Trenton waited for her to explain what she meant, but she had turned back to listen to the patriarch.

"As you know," Wilhelm continued, "since the disappearance of the holy beast that protected our city, we have been under regular attacks from the new dragons."

Around the room the grumbling grew louder. The voices definitely had a hostile edge to them.

Trenton hunched his shoulders. "Keep your head down," he whispered to Kallista. "This could get ugly."

"This latest beast," the patriarch continued, "appears to be much larger and more powerful than previous ones, and it flies after dark. Therefore, new rules are being put into place, effective at once. Until further notice, no one may leave the city for any reason without the Order's express consent. No one may travel outside without a member of the Order accompanying them. All hunting and gathering is suspended. Guards have been placed at all exits, and they will enforce these rules by whatever means necessary."

"We'll starve!" someone shouted.

Martin reached for his sword, his eyes scanning the audience for whoever had interrupted, but the patriarch touched his sleeve. "We understand this will be a great hardship for all. But there is hope. We believe this new dragon may be a leader. We hope to reach a binding with this sacred beast so that our city may once more be at peace. Holy offerings are being doubled. We will be collecting food and valuables from the city."

It was a good thing they'd gone out for metal the night before.

"Finally," the patriarch said, "threatening or in any way plotting against any dragon or dragons is deemed a capital offense, punished by immediate execution of the person or persons involved."

As soon as the patriarch finished speaking, people leaped from their seats. Their frightened conversations quickly turned to shouts.

"It's the newcomers' fault!"

"They angered the dragons."

"Give the outsiders a necktie party."

Plucky said something to Trenton, but he couldn't make out a word. She pushed him and Kallista toward the door as people recognized who they were and began throwing punches. A boot kicked Trenton's leg as a fist slammed into the back of his head. Kallista screamed as someone yanked her hair. She elbowed a man in the ribs, then found the woman who'd pulled her hair and jabbed a finger in her eye.

"We have to get out of here!" Trenton yelled, forcing his way through the crowd.

Then they were surrounded by a group of Whipjacks clearing the way with clubs and knives.

"This way," Slash said. He shoved them through a door and into the streets as the rest of the Whipjacks blocked the crowd from following them.

"In there!" Slash yelled, pointing at a small doorway down the street.

Trenton looked for Plucky, but she was gone.

"Go on!" the Whipjack shouted, pushing him in the back.

The crowd streamed out the front door of the building and headed around the corner.

The Whipjacks had to get off the streets before they were spotted. Trenton and Kallista ran to the door and tried the knob. It was unlocked.

They stepped inside and found themselves in a small medicine shop. A figure stepped out of the shadows at the back of the room.

Cochrane. How had the dimber damber arrived there so quickly?

Before Trenton could ask, Cochrane walked forward and locked the door behind them. "How quickly can you have your dragon repaired?"

"A week," Trenton said. "Maybe sooner if we hurry. But how are we going to do anything when all the people want to kill us?"

"Leave that to me," the Whipjack leader said. "I want you ready to leave tomorrow night."

"That's impossible," Trenton said. "The patriarch said—"

Cochrane glanced through the shop's small display window and pushed them deeper into the shadows. People were shouting in the streets. Fights were breaking out everywhere. It was clear from the way the people were trying doors and looking in windows that they were searching for Trenton and Kallista. The expressions on their faces were equal parts fear and anger.

"You knew what the patriarch was going to tell the people," Kallista said, "and how they would react. You must have a plan. What is it?"

"We can't talk here," Cochrane said. "There's a hidden door at the back of the store. It opens into a tunnel. Follow the passage down and to the right until you reach the canals. Once you reach the wharf, you'll be safe enough. Meet me in the library in an hour."

23

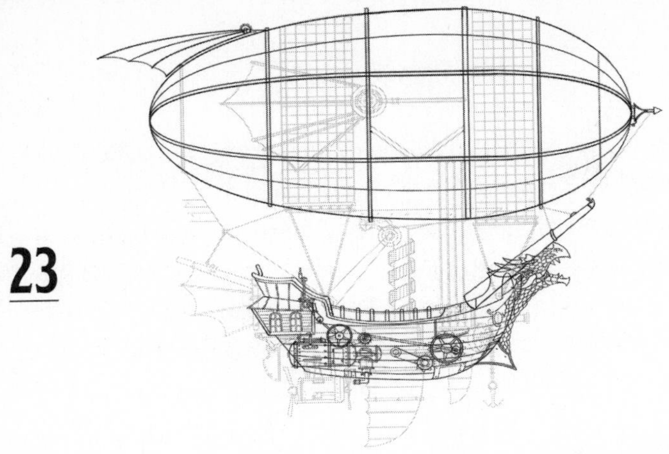

It had only been twenty-four hours since Trenton had last been to the library, but it had changed dramatically. Notes were hung up on the walls, maps were spread out on one table, and what looked like a timeline was draped over the back of a chair.

"What is all this?" Trenton asked, glancing at the notes.

Kallista began pulling papers off the walls, stuffing them into a wooden crate. "Help me put these away before Cochrane gets here."

Trenton stopped in the center of the room. "Tell me what's going on."

She reached around him to grab a map, but he stepped in front of her. "I don't want the dimber damber to see this," she said.

"Okay," he said as she pushed past him, nearly knocking him over. "I get it. I'll help you. But you have to tell me what's going on. You promised to help me build the machines, which you haven't. You claim you want to find your father, but you haven't touched the dragon for days. You don't eat, and you barely sleep. Tell me what's wrong."

Kallista pointed to a stack of maps. "Roll those up, and I'll talk while we work."

Trenton began collecting the maps. He expected them to be of the local area—and a few were—but most of them were of places as far away as the other side of the world. He rolled them into a tube and put them in the crate. "Okay, talk."

Kallista scooped up a pile of notes and leaned against the table. "Have you ever wondered where the dragons came from?"

Trenton paused in the act of pulling sheets from the walls. "Not really. Why?"

"Think about it for a minute. What are the possibilities?"

Trenton rubbed his chin. When he and Kallista first discovered that dragons were real, he'd been so amazed it had never occurred to him to wonder where they came from. Since then, he'd spent most of his time trying to make sure they didn't eat him.

He shrugged. "From other dragons, I guess. You know, where most animals come from. Maybe eggs or something."

Kallista's lips pulled down, making it clear he hadn't passed her test. "Eggs. Well, let's assume that no one noticed dragon eggs suddenly showing up around the world. Where did those eggs come from? You have to have mommy and daddy dragons to make baby dragons. But no one noticed any dragons or dragon eggs before, did they?"

Okay, so maybe that wasn't the best answer. He tried again, this time giving it more thought. "What if they existed all along, but somewhere people never looked? Like a remote country. Or maybe . . ." He let out a thoughtful breath. "An island. Like a really remote island no one has ever been to."

"Better," Kallista said, and he mentally patted himself on the back. "Except, according to the stories my father found in Discovery and here, dragons began appearing all over the world at nearly the same time. That would be extremely unlikely if they all came from the same remote island."

Trenton opened his mouth, but she wasn't done.

"Not only that, but the dragons didn't appear in ones or

twos. If they had, the cities could have fought them off. Oh, there would have been damage—fires and deaths—but we would have fought back. Based on what I've read, the dragons showed up in swarms, overran the cities, and moved on to the next place. It wasn't random either. They focused on the biggest cities with the best defenses first. It was so coordinated it's like they could communicate with one another."

"Huh," Trenton muttered. He wondered if Kallista had been talking to Ander about communicating with dragons. He scrunched up his face trying to come up with a scenario in which hundreds, or more likely thousands, of dragons could have shown up across the world at the same time. He couldn't think of anything. "I give up. Where did they come from?"

"No idea," Kallista said. "I haven't figured it out, and from what I can tell, neither had my father. But he was looking."

Trenton studied the table. "Did you discover his journal? Or more letters?"

Kallista gathered up the last few notes and put them on the pile in the crate. "Nothing that easy. If he was keeping notes, he took them with him. I had to figure it out by following the trail of his research. Based on the books and stories he dug up and restored, he seemed focused on nonfiction, with an emphasis on the wars, local politics, pack animals, and inventors who were alive when the dragons appeared."

Before Trenton could ask, she shook her head. "I have no idea how those all tie together. But I'm sure those were the books he was reading. I've found a few of his notes jotted in the margins."

"Why not ask Cochrane?" Trenton asked. "He spent the last two years with your father."

"And don't you think it's odd that he never mentioned

anything about that part of their research?" Kallista picked up the crate. "Think about that while I hide this."

She disappeared into the shelves of books, and Trenton considered what she'd said. *Was* it odd that Cochrane hadn't mentioned it? Or was it just that they hadn't asked? Sure it was interesting to wonder about the origins of dragons, but it wasn't going to help fight them.

Maybe Cochrane and Leo *had* been looking into the subject at some point, or maybe Leo had researched it on his own—kind of a pet project—but ultimately he must have realized that the most important thing to study was how to fight the dragons. *Weapons.*

In fact . . .

As Kallista came back, he met her in front of the shelves. "Did it ever occur to you that your father read about wars and inventors because he was researching weapons to fight the dragons? Cochrane told us they were studying how to make gunpowder."

"Do you know how many books I've found about gunpowder?" She formed her fingers into a zero. "And for all Cochrane's talk about researching the subject, do you know how many times I've seen him here looking for more information?" She kept up the zero.

Trenton waved his hands in the air. She was searching for reasons to be suspicious. "That's probably because he has all the books he needs in his workshop. I'll bet he's been doing experiments there. That's why you haven't seen him here." He crossed his arms in front of his chest. "Give me one reason why we *shouldn't* trust Cochrane. What has he done that's even slightly questionable?"

"Name one thing he's done that *should* make us trust him." Kallista raised her palms. "Look, I understand that you like him.

He kept us out of prison. He showed us the library. He's letting you build things. But each of those actions can be for *his* benefit instead of ours. All I'm saying is, let's be careful who we trust. Is that too much to ask?"

Maybe not. But at what point did being careful turn into being paranoid? Trenton wondered if he could trust anyone. Kallista was keeping secrets. Ander might be a spy for the Order. Cochrane could be hiding something. At this point, the only person Trenton felt like he could completely trust was Plucky. And she had shot the two of them down and gotten them into this whole mess in the first place.

He pulled out his pocket watch and checked the time. The dimber damber would arrive in a few minutes. "Let's ask him when he gets here. Give him a chance to explain."

"Maybe," Kallista said. "But for now, I'd like to keep my research to myself. Can I trust you to not say anything?"

She didn't mention it, but Trenton knew she was remembering how he'd broken his promise and told Simoni about the dragon. "I won't say anything. If you really want to find your father, though, you should be working on Ladon. You'll never track him down otherwise."

Kallista sat, folding her hands on the table. "Why did my father leave?"

"Like Cochrane said, because he figured something out and went to research it."

"But why now? He had to know it was only a matter of time before I showed up."

Trenton slumped into a chair across from her. "Look, he loved you. And he probably wanted to wait but . . ." He sighed. "Leo Babbage isn't like other people."

Kallista clenched her fists, her face going red. "You think I don't know that? Trust me, I get that he's not an ordinary father. Sometimes he'd get so caught up in his work that I wondered if he even knew I was alive. But he never forgot about me. Not once. Even when his own life was in danger, he left clues for me to follow. He could have come straight to Seattle, but he walked through woods filled with dragons, creating a signal and hanging up a compass so I wouldn't get lost. He designed an entire flying dragon just so I'd be safe and so I could follow him.

"I want to find him so much it's killing me inside. But it's more than that now. Ever since you found that first talon, I've been viewing this as just another one of my father's games. He leaves me clues, and I follow them until I get the prize."

She stood up and began pacing the room. "I always thought *he* was the prize. That finding him was the goal of the game. But what if it's not? What if the point of his clues wasn't about finding him? What if it wasn't even about saving the city from the dragons?"

Trenton sighed, leaning back in his chair. "I don't get it."

"What if the whole purpose of my father's final game isn't the destination, but the journey? What if the real prize is this?" Kallista waved her hands at the books around them. "The first time I saw this library, it occurred to me that with every step we've taken, my father has been teaching us. In Discovery, it was about learning the truth behind the lies, about understanding that creativity is good, free communication is vital, and that even if it's done with the best of intentions, a government that lies to its people is dangerous and wrong."

He could see that. Clearly the clues to building the dragon had been placed in key locations around the city where the two of them would discover that everything they'd been told for years were lies.

"Then there was the dragon," Kallista said, the speed of her steps matching the speed of her words. "My father intentionally designed Ladon to teach me that I couldn't do everything on my own. It was like he was taking me by the hand and saying, 'I may not have done a very good job of showing you that people are every bit as important as knowledge and technology, but I'm going to do it now. If you're going to fly this dragon, you are going to have to make a friend.'"

Trenton's chest grew warm. It hadn't always been easy for him to get along with Kallista. Maybe it hadn't been easy for her either. But it was nice to know she considered him a friend. "And you think that's why he brought us here? That there's something we're supposed to learn?"

Kallista's face twisted until Trenton barely recognized her. "For some reason, he felt he had to leave this city. I wish he hadn't. I wish he'd waited for me. There's nothing I want to do more than go out and look for him, but I can't. Not until I understand what he wanted me to learn."

"Hey there," Cochrane said, walking into the library. "Sounds like you two beat me here." He stopped inside the door, looking from Kallista to Trenton. "Is everything all right? You both seem a little tense."

Kallista stared at Trenton, silently pleading with him not to tell the dimber damber what they'd been discussing. It was probably all a misunderstanding that could be cleared up with one or two questions, but Kallista had supported him when he'd made big decisions in the past, and he thought it was the least he could do for her now.

"Just worried about what's going to happen next," he said. "Did you see the way that crowd attacked us?"

Cochrane's face cleared. "They're frightened. When people get scared, they search for leadership. Once they realize that leadership is coming from the Whipjacks instead of the Red Robes, everything will be fine."

Kallista gave Trenton a look he couldn't read.

"I'm not so sure about that," he said. "Did you see that dragon last night? It was a monster."

"I did. Which is why I'm here." The dimber damber walked to the table, pulled out a chair, and sat next to Trenton. "The appearance of this giant changes our plans."

"You want to stop building the weapons?" Trenton asked, more than a little disappointed.

"Just the opposite," Cochrane said. "After the appearance of that monster, it's clear the dragons will never leave us alone. We have to fight sooner, harder. We have to show these monsters we won't be intimidated. As of today, I'm doubling the number of people working on the weapons."

Trenton's heart thrummed. "What do you want us to do?" he asked, dreaming of how he could build bigger and better weapons. Things even Leo Babbage hadn't dreamed of.

The dimber damber offered him a smile. "Take me to your city."

24

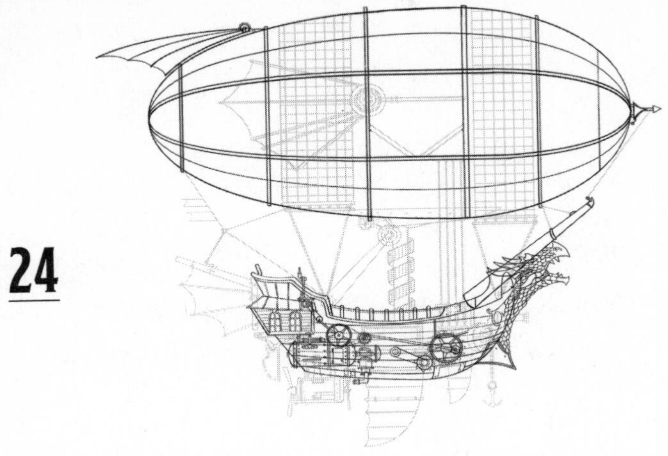

For a moment, Trenton thought he'd misheard. "Our city? You mean Discovery?"

Cochrane nodded. "When we only had a few dragons to deal with, we could have fought them ourselves. But now, with this new dragon—and who knows how many more on the way—we're going to need more help."

Kallista stared at him. "You want to put the people of Discovery in danger too?"

"That's just it," Cochrane said. "They're already in danger. Only they don't know it yet. They've already had one dragon attack. What would happen if they had another? Or two, or three, or more?"

Trenton had worried about that himself. The city leaders had built a new gate over the mountain entrance. But would it stand up to a determined dragon? Especially one as big as this new monster? If it managed to get inside Discovery, there was nothing to stop it from killing everyone in the city.

"Why do you care about the people of Discovery?" Kallista asked. "They've never done anything for you."

"A fair point," Cochrane said. "Don't think it hasn't occurred to me that for a hundred and fifty years they've lived in peace and plenty while we've died in our hole. But this isn't about one city versus another. It's about dragons against humans. We have the weapons, and they have the most defensible place to launch them from. We both need each other."

It made sense. The weapons Trenton and his team were building would be much more effective if they were shooting them from a high vantage point. And as secure as Discovery was—and maybe because of their security—they'd never developed any kind of offensive technology. At least not for a long time.

Traveling back to Discovery would be dangerous, but it could be even more dangerous not to. "How soon do you think we should leave?" he asked.

"As soon as your dragon is ready to fly—tomorrow."

Kallista frowned. "The patriarch said no one is allowed to leave the city."

"Leave that to me," Cochrane said. "I'll tell the Order the trip is to scout out any invaders that might be coming. That it's vital to our defense."

"The army. *Right.*" Trenton had nearly forgotten that was their cover story for building the weapons in the first place. "When do we tell everyone what the weapons are really for?"

The dimber damber smiled. "As soon as people realize the Order is no longer capable of protecting them. We'll be the ones with the weapons and the plan. The Red Robes will have no choice but to go along."

"Why not take the airship?" Kallista asked.

"Until it has working weapons, it would be a sitting target for any dragon we might encounter. Don't forget it's filled with flammable gas. Besides, your machine is faster and more maneuverable."

Trenton looked at Kallista and shrugged. "I'm in if you are."

Cochrane shook his head and pointed to Trenton. "I need *you* to stay here and continue to build weapons. We're going to need them as soon as possible. Kallista and I can fly the dragon to your mountain. We'll explain the situation. Warn the people of what's coming. If they choose to fight with us, we can bring your weapons to their city. If they choose not to, at least they'll have advance warning of what's on the way."

Trenton nodded. It made sense. But Kallista spoke up.

"It won't work."

Cochrane frowned. "What are you talking about?"

"You can't fly the dragon," Kallista said.

"Not yet. But you'll teach me what I need to know. It can't be that hard."

"Even if you knew how, you still couldn't fly it," Kallista said. "You're too heavy."

"So I won't eat dinner tonight." The dimber damber laughed. "I might not be as light as either of you, but I weigh a lot less than the supplies you carried here."

"It's not just the weight; it's where it placed." Kallista pulled out a sheet of paper and sketched an outline of the dragon. "Here are the controls, where the drivers sit," she said, noting a spot just behind the dragon's neck. "And back here is where we store the fuel and supplies. If you put an adult in one of the pilot seats, it would overbalance the front."

Cochrane's eyebrows knitted together. "Then we add more ballast to the back."

Trenton did the math in his head. "That would make it too heavy. You'd never get off the ground."

"So I ride in the back with the supplies, or we move the controls, or change the design," the dimber damber fumed. "There has to be a way."

For someone with the skills to design the weapons he had, Cochrane didn't seem very good at math. Trenton wondered how much designing the dimber damber had done and how much Leo Babbage was responsible for. He pulled a pencil out of his pocket, jotting formulas on the sheet of paper. Kallista was right. No matter what he tried, there was no way to carry an adult on the dragon. Almost as if Kallista's father had planned it that way intentionally.

"Without a major redesign, it's just not possible," he said. "You'll have to stay here and oversee the weapons while Kallista and I go back to warn the city."

Kallista took a deep breath. "I'm not going."

"What are you talking about?" Trenton asked. "You have to go. I can't fly the dragon by myself."

"No." She set her jaw, and he knew he wasn't going to be able to change her mind. "I'll stay here and oversee the weapons. That will give Dimber Damber Cochrane time to finish figuring out the gunpowder. Without that, the weapons will be useless anyway. We'll have to train someone else to take my spot."

Trenton stared at her. Why was she being so stubborn? Was this about not trusting Cochrane? Or was she determined to finish her research? Either way, he could tell by the lines on her forehead that her mind was made up.

"Weasel," Cochrane said at once. "He's strong, smart, and he's good with his hands."

"No," Trenton said. "I don't trust him, and I won't fly with him."

"Then who?" Kallista asked.

Trenton thought. He didn't like the idea of flying Ladon without Kallista at the other set of controls, and he liked the idea of her staying behind by herself even less. But if he was going back to Discovery, it needed to be with someone he trusted. Someone smart and mechanical. Someone who could pick up the nuances of flying quickly, who could figure out how things worked. Someone like—

He snapped his fingers. "Plucky."

• • •

The next day, Trenton and Plucky were seated on Ladon inside the bay. Working around the clock, with everyone at the forge focused on making fan blades, and Trenton, Kallista, and Plucky installing them, they'd managed to finish the repairs in just over twenty-four hours.

"Okay, let's try this again," Trenton said. "Front left leg, back right leg, front right leg."

"Back left leg," Plucky said. "I know. I'm not beetle-headed."

"Sorry." Trenton held up his hands. He reminded himself that just because she talked differently, it didn't mean she wasn't smart. He rubbed his palms on the front of his shirt and looked down at Cochrane, who was watching them. "Okay," he said to Plucky, "start the engine."

Plucky pressed the ignition, and the engine started at once, running perfectly. He wished he could say the same for the rest of their projects. It seemed like everything else he was working on ended up having at least one major bug.

Plucky looked back, a hopeful expression on her scarred face. "All right?"

"Just plummy," Trenton said. Now he was even starting to talk like them. "Let's take it slowly." He bit his tongue to keep himself from repeating the instructions one more time.

"Front left," Plucky muttered. She pushed the lever on her right forward. Ladon lifted his leg forward.

"Set it down," Trenton said. He swung the tail to keep the wobbling dragon balanced.

Plucky gently set the leg down while at the same time lifting the back right. It was so smooth it could have been Kallista at the controls. Trenton barely had to move the tail at all.

"Front right, back left," Plucky mouthed, pushing and pulling the controls with careful concentration.

They were doing it; they were actually walking.

"Great job!" Trenton shouted.

Plucky smirked. "I've had some practice with mechanical legs."

Around the room, workers stopped what they were doing to watch. The dragon moved across the bay, giant feet clanging against the floor. A worker standing on the gondola of the airship began to applaud. Soon everyone in the room was clapping.

"Okay, let's stop," Trenton said as they neared the wall.

"No need," Plucky called, turning the dragon.

"Hold on, I've haven't shown you how to steer yet," Trenton called.

"No worries, pigeon." Plucky looked back at him, grinning. "Piece'a pie."

"Look out!" Trenton yelled. They were going too fast, and the wall was coming up quickly.

Plucky turned around and gasped. She jerked the controls, sending them far off balance to the right.

Trenton whipped the tail around to keep them from falling at the same time that Plucky overcorrected. Now they were tipping left.

"No!" He yanked the tail back, putting all his weight over the right side of the dragon, but it was too late. They were going over.

"Hang on," he called. Realizing Plucky hadn't strapped in yet, he yanked off his harness and leaned forward to grab her. With a groan of metal, the dragon toppled. Trenton threw his arm around Plucky, grabbing the back of her seat for support. He closed his eyes, waiting for the crash of metal on stone.

There was a bang, a screech, and then, miraculously, they stopped.

Trenton opened his eyes. Ladon was leaning against the wall, two legs on the ground and two hanging in the air.

Plucky looked back at him, her face a sickly gray. "Sorry," she whispered.

Slowly Trenton released his grip on her shoulders, amazed they were both alive. "No problem," he said, trying to catch his breath. "Let's get down and take a break for a minute."

Back on the ground, he tried to keep his legs from shaking as he walked back to the table. "Rig a pulley up to the dragon and get it on all four feet," he called. "Carefully!"

"Got a minute?" asked one of the workers as Trenton collapsed into his chair.

He took a deep breath and released it slowly. "Sure. What do you have for me?"

"Cannon mount's not working right on the armored vehicle," the man said, wiping his face with a gold-and-silver scarf.

Trenton rolled open the plans as the man explained the problem. He studied the diagram, comparing it to what they'd already done.

It was a solid design—one he was proud to work on. A rear-mounted steam engine powered the gears that turned two metal wheels at the front of the car.

The wheels in the front were twice as large as the ones in the back to provide a more powerful ratio when going up hills or rough terrain. Heavy metal shields protected the sides and rear, while an angled, plow-shaped battering ram on the front provided a way to clear brush, trees, or even small boulders.

Metal viewports could be slid open so the driver and passenger could see what was coming from the front and above while also sliding shut in the event of an attack.

But the most impressive part was the rear cannon. Due to a raised rotating turret, the gunner could fire in any direction while still being protected from fireballs.

The turret, which was also steam-powered, rotated on a C-ring filled with ball bearings. Except apparently it wasn't rotating at all.

Everything seemed to meet the specs, but clearly it wasn't working. For a minute he considered taking it to the library to have Kallista take a look. Then he shook his head. If he was going to be a real mechanic, he needed to stop going to her for advice.

"Let's see," he said, tracing his finger over the lines. They connected there, there, and there. The bolts and brackets looked right. The bearings were the right size. He stopped, looking from the plans to vehicle being built. "Bring me the C-ring," he called.

Two men grabbed the heavy metal ring and carried it up to the table.

Trenton examined it carefully. He looked at the plans and back at the ring. "The diagram is upside down," he said. "The mount will never turn with it that direction."

The two men looked at the ring, bursting into surprised grins.

"Everything all right?" Cochrane asked, walking up to the platform.

"It is now," Trenton said. Sliding the plans back so the dimber damber couldn't see them, he made a note regarding the correct direction for the ring. Leo Babbage would never have made a mistake like that.

Out of the corner of his eye, Trenton spotted Ander entering the bay. He hadn't been back to work since the Order made their announcement. Still dressed in his red robe and wearing his sword, Ander approached Cochrane and whispered in his ear. Cochrane nodded and hurried out the door.

"Ready to get to work?" Trenton asked Ander.

Ander climbed onto the platform and looked at the men and women hooking ropes and pulleys up to Ladon. "You're still leaving tonight?"

Trenton shoved aside his plans. How did Ander know what he was doing? He'd assumed the dimber damber would find a way to sneak the dragon out. "I think so." He rubbed a hand across his mouth. "Is the Order, um, okay with me going?"

"It is important that our city be prepared for any attack," Ander said. He looked thoughtfully at the mechanical dragon, as though estimating its capabilities, then pulled Trenton aside. "Tell me the truth. What is the real reason for your trip?"

The back of Trenton's throat went dry. "To protect the city, of course."

The muscles on the sides of Ander's neck twitched. For a moment, Trenton thought he was going to go for his sword. Instead he placed his hands on Trenton's shoulders, looking into his eyes. "We need to be honest with each other."

"Honest?" Trenton asked, the scorn in his voice clear. "The way you've been honest with me about why you're really here?"

Ander took a deep breath. He released Trenton's shoulders, then lifted his black cap off his head and studied it for a moment. "I took a sacred oath not to reveal the plans of the Order. I'm about to break that oath now because I feel it's necessary for the safety of my city and yours. The patriarch doesn't trust you or your friend. And he definitely doesn't trust Dimber Damber Cochrane. He sent me to spy on you."

"I knew it," Trenton muttered. "What have you told him?"

"Only that you seem sincere in your efforts to protect the people of Seattle," Ander said. "It's just that I'm not sure what you are protecting them from." He looked around to make sure no one was listening. "I've told you the truth. Now you must tell me something—did you and your friend kill the green dragon?"

Trenton could hardly believe what he was hearing. "I thought the Order believes dragons are immortal."

"We do. Our entire belief system is based on the fact that dragons are gods. Suggesting otherwise is blasphemy. I could be expelled just for asking the question. But if dragons *can* be killed . . ." Ander stared at Trenton, his blue eyes unblinking. "I must know the truth."

Trenton bit the inside of his cheek. He and Kallista had been condemned to life in prison simply for attacking a dragon. What would the Order do if they knew the two of them had actually killed one?

"No," he said softly. "We didn't."

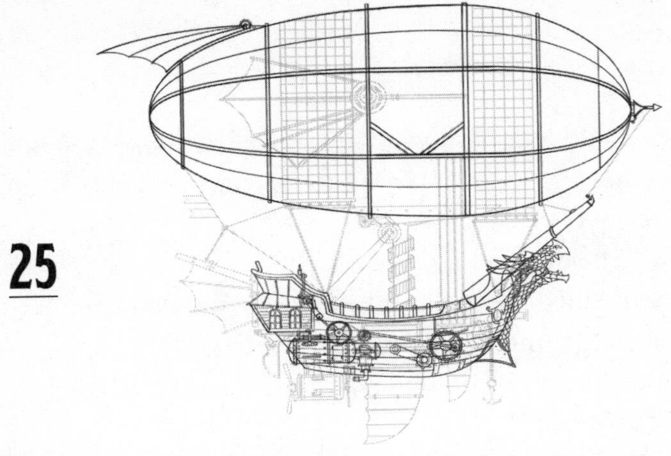

25

Easy," Cochrane whispered. "Easy does it."

Slowly the men and women working the hoist lifted Ladon out of the bay doors and swung him around to land on the ground nearby. Even with the ropes and pulleys greased, every so often a single squeal echoed through the night air, causing each person standing outside to glance upward in terror.

Even with the new rules, two guards had already disappeared. A few people suggested they'd abandoned the city. But to go where? Most people agreed they'd been snatched up by the dragon. Several people even claimed to have found bits of bloody clothing, though that was impossible since no one could go outside.

The Order wasn't saying anything, but Plucky claimed to have heard they'd left out the biggest peace offering ever—three full deer carcasses and a dozen rabbits. The black dragon flew down, ate them in a single mouthful, then went hunting for the people who had left them out.

The worst part was that the monster hunted during the night and the day. There was no safe time to avoid it, so Cochrane had made the decision for Trenton and Plucky to leave just after sunset.

"There you go," the dimber damber said when the mechanical dragon was safely settled on the ground. "Everything's set."

"Thank you," Trenton said, shaking the man's hand. He

and Kallista could have flown out of the bay on their own, but with Plucky having no actual flying experience, it would have been too great a risk.

"Be safe," the dimber damber said.

Trenton nodded. "If we fly all night, we should arrive just before dawn." He turned to Plucky. "Ready to go?"

For once Plucky had no quick response. She simply licked her lips and nodded.

"All right, then," he said, glancing once more at the sky. The clouds were low and dark, threatening a storm. Good news because it would give them plenty of places to hide. Bad news because it would be harder to fly a steady course. And they wouldn't see an attacking dragon until it was right on them.

As he started toward Ladon, Kallista appeared on his left. "Not going to say good-bye?"

"Hey," he said, relieved and a little surprised that she'd shown up. "I didn't know if you'd come."

Kallista smirked. "I'm a Babbage, not a monster." She reached out and adjusted his flight helmet. "Got your compass?"

Trenton patted the pocket of his leather coat. "One hundred and fifty degrees until we see the mountain." He edged away from Plucky and whispered, "Be careful. I don't think Cochrane is hiding anything, but if he is, and you find out . . ."

Kallista nodded. "Tell all my friends back home hello for me." It was a joke because, other than Trenton, she didn't have any friends. "Maybe your girlfriend will take you on a picnic or something."

Trenton poked her shoulder. "Simoni was never my girlfriend."

Then suddenly the two of them were hugging. "Look out for dragons," Kallista whispered, squeezing him fiercely. "If you see any, run. You won't have me there to save your skin."

"Or to randomly decide to attack them," Trenton said.

Kallista pushed him away and gave him a fake snarl. "Or to keep you from blowing up the boiler."

Trenton searched for a good response but then settled on "I'll be back soon." The two of them nodded awkwardly, then he turned and climbed the ladder.

Plucky was already in the front seat, giving everything a quick scan.

Trenton noticed she'd adjusted her leg braces to allow her to fit more comfortably behind the controls. Once again he was amazed by her mechanical talent. Especially since she'd never had any formal instruction.

Trenton checked to make sure she was locked into her harness and that her flight helmet was pulled snugly over her ears. He tapped her goggles, and she pulled them down over her eyes. "Okay," he said. "Let's do this."

Plucky pushed the ignition while Trenton studied the sky for any sign of movement.

"Straight ahead," he said, extending the wings. "Do your best to keep us level, and I'll get us up into the clouds."

Plucky tried to speak but couldn't seem to get the words out. She looked terrified.

Trenton patted her on the shoulder. "You're going to be fine. Just remember right leg, left leg."

She nodded and moved the controls.

Hand on the tail lever, Trenton guided her through walking, trotting, then running. Wind lashing at his face, he pulled back on the controls, and the dragon leaped into the air, landed hard, tilted, then leaped again.

Trenton yanked all the way back on the lever, and the ground pulled away.

Plucky leaned over the side, mouth agape.

"What do you think?" Trenton asked, gliding just below the clouds so she could appreciate the view.

Plucky shook her head and placed her hand over her heart. "Rummest sight I ever seen. Feel like a cheeping sparrow, I do."

"Well, get used to it," Trenton said. "We're going to be up here for a while."

Ten hours later, dawn had painted the tops of the eastern mountains a faint pink. Stifling a yawn, Trenton tapped the steam release valve until the pressure gauge was a good ten marks below red. No need to get anywhere close to the danger mark on this trip. He rolled his shoulders, relieved that they hadn't seen a single dragon during their flight.

"Not falling asleep, are you?" he called.

Plucky looked back, a wide grin splitting her face. "Don't think I could nod off up here if I'd flown for a week."

Trenton matched her grin. He'd almost forgotten what it was like to soar through the sky for the first time. Off to the left he saw what he'd been looking for. "There it is!" he called, pointing.

"Which one?" Plucky asked, squinting. "Lots'a mountains over there, yeah, yeah?"

"The one with the black spot near the top," Trenton said. Before he and Kallista had left, the city leaders had said they were planning on cleaning up the huge piles of dirt and rock that had been spewed from years of mining and digging in the mountain. It was one of the things Leo had mentioned in his letter that would attract dragons.

Trenton had to admit the city had done a pretty good job. Even knowing what he was looking for, it was hard to spot the tailings. Of course, the fact that it had snowed recently helped.

Taking Plucky's head in his hands, he turned her until she was facing the entrance to Discovery.

"Got it," she yelled.

"Turn us easy to the left," Trenton said, "and I'll take us to the right altitude. The landing may be a little rough since you've—"

A shape rose out of the trees to their right, and the words died in his mouth. "Dragon," he shouted. "Turn, turn, turn."

Plucky looked back, and her hands trembled on the controls. Ladon tilted crazily back and forth.

Trenton grabbed her by the shoulder. "Focus on where you're going."

The creature wasn't big enough to be the black dragon, but any dragon was dangerous enough to kill them. Especially with Plucky's lack of experience.

Tightening the release valve until the needle was several lines into the red, he pushed the throttle as far forward as he dared. Ladon's wings flapped so hard that Trenton bounced against the straps of his harness. He could see Plucky doing the same. He dove until they were just above the tops of the trees and risked a glanced behind him.

The dragon's scales flashed red against the green of the forest, making it easy to see the black gouges on its face and neck. A tattered piece of skin flapped where its wing had been torn. There was no doubt it was the dragon he and Kallista had fought several weeks before. If he survived, he would be sure to point out to Kallista that it wasn't dead after all.

The dragon hadn't seen them yet, but as soon as it turned it would. Trenton eyed their approach to the side of the mountain, which was getting closer and closer every second. The entrance to Discovery was at least twenty-five hundred feet above them, but if they rose now, there was no way the dragon could miss seeing them.

"Gotta pull up right quick," Plucky squeaked.

"Just keep flying straight," Trenton yelled back. Hand on the flight stick, he waited until they were mere yards from crashing, then yanked upward. Like a fish leaping from a pool, Ladon jumped upward. Snow and rock blurred by just beneath their wings.

"Rust!" Plucky cried, hands locked on her controls.

Trenton glanced back. The red dragon banked in their direction, but he couldn't tell if it had seen them or not. The entrance to the city was coming up fast, but they were approaching the ledge at a terrible angle. Gripping the flight stick in one hand and the throttle in the other, he leaned forward. "When I say so, move those leg controls faster than you ever have."

The ledge was coming up in three, two, one . . .

"Now!" Jamming the flight stick forward, he pulled the throttle all the way back. The effect was like trying to launch into a somersault from a full sprint.

Ladon's claws crashed against the snow-covered ledge, sending up sparks, and Trenton could only pray they were far enough away that the red dragon hadn't noticed.

Plucky pounded the leg levers back and forth, but it wasn't enough. Ladon's nose tilted toward the ground.

Trenton flung the dragon's tail down in a squeal of metal. He yanked the wings back, trying to slow them down.

The dragon jumped, tripped, caught its feet, and tripped again. The gate at the city entrance was shut. They weren't going to have enough room to land.

"Look out!" he yelled, dragging Ladon's tail on the ground.

Digging the dragon's claws into the rock, Plucky ducked her head.

They jounced, jumped, skidded, and crashed headfirst into the gate.

When Trenton looked up, he saw that Ladon's head was jammed between the bars. "Are you okay?" he gasped.

"Not sure," Plucky said. "Let me draw air and make sure I haven't croaked."

Looking around, Trenton didn't see any sign of the red dragon. He patted Plucky on the shoulder. "Congratulations on your first landing."

Beyond the gate, two figures crept out of the shadows. "Trenton?" a voice called hoarsely. "Is that you?"

Trenton squinted into the darkness. "Angus!" He never thought he'd be so glad to see the boy who'd caused him so much trouble back when he was in school.

"It *is* you," Angus said. He and another man approached the bars. Both of them wore security uniforms and carried long metal spears. The spears were new. Trenton wondered what else might have changed since he'd been gone. "I thought for sure you'd been eaten by a dragon by now."

"And I thought for sure you would have choked on your own arrogance."

The man next to Angus snorted with laughter.

"Who's that with you?" Angus asked, peering up to get a better look.

"I'll tell you when we get inside," Trenton said. "Can you open the gate? We need to meet with the city council right away."

Angus frowned. "You'll need an appointment for that."

"I'm sure I will." Trenton grunted. Apparently Angus was still as annoying as ever. "Now, the gate?"

The man next to Angus scratched his head. "I think you're going to have to get your dragon's head out of the bars before we can open it."

Trenton looked at the metal wedged against metal and shook his head. "That could be a problem."

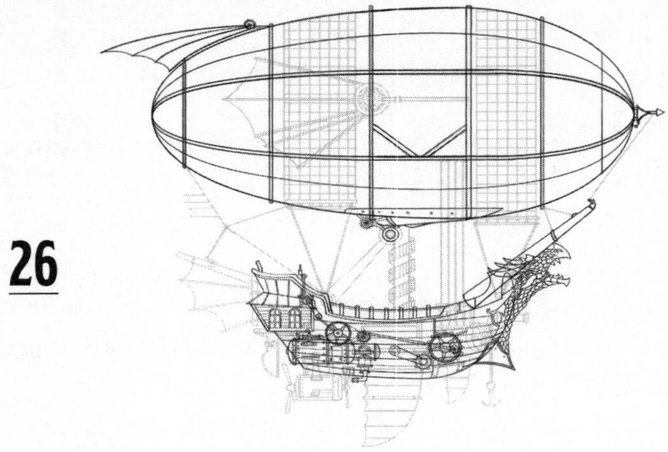

26

It had only been about a month since Trenton left home, but somehow everything felt different.

Part of it was the many actual changes that had been made. The giant fans at the center of the city had not been repaired after the dragon attack. Instead, the entire exhaust system had been ripped out, replaced by railings at each level. You could stand and look all the way from the top level down to the mines. With filters no longer needed to clean the outside "poison," the vents running along the walls were more than enough to draw in and circulate fresh air.

A huge freight elevator, nearly big enough to hold Ladon, had been rigged along one side of the circular opening to transport people and equipment. People were allowed to move freely from one level to the next with no passes required.

"The city council has gone crazy," Angus said as they got on the elevator and started down. "You can eat whatever foods you feel like on whatever days you choose—unless there are shortages. People are painting their apartments random colors. They're making up stories, creating music, drawing pictures. The new chancellor is even suggesting this year's graduating class might be allowed to choose their own training. My father says everything will be falling apart in less than a year."

Trenton couldn't help grinning as he imagined what Angus would think of Seattle.

"What are they doing there?" Trenton asked as they passed the second level. The area, which had been dark and deserted when he and Kallista built Ladon, was now brightly lit and filled with people and the sounds of machines.

"The council wants to restore all the factories and buildings," Angus said. "No one actually wants to live there because there are no shops, and"— he pointed upward—"you know . . . the *outside*."

He spoke of what Trenton now thought of as the real world in a hushed, fearful tone, and Trenton wondered if everyone in the city felt the same way. When he'd first met Kallista, the thought of leaving the safety of the mountain had been terrifying. Now he couldn't wait to explore the rest of the world. Assuming they survived the dragons.

Plucky suddenly let out a gasp. "Rust and corrosion!"

They were passing through the food-production level, and Plucky stared out at the rows of trees, grains, and other plants with an expression of shocked wonder.

"Stop the elevator for a minute," Trenton said. Plucky held back as the doors opened, but Trenton took her hand. "Come on. It's okay."

Trenton had been devastated the day he'd learned he was being assigned to train in food production. He'd done everything he could to get reassigned. But now he took pride in showing Plucky around the farms, orchards, and fish tanks.

Plucky's head spun left and right as though someone had installed ball bearings in her neck. "Look at this," she said, clanking off in one direction. "What's that?" she said, heading in another. "Never seen so much rum belly timber in me life, I haven't."

Angus elbowed Trenton in the ribs. "What's wrong with her legs? And why does she talk like that?"

"I have no idea what you mean," Trenton said, then walked over to show Plucky how the hydroponics worked.

Without any warning, a dark-haired boy came running toward Trenton.

"You're home!" Clyde barreled into Trenton and nearly knocked him over. "When did you get here? You look great. Well, great for you. I mean you're no ladies' man like me." He looked around. "Speaking of ladies, where's Kallista? She didn't dump you here by yourself, did she?"

"She's working on another project," Trenton said. "I flew here with my friend Plucky."

Plucky came back from examining a crop of potatoes. The drive spring in her leg braces sproinged, and she began winding it up. "Hello."

Clyde looked Plucky up and down, then gave her a half bow. "Good to meet you. Let me know if Trenton's not getting you enough to eat, and I'll hook you up with the good stuff." He rolled his eyes. "Hopefully the two of you aren't a thing, because if you are, I have to warn you that my pal Trenton is not exactly polished in the social graces."

Plucky looked at Trenton with a bewildered expression.

Trenton shook his head. "Ignore him. He means well."

"Your mate's a bit of a word pecker, aint he? Never heard so much rigmarole in me life." She nodded at Clyde. "How dost do?"

Now it was Clyde's turn to raise his eyebrows.

"It's called the Cant," Trenton explained. "It's a coded language for thieves and murderers."

Clyde and Angus both took an involuntary step backward, and Trenton and Plucky laughed.

"Trenton?" Simoni walked out of the trees carrying a bushel of apples. Dropping the bushel and sending apples rolling everywhere, she ran forward and threw her arms around his neck.

Feeling his face blush, Trenton hugged her back. She looked every bit as beautiful as he remembered.

"How long have you been here?" Simoni asked. "What did you see outside? Is the world really overrun with dragons?"

"I don't know if I'd say overrun," Trenton said.

"One's more than enough," Plucky said, picking up an apple and taking a bite. Juice dripped down her chin as she munched hungrily on it.

"That's Plucky," Trenton said. "These are my friends, Simoni and Clyde."

Plucky said something that might have been "Hello." It was hard to tell with her mouth full.

"There *are* quite a few dragons outside, and more arriving," Trenton said to Simoni. "That's why we're here. We discovered another city. Well, actually, Leo Babbage discovered it, and he gave us directions."

"You found Kallista's father?" Simoni said, bouncing up and down. "That's wonderful."

Clyde eyed the apples around his feet. "Maybe it'll make her less grouchy."

Trenton grinned. Kallista and Clyde had never gotten along very well. Then the grin faded. "Actually, we haven't found him yet. He did go to the city, but he left before we arrived. Kallista's still there, trying to figure out where he went."

He looked at Plucky, who was starting in on another apple, and remembered why he was there. "Listen, I want to talk with you more, but we need to meet with the city council right away."

"We get it," Clyde said. "Too important for your old friends."

Simoni poked him. "Ignore Clyde. Go have your meeting."

She touched Trenton on the arm, and he couldn't help remembering the times they'd spent working and playing together in the orchard. "We're all really proud of you."

If Trenton's face had been warm before, it felt like it had just burst into flames. "Thanks," he said, turning away quickly.

• • •

Word of their arrival had spread, because as soon as the elevator gates opened on the city level, Trenton's father rushed forward and wrapped his arms around him.

"I've been so worried about you," he said, pulling Trenton close. "We didn't hear anything for weeks, and then when the dragon . . ." He grabbed Trenton's shoulders. "You know there's another dragon? A red one. The guards have seen it in the area."

"I know," Trenton said. "There's more than one, but we can talk about that later." He turned to his mother, knelt by her wheelchair, and hugged her. "How are you feeling?"

"Better now that you're home." She ruffled a hand through his shaggy hair. "You need a haircut. And a good meal. What have you been eating out there?"

"I'm fine," he said. "I've been working on some things that are important to the safety of our city."

"What kinds of things?" his father asked. "Should I get the chancellor?"

"As soon as possible," Trenton said. "We need to meet with her and the city council." He gripped his father's arm. "There are some bad things going on outside."

Trenton's father nodded. "We'll gather the council immediately. We should have everyone at City Hall within the hour."

Plucky stepped out of the elevator and gazed up at the tall buildings.

Trenton's mother leaned forward in her chair. "Who is your friend?"

"This is Plucky. She's a member of a group called the Whipjacks, and she lives in the city where Kallista and I have been staying for the last couple of weeks. She was brave enough to help me fly here even though she only had a few hours to practice."

Trenton's father stepped forward and shook Plucky's hand. "It's a pleasure to meet you."

Plucky nodded. "Your son's a rum good mechanic and a plummy flyer."

"What are those *things* on your legs?" Trenton's mother demanded.

Trenton and his father exchanged a look, but Plucky only grinned.

"These here is me metal walkers, mum." She gave the key on the side a couple of twists and circled the wheelchair, sproinging and clicking. She nodded at the wheelchair. "I can makes you a pair for your pegs if you like. Gets you up and walking around faster'n a cat with its tail a'fire."

Trenton held his breath, waiting for his mother to explode. Her nostrils flared for a moment, then her mouth twitched slightly. Trenton would have sworn she was biting back a smile if he didn't know better. "We'll see you and Trenton for dinner tonight after the meeting. I'd like to hear more about your city, Plucky."

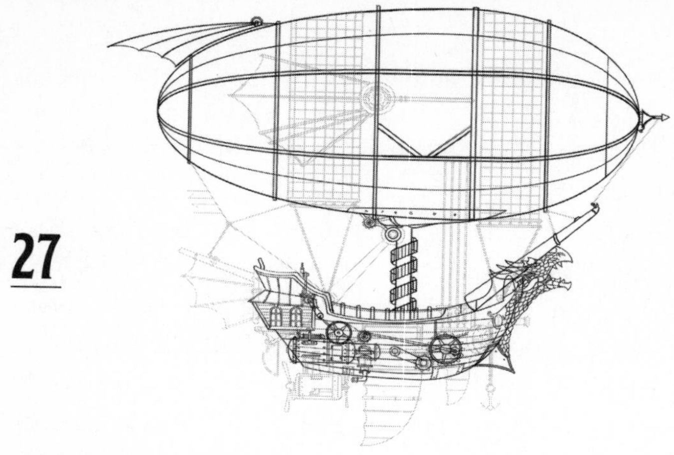

27

Although he'd been the topic of discussion there more than once, Trenton had never actually been inside the city council chambers. Walking around the polished metal table, he admired the many sculptures and paintings. He turned to Chancellor Huber. "Are these . . . ?"

The chancellor nodded. "When we opened up the room where so much incredible art had been locked away for far too long, the first thing we did was offer everything we could identify to the families of the artists who created the pieces. But some of them were so spectacular we asked if we could keep them here at the city council. As a reminder of why creativity must never be banned again."

"A big mistake, if you ask me," said a gruff voice. Mr. Darrow, Angus's father and the city's former head of security, took a seat on the other side of the table.

"What's *he* doing here?" Trenton whispered.

"We took a vote to decide who should sit on the city council," Chancellor Huber said. "He barely had enough supporters to make it in." She sniffed and shook her head. "Your father received ten times as many votes."

"My *father's* on the council?" Trenton asked. His father was a coal miner who, like Trenton, had once dreamed of being a mechanic. Trenton had no idea his father had any interest in politics.

"Your father is the *head* of the council," Chancellor Huber said.

Marshall Darrow and his father on the council, surrounded by *creative* artwork? It was like he'd returned to a completely different city. He did see one thing that looked familiar, though. A silver dragon's head with a glittering glass ball clamped between its teeth.

"Isn't that from Chancellor Lusk's walking stick?" he asked.

Chancellor Huber nodded. "It's all we found of him after he was . . . after the dragon . . ."

Trenton shuddered, remembering the last time he'd seen Lusk, disappearing down the throat of the monster.

"Are those dragon scales, then?" Plucky asked, pointing to a pair of thick green diamond shapes.

Trenton realized he'd never told her that he and Kallista had killed the dragon, but she didn't seem surprised.

Chancellor Huber nodded. "We kept them as a reminder. This time, instead of hiding from what endangers us, we want to use it to make sure it never happens again."

Trenton's father walked into the room. He closed the door and took a seat at the head of the table. "All right, son, tell us what's happening in the outside world."

For the next two hours, Trenton told them everything he and Kallista had seen—about the city of Seattle, the Order of the Beast, the Whipjacks, and, most importantly, about the dragons.

When Trenton had finished, Chancellor Huber, who had been taking notes on pieces of real paper, set down her pen and folded her hands in front of her. "What are you proposing?"

"It's not what I'm proposing," Trenton said. "It's the people of Seattle. They want to fight the dragons. Dimber Damber Cochrane, the head of the Whipjacks, worked with Leo Babbage to design a bunch of powerful weapons, and they think they've discovered a weapon our city's founders used. It's a substance called gunpowder that would allow us to shoot metal balls at the dragons and create explosions. They're asking the people of Discovery to join them in the fight."

Mr. Darrow frowned. "We tried fighting the dragons before, and it nearly destroyed the city." Several of the people on his side of the table nodded.

"I'm not sure we're ready to enter into another battle at this time," Chancellor Huber said. "We're still trying to recover from the last attack. And while Seattle might have weapons, we do not."

"You may not have a choice," Trenton said. "More dragons are coming, and they are even more dangerous than the green one Kallista and I killed. The one over Seattle is twice as big as any dragon I've seen. There's a gold one that can zip around so fast it's hard to see, and the red dragon just outside our mountain breathes acid."

"All the more reason to seal our entrance and wait it out," a woman next to Mr. Darrow said.

Trenton's father leaned back in his chair. "Look how that worked out for us last time."

Mr. Darrow glared. "It kept us safe for a hundred years."

Trenton took a breath, not sure how much he believed what he was about to say but knowing it had to be said. "There are people in Seattle who believe the newest dragon has come looking for the one we killed. If it finds us here, no gate is going to keep it out. Even sealing the entrance may not be enough. If you'd seen the size of the beast you'd understand."

"He's not telling you any clankers," Plucky said. "The

monster will get in, yeah, yeah? And when it does, that big opening we come down will make a plummy passage for the beast and the rest of its mates to turn this whole city into a rum feast. See what I'm saying now?"

Trenton was impressed that she'd noticed the same thing he had. With the giant exhaust fans gone, any dragons that got inside would have unimpeded access to any part of the city they wanted.

Still, the committee seemed unconvinced. "What do the people of Seattle want from us? Food? Supplies? People?"

"None of that," Trenton said. "In the past, Discovery was safe because the dragons didn't know we were here. Seattle was safe because they had formed a kind of truce with the beasts. Since the death of the green dragon, all of that has changed. The dragons know about us now. And the people of Seattle haven't been able to form another pact."

He looked from one member of the committee to another, hoping to make them understand. "It's only a matter of time before both of our cities are attacked again. We can hide, like we've done for over a hundred years, leaving the people outside to fend for themselves and hoping the dragons leave us alone. Or we can combine our forces. The Whipjacks want to bring their people here. This is the best location to fight from. With our supplies and their weapons, we stand a real chance of driving the dragons out for good. It's the first step in taking back our world."

"Absolutely not," Mr. Darrow said.

"We don't have the food or the room to support another city," a man beside him grumbled.

"Yes, it would put a strain on our resources," said Trenton's former sixth-grade teacher. "But we also don't have weapons if the dragons attack us. That gunpowder could save our lives."

Soon everyone in the room was shouting.

Chancellor Huber banged her fist on the table.

"Quiet," Trenton's father yelled. "Everyone calm down."

"We will discuss this among ourselves," the chancellor said. "I'll take a vote in the morning."

• • •

That night at dinner, Plucky chewed and gulped as if she'd never seen food in her life. Trenton guessed maybe she hadn't. At least not like this.

"More potatoes?" his mom asked.

"Yes, please," Plucky said around a mouthful of chicken. "Best taters I ever had."

"I guess they don't have as much food in Seattle as we do?" Trenton's father said.

"Never ate this much grub at one time in me life," Plucky said, smearing her potatoes with a huge slab of butter. "Bust a gut if I ain't careful."

Trenton pushed his peas around on his plate. The meal *was* delicious—he'd almost forgotten how good real food tasted—but he found that his appetite wasn't as big as he'd expected.

"What's wrong?" his mother asked. "You've barely eaten anything. Are you feeling all right?"

"I'm okay," Trenton said. Coming back home, he'd realized that all his life he'd taken this city, his safety, his friends, and his family for granted. Now that he understood what he had, he appreciated it more than ever.

But he also felt guilty.

"Today in the council meeting, people were arguing that we couldn't afford to feed another city's people. A month ago, I would have agreed. But if we all got by with as little as the people of Seattle do, we'd have enough for *two* more cities. Maybe even more."

His mother nodded. "It's hard to appreciate what you have until you go without it for a while. And when they don't appreciate it the way they should, folks are afraid of losing what they have. We've been spoiled here."

Trenton set his fork beside his plate. "It's not just the food. In Seattle, everyone has to watch their back. You don't know who you can trust, and even friends are willing to cheat friends if it gets them ahead."

"Things aren't perfect here, and they never will be," his father said.

"I know. But even at the worst of times, even when creativity was against the law, people did what they did to protect the city. I don't know. It just feels like on the outside everyone's looking out for themselves, and I don't know if that's because things are so much harder there or because people here really are different."

He looked at Plucky and felt his face go red. He'd completely forgotten he was talking about her city. Her people. "I'm sorry," he said.

Plucky shook her head. "Ain't no need. Rule'o the Whipjacks is filch whats you can when you can. But that ain't just us. Everyone there'll knap what they can if given half a chance." She poked at the last of her potato, then pushed it aside. "I ain't never seen this kind'a generosity before."

Trenton's mother turned in her chair to face him. "Caring doesn't stop with the people you see every day. Selflessness crosses all borders."

This was a side of his mother he wasn't used to. For so much of his life, he'd viewed her as an angry, selfish person. But more and more he was realizing that even though they argued about many things, much of what she did was because she wanted the best for him. At least what she viewed as best.

"Where does selflessness stop, though?" he asked. "Who knows how many people are out there in as bad of shape, or worse, than Seattle? When we thought everyone outside the mountain was dead, it didn't matter. But now that we know . . . Can we really ignore everyone else and go on with our lives? That would make us the same kind of monsters the dragons are."

Trenton's father wiped his mouth and stood up from the table. "Trenton, come for a walk with me. Plucky, stay here and relax. Celia's never had a girl to spoil, and I think she likes it."

Outside, Trenton's father led him to the freight elevator, and together, the two rode toward the second level. "About these weapons of yours . . ."

"They aren't exactly *my* weapons," Trenton said. "Leo Babbage and Dimber Damber Cochrane worked on the designs. I'm just the one in charge of putting them together."

His father nodded. "They must have a lot of confidence in you."

Trenton scuffed his feet on the elevator floor. "I'm pretty good at it. I got the airship flying, with Kallista's help, and I'm just about done with an armored vehicle that will be able to fire a cannon on the move."

"You know that your mother is biting her tongue to keep from telling you how dangerous your work is, right?"

Trenton bristled. "Not as dangerous as the dragons."

His father held up his hands. "I know. I know."

The elevator stopped, and the two of them got off. With work done for the day, the floor was dark and deserted. Except for the signs of new construction, it felt almost the same as the day Trenton and Kallista had found it.

"You think these weapons can stop the dragons?" his father asked. "The founders tried it once and failed."

"Maybe they didn't know what they were up against. Even if they did have gunpowder, they didn't have the weapons I've been working on," Trenton said. "I know one thing, though. If we don't try now, while we have the advantage, it may be too late."

His father walked to a bank of switches and turned on all the lights strung above the buildings. With everything lit up, it was clear how much the workers had managed to accomplish in just over a month. Several of the factories looked like they were already in operation, and even more appeared to be close to it. "This is the project I've been working on."

Trenton stared at his father. "You?"

"Thought I was only a miner?" His father chuckled.

"Not *only*. But you're not an engineer."

"I'm not," his father agreed. "But I understand enough to work with machines. Even though there's a lot left to do, we're on track to double energy and production in the next year." He pulled some papers out of his back pocket and jotted down a few numbers. "If we turned some of this into housing and added some food production stations here and on the next level, I think we could handle a pretty sizable increase in population."

Trenton's heart began to race. "What about coal?"

"That's an interesting thing." His father grabbed a lantern and led him to a mine shaft Trenton recognized. It was where he and Kallista had discovered the material to make Ladon's wings. "We've discovered two more seams here. I guess the founders abandoned them when they closed off the level. It looks like they still have plenty of coal left in them. In fact . . ." He stopped at the end of the shaft and pointed at a wall of piled rocks. "There may be even more back here. Once we dig through it."

"Looks like they had a cave-in," Trenton said, thinking about how his mother had nearly lost her legs.

His father shook his head. "No, these were put here on purpose. My guess is they used the end of the tunnel as a dumping ground when they dug out the next level. "Or . . ." He held the lantern below his chin, the play of light and shadow giving him a monstrous appearance. "This is where they buried the dead bodies. Booo-o-o," he moaned, waving his hand like a ghost.

Trenton laughed uneasily, trying not to think about how that might become a reality if the council didn't approve their plan. "Do you think the council will agree to fight?" he asked.

"It's going to be close," his father said, lowering the lantern. "There are a lot of people on both sides of the issue. I guess we'll have to wait until tomorrow to find out for sure."

28

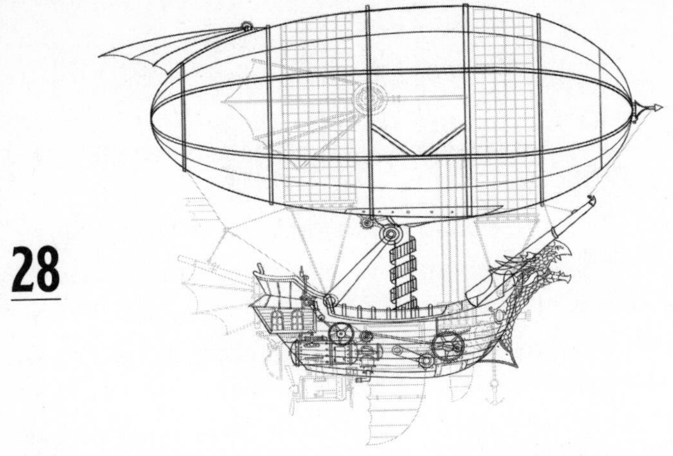

Early the next morning, Trenton and Plucky waited outside the council chambers while the members voted.

Plucky paced around the hallway, giving one-word answers when he tried to talk to her. Not that Trenton could blame her. Now that she'd seen what Discovery was like, could she ever be satisfied with Seattle?

"They're good people," he told her. "They'll do the right thing."

She glanced at him before looking quickly away. "'Course."

"Sorry about my family last night," he said. "My father can be a little intense. And my mom . . ." He shrugged his shoulders.

"Love yer mum. Wish she was mine." Plucky walked down the hall, looked out the window, and turned around. "Maybe it's best the council says no, yeah, yeah?"

Trenton stared at her. "What do you mean?"

She rubbed a hand across her mouth. "Back home we gots no choice but to fight, right? We ain't got much, but we gots to protect what we has. But here . . ." She waved her hands. "If I lived here, I'd pile up as many rocks against the door as it takes to keep 'em from breaking through, and I'd never comes out again."

"I'd think you'd be all for fighting the dragons," Trenton said. "I mean, they killed your parents."

Plucky tried to swallow and ended up choking. "I'm a great

liar, I am." She swiped at her eyes. "Ain't been a dragon attack in our city for fifty years."

"I know," Trenton said. Then it hit him. What had been bothering him since Ander said the same thing while they were looking for silver. "If there hasn't been a dragon attack, how could . . ." He pointed toward her legs, searching for an answer that made sense. "How did . . . ?"

Plucky put her hands over her face. "My mum and da weren't killed by no dragon. It was me. I knocked over a lantern when I was a tot. Started a fire what burned up me whole family. I was the only one who didn't croak."

Trenton stared at her. "Why would you lie about something like that? Do the Whipjacks know? They must."

"'Course," she said, still covering her face. "Lots'a folks call me a monster. I didn't want you . . ." She shook her head.

As Trenton struggled with her revelation, the door to the council room opened, and his father waved them inside.

Chancellor Huber straightened her notes and asked them to take a seat. "After much discussion," she said, "we have reached a decision."

Trenton looked at the faces around the room, trying to read their expressions.

"By a slim majority," the Chancellor said, "we have agreed to join the people of Seattle in fighting the dragons."

Slumping back in his chair, Trenton realized he'd been holding his breath. He sucked in a deep lungful of air and nodded. "Thank you."

The chancellor held up a finger. "However, this does not mean we will take in the entire population of Seattle."

"Darn right, we won't!" Mr. Darrow growled.

Confused, Trenton turned to the chancellor. She looked slowly around the room. "We were able to pass a motion to fight the dragons. But only if we agreed to take in just enough men and women to transport and operate the fighting machines. At the moment, our food supplies are still dangerously low. Once the battle with the dragons is over, we will decide how many people we can take in permanently."

"But what about the rest of the people?" Trenton asked. "The ones who can't fight? What about the children? We're just going to leave them there? They'd have no defenses at all."

His father stared at the table. "I'm sorry. It's the best we could do."

"If we'd had a little more warning—" the chancellor began.

But Trenton wasn't listening any longer. He jumped up from his chair and stormed out of the room. Slamming the door behind him, he stomped down the hall and out the front entrance. Tears stung his eyes.

Clyde, Simoni, and Angus were waiting for him.

"We heard about the meeting," Simoni said. "Everyone's been talking about how you are trying to help the people from the other city."

"Haven't noticed anyone helping *us*," Angus said.

Simoni gave him a dark look, then turned back to Trenton. "Have they voted yet?" She looked at his face and shook her head. "They have, haven't they?"

Trenton stared at the ground, hands balled into fists. "They voted."

"Well?" Clyde asked. "Are you bringing in a new city full of beautiful girls ignorant of my irresistible charms?"

"You mean a bunch of beggars," Angus said. "Coming to steal our food and take over our city."

Trenton charged forward, grabbing Angus by the front of his shirt. For years, the bully had used his size and his father's connections to get his way. But weeks of working with his hands had built up Trenton's muscles. He pushed hard, causing Angus to stumble backward. "Take it back or I swear I'll—"

Angus raised his fists, but Simoni stepped between them, moving closer to Trenton until she was looking into his eyes. "What happened? Did they vote not to let the people in?" Tears wet her cheeks, and Trenton had to turn away.

"No," he said between gritted teeth. "They were much more generous than that. They voted to let in all the weapons and enough people to operate them—exactly the minimum to help protect our city. The rest, including the elderly and the children, are on their own."

"No," Simoni cried.

Clyde shook his fists. "They wouldn't do that."

"They would and they did," Trenton said.

Angus nodded. "It makes sense. We have to look out for ourselves first."

It was all Trenton could do to keep from punching him.

"Hold on," Trenton's father said. He raced down the steps to join the group. "Try to understand. The people of this city have been through a lot. The last thing they want to hear about is dragons."

Trenton spun around. "You want to see people who have gone through a lot? Try looking at people who have to sneak out in the woods every day, hoping they don't get attacked or killed, just to get enough food to feed their families. Look at people living in damp holes with rats and filth, with roots sticking through the walls."

"I know," his father said. "We did the best we could in there. The chancellor and I just didn't have the votes. I'll put every man I have on getting things ready for when the people of Seattle arrive. There'll be housing and food for the fighters." He took his son's shoulders, waiting until Trenton met his eyes.

"Once we show people here that there's enough for all of us—when they realize the outsiders aren't the enemy—they'll be in a more giving mood."

Trenton nodded. There was nothing else he could do.

"Build those weapons and get them here as quickly as you can," his father said. "You and I know what a great mechanic you are. Now prove it to the rest of the city. I might have a little something up my sleeve too."

"Like what?" Trenton asked, wiping his eyes.

His father squeezed his shoulder. "Make it back here safely and you'll see."

In the time they'd been talking, the rest of the council had left the building; no doubt they didn't want to discuss what cowards they were.

"Plucky?" Trenton called, wondering if she had gone too. He went back into the council chamber and found her standing on the far side of the table, facing the wall.

"Are you all right?"

She tucked her hands into her jacket pockets and turned around. "Plummy."

Trenton put his hand to the back of his neck, trying to rub out the huge knot in it. "Let's get back to Seattle and give them the news."

• • •

If there had been any question that the number of dragons was increasing, the trip back to Seattle answered it. Even staying close to the trees and flying at night, they had three dragon sightings and heard what they thought were two more. Several sections of the forest were in flames, and the smell of smoke and sulfur hung thick in the air.

Trenton was so angry he almost wished they would be attacked just so he could take his frustrations out on something.

Plucky was silent nearly the entire flight. Not that Trenton could blame her. It was like his mother had said. It was easy to be generous with people you saw every day. But people were far less likely to help those they didn't have to look in the eye. Instead, he'd be the one to look Cochrane in the eye and tell him he had two choices. He could bring his weapons to Discovery, leaving most of his people defenseless, or he could stay and fight on his own while the city in the mountain once again hid itself away.

He wouldn't be surprised if the people of Seattle chose to ignore Discovery's offer and fight on their own. If they did, he'd decided he would stay and help them. Kallista could do whatever she thought was best.

As they were nearing Seattle, he tapped Plucky on the back. "About what you said before we went in the council room . . ."

Plucky turned around, her eyes guarded behind her flight goggles.

"I don't care if you lied. You were a little kid. It wasn't your fault. I would never think of you as a monster. I think you're one of the most courageous people I've ever met."

She blinked and took a deep breath. "Thanks."

Reaching the city, they circled twice, looking for any sign of the black dragon, then landed beside the sliding bay doors. Plucky glided them in perfectly, running at just the right moment and slowing them to a walk and then a stop.

A moment later, the doors hidden in the ground slid open, and a group of workers came outside to hook Ladon to the hoist.

As Trenton climbed down the ladder attached to Ladon's leg, Cochrane hurried to meet him. "You made it there?"

Trenton nodded. He reached up to help Plucky down, but

she jumped past his outstretched arms, clanging as she hit the ground.

"How'd she do?" Cochrane asked.

"Perfect," Trenton said. "By the end, she didn't need my help at all."

"Excellent." The dimber damber waved them to the open bay doors. "Let's get down below, and you can tell me all about it. Plucky, I'll meet with you separately."

Following the Whipjack leader through the tunnels, Trenton tried to think of the best way to present the council's decision, but there was no good way to say it.

When they reached his office, Cochrane dropped into his chair and grinned. "Take off your coat. Sit down. Can I get you anything to eat or drink?"

Trenton slumped into a chair. "No, thank you."

Cochrane leaned forward, eyes sharp. "What's wrong? Did they say no?"

"We told them everything you said—about fighting the dragons together and the need to protect their city." Trenton fought back the lump blocking his throat. "But they voted to only allow in the weapons and enough people to operate them. They say the rest of the people have to stay here."

He waited for the dimber damber to explode. He couldn't blame him.

Instead Cochrane began to laugh.

Trenton looked up. "You aren't mad?"

"Mad?" He clapped his hands. "I never wanted to take the whole city to your mountain. How could we? This is a military operation. We need to move fast. Civilians will only slow us down. We'll tell the Order the invading army is nearly here and that we need to go now in order to face it head-on and protect the city."

"But what happens to the people left behind?" Trenton asked. "What if the dragons attack while we're gone?"

"We just have to make sure they don't. We'll draw so much attention to your mountain that every dragon for miles will go straight to it." He leaped out of his chair and began pacing the room. "How long will it take you to finish the weapons?"

"I'm not sure. I'll need to see how things went while I was gone." Trenton did a quick count in his head. "Three weeks, maybe four?"

"I'll give you two," Cochrane said. "Anything you can't finish by then, we work on there. You said Discovery has good tools, didn't you?"

"The best. But what about the gunpowder? Have you figured out the formula?"

"Any day now. Any day."

Trenton sucked on his lower lip. "Are you sure it will be safe to leave everyone else here?"

"Positive." Cochrane slapped him on the back. "Trust me. The people of this city will be thanking you for years to come."

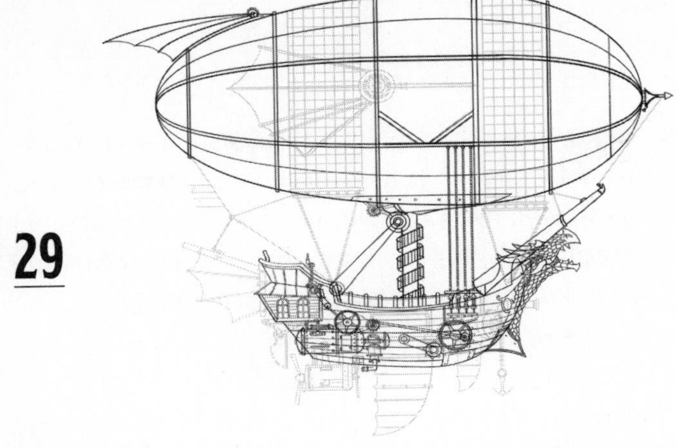

29

Trenton had never worked harder in his life than he did during the next two weeks. Even during the days when he'd spent all morning learning food production and all night building Ladon, he hadn't felt so exhausted, or so exhilarated.

True to her word, Kallista had headed up the work while he was gone, fixing several problems he'd been struggling with and keeping things on schedule. Now that he was back, she'd returned to her studies, but he didn't mind.

There was something about seeing new machinery come together under his direction that made his pulse race. He found he could get by on six hours of sleep a night. Then four. The idea of his inventions protecting the people of Discovery filled not only his waking thoughts but his dreams as well.

The fighting machines came together like soldiers lining up for battle. He not only fixed the problems in the design of the horsecycles, he improved them—adding two small side-mounted cannons, heavier armor, and widening the distance between the front legs for greater stability.

Cochrane found a drawing of something labeled a telescope in one of his books, and Trenton worked with a glassblower to build a dozen of them. Peering through them, you could see things that were miles away as if they were right next to you. They would be perfect for spotting dragons.

His greatest success might have been the airship, though. Imagining it would be at the front of airborne battles, he outfitted it with spotlights, two catapults, a gun that shot weighted nets, and a pair of small, lightweight cannons, awaiting only Cochrane's promised gunpowder to make them complete. The only reason he stopped adding features to the airship was because the weight was getting to be too much.

With three days to go until they would leave for Discovery, he called over to Slash, who had been working as his head of inventory and inspection.

"Can you give me a rundown on where we stand?"

Slash pulled a sheet out of his pocket and read down the list. "The airship is plum set. We've finished all but four of the rusting horsecyles. The explosive metal spheres—just waiting on gunpowder. We have two armored vehicles a'done and polished, and two more we hopes to have cracking afore we leave."

"What's the delay?" Trenton asked. Having only half of their armored vehicles would be a big loss.

"Can't get the parts," Slash said, tugging on a ring stuck through the skin of his wrist. "The scrap pile's just about bare."

They'd have to find a way to get more metal in a hurry. "Okay," he said, making a note. "How about cannons?"

Slash shook his head. "Way behind schedule. Ain't got no more copper. And without copper . . ."

"I know, I know," Trenton said. The ideal metal for cannons was bronze, an alloy made of copper and tin. They had plenty of tin, but without copper there wouldn't be any bronze. "What about iron? I know it has a greater chance of exploding, but at this point, I'll take whatever I can get."

Slash folded his arms across his chest, biceps bulging under his red-and-black shirt. "Rum out."

"Anything I can do to help?" Ander asked.

"Maybe," Trenton said. He'd expected that after the Order's decree, Ander would be too busy making offerings to the dragon to help him. He also thought he'd lose Plucky after what had happened in Discovery. And yet while Ander often wore his red robe, sword, and hat, he and Plucky had proven to be his two hardest workers.

He jumped down from the platform and headed toward the dwindling scrap heap. "Come help me sort through this stuff and see if there's anything worth using."

Together they began examining every bit of scrap metal, looking for anything that could be melted down and turned into parts.

Ander picked up a square of iron too rusty to be of any use and tossed it aside. "Dimber Damber Cochrane says you will be leaving in a few days to fight the enemy. Do you think that is the best strategy?"

Trenton pretended to study a fitting. He hated lying to Ander. Especially after Ander had been honest with him. But he suspected the Red Robe knew more than he was letting on. Had the patriarch told him to ask this? Was the Order growing suspicious?

"You'd have to ask Dimber Damber Cochrane. I don't know anything about strategy. I'm just focusing on building weapons."

Ander moved closer, speaking softly so only Trenton could hear. "I suggest you take time to consider your strategy. It could make all the difference."

"What do you mean?" Trenton asked.

Ander turned his back to the rest of the workers. "Cochrane has been meeting secretly with someone inside the Order."

"Who?"

"I don't know." Ander ran his hand along the hilt of his sword. "I've never actually seen the meetings. I've only spotted him leaving from them. I don't dare ask the patriarch in case he's involved. But whatever they've been discussing is extremely secret, and I'm pretty sure it involves what we're building here. I found a scrap of paper Cochrane left behind on accident. It was covered with numbers that matched the count of the weapons you're building."

Why would the dimber damber secretly be discussing weapons with someone in the Order? Wasn't the whole point to keep them in the dark? Trenton noticed Weasel going through scraps of metal nearby and waved him away. "Get back to the forge."

Weasel sneered, shrugged his shoulders, and walked away. Had he overheard them? It didn't matter. He was too dense to understand what they were discussing.

Ander rubbed his hands on the front of his robe. "Something's going on, but I don't know who I can trust anymore. Is there anything you aren't telling me?"

What was he supposed to say? Trenton didn't want to get caught up in the politics of someone else's city. Besides, even if the dimber damber wasn't being completely truthful, he was doing it for the benefit of everyone here. The ordinary citizens might not understand why they were building weapons. They might not approve of fighting the dragons. But it was for their own good.

He heard the words in his head, and all at once he remembered sitting in the library with Kallista, talking about the things her father had taught her. *Even with the best of intentions, a government that lies to its people is dangerous and wrong.* Was that the case here? Were the lies really necessary, or was Cochrane using them to gain more power for himself?

Ander glanced around, making sure they were alone, then whispered. "Things are more complicated than you understand."

"In what way?"

"Things are changing. For the last fifty years the Order ruled the city, but now the people are relying more and more on Cochrane and his Whipjacks. But should they? Is he really looking out for their best interests?"

Trenton folded his arms across his chest. "You're just mad because the Order of the Beast no longer controls the people of this city the way they control the dragons."

Ander's brow furrowed. "No one *controls* the dragons. Anyone who says that is mistaken." He gripped Trenton's arm. "Tell me the truth. Are these weapons really to fight an army? Or are they being built to fight the dragons?"

It was like being back in Discovery again, back when he and Kallista had been discovering that everything they knew about their city was a lie. Back then, he'd wanted to tell someone the truth, and look how that had turned out. Still, he had to trust someone.

Hoping he was doing the right thing, Trenton leaned in close. "*If*, and I'm not saying this is the case, but *if* the Order is unable to stop the dragons from attacking the city again, the people are going to need a way to defend themselves. These weapons are being built to keep the city safe. That's all that matters."

Ander worked his jaw, his eyes shifting left and right. At last he seemed to come to a decision. "Cochrane's been lying to you."

"About what?"

"Hey," Slash called. Trenton turned to see the Whipjack standing by Weasel near the forge. "We're all outta metal here."

Trenton shrugged. "What do you want me to do about it?"

"Maybe it's time for another salvage run," Weasel suggested.

Trenton snorted. The kid really was dumb. "How exactly

are we supposed to do that when the Order won't let us leave the city?"

Slash shot a mocking grin toward Ander. "You think them Red Robes tell us what ta do? Leave that to Cochrane. He'll work it out."

Ander gave Trenton a meaningful glance and whispered, "We'll talk soon."

From down the hallway came the sound of running feet. Kallista raced into the bay, her face red from exertion. She headed directly for Trenton.

"I need to talk to you," she called, panting.

"Sure," Trenton said, stepping away from the scrap heap.

Kallista glanced at Slash and Weasel. "Not here. Come with me."

Trenton turned to Ander, who'd been watching their conversation with obvious interest. "I'll be back in a while." He nodded at Slash. "Figure out what we can make with the pieces we have left. And maybe you're right—maybe Cochrane can figure out a way for us to make another salvage run."

Kallista led Trenton back to the library. As they walked through the door, she disappeared into the shelves.

"What are you doing?" Trenton asked.

"Making sure no one's hiding in the back," she called.

Trenton groaned and dropped into a chair. "You really think someone wants to spy on all your *valuable* research?"

Kallista came back from the shelves carrying her crate of notes. "That's exactly what I think." She dropped the box on the table. "Someone's been going through my things."

"What are you talking about?" Trenton asked. Was there anyone in this city who wasn't paranoid?

"Someone's been coming into the library when I'm not

here," Kallista said. "They've been sorting through my notes and moving my books around. They've even taken a few."

"Is that all?" Trenton would have laughed if he hadn't been so tired. "Why would anyone care about your notes?" He had a thought. "Did it ever occur to you that Cochrane might have come here researching how to make gunpowder? You said yourself it was suspicious that he hadn't been in the library."

"That's because there aren't any books here about gunpowder. So why would he be looking through *my notes* for how to make gunpowder?"

"Think about it." Trenton held up his hand, ticking off the points on his fingers. "You've been following your father's research. Your father was studying inventors and looking for a secret weapon the founders of Discovery developed. Cochrane is researching how to make gunpowder. Gunpowder is the secret weapon. Cochrane came to the library, saw your notes, realized you were both looking for the same thing and checked to see what you'd found. If you'd been here when he came in, I'm sure he would have asked you himself."

He pushed back his chair and got up to leave, when Kallista said, "Gunpowder isn't the secret weapon."

Trenton paused. "You can't know that."

"I do. And you would too, if you hadn't been blinded by Cochrane's flash and charm." Kallista pushed the crate aside. "Why was Discovery founded?"

"To escape the destruction going on around them." Trenton eyed the door, anxious to get back to work.

Kallista stared at him. "And . . ."

It took him a moment to come up with the answer. Considering what he'd been doing for the last month, it should have been obvious. "To come up with a way to fight the dragons."

Kallista nodded, watching him as though waiting for him to

understand. "Remember when we went to the first level of the city back in Discovery?" she said at last. "How we were confused by the thirty years missing from the records?"

Of course he did. There seemed to be two different dates for when Discovery was founded. The city leaders had done everything they could to hide the real date, even going so far as to remove the first pages from the Book of Chancellors.

"That's when they were working on their weapons," Trenton said. "Like we are now. The whole point of naming the city Discovery was because they were trying to discover a way to fight back. And now we know that what they were working on was gunpowder."

Kallista stared at him, face expectant, like a teacher who had called on a student and was waiting for an answer. But what did she want? He'd explained everything perfectly. The founders created Discovery to find a way to fight the dragons. They spent thirty years coming up with a secret weapon. And the weapon they developed was—

All at once it hit him. He dropped back into his chair. "They couldn't have been developing gunpowder because it already existed at that time."

Kallista nodded and let out a deep breath.

"How long have you known?" Trenton asked.

"From the first time Cochrane told us. As soon as he mentioned how cannons and explosives had been used in the past, I realized gunpowder couldn't have been the secret weapon the founders of Discovery were working on."

"We need to tell him," Trenton said.

Kallista shook her head. "He already knows."

Trenton was confused all over again.

Kallista put her hands flat on the table in front of her. "According to Cochrane, he and my father have been working together for two years. There's not a chance my father would have believed the people of Discovery were trying to develop gunpowder. So either Cochrane knows it too and has been lying to us the whole time, or my father never told the dimber damber what he was actually researching. Maybe both. Either way, I don't think we can trust Cochrane or any of the Whipjacks."

Trenton felt so stupid. How had he not picked up on any of this sooner? Is that what Ander meant about Cochrane lying? "Why would he tell us they were working on gunpowder if it wasn't true?"

"I don't know. I've spent weeks in here trying to figure out what my father was doing and why he left. I'm so close I can almost feel him watching over my shoulder. But there's something I'm missing. Something big." Kallista pressed her forehead to the table. "I've always tried to do things by myself. Maybe it's because of the way I was raised. Or maybe it's just part of my personality. I've looked at this from every angle, and . . . I don't think I'm seeing things clearly anymore."

"What are you saying?"

Kallista looked up. She reached across the table and took his hand. "I need you to help me figure out what my father is trying to tell me."

"Of course I'll help," he said, nearly laughing. "Why did you wait so long to ask?"

She quirked her mouth in a twisted half grin. "Says the boy who hates coming to me for help with his machines."

"Low blow." Trenton snorted. "Okay, I guess we both like to solve our own problems. We can start tonight. I'm out of metal anyway."

Something moved out in the hallway, and they both spun around.

"Who's there?" Trenton called.

There was more noise, but the sound was muffled by the narrow tunnel.

Kallista leaped out of her chair. She raced into the tunnel with Trenton close behind. Up ahead, they heard a splash.

"Stop!" Kallista shouted. But it was no use. By the time they reached the water, nobody was there.

"Look!" Trenton called, pointing downstream. Disappearing around the bend was a figure in a boat.

"Could you tell who it was?" Kallista asked.

"No," Trenton said. "It's too dark." Looking down, he noticed something caught on a jagged edge of the wall. It was a small piece of fabric. He picked it up to get a better look.

It was a scrap torn from a robe. A red robe.

30

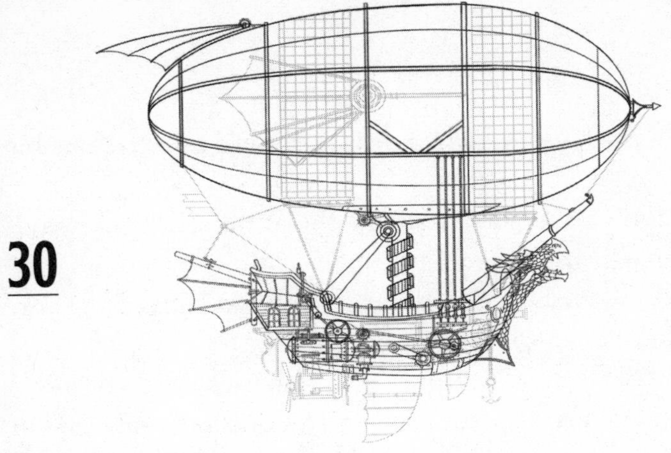

When Trenton got back to the bay, Cochrane was waiting for him.

"Great news!" the dimber damber called, his face beaming.

Trenton looked up at him, wondering if he could trust a word that came from the man's mouth. How many of the things he'd said over the past months—the compliments, the advice, the encouragement—had been lies? And if they were, what was he really after?

"What's the news?" he asked, his lips feeling like wood.

Cochrane didn't seem to notice anything strange. He reached into his pocket, pulled out a small cloth bag, and handed it to Trenton. "See for yourself."

Trenton opened the mouth of the bag and looked inside. It was filled with a gritty, black substance.

"Careful." The dimber damber chuckled. "There's enough in that bag to blow both of us to bits."

"Gunpowder?" Trenton asked, staring at the bag. "You figured out how to make it?"

"I did," Cochrane said. "I knew the ingredients. It was just a matter of getting the right proportions."

What did this mean? Had he really finished figuring it out at the same time Trenton and Kallista were discussing that very thing? It seemed like a big coincidence. Or had he known about it all along? And if so, why had he waited until now to share his discovery?

"You don't seem very excited," the Whipjack leader said, studying him closely.

Trenton looked up. "No, I am." He handed the bag back. "It's just that I have a lot on my mind."

"Slash told me," Cochrane said. "I understand you need more scrap. I can arrange for you to go on one more salvage run tonight."

"Tonight?" Trenton had promised Kallista he'd help her work on her research.

"We've only got two more days before we leave." Cochrane tugged on his beard. "Are you sure you're okay? You don't look well. You've been putting in a lot of hours, I hear."

Until Kallista's revelations, Trenton had felt fantastic. Now he could feel the lack of sleep catching up with him. With no idea who he could trust or what anyone was really up to, he needed his mind sharp. But all his thoughts were blurred by a haze of fear, doubt, and exhaustion.

Cochrane put a hand to Trenton's forehead. "You seem warm, lad. Go back to your room and rest until tonight. I'll have the crew top off the hydrogen in the airship." He tossed the gunpowder bag in his hand. "Might even see if we can ready the cannons and assemble some explosives. Tonight you'll be captaining a fully armed vessel."

"Me?"

"Don't see why not," Cochrane said. "Saints know you've earned it."

• • •

That evening, Trenton woke to a knocking at his door.

"Ready?" Slash asked, leaning inside.

"Is it time?" Trenton rubbed his eyes. It felt like he'd just laid down.

"Been dark for mor'na hour," Slash said. "Dimber Damber said to let ya nod long as we could, right? But it's time to bolt."

Trenton pulled a black shirt over his head, tugged on his shoes, and followed the Whipjack down to the bay. When they got there, the members of the crew were already in their places. Trenton and Slash climbed the ladder to the airship.

"You takes the wheel, and I'll tell the crew ta open the doors and cast off, right?" Slash said.

Trenton stopped outside the door to the captain's cabin. "Where's Cochrane?"

"Not coming," Slash said. "He's roughing out the arrangements for our plan."

Trenton nodded. That made sense. So why did it set the hairs on the back of his neck on end?

As he entered the cabin, someone approached him and handed him a piece of burnt wood. "For your face and hands."

Trenton nodded, then took a second look. "Kallista? What are you doing here?"

"I volunteered. I thought it would be a good idea for us to stay together as much as possible," she said. "Until we know what's really going on."

"Yeah, that's good," he said. It actually calmed his nerves a little to know she was there.

"Show me how this all works," Kallista said as Trenton blackened his hands and face.

It didn't take long to walk her through the controls. She'd seen them in the plans, and everything was fairly self-explanatory. He showed her how to start the engines and the basic elevation and steering processes.

Overhead, the doors slid open, and Slash stuck his head through. "Ready to cast off, Cap?"

"Let's go," Trenton said.

Hands on the wheel, he guided the airship slowly toward the bay's double doors. Having watched Cochrane's mistake, he kept well away from the walls. Still, he felt a huge sense of relief when he reached the opening and rose into the night sky.

Once they were airborne, it was simply a matter of following the compass heading he'd seen Cochrane take and watching for the ruins of the factory to appear.

"You want to take the wheel?" he asked Kallista. "I'm going to look take a look around."

She nodded. "Is something wrong?"

"No. It's just . . . a feeling, I guess." He stepped back from the wheel and climbed the ladder, making his way into the envelope. The pressure appeared to be fine, and everything was in working order. Down below, the engines were running smoothly.

"Everything rum?" asked one of the men, keeping an eye on the equipment.

"Plummy," Trenton said. Still, he had an uneasy feeling.

He took the stairs to the gondola and found Ander standing on deck. "I notice you're not wearing your robe," Trenton said.

Ander grinned, teeth brilliant white against his camouflaged skin. "Not exactly the right outfit for blending into the night, is it?"

"No," Trenton said. "I guess not. Of course you might have had to change out of your robe if was damaged somehow. Maybe torn?"

Ander's smile disappeared. "What are you talking about?"

Trenton locked eyes with him, trying to replicate the boy's icy stare. "I can't believe you followed Kallista and me. I thought we were friends."

"Today? I didn't follow you. I didn't leave the bay."

"Nice try." Trenton held out the torn piece of cloth.

Ander took the fabric and rubbed it between his fingers. "This is from a robe of the Order. There's nothing else like it in the city."

"Of course it is," Trenton said. "It must have snagged on a rock when you were spying on us."

Ander moved forward until their faces nearly touched. "I was working with Slash the whole time. Ask him."

"Ask me what?" Slash said, approaching the two of them.

"Nothing," Ander and Trenton answered in unison.

The Whipjack looked from one to the other, then spit over the side of the rail. "Who's watching the ship?"

"Kallista's steering," Trenton said. "The rest of the crew is keeping an eye out for dragons."

Slash nodded. "Rum girl, that one. Wanna have'a look at the cannons, then?"

"Sure," Trenton said.

As he walked away, Ander leaned in behind him and whispered, "We need to talk."

Trenton ignored him.

There were two cannons on deck—one mounted on each side of the gondola at the front of the ship. A pair of wheels allowed the weapons to be aimed left, right, up, or down and locked into place. Wadding, powder, and various tools were placed nearby, along with a sponge in a bucket of water. The barrel needed to be cleaned after each firing.

"Both of 'em is loaded and primed," Slash said with a grin.

"All you gots to do is lights the wick and cover yer ears." He placed his hands over his ears to demonstrate.

It was good to know, although Trenton didn't anticipate needing to use that knowledge anytime in the near future. He couldn't imagine any situation where he'd be the one firing cannons at dragons.

Slash nodded to a small box on the deck. "Got'a half dozen explosives in there. Just in case."

The idea of having gunpowder so close to an airship envelope full of flammable gas didn't exactly thrill Trenton, but he knew it was necessary.

"Factory's in sight," said a Whipjack from the front of the airship.

Trenton headed back to the cabin and guided the vessel to a spot near where they'd explored last time. Taking them down to about a hundred feet above the ground, he dropped anchor and gave out assignments.

"Want me to take the wheel while you go down?" Ander asked.

Trenton thought about the idea of having the Red Robe controlling the airship while he and Kallista were on the ground and shook his head. "I'll have Kallista take the controls. You and Slash come with me. And I want two crew members up here with telescopes at all times. I don't want another surprise visit like we had before."

For all his concerns, the metal salvaging went better than Trenton expected. They found a large cache of iron pipes and enough copper to finish the cannons. They had everything loaded up in less than two hours.

During the salvage operation, Ander followed Trenton around the ruins. He tried to speak to him several times, but whatever the spy was up to, Trenton wanted nothing to do with the Red Robe.

As they pulled in the nets and shut the hatches, a stiff, easterly wind picked up, making the ship sway beneath their feet.

"Let's get back to the city," Trenton said. "It looks like a storm's blowing in."

Ten minutes later, heavy raindrops began pounding against the front viewports. Lightning flashed, and the wind increased. It took both Trenton and Kallista's full efforts to keep the ship on a straight course.

Trenton stuck his head outside and yelled to the people on the deck. "Hang on to something. I don't want anyone going over the side." He eased back on the throttles, trying to control the sway. As he did, Ander stepped into the cabin.

"Listen to me," Ander said. "We don't have much time to talk. They've been watching you for weeks, and it's only going to get worse until—"

"Not now!" Trenton yelled. "Can't you see we're busy?"

"Who's been watching us?" Kallista asked. "And why is it going to get worse?"

"Don't listen to him," Trenton growled, dropping them fifty feet to see if he could escape the turbulence. "We can't trust him."

"Yes, you can," Ander said. "I swear my life on it."

Trenton shook his head.

Ander clenched his jaw. "I promise on the holy dragon that you can trust me. That's the most sacred vow a member of the Order can make." He glanced quickly toward the door. "You have to tell me right now. Did the two of you kill the green dragon?"

Kallista glanced toward Trenton, and he shook his head. "I already told you. No, we didn't."

"What does it matter to you?" Kallista asked.

A gust of wind slapped the airship like a giant hand, and Ander grabbed the stair rail for support. "I haven't been following you, but I *have* been following the dimber damber. Long before you got here. I think I know what he's up to. Only it doesn't make sense unless you killed the green dragon and he can prove it."

"We did," Kallista said.

"Be quiet," Trenton warned. But she ignored him.

"We killed the dragon. But it was in self-defense. It attacked our city. We didn't have any choice."

"No one can prove it, though," Trenton said. "If you tell anyone, we'll swear you're lying."

"I know where that piece of robe came from," Ander said. "I'm going to check as soon as we get back. If I'm right, I'll let you know tonight."

He looked out the forward window. They were nearly to the city, but the pouring rain made it almost impossible to see. "I know about the stranger who came to the city two years ago. I know it was your father."

Kallista grabbed the front of his shirt, her foot slipping in a puddle of water, and the two of them nearly went down. "You saw my father? What happened to him? Where is he?"

"He found out what Cochrane was up to," Ander said. "I didn't realize what it all meant until today. But now—"

A blaring horn split the night air, drowning out his words. Trenton looked at the rope over his head. He hadn't pulled it. Someone else on the ship had. Outside on the deck, men began to shout.

"Rope's broken loose!" someone screamed. "It's going to rip the envelope!"

31

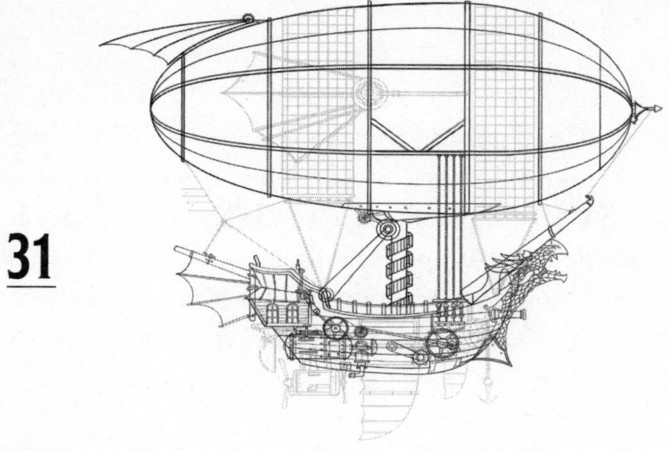

Trenton burst out of the cabin to find an entire section of rigging flapping loose on one side of the ship. Ropes whipped against the surface of the envelope, including one with a large piece of jagged metal attached to the end.

One of the brackets had ripped out of the deck, and the wind was slapping it wildly against the taut fabric with a loud *boom, boom, boom*. A square of torn silver cloth snapped back and forth. It was a miracle the whole envelope hadn't ripped open. Several crew members were trying to grab the ropes, but they were too high to reach.

"How did this happen?" Trenton screamed.

Slash stared up at the growing tear with fascinated horror. "No idea. But it's gonna blow any second."

Kallista ran out behind Trenton, grabbed his shoulder, and jumped for the end of one of the swinging ropes. Her fingers brushed against it, but the wind snatched it out of her hand before she could grasp it. As she landed on the deck, the gondola shifted, and she would have flipped over the railing if Trenton hadn't grabbed her.

"Jump!" someone yelled. "We're going down."

Trenton looked over the side of the gondola. They were still at least two hundred feet above the ground. No one would survive the fall. He looked back up at the ripped fabric. Right now the tear was small and only on the outside of the envelope. But with the way the metal bracket was bouncing, it was only a matter of seconds before it broke through to the hydrogen. Once it did, the entire thing would rip to shreds.

There was another set of rigging ten feet from the one that had torn lose. If he could get up there before the bracket—

He turned to run for the rigging when Ander raced past.

"Give me a boost!" he yelled, climbing onto the wet railing.

Trenton cupped his hands, and Ander stepped into them, launching himself up the rope. Wind blasted the ship, sending sheets of rain into the crew's faces as they watched Ander climb.

Kallista pointed at the ropes. "The wind's blowing toward us. We've got to turn around and use the ship as a shield."

"Right." Trenton ran into the cabin where one of the crew was frantically yanking at the controls. The floor bucked under his feet, and he nearly fell.

"Stand back." Trenton shoved the man aside. He wanted to lower the ship, but he was afraid the sudden shift might knock Ander from the ropes. Instead, he carefully turned the wheel, using the wind and the rudders to ease the ship around. "Hold it steady on this course," he told the crewman.

Gripping the wall for support, Trenton made his way back outside.

Ander was nearly even with the bracket, but the rip was definitely bigger and the metal was ripping it more with every bounce.

"Grab the rope!" Kallista shouted.

Having reached the point where the rigging met the material of the envelope, Ander hooked his left arm and leg in the rigging. He swung his body toward the swinging rope and, at the last second, snatched at the bracket. The metal brushed against his fingers, spun, and slipped away.

Trenton was sure they'd lost their chance, when the wind gave the ship a large shove. The rope flipped around, and Ander grabbed the jagged metal.

Stretched between the rigging and the hanging rope, Ander seemed on the verge of losing his grip. Then, carefully, an inch at a time, he pulled the bracket back to the rigging and tied it in place.

On the deck below, the water-soaked Whipjacks let out a cheer. They were all clapping their hands and grinning when Ander slipped from the ropes. One second he was grinning down at them, and the next, his hand slipped on the wet rigging. He reached out to grab something, but his body was already swinging away from the envelope.

Hands dangling in the air, he hung upside down. His leg slid, dropping him another foot. Someone on deck screamed. Given his position on the side of the envelope, Ander was hanging far past the edge of the gondola. If he fell, he'd drop straight to the ground.

Trenton watched in horror as Ander's foot began to slide again. The boy clawed for purchase, but there was nothing in reach. He kicked for the ropes with his other leg, slipped, and lost his hold completely.

Someone screamed, "He's going down!"

Trenton dove across the deck. His body slammed against the railing, and he leaned outward, stretching his arms. Ander's body brushed against Trenton, and he clawed for anything he could get hold of. Soaked clothing slipped through his fingers.

He was going to lose him.

Then Ander reached out and grabbed for Trenton. Their hands locked around each other's arms. The weight lifted Trenton's feet off the deck, and his body started to tip over the rail.

"Hang on!" Kallista yelled. She grabbed his feet, and for a moment, his body balanced precariously on the railing. Trenton strained to hold on to Ander while shifting as much of his weight backward as he could.

Kallista pulled. "Someone help me."

People grabbed his feet. Arms reached around and over him. Hands gripped Ander's arms and upper torso.

And then they were both sitting on the deck, panting. Rain dripped down Ander's face as he reached out to grip Trenton's shoulder. "You saved me."

Trenton pushed his wet hair out of his eyes. "You"—he gasped—"saved . . . all of us."

Taking Kallista's hand for support, Trenton pulled himself to his feet. "Somebody shut off the alarm," he yelled as the two of them walked down the stairs into the cabin. The storm was mostly over, but they had flown several hundred yards off course, and he needed to get them back to the city.

He turned the wheel to correct their course and pushed the altitude lever to start down. Slowly, the clouds and stars began to swing upward.

Trenton glanced over his shoulder at Kallista. "That was too close."

Kallista's jaw dropped, her eyes stretching wide. She pointed out the forward window.

Trenton turned around and saw an enormous black dragon flying straight toward them.

• • •

Kallista pushed past Trenton, spinning the wheel left and jamming the altitude control back up seconds before the dragon belched a cloud of flame at them. If she had reacted an instant later, or if the dragon had breathed its fire an instant earlier, the entire ship would have gone down in flames.

As it was, the attack scorched the forward starboard side of the gondola, sending flames roaring over the railing as the wood immediately caught fire. Screams sounded from down below, and two Whipjacks burst out of the stairwell.

As Kallista evened the ship out, Trenton peered through the window, trying to see where the dragon was. "There," he said, pointing. "It's circling to the right." He picked up a lantern and raced for the stairs. "Get me a clear shot and then get us down to the ground."

Wisps of black smoke were drifting up the stairs. Clutching the lantern in one hand, he ran to the starboard cannon. Most of the crew on deck were running around in mass confusion and terror. Trenton shouldered his way through them until he reached the cannon.

Although he had fought dragons before, he'd never faced anything like the horned behemoth heading straight at them. Its brilliant green eyes cut through the darkness, and it took all of Trenton's self-control to keep from giving in to the panic that clutched his heart like an icy glove.

He set the lantern at his feet and spun the wheels to aim the cannon. Even as he watched the enormous beast closing in on him, he mentally noted that if he survived this he'd need to come up with a quicker way to adjust the cannon.

With the dragon less than a hundred yards away, he ripped the cover off the lantern, tilted it, and lit the fuse. "Somebody get on the other cannon," he called, then clapped his hands over his ears. A second later, the cannon bucked against its bracket. Smoke and flame exploded from the end of the barrel.

The cannonball went wide.

The dragon opened its jaws, the beginnings of a fireball glowing in its mouth.

Trenton's heart sank, but then the dragon tilted its head at the sound of the explosion. Trenton watched as the creature's entire body followed along with its head. The beast's right wing rose directly into the ball's path.

The cannonball bounced off its leathery wing enough to alter the dragon's path. The fireball that would have incinerated Trenton passed harmlessly next to the airship.

Grabbing the lantern, Trenton raced to the other side of the ship. He watched, fascinated, as the dragon dove beneath them, then made a wide, looping turn back in their direction. Why didn't it simply turn its head and blast them?

Unless it couldn't. He stared at the armor-like scales encasing its neck. Was it possible the dragon *couldn't* turn its head?

Grabbing the lantern from Trenton, the Whipjack manning the cannon lit the fuse. The shot was high, and the cannonball sailed past the dragon.

Having learned from the previous attack, though, the dragon dove at the sound of the explosion. It tried to rise but couldn't get an angle to blow flames at the airship. Instead, it raised its curved horns and gouged the side. Wood splintered, sending gouts of flame into the air as the gondola swung wildly.

Trenton clung to the railing, waiting for the swinging to stop. From the forward section of the deck, someone fired the nets as the dragon passed beneath them, but they bounced harmlessly off the monster's back.

Kallista was angling the airship toward the ground in a perilously steep descent. Half the gondola was in flames, so there was no time to lose.

It would take too long to reload the cannons, and the dragon was still circling the ship. Somehow he had to buy Kallista the time she needed to get the ship to the ground. Searching for any kind of weapon, his eyes stopped on the wooden crate on the deck.

Explosives.

Taking as many of the small metal spheres as he could cradle in the front of his shirt, Trenton grabbed the lantern and raced across the deck to the other side of the ship.

"Get us on the ground," he called to Kallista as he ran past the cabin door.

Stopping at the railing, he tried to peer through the acrid smoke that was getting thicker and thicker. For a moment, he couldn't see the dragon. Then he spotted a huge black shape gliding toward the aft of the airship.

He dipped the fuse of the explosive into the lantern's flame, holding his breath as the end caught and sputtered. There was supposed to be a five-second delay, but if the fuse had been designed wrong . . .

Five, four, three, he counted silently, walking toward the back of the ship. He cocked his arm. And fired.

The throw was off to the right, but it actually ended up being in his favor. The tiny bomb exploded in a miniature sun of heat and metal.

Roaring, the dragon turned and missed the airship completely.

Trenton ran to the front of the ship, watching as the dragon came out the other side. He readied another explosive. The dragon circled to attack again, and Trenton tried to be patient. Drops of sweat and soot trickled into his eyes as he waited for the dragon to come into range. Smoke filled his lungs, and his throat burned.

The dragon rose toward them, its wings filling the night.

He lit the fuse.

Five . . .

Four . . .

Three . . .

One more second and the dragon was right on top of the ship. It opened its jaws wide, and Trenton flung his sphere as hard as he could.

This time his aim was perfect. Ball and dragon met just as the bomb exploded. A burst of fire went off inside the dragon's mouth. Metal shards peppered its tongue and face.

Howling in pain and surprise, the dragon turned away. Trenton watched in shock as the huge beast beat its wings and disappeared into the clouds. Banging sounded from behind him, and he turned to see Kallista pounding on the front window of the cabin, pumping her right fist in the air.

He'd done it. He'd actually fought off the dragon.

A moment later, they crashed to the ground. Flames and sparks shot into the air. He heard a loud hissing overhead. A piece of wood had pierced the envelope and hydrogen was flowing out of it. The cloth at the edge of the rip flapped with the force of the escaping gas.

"Everybody off the ship!" he screamed. He ran toward the cabin door just as Kallista stumbled out of the smoke-filled room. He wrapped his arm around her waist.

Together they reached the railing and tumbled over it to the ground below. Above them, a flame finally touched the gas, but, miraculously, instead of exploding, the gas shot a geyser of fire high into the air.

Gagging and vomiting, the crew backed away from the ship. The flames chewing away at the gondola smoldered, then flickered out.

A few yards behind them the double doors of the bay rumbled open.

Plucky's head popped over the side. "Saw what happened with me own peeps," she said. "Everyone all right?"

"Yeah," Trenton croaked, wiping his mouth with the back of his hand. "We're all right."

Quickly he counted the black-clad figures around him: *one, two, three, four, five, six, seven, eight, nine, ten . . .*

He looked around, thinking he must have missed someone. Counting himself, there were eleven. There should have been twelve. He counted again. Still eleven. Heart pounding, he started back toward the ship.

"Pull up," Slash said, gripping his shoulder. "Could still be gas, chum."

Trenton ducked out of his grasp and raced toward the smoldering wreck. He'd missed someone. He was almost back to the airship when he saw the body lying spread-eagled on the ground.

"No!" he screamed running toward it. *"No!"*

Before he even reached the body, he could see the blond hair lying against the ground.

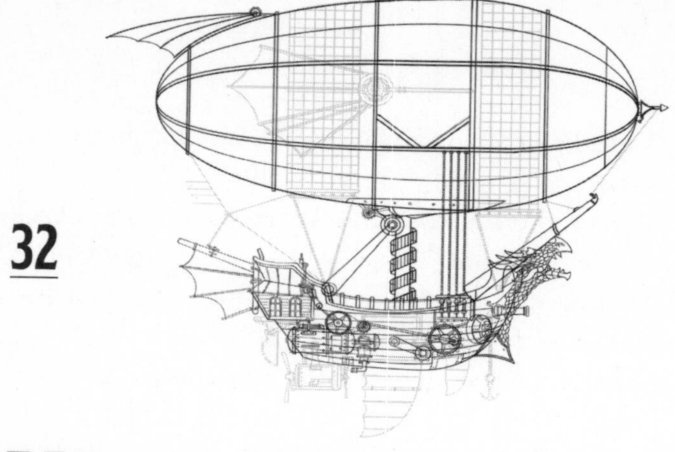

32

Not your fault," Slash said, patting him on the shoulder.

Trenton sat at the table, his face buried in his arms. It had taken all his strength to drag himself down to the bay the next morning. As soon as he saw the charred hull of the airship on the floor of the bay, he dropped into a chair and burst into tears.

"Ya done everything ya could," Plucky said. "It weren't your fault."

"I failed," Trenton croaked. "I didn't bring my crew back alive."

"Ya brung ten o'em," Plucky said. "Got the ship down in one piece, didn't ya?"

"Give him some time," Cochrane said. "We gots a load'a metal spread out up top to salvage. And work to be done."

Footsteps moved away from him, and Trenton was alone. Then a soft hand touched his back, rubbing gently. He thought he was done crying, but fresh tears welled in his eyes and ragged sobs tore from his throat.

"I know, I know," Kallista said softly.

"He wanted to h-help me," Trenton cried, "and I wouldn't listen to him."

Kallista squeezed his shoulder. "You did what you could. If it wasn't for you, he would have died after securing the rigging.

You risked your life to save his. Don't think he didn't know that."

Trenton sat up, hot tears burning on his cheeks. "The Order of the Beast buries their own. They said I couldn't attend."

Kallista nodded. "It's not right. But there's nothing we can do about that, either."

Trenton glared at the burned airship. "He didn't fall on his own."

"What are you talking about?" Kallista said. "He fell overboard when the dragon gored the ship."

"Did you see him fall?"

"No, but—"

"Do you really think it was an accident that the rigging ripped loose just as Ander was about to tell us about your father?" Trenton said. "Even with the storm, there's no way the rigging should have ripped loose like that. Someone ripped the bracket out to divert our attention. When that didn't work, they threw him over the side during the dragon attack."

Kallista looked from Trenton to the ruined ship. "You really think someone would risk their life to kill Ander? There had to be an easier way."

"They would if Cochrane commanded them to. They probably would have done it at the factory, but Ander stuck close to me the whole time. We were nearly back to the city. They were probably desperate."

"But why? What was so important that someone was willing to kill him over it?"

Trenton rubbed his eyes, remembering how Weasel had seen him and Ander talking. Right after that, the dimber damber had arranged for them to take out the airship. "Ander said your father found out something about Cochrane. Whatever it was made your father leave, and it got Ander killed." He stood up. "Let's get out of here."

"Where are we going?" Kallista asked.

"To the library. We're going to find out what your father discovered."

• • •

"Okay, tell me one more time," Trenton said, pushing aside the stack of notes he'd been studying.

"Tell you *what?*" Kallista frowned so hard that lines formed on either side of her mouth. Her nostrils flared as she breathed, and her eyebrows squeezed together in a way that told him he was about to go too far. But they'd gone over every book Leo had read, every note he had doodled in a margin, every subject he'd researched, and all of it piled, sorted, and diagrammed amounted to nothing.

"I don't know." Trenton rubbed his face. "Tell me about the maps."

"No," Kallista said.

"No?"

She hunched her shoulders, the crease in her forehead so deep it could have held a pencil. "I'm sick of the maps."

"All right." Trenton exhaled and looked around the room. "How about the timelines?"

"No."

"The inventors?"

Kallista shook her head.

Trenton drummed his fingers on the table. "What do you want to talk about?"

"Nothing," she said. "I told you. I've gone over it a hundred times, and there's nothing here. I'd know if there was."

She was right. He didn't know why he'd thought he could

solve her problem or why she'd thought he could help. Kallista was probably smarter than he was. She was definitely more stubborn. And after playing thousands of hours of games with her father, she knew him better than anyone else.

"How about the games?" he said. "Would you tell me about those?"

The crease shrunk a little but didn't go away.

He took that as a positive sign. "You know. When you started playing them? How they worked? Maybe your favorite one?"

"I didn't have any favorites," Kallista said. "They were all hard and frustrating. At least while we were playing them. As soon as I figured out one of his tricks, he'd add another, more difficult, one. The only good part about a game was when I finally solved it and he gave me a prize."

Trenton leaned forward. His parents had never played games with him, and he found the idea fascinating. "So they were all hide-and-seek-type games, like the one he set up for us with the pieces of Ladon?"

"Not always," Kallista said. "Sometimes there were things I had to find. Sometimes there were puzzles. But sometimes the thing I was looking for had been right in front of me, and the trick was figuring out it was there at all."

That didn't help much. "Was there anything that all the games had in common?"

Kallista propped her elbows on the table, resting her chin in her hands. "Not really. Except that they always started with a single clue."

"What kind of clue?"

"You know, a message or something telling you the game had started. You'd have to figure it out from there yourself."

Trenton nodded. "Like the talon. Once we found that, it

led us to the aquarium, which led us to Chancellor Huber, and everything came together after that. Okay, this is good."

"How is this good?" Kallista snorted, and the line on her brow began to form again. "We don't know what the first clue is. If we did, we wouldn't be sitting here, banging our heads."

Trenton flipped through her stack of notes. "Well, which of these came first? You always say that your father does everything for a reason. What's the first piece of information you discovered?"

"The letter he left for me," Kallista said immediately.

"Great," Trenton said. "Where's the letter? Let's look at it again."

Kallista fished through the box and pulled it out. "I've read it a thousand times. There's nothing in it. He probably knew Cochrane would read it, so he put the first clue somewhere else."

"Or he disguised it in a way that Cochrane wouldn't know it was a clue." He examined the letter closely, turning it upside down and side to side. "Have you checked for invisible ink? Maybe near a flame? Or maybe it's another code where we have to count the words."

"I've tried heat, chemicals, codes, number variations, anagrams. I've counted letters, words, and syllables, forward and backward."

"Well, that's a good start."

Kallista snorted and flapped her hands. "Trust me, if I didn't find anything, you won't either."

She was right, of course. But that didn't mean Trenton was going to give her the satisfaction of admitting it. Tugging on his left earlobe, he carefully read the letter, hoping a secret message might pop out at him. He squinted his eyes to see if anything looked different, but then he couldn't make out the words at all.

By the time he got to the last paragraph, he knew he wasn't going to find anything.

> *Please know that I am thinking of you always. Do not come looking for me. Stay and help Cochrane build the machines we have designed. Unlike the plans I left for you in Cove, these schematics will provide you everything you need to know.*

He smiled, remembering how frustrated he and Kallista had been when they discovered the blueprints for the dragon were missing key parts. Minor things like the wing and the engine. They'd been so excited to discover the answers for themselves. And, along with those answers, they'd discovered the truth about their city. Now he'd be thrilled to find a set of plans with a blank area because he'd know that once he found the missing part, he'd have his answer.

"I told you," Kallista said, when he finished reading. "There's nothing there."

What he wouldn't give for a set of diagrams with a missing piece. Except Kallista had said that once you figured out the trick the first time, her father would change it for the next time. So even if he had hidden something in the plans . . .

Plans.

Trenton looked back at the last line again.

> *Unlike the plans I left for you in Cove, these schematics will provide you everything you need to know.*

These schematics will provide you everything you need to know . . .

But he'd looked over the schematics hundreds of times.

There were no missing parts. And if there had been, Cochrane would have discovered them by now.

Unlike the plans I left for you in Cove . . .

What if Leo had found a *different* way to hide clues in the plans? A way Cochrane wouldn't have discovered? Was there anything in the plans Cochrane didn't know about?

Yes. There was.

Trenton jumped up from his chair, banging his knees into the table so hard he nearly knocked it and Kallista over.

"I know where the clue is!"

"What?" Kallista grabbed the letter and turned it around. "Where? What did you find?"

Trenton ran for the tunnel. "Stay here," he called over his shoulder. "I'll be right back."

He raced all the way back to the bay, jumped up on the platform, and grabbed every set of diagrams Cochrane had given him.

"Trenton, come here for a minute," the dimber damber called. "I need your help."

"Not now," Trenton yelled. "I'll be right back."

Halfway to the library, he detoured and headed to Cochrane's office. He was worried the dimber damber's workroom might be locked, but it wasn't. Searching through the drawers of the tool bench, he pulled out every set of schematics he could find, making sure he had the ones for the vibrating chair and the chain-making machine.

Tucking them all under his arm, he hurried to the boat and floated impatiently down to the crack in the wall. By the time he got there, Kallista was furious.

"Where have you been? Why you did you run off like that? You took the only boat so I couldn't even follow you."

Trenton dumped the plans out onto the table.

"What are those?" Kallista bent over the papers, then frowned. "The diagrams for Cochrane's weapons? I've seen them all before."

"Not as many times as I have," Trenton said. "Give me some paper and a pencil."

Opening the schematic for the horsecycle, he copied the pair of squiggly lines representing the throttle cables that had been too long and a ninety-degree angle for the bracket that had been in the wrong place.

"I don't understand," Kallista said.

The next sheet of paper was the Envelope Inflation Method. He carefully copied out the pair of wires that had been too thin.

"Hang on," Kallista said. "Are those . . ."

By the time he copied the backward C-ring from the armored vehicle schematic, she'd grabbed her own set of plans.

When you knew what you were looking for, it became obvious. Each set of plans had one or two mistakes in it. Nothing obvious enough for Cochrane to pick up on, but something skilled mechanics, like Trenton and Kallista, were able to spot quickly.

By the time they'd gone through all the plans, they'd drawn twenty different shapes.

"It's a puzzle," Kallista said, tearing the papers so that each shape they'd drawn was on its own piece.

It took them awhile to figure out where the pieces went, but once they realized the two squiggly lines represented the canal, the rest came together easily.

"It's a map of the library," Trenton said as Kallista slid the last piece into place.

Kallista studied the map for a minute before pointing to a specific image. "I know right where this is." With the speed of someone who'd spent endless hours exploring the dimly lit room, she led Trenton through the labyrinth of shelves to a badly leaning brick wall.

She grabbed a large metal bookcase and shoved. "Help me move this."

Together, the two of them bent their knees, pressed their backs against the shelf, and pushed. With a loud screech, the bookshelf slid aside. Behind it was a carefully carved out hole in the bricks.

"Just like where he hid the stuff about the dragons," Trenton said.

Side by side, they dropped onto their hands and knees and peered into the hole. "There's something there," Kallista said. She reached inside the hole, cupped her hands around a dark object, and pulled out a charred box. It collapsed into a pile of burned wood and ashes in her hands.

"I don't understand," Kallista said.

Trenton pressed his face to the hole to see if there was more, but the hiding space was empty.

"You were right," a voice said from behind them. "They are smarter than I gave them credit for."

Trenton and Kallista turned to find Martin, second in command in the Order of the Beast, leaning against a shelf.

"They even surprised me a little," Cochrane said, stepping out of the shadows. "It's really sad we have to kill them."

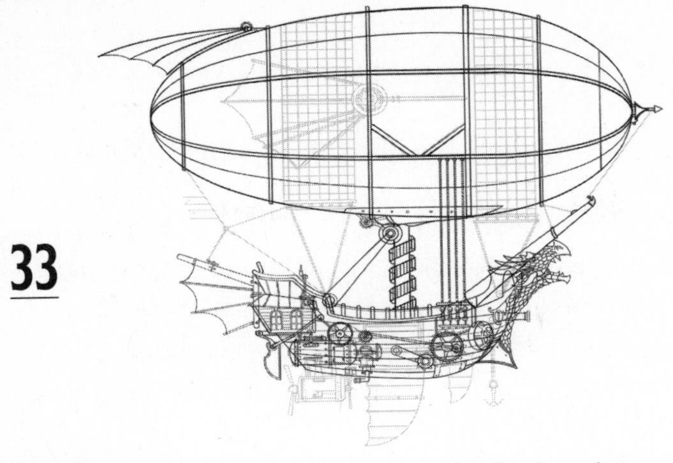

33

Floating down the canal, wedged in the boat between Kallista and Martin, Trenton twisted his hands, but the ropes tied around his wrists only dug in deeper. Cochrane had taken all of their belongings and tied their hands behind their backs.

"How did you figure out that the clues were in the plans?" Trenton asked.

Cochrane chuckled. "You really think you're that much smarter than me?"

"I don't think it. I know it," Kallista said.

"I'd make you pay for that remark," the dimber damber said, "but in the next few days you'll be enduring pain you can't even imagine. There's no need for me to add to it."

Slash and Weasel were waiting at the edge of the canal. The moment the boat stopped, they yanked Trenton and Kallista out. Cochrane climbed out too, but Martin remained in the boat. "I'll tell the patriarch what we've *discovered*," he said with a nasty grin.

As the Red Robe pushed back into the canal, Weasel and Slash spun Trenton and Kallista around and shoved them in the back.

"How *did* you figure it out?" Trenton asked. He'd always known Cochrane wasn't the inventor he'd claimed to be. Now he was beginning to think the man had no mechanical knowledge at all.

Cochrane shrugged. "I didn't, actually. I didn't need to. Once we searched Babbage's room and didn't find his notes there, it only stood to reason he'd hidden them somewhere nearby where he could access them on a regular basis. The obvious choice was the library. We simply ransacked it until we found his notes and then burned them."

Kallista squeezed her eyes shut. "Then you stood back and watched while we searched for them."

"It was a good way to keep you from snooping around places where I didn't want you."

"Is that where you learned to make gunpowder?" she asked. "Obviously you didn't figure it out for yourself."

Cochrane's eyes narrowed. He turned to Slash. "One more smart word out of her mouth and you can make it her last."

The Whipjack jangled the metal rings in his arms and smiled.

"I *had* hoped the formula for making gunpowder was in Leo's notes. When I discovered it wasn't, I had to use *other* methods to get the information. I have it now, and that's what matters."

Looking around, Trenton realized they were headed for the bay. Was Cochrane taking them there to work as slaves, finishing the last of the weapons before they went to fight the dragons?

"What *was* in my father's notes?" Kallista demanded.

Cochrane pouted. "Say please."

Kallista glared at him. "Please."

"See." Cochrane nodded at Slash. "Bad children can be taught manners. They just need the right motivation."

Slash hooted.

"Nothing of any great importance," Cochrane said to

Kallista. "Lunatic ramblings, mostly." They turned down the passage that led to the bay. "Our research together actually started out to be quite promising. That part of my story was true. I did meet him in the woods, and I did bring him back here. He was fascinated by the library, and I was fascinated by his ability to come up with the most amazing inventions. Then, when he told me about your city in the mountains, I knew it was the perfect place to launch my attack against the dragons."

They walked into the bay, where all the weaponized machines Trenton had been working on were lined up side by side, ready to be lifted out of the double doors and taken into battle.

"The people of Discovery will never help you fight the dragons without me and Kallista," Trenton said.

Cochrane put a hand to his mouth and giggled a little. Slash grinned. "Well, the thing about fighting the dragons was sort of a lie," the dimber damber said. "I mean, yes, we will fight them if we have to, but Martin thinks it might not come to that if we make certain concessions."

Trenton looked at all the machines he'd worked so hard on. "So these were all a lie too? A way to keep *me* occupied?"

"Not at all," Cochrane said, shocked. "These were the key to my plan. Babbage designed them. But once he was no longer available, I needed someone with your special talents to bring his designs to fruition. Perhaps we could have figured them out over time by ourselves, but I must say I enjoyed watching someone from Discovery building the weapons, considering what we have planned for the city."

He patted Trenton on the back, and Trenton jerked away from his touch.

"As soon as I saw you admiring the machines in my office, I knew you valued technology—a boy who placed machines in such high regard that he'd choose them over human companionship. And my strategy worked more perfectly than I could have imagined. She ignored you to search for her father, and you ignored her to build my weapons. Until recently, I never had to worry about the two of you working together to figure out what I was up to."

"What *are* you up to?" Kallista asked. "If you didn't build these machines to fight the dragons, what did you build them for?"

Cochrane shook his head. "I'm surprised children as *smart* as you two have to ask. I'm going to use your machines to attack your city and take it for myself. It will be the new Whipjack headquarters."

Trenton's stomach clenched, and his chest burned. All his time. All his energy. He'd been so proud of what he was doing only to discover he'd used his talents to build something that would destroy everything he loved. He bent over, feeling like he was going to throw up.

"Don't take it so hard," Cochrane said. "You're only half to blame. Babbage designed the machines. You only completed his designs."

"My father would never build something to hurt other people," Kallista spat, her face turning red.

"It did take some persuasion," Cochrane admitted. "But I'm good at that sort of thing."

"And what about the Order of the Beast?" Trenton asked, his head spinning. "They're in on it too? Is that what Ander found out? Is that why you killed him?"

"Ander had been putting his nose in places it didn't belong. His accident was very well timed, don't you think, Slash?"

Slash and Weasel looked at one another before bursting out in laughter.

"As it happens," Cochrane said, "Patriarch Wilhelm and his

followers are still true believers. In fact, they presented a bit of a thorny problem for me until I realized I could use them as well. At this very moment, Martin is on his way to tell the patriarch that he knows for a fact the two of you murdered their sacred green dragon."

"It will never work," Trenton said. "You don't have any proof."

"Actually, I do." Cochrane looked toward the top of Ladon, put his fingers in his mouth, and whistled. "Can you come down here for a second?"

Clanging sounds came from inside the hatch, then a head peered out.

"Plucky," Trenton whispered.

Slowly Plucky climbed down the ladder. When she reached the bottom, she stuck her hands in her pockets, ducked her shoulders, and slouched over to where the dimber damber was standing, clicking and sproinging the whole way.

Cochrane held out his hand. "Do you have that item you've been holding for me?"

Plucky dropped her head and pulled her hand out of her pocket. In her palm was a green dragon scale from Discovery's council chamber. That's what she'd been doing when he went back to look for her—she'd been stealing it.

"Why?" he whispered.

When she didn't answer, Cochrane spoke for her. "Clearly I had hoped to be the one to visit your city and scope it out in advance of attacking it. Weasel or Slash would have been my next choices, but Plucky came through just fine."

He grinned at Plucky cowering before him. "Poor girl was thrilled when you offered to let her fly back to your city with you. You know, she actually refused the job at first. Until I explained that people in a city as magnificent as yours would never have a place for a girl like her—a cripple whose mistake killed her own family. I told her that if she didn't do what I wanted, the Whipjacks would force her out of the city. She'd have nowhere else to go."

He placed a hand on her head and sniffed. "And it turns out I was right. Your people are happy to take our weapons and soldiers. But a child? No, she would be out on her own if it wasn't for someone as generous as myself. After that, she was more than happy to give me a detailed map to your city. Even better, she knows how to fly your dragon. That will make an especially nice addition to my arsenal, won't it, Plucky? You'll train Weasel to fly with you, and the two of you will become part of my magnificent army."

Plucky shook her head, and Cochrane scowled. "Excuse me?" the dimber damber said. "Did you just disagree with me?"

"No, sir," the girl said, eyes on her feet. "Problem is, the dragon don't run."

"What are you talking about?" Cochrane demanded.

"I'll show you." Plucky clanged across the floor and climbed the dragon until she was in the driver's seat. Settling in, she pushed the ignition button. Black smoke poured out of the dragon's mouth, and a terrible clanking came from inside. A moment later, the entire engine seized and died.

"Trenton musta done something to the inner workings," Plucky called down.

What was she talking about? He hadn't touched the dragon since they got back from Discovery. Why would she lie about that?

Cochrane spun around to glare at him.

Trenton shrugged, forcing a cocky grin onto his lips. "Didn't think I was going to let you take all my machines, did you?"

The dimber damber drew back his hand, and Trenton

flinched, waiting to be struck. Slowly Cochrane lowered his hand. "No matter. Once I get to Discovery, I can force your people to build me all the dragons I want." He stroked his beard and grinned.

"They won't do it!" Trenton shouted, fighting to free himself from his bands.

"They won't have any choice," Cochrane said, waving aside protests. "If I were you, though, I'd be far more worried about what Wilhelm the Divine is going to do." He fingered the green dragon scale Plucky had given him. "The Order can't have people walking around claiming dragons are mortal, now can they?

"As for you . . ." He turned around to look for Kallista and saw that she had edged over to one of the unfinished armored vehicles. "What are you doing over there?" he yelled. "Slash, bring her back."

The Whipjack grabbed her roughly by the arm, pulled her back to Cochrane, and spun her around. Her wrists were covered in blood, and the rope binding them was nearly cut in half where she'd been rubbing it against a sharp piece of metal.

"Wouldn't want you running off," Cochrane said. "After all the time you've spent looking for your father, I think you deserve a little time with him. Enjoy it while you can. I hear the Red Robes have something special prepared for you."

34

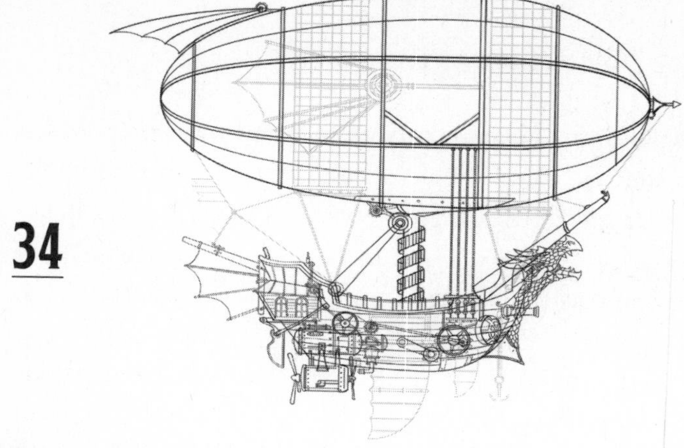

It took a moment for the dimber damber's words to sink in. Then Kallista gasped. "My father? He's *here?*"

Trenton glared at Cochrane, trying to decide how much of the man's words he could believe. "But the letter . . ."

"The letter." Cochrane nodded. "Let's just say he didn't exactly write that of his own free will. Same with the weapon designs, though the airship was his idea. I think he rather liked that. The rest of my arsenal—gunpowder in particular—took some motivating. When I told him his daughter was here and what I'd do to her if he didn't cooperate, things moved a lot more quickly."

"Where is he?" Kallista demanded. "Take me to him."

"Oh, I will," Cochrane said, grinning. "It's actually sort of ironic that all the time you were trying to find his trail in the library, Trenton here has been practically right on top of him."

Trenton looked around. "What are you talking about? I'd have seen him if he was here."

"All the time you've worked in the bay, and you've never wondered what this room was? Before Leo Babbage arrived and I assumed the power of which I was so deserving." The dimber damber nodded to his lead Whipjack. "Tell them, Slash."

"It's a prison," the man said, spitting on the ground.

Cochrane nodded. "Filled top to bottom with cells. You might have noticed the remains of the bars embedded in the walls? And the high-pressure hose to wash the criminals down when their stink got too bad."

Trenton nodded. He'd noticed the metal stubs in the walls but hadn't given them much thought. And he'd even used that hose to wash the salvaged parts.

"I removed the cells when I took power. It's surprising what loyal followers freed prisoners make. The only cell I left was the one used for solitary confinement. That's where I've been keeping our houseguest." He looked down at the bars in the floor, and Trenton gasped.

The grate? Where he'd dumped ice-cold water, along with all the dirt and sludge from the salvage? But the stink, and the huge, hungry-looking rats . . . No. Leo Babbage could not possibly have been down there all this time.

"You said it was a sewer," he whispered.

"It *is* where we keep the sewage," Cochrane said. "And now you both can take your rightful place there. Slash, take the girl down to meet her father."

Wrinkling his nose at the stench, Slash lifted the grate. He pulled out his knife to force Trenton and Kallista inside. Kallista didn't need any urging, though. Running down the slime-coated stairs, she called out, "Father!"

Trying not to slip, Trenton hurried after her, Slash following him. The lower he went, the more unbearable the stink became. Green and yellow fungus climbed the walls, and the floor was damp and slick. The narrow passage was so low he had to duck his head. The only light came from a few sputtering gas lanterns bracketed to the walls.

The downward sloping passage curved left, then right. Through the crumbling walls, Trenton could hear what he thought was the river. Something skittered near his feet, and Trenton looked down to see a rat at least a foot long glaring up at him. Slash kicked at it, and the rodent hissed before scurrying away.

"Father!" Kallista's cry echoed off the walls.

A wet cough answered her.

Slash chuckled. "Sounds like he's still alive."

They turned a corner, and the passage ended in a cell door. Kallista knelt on the floor, sobbing. Her arms stretched through the bars, cradling a bearded man dressed in rags. His face was a mass of cuts and bruises, and his arms and legs were so thin Trenton could make out every bone. But even with all that, the resemblance was impossible to miss.

For the first time since finding the metal talon trapped in the feeder belt of the coal mine, Trenton was looking at Kallista's father, the great inventor Leo Babbage.

• • •

After everything he'd heard about Leo Babbage, Trenton expected him to greet Kallista with a checklist of things he thought she should have accomplished. Instead, the two of them sat on a small cot in the locked cell, father embracing daughter.

"I'm so sorry," Kallista said, burying her face in her father's chest. "I should have figured out the clues faster, found you sooner. Then maybe you wouldn't be here."

"Nonsense," Leo said, patting her shoulders as he rocked her back and forth. "You were brilliant. Everything I expected you to be. Everything I hoped for."

"Really?" Kallista looked up, eyes red and cheeks wet. "You're not just saying that to make me feel better?"

Leo snorted exactly the way Kallista always did. His eyebrows knitted together, and Trenton recognized the same vertical line running down the center of his forehead.

Kallista's hair had fallen over her eyes, and her father brushed it back. "Since when have I ever said anything that wasn't true simply to soothe your feelings?"

Kallista wiped her eyes. "Never, that I can remember."

"Then, based on previous observations, it would be safe to assume that I am not doing so now."

"Since when have I ever been able to predict what you'd do in the future based on your previous actions?" Kallista asked, a mischievous gleam in her eye.

Leo raised a crooked finger, thought for a moment, then put it down. "Good point."

Kallista gasped. "Your hands. What have they done to you?"

Leo held up his hands to his face, studying his twisted and swollen fingers. "The man who refers to himself with the pompous title of dimber damber has a rather harsh way of dealing with his prisoners. The first time they caught me trying to escape, they broke my leg. The second time, they decided I couldn't pick locks if they broke my fingers."

"No." Kallista wept, cradling her father's hands.

"Now, now," Leo said. "No need to cry. I set them myself. Even with my twisted digits, I'm still twice the lock picker you are."

Kallista sniffed, wiped her eyes, and managed a small smile. "In your dreams."

Sitting on a narrow stone bench across from them, Trenton watched the two trade barbs and grinned. Even under such awful circumstances, it was great to see Kallista reunited with the father she'd worked so long and hard to find.

Seeming to notice him for the first time, Mr. Babbage looked Trenton up and down. "Have I met you before?"

"No, sir," he said. "I'm Trenton Coleman."

"Ray and Celia's boy. Of course. I knew your father very

well. You inherited more of your mother's features. How is she these days?"

"She's . . ." Trenton paused, remembering how badly his mother had treated Kallista.

Kallista bailed him out. "Trenton is the one who found the talon you planted in the coal shaft. We built the dragon together."

"Is that right?" He looked from Kallista to Trenton. "The two of you. Interesting."

"What?" Kallista asked, a line in her forehead starting to form. "What's interesting about that?"

"Nothing at all." Leo began to chuckle, which turned into a wet, hacking cough that shook his entire frame.

"You're sick," Kallista said, patting him on the back.

"Nonsense." He pressed the side of his fist to his mouth until the coughing stopped. "It's just this damp air." He swallowed and took a deep breath. "So, tell me what's been going on up there. Do Cochrane and his slimy cohort, Martin, still plan on taking over the world?"

"You know about that?" Trenton asked.

"Of course," Leo said. "It's the reason I tried to leave. He caught me before I could get away, and I've been here ever since. At least I had the chance to hide my notes first. You've read them, I assume?"

"No," Kallista said. "We followed your clues and found the hiding place, but Cochrane had already discovered it and burned your notes."

Leo scratched his matted hair. "I was afraid of that."

"What was in them?" Trenton asked.

"Information gathered from my research." He tapped his head. "Nothing I don't have stored up here."

"Until Trenton figured out about the errors you placed in

the schematics, I was trying to figure out where you'd gone by reading the same books you read," Kallista said.

"Really? Very clever." Her father's eyes lit up. "Tell me what you've found, and we'll see how it compares to what I put in my notes."

Kallista sat up straight, chewing her lower lip as though she were about to take a difficult exam. "All right. Well, first of all, you started by trying to figure out where the dragons came from."

"Not just where, but how and why," her father said. "*Why* could be the most important question of all because . . . ?" he prompted.

"Because the sudden appearance of massive numbers of dragons throughout the world is, um, unlikely to be a random or natural occurrence," Kallista finished.

Leo nodded proudly.

"Several key indicators point to the likelihood of a single, specific cause," Kallista continued more confidently. "Rising tensions and political alliances, specifically in Europe but spreading across the world, appear to have been leading up to what could have been a worldwide war."

"Oh, no doubt about it," her father said. "The race was on to see who could build the biggest ships, the strongest navy. It started with Britain and Germany but quickly spread to the rest of the world, including—"

"Hang on," Trenton said, waving his hand. "This all sounds really smart, but what does it mean?"

Leo gestured for his daughter to explain.

"Basically," Kallista said, "most countries thought there was going to be a big war sooner or later. They started building up weapons, mostly ships. The United States began recruiting the best scientists of the time. People like Edison, Tesla, and Bell. Probably to invent weapons of their own."

"Like the group that founded Discovery?"

"Precisely," Leo said. "In fact, I learned that among the founders of Discovery were several key scientists hired to work on a secret invention. Most likely an advanced weapon of some type. I believe they continued to work on this weapon after sealing themselves inside the mountain. At least until the failed attempt at fighting the dragons."

Trenton nodded. That made sense. If the scientists were already working on a weapon before the dragons attacked, they'd obviously continue to work on it afterwards. "So those guys you mentioned—Edison and Tesla—they were some of the founders of Discovery?"

"No," Kallista said. "They were working on another project in a place south of here called California. It was probably a weapon too."

"But something may have gone wrong with it," Leo added. "In the outside year 1906, a few years after the scientists started their secret project in California, there were an unusually large number of natural disasters around the world—earthquakes, fires, floods, volcanic eruptions. Right after that, the dragons started appearing."

Trenton leaned against the wall, stunned. "You think the weapon they were inventing was . . . dragons?"

Leo and Kallista both burst into startled laughter.

Leo shook his head. "Hardly. Creating an entirely new species in a few years would be impossible. They weren't attempting to 'invent' dragons, but whatever they did invent could have had the unintentional effect of either attracting, or more likely, releasing the dragons. The disasters seem unquestionably tied to the creatures' appearance. And the largest earthquake of all was almost exactly where the inventors were working."

"San Francisco," Kallista chirped.

"Which is where I intend to go as soon as we get out of here," Leo said.

A sudden silence filled the cell as Trenton and Kallista looked at each other.

"There's something we need to tell you," Trenton said.

Kallista squeezed her father's hands. "I don't think the Order is going to let us live. They can't risk us telling anyone the dragons are not immortal."

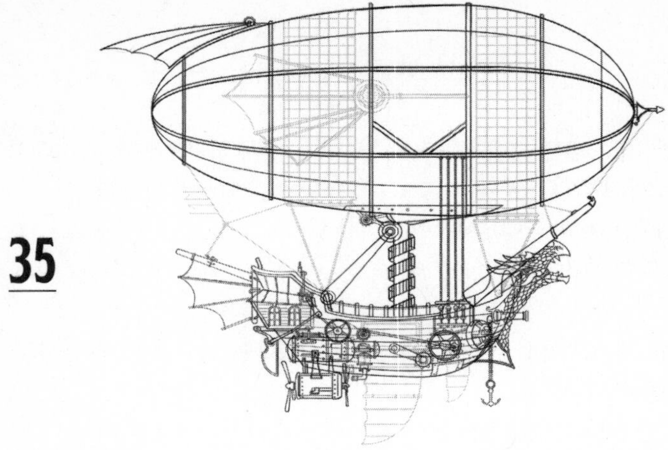

35

Later that night, someone in the bay above them hosed off the pile of parts Trenton had helped scavenge from the factory. Ice-cold water roiled down the stairs and into their cell, carrying with it dirt, grease, and small, random bits of metal.

All three of them stood on the bench, the highest spot in the room. But the frigid water still rose almost to their calves before slowly disappearing down the drain in the floor.

"I'm s-s-so s-s-sorry I was doing that before," Trenton said through chattering teeth. "I had n-n-no idea."

Leo nodded as Kallista rubbed his arms, trying to keep her father warm. "I d-d-don't blame you."

The clanging and clashing sounds of tools and machinery lasted all night and into the next day before suddenly stopping. A few hours later, they heard the sound of machines being moved above them. Trenton and Kallista tried screaming, hoping someone would rescue them, but it was no use.

"The acoustics of the tunnel direct sound down to us," Leo said, "and effectively block sound going the other way. Even if anyone did hear you, who is going to help?"

He was right. No one would help them. Trenton was going to die far away from his friends and his family, who were going to be attacked by the very weapons he'd helped create. It turned out his mother had been right all along. His mechanical skills and creativity *were* going to end up hurting the city.

After several hours of silence, Kallista said, "I think they've left for Discovery."

Trenton dropped his head into his hands. His family, his friends—they were going to let Cochrane in, thinking the Whipjacks would help them fight the dragons. By the time they realized what he was really there for, it would be too late.

The next day made it clear Kallista's guess had been right. There were no more sounds of work above them. No sounds of anyone at all. They were alone, except for a scrawny-looking man who came down with a small amount of food and water for them.

All they could do was wait to see what the Order would do to them. They could be locked up for weeks or hours; there was no way to tell.

Kallista and her father swung between long stretches of brooding silence and intense rounds of scientific debate that were mostly over Trenton's head. One time they went on for two hours discussing whether the dragons could actually communicate with each other.

"They are definitely cold-blooded reptiles, which makes any sort of pack activity highly unlikely," Leo said.

"True," Kallista said. "But you said yourself in one of your margin notes that they have alpha males who stake out their territory and defend it vigorously. So the fact that there are several dragons in the same area either means they're still determining who the alpha is—though my bet is on the black dragon—or that they have reached an agreement between themselves. Which points to their ability to communicate with each other."

"Bah," Leo said, throwing his hands in the air. "They are nothing but giant flying lizards."

"And, as I'm sure you know," Kallista said with a victorious grin, "there are several types of lizards capable of basic communication, not only between themselves, but with different species."

Trenton, who had been stretched out on the bench, trying to remember what his mother's cooking tasted like, chimed in. "The Order of the Beast believes that dragons can understand human speech and that some humans can understand dragons. Ander said they talk to each other. He said the black dragon who attacked the airship is here looking for the missing green dragon."

Kallista and her father looked at each other.

Leo shook his head. "Sounds more like mythology than science. The odds of dragons being intelligent enough to understand human speech . . . Well, let's just say in all the years the world has existed, it has never occurred. Many animals can mimic human speech, even understand basic commands, but you're talking about a species evolving the actual ability to communicate with humans in less than two hundred years. It's impossible."

Trenton agreed. He hadn't really believed Ander anyway.

The third morning after they'd been locked up, Trenton awoke to find Kallista kneeling in front of the cell door, fiddling with the lock. Her father leaned over her shoulder, giving her advice.

"What are you doing?" Trenton asked, walking over to get a better look.

"Shh." Kallista's brow furrowed in concentration. From inside the lock came a soft tapping sound.

"A little to the left," her father whispered.

Looking over their shoulders, Trenton saw that she was holding a pair of thin metal tools. She was trying to pick the lock.

"I think I've got it," Kallista said. She slowly raised her right hand.

"Gently, gently," her father said. "As though you are balancing an egg on the tip of a spoon."

An audible click sounded, and Trenton thought she'd succeeded. Then Kallista sighed, dropping the end of her broken tool on the cell floor.

"Not your fault," her father said. "The metal was too corroded."

Kallista slammed her hand against the bars. "If I had my tools, I'd have the door open in a snap."

Trenton examined the broken pick. Like her father had said, the slim piece of metal was rusted and falling apart. "Where did you get this?"

Kallista walked back to the bench. "I made it out of the scraps that washed down with the water the other night."

Scraps? Why hadn't he thought of that? Trenton hurried to the drain, looking for any more metal they could use. The only thing he found was a bolt, six inches long and roughly the diameter of his pinkie, caught in the grate. "Is there anything you can do with this?"

Kallista rubbed her eyes. "It's too thick."

"Maybe we can find something else the next time they run water down the drain," Trenton suggested. "I can help you look."

"No one's working in the bay anymore. There won't be any parts to wash down."

It had been too much to hope for. Collapsing on the bench

beside Kallista, he realized they were not getting out of the cell until the Order came for them.

A few hours later, a group of men and women in red robes and black hats arrived to lead them to their fate.

• • •

Taking his first breath of clean air outside the underground cell was like drinking a cold glass of water. Trenton filled his lungs again and again, wishing he had some way of getting the stench out of his hair, skin, and clothes.

Knowing this could be his last day alive made him want to relish his final hours or minutes—whatever he had left—even more.

"So that's the dragon," Leo Babbage said as they walked through the bay. "It looks exactly as I imagined it."

"We named him Ladon," Kallista said.

Leo nodded. "After the dragon in the Garden of the Hesperides."

Trenton shook his head. They were quite a pair.

He glanced at the charred airship, wishing he'd destroyed more of the Whipjacks' weapons. Cochrane had salvaged both cannons, leaving only an empty net cannon and a catapult on the blackened deck. Neither of them were needed for an attack on Discovery.

The giant bay looked strange now that all of the workers and machines were gone. Trenton would be happy to never see this place again. All the happy memories he'd had of building, leading, and creating had been corrupted for him. All he wanted to do was get out as quickly as possible.

"Do you think they've reached Discovery yet?" Kallista asked.

"I don't even want to think about it," he said, but he couldn't help it.

Travel between Seattle and Discovery was only a few hours when flying; how long would it take on foot? Two days? Three? Would all the equipment help the Whipjacks travel faster or would it slow them down?

If only he had some way to reach Discovery first, to get word to his family, to warn them.

When they reached the center of the city, they were marched up the marble stairs and into the hall of the Order of the Beast. Hands bound behind their backs, they ducked their heads as the citizens screamed and spit at them. Clearly they still blamed the outsiders for what had happened to their city. And maybe they were right to. After all, even if he and Kallista hadn't known what they were doing, they had killed the green dragon and destroyed the city's peace.

Would the citizens feel any different if they knew what the Whipjacks had done? What they were planning?

Trenton's stomach sank. They'd never believe him even if he told them.

This time, only members of the Order were inside the hall. Maybe the Order didn't want the ordinary citizens to know what they were doing. Or more likely, they didn't want anyone knowing the dragons were mortal.

At the front of the hall, a woman announced the patriarch. The old man, looking so tired and stooped that Trenton would have felt sorry for him under other circumstances, walked to the center of the platform and stood at the podium.

He glanced down at a paper in his hands, then tossed it aside and sighed.

Maybe he'd changed his mind. Maybe he wouldn't go through with giving them to the dragons after all.

But when the patriarch stared down at the three of them, his expression told Trenton everything he needed to know.

"You have been charged with killing a holy dragon," he intoned. "The greatest sacrilege possible. Through your actions, you have defiled all mankind."

"Which proves your beliefs have been wrong all along," Leo said. "I should think you would thank us for showing you the light."

The old man showed no sign of having heard him, but several of the members glared at Leo, hands on their swords.

"You are hereby exiled from the city," the patriarch said.

Trenton thought he must have heard him wrong. "Exile? You're letting us go?"

"You will be taken to the place of the offerings. There you will be chained to the unmoving stone and left for the holy ones. The dragons will determine your fate. They will either spare you . . . or not."

"You're insane!" Kallista yelled.

Ignoring her outburst, the patriarch turned to the other members of the Order. "Are there any here who object?"

"I object," Trenton shouted.

"You know this is wrong," Leo said. "Think what you're doing."

"Very well," the patriarch said calmly as the Red Robes remained silent. "Take them outside."

36

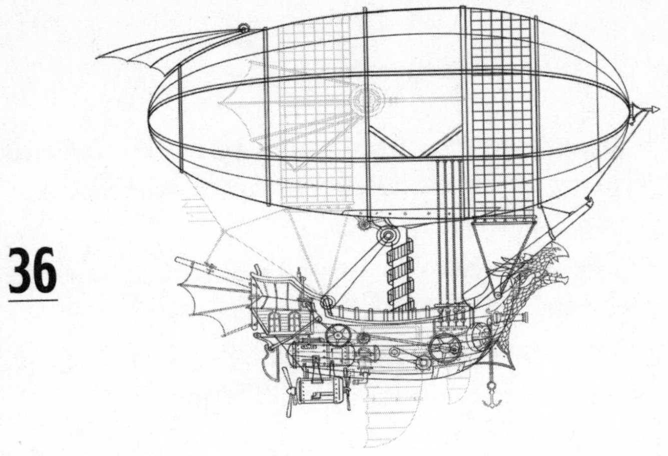

Outside, the sun was beginning to set. Trenton glanced up at the beautiful orange-and-red sky. He'd never seen a sunset before leaving Discovery. Now he wondered if this was the last one he'd ever witness.

Just beyond the Whipjacks' jousting area was a wooden platform covered with rows of chairs. A "viewing area" Trenton realized. It was close enough that the members of the Order could get a good view when the dragons came for Trenton, Kallista, and Leo, but far enough back that they could retreat inside the city if necessary.

The Red Robes led them past the viewing area to a patch of ground burned so black it appeared from a distance to be an actual hole in the ground. In the center of the patch was the circular stone pedestal Trenton had noticed the first night he'd gone up in the airship. The place of offerings. The pedestal was two feet high and ten feet across. The black stone had been polished until its surface was like glass.

The guards marched them onto the pedestal, locked thick brass bands around their waists, then ran a chain through the bands and into a ring sunk deep into the stone. When the prisoners were safely secured, a robed man cut the ropes from their hands and stepped off the pedestal.

"As decreed by the patriarch, you are placed here for

judgment. If the holy beasts refuse to come, you will be released and exiled from our city. If the holy beasts *do* come . . . may they have mercy upon your souls," he said.

"What are we supposed to do now?" Trenton asked a motherly looking woman.

"You may now put your body and soul into a state of readiness in whatever manner you wish. It won't be long."

How could she know that?

The woman moved to the viewing area with the others.

Kallista examined the lock at her waist and the one at the end of the chain binding them all to the pedestal. "If I had my picks, I could have these open in seconds."

"You don't happen to have that exploding-clock hat you used to pick the locks at the museum, do you?" he asked, trying to lighten the mood.

No one laughed.

Maybe there was something else she could use. A rock or a twig. He checked the area around them, but the stone platform was completely bare, and the chain didn't stretch far enough for him to reach the ground beyond it.

"Good-bye," Kallista said. "Thank you for being my friend."

"No. Don't say that. We're not going to die here." Trenton pulled at the band around his waist until his arms shook. He yanked at the chain. It was brand-new, not a flake of rust or spot of corrosion on it.

Back in the viewing area, the men and women of the Order had taken their seats.

"Maybe the dragon won't come," Trenton said, a jagged ball of ice tearing the inside of his stomach. "Maybe it won't come at all. For all we know, it could be miles from here."

A robed man stood and raised a long gold horn to his lips.

A mournful note floated across the air. A moment later, a distant roar answered from the woods.

Kallista threw her arms around her father. "I love you."

"I love you too," he said, hugging her back.

This couldn't be happening. Not like this. Were they really giving up? Looking around desperately, his eyes stopped on the chain. Something about it was off. Grabbing it, he saw that one of the links was not quite perfect, the two welded ends were mismatched just enough to ruin the perfect oval.

The links.

The brand-new chain.

With a flash of perfect clarity, he recalled Kallista standing in the dimber damber's office, commenting on his chain-making machine. The one Leo Babbage had intentionally designed wrong.

The links don't line up, she'd said. *One of them isn't even completely closed.*

"The chain!" he shouted, running the links through his hands.

Kallista and Leo stared at him.

"This chain was made with Cochrane's machine. Find a link that isn't closed all the way."

For a second neither of them moved. Then they both dropped to the ground, searching for a broken link.

The dragon roared again. This time it was closer.

"I've got one," Kallista yelled. She held up a section of chain with a link that hadn't quite been welded closed.

Trenton grabbed one side of the chain. "Pull."

Kallista and Leo took the other side. Straining with all their combined might, they pulled at the chain. Trenton stopped and examined the link. It hadn't budged. The metal was too strong, and the opening between the ends was too small to slip another link through it.

"The holy beast comes!" someone shouted from the viewing area.

Trenton looked up. A dark shape was silhouetted against the sky, quickly getting larger.

"We need something to pry with," Kallista said.

Trenton reached into his jacket pocket, searching for anything he could use to twist the chain. His fingers closed around the bolt he'd taken out of grate in the prison cell.

He jammed the bolt through the link and twisted, but the whole chain turned. "Wrap it around the ring," he said.

Kallista wrapped the chain twice around the base of the ring anchored into the rock. She and her father each grabbed an end, locking it in place.

Trenton twisted the bolt. It slipped in his sweaty fingers, and his knuckles smashed against the stone. Blood dripped down the backs of his fingers.

The dragon roared again. It sounded like it was right on top of them.

"Let me," Kallista said.

"No. I've got it." He wiped his hands on his pants, then slammed the bolt through the link. Closing his eyes, he pushed as hard as he could. He thought he felt something give when the bolt slipped out of his hands again. He opened his eyes in time to see the bolt roll across the platform and bounce off the edge.

He dove after it. The chain pulled him up short. It was gone.

"You did it!" Kallista cried. She unwound the chain from the ring and pulled the two links apart. She yanked the end, pulling the chain out from the bands around their waists.

Leo's head jerked back, his eyes wide. "Run!"

Trenton looked up to see the black dragon swooping toward them.

Kallista and Leo started toward the far side of the pedestal, but Trenton grabbed them. "No, this way," he yelled. Without looking back, he ran straight for the viewing area. Several of the people got to their feet, but most of them remained in the chairs, eyes locked on the sky.

He risked a glance over his shoulder. Leo was falling behind. Kallista had one of his arms draped over her shoulder, but he was struggling to keep up. Leo yelled at her to leave him. The dragon was just above them.

Spinning around, Trenton threw up his arms and screamed at the beast, "You want to fight? Come get me. I'm the one who killed your brother."

Whether the dragon understood his words or simply thought Trenton would make a better target, it swooped over Leo and Kallista and flew straight at him.

He turned and ran toward the members of the Order, who were standing up once they realized the prisoners were free. Trenton was nearly to the chairs when a shadow dropped over him.

The man with the horn lifted it to his mouth as if he could somehow send the creature away.

Looking up, Trenton saw the dragon open its fang-filled maw. A flash of orange lit the dark opening of its throat.

Trenton planted his foot and cut to the left. The dragon, unable to turn quickly, continued straight. A ball of flame passed close enough that Trenton felt the hair on the back of his neck curl. An instant later, the platform and everyone on it disappeared in a fiery inferno.

A pillar of black smoke plumed into the air, and Trenton searched for any sign of movement among the charred ruins.

The Red Robes had tried to kill him, but that didn't mean he wanted them all dead.

"Move!" Kallista shouted as the black dragon circled toward them.

Trenton spared one last glance at the ruined platform. There was no sign anyone had survived the blast.

"This way," Trenton called to Kallista and Leo, guiding them toward a door in the ground. A second after they disappeared into the earth, pulling the door closed after them, another explosion sounded from above and the door burst inward. Bricks tumbled to the ground around them. Racing through the passageways, they tried to put as much distance between themselves and the furious beast as they could.

After a few minutes, Kallista stopped to let her father rest.

"Are you okay?" she asked as he clutched his chest, coughing.

"Fine. Just need . . . to catch . . . my breath."

She whirled around to face Trenton. "'Come get me. I'm the one who killed your brother.' Did you really just challenge a dragon to fight you?"

Trenton bent over, hands on his knees. "Yeah. I guess I did."

"And I thought *I* was the crazy one."

"Oh, you are," Trenton said.

When they'd recovered enough to keep moving, Kallista asked, "Where to?"

"The bay," Leo said at once. "You've got to warn Discovery."

It took them several minutes, but eventually they found the passage that led them to the bay. Once they were inside, they barred the door that was the only way in or out, except for the double doors in the ceiling. Trenton didn't think anyone from the Order had survived the attack, and if they had, they probably wouldn't be in any shape to come looking for them, but he didn't want to take any chances.

Trenton climbed up the ladder to check on the damage to Ladon while Kallista cared for her father. He climbed over the seats, wondering what Plucky had done to the dragon and why. The hatch to the turbines was open. He looked inside and felt the blood drain from his face.

The fans were a mess. It looked like Plucky had taken a sledgehammer to them. Bits of broken blades were strewn everywhere. Even the main shaft was bent. It would take weeks to fix the damage.

Scrawled on one small spot was a message written in soot.

I'm sorry I betrayed you. I couldn't let them take your dragon too.

P

37

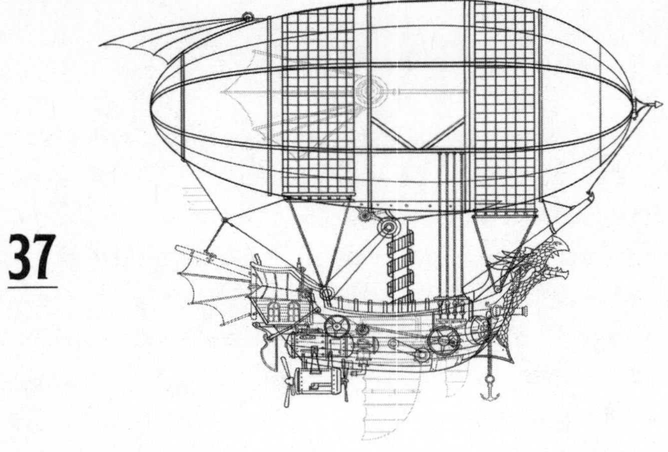

Leo Babbage started up the ladder. "Let me have a look."

"Get down from there," Kallista said.

"I'm fine." He reached the top of the dragon, muttering, "Just because I have a cough doesn't mean I'm on my deathbed."

Sitting at the base of the dragon, Trenton put his head in his hands.

"How bad is it?" Kallista asked.

"The shaft is bent, and all but a couple of the fans are smashed," Trenton said. "I'm surprised it started at all."

Kallista sat beside him. "Why do you think she did it?"

"Did what? Help Cochrane betray us or destroy the dragon so they couldn't take it with them?"

She puffed out her cheeks and exhaled. "Both, I guess."

"No idea. Why does anyone do what they do?" he asked. "The more I see of people, the less I understand them. Why did Cochrane have to attack Discovery when the people would have let him in anyway? Why didn't the city council vote to let all the people of Seattle in when they had more than enough room and could have stretched the food supply to make it work?"

Kallista ran her hand across the golden alloy of Ladon's leg. "Why didn't you and I work together when it turns out we both had what the other needed?"

Trenton couldn't help laughing, even though there was nothing funny.

Leo climbed slowly back down the ladder.

"What do you think?" Kallista asked.

Her father coughed into his fist. "It's bad, all right. By ourselves it could take as long as a month to fix it. If we could recruit some of the people of the city to help us, we might be able to fix it in a week or two."

"Fat chance of that," Trenton said.

Leo glanced at the burned-out airship. "We'd have a better chance of getting that thing airborne in less time."

Trenton tugged at the band still locked around his waist. "It would still take way too long. If the Whipjacks aren't at the city already, they will be soon."

"If only we had some way to send a message," Kallista said.

Leo sat down beside her, both of his knees popping. "Before the dragons came, you could talk to someone miles away with something called a telephone. Before that, telegraphs let you tap out a message in code. Even before that, there were many ways of communication—letters, smoke signals, homing pigeons."

Trenton had no idea what most of those things were, but it didn't matter. "None of that is going to help us. Maybe we could start a fire for smoke signals, but we'd have a better chance of getting the dragons' attention before anyone in Discovery noticed us."

"How long would it take you to build one of the fighting machines?" Kallista asked. "Like the horsecycle?"

"Too long," Trenton said. "If only there was a way to replace Ladon's turbines. The rest of him works perfectly."

Leo scratched his head. "Without the turbines, you've got no power. Although there are still two good fans. If you ripped off the broken ones and replaced that bad bit of drive, you'd probably have enough power to run the basics. Move the legs, spread the wings—that sort of thing. You could actually stay airborne, once you got him up."

What was the point? "That doesn't do us any good unless you have some way to get him in the air. It can't be done," Trenton said.

"Get him in the air," Leo murmured. He stood and began pacing the floor.

"Do you have an idea?" Kallista asked.

"No. But to a truly creative mind, 'can't be done' just means 'look for another way.' Why don't you two climb up there and get the remaining turbine fans working while I look for another way to get you airborne."

Trenton looked at Kallista. "Is he serious?"

Kallista grinned. "My father doesn't do anything without a reason."

• • •

Ripping out fan blades wasn't nearly as hard as building new ones and putting them in. Still, it wasn't simply as easy as pulling off a few bolts. Trenton had to disconnect the driveshaft, remove the entire fan mechanism, throw in a connecter to hold the shaft together, then start all over with the next one.

Also it turned out the driveshaft wasn't as badly bent as he thought. They had to remove a small piece of it, but with the removal of the fans, they were able to move the entire shaft back eighteen inches to make up for the missing piece.

Halfway through the job, Trenton heard pounding and drilling above his head. He stood up to take a look, but Kallista called him back. "He works better when people stay out of his way."

"What's he doing?" Trenton asked. They were inside the

engine, so it wasn't like her father was installing a new power source.

"Honestly," Kallista said, "I have no idea."

Forty-five minutes later there was a huge crash.

Trenton jerked around, but Kallista only shook her head. "Let him work."

Then, just as they were bolting the final piece of the drive-shaft back in place, the air shook with a noise that sounded like a cow had accidentally swallowed a tuba.

"I don't care what you say," Trenton said. "I want to see what's going on." He grabbed his tools and climbed out of the hatch. The first thing he noticed was that Leo had removed the winches from the burned-out airship, installing them on either side of Ladon's operator seats. Several hundred feet of thick cable spooled out from the winches and spread across the floor of the bay.

The next thing he saw was that the airship itself looked like someone had taken a saw to it. One side of the railing was completely torn away, and an unburned section of the hull had been cut out and turned around to form a ramp. Something else was missing, but he couldn't quite put his finger on it.

Leo Babbage himself was sitting on the ground, attempting to play a battered horn.

"What is all this?" Trenton asked.

Leo looked up, his black hair curled over his head like a crazy halo. "Trumpet. From outside year 1860, I believe. Isn't it a beauty? Did a little scouting around outside and discovered it in one of the Whipjack's abandoned homes."

Kallista climbed up beside Trenton and looked down at her father.

"Has he gone completely crazy?" Trenton asked her.

"I honestly don't know," she said. She called down to her father. "Why are there winches on the dragon?"

Leo waved a hand and produced a tortured note from the trumpet. "Fire up the engine, and let's try them out."

Trenton looked at Kallista, who shrugged.

They climbed into the seats. Kallista started up the engine. The turbines shook hard enough to rattle the whole dragon for a moment, and Trenton held his breath. Then they evened out, running as well as could be expected for a quick patch job.

Kallista raised Ladon's feet and set them back down. She nodded Ladon's head in a friendly greeting to her father.

Trenton extended the wings, tilted them back and forth, and retracted them. With fewer than half of the normal fans working, Trenton had to slow the fuel feeder down to keep from overloading the engine, but everything worked fine. Not that they had anywhere near enough power to get airborne, but he hadn't expected they would.

"Now the winches," Leo called. He set down his horn, walked to the end of the cable, and took hold. "Reel me in!"

Trenton reached forward and pulled the handle to reel in the spool. Instantly the cable began to wind up.

"Wahoo!" Leo called, his feet sliding across the bay floor. "Now release it."

Trenton pushed the handle forward, and the line spooled out. They repeated the process with the other side, and Kallista shut off the engine.

"Are you ready to tell us your plan?" Kallista asked.

"Come on down," her father said.

He took a seat at one of the worktables and motioned Trenton and Kallista to take the chairs next to him. He then opened a piece of paper and sketched out a reasonable replica of the dragon. "The most difficult part of flying is getting up in the air in the first place," he said, drawing a line representing what Trenton assumed was the ground beneath the dragon.

Trenton scratched his cheek. "Good to know."

Kallista glared at him.

"It *is* good to know," Leo said, "because it helps narrow the problem. Once you are in the air, you'll have enough power to stay there. You should be able to steer and control your altitude. And of course landing takes almost no energy at all."

He drew a pair of upward-pointing arrows under the wings of the dragon. "We tend to think of upward force as vertical, but in flying that's not the case. By angling the wings in the right direction, a good tug forward will get you up in the air. Let me demonstrate."

He stood, grabbed Trenton's hands, and yanked him forward. Trenton flew up out of his chair.

"What was that for?" Trenton asked, rubbing his arm. "You practically pulled my shoulder out of its socket."

"Exactly. The initial pull will be quite forceful, which is why I made sure to make the mounting brackets extra-strong." He sat down and sketched the winches on either side of Ladon, drawing the cables out and up as though an outside force was pulling them. "Of course, one or both of the cables could snap, but we'd find out about that rather quickly."

Kallista looked from the picture on the table to the cables laid out in front of Ladon. "Wait, are you talking about pulling Ladon up in the air with those?"

"Of course," Leo said. "Why else would I have installed them?"

Trenton stared at the inventor, wondering if this was another of his games, but Leo was completely serious. "Okay, I'll play along. What are you going to use to pull us up in the air? It's not like we have a second—"

He looked from the drawing to the sliding doors overhead. Then he saw the horn lying innocently on the floor. All at once the pieces came together, and he realized what was missing from the airship. He jumped out of his chair and looked around. There it was—directly beneath the overhead bay doors.

"Oh no," Trenton said. "We are absolutely *not* going to do that."

"What?" Kallista asked. "What are we not going to do?"

Trenton wanted there to be another explanation. He looked at Leo, silently begging him to tell him he was wrong, but the inventor simply grinned at him like he'd presented Trenton and Kallista with the best gift ever.

It took two tries before he could finally get the words out of his mouth. "He wants to hook Ladon up to a real dragon."

38

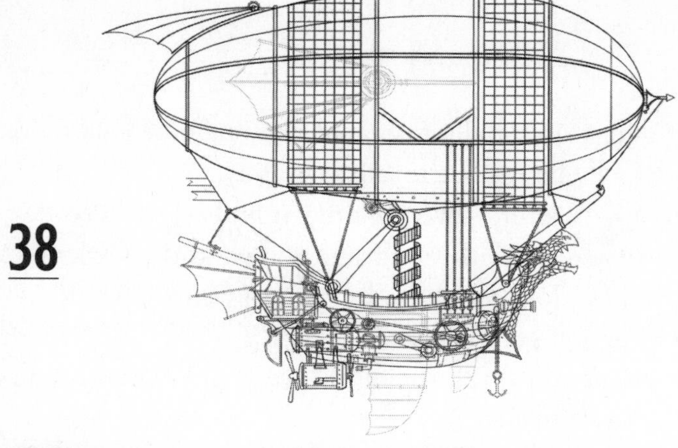

There is no way this will work," Trenton said. "If we're lucky, we'll crash into the ground. If we're unlucky, we'll be eaten alive."

"You don't have to do it," Kallista said. "We can wait to repair Ladon and fly back then."

While Discovery was attacked by weapons *he'd* built? "No," he said. "I just wish there was another way. One that had even half a chance of working."

"I think it *will* work," Kallista said. "Or at least it has a good chance of working. My father's crazy. I freely admit that. It's why he upset so many people back home. He doesn't follow the rules. Sometimes I think he intentionally refuses to even learn the rules in the first place. But that's also why so many people loved him. He's willing to try things no one else would even dream of."

They were sitting on the dragon, looking up through the double doors of the bay as the night sky slowly began to lighten. Two long cables snaked down through the ceiling doors. One side of the cables was attached to a pair of hooks which Leo would shoot at the dragon's wings using the catapult. The other side of the cables was attached to Ladon's winches.

Leo was outside, both he and the catapult covered in soot. Trenton and Kallista had tried to convince him to come with them. Surely they could find a way to get him on the dragon.

They could dump almost all of the fuel; the engine would burn a lot less with only half of the turbines anyway.

But Leo was insistent that the dragon had never been designed to carry adults. With Cochrane gone and the Order either destroyed or close to it, the citizens of Seattle would be looking for direction and new leadership.

"What makes you think they'll follow you?" Trenton had asked. "They hate outsiders."

"I won't leave you here," Kallista said. "I'm not going to lose you again."

Leo only chuckled. "With the Whipjacks gone, there's no one to keep the lights on and the water flowing. Who do you think taught Cochrane and his friends how to set up everything in the first place? To these people I will be a wizard—one whose magic is the power of technology."

Trenton wasn't sure what a wizard was, and he suspected magic was something in the fantasy books Leo had collected back in Discovery. But he also realized that the chances of Kallista and him surviving what they were trying to do wasn't much better.

And, truth be told, Leo's health wasn't good enough to survive the trip even if they did manage to get airborne. Kallista must have realized the same thing, because once she understood he wasn't going to change his mind, she hugged him and told him to be careful.

The general plan was that Leo would blow his horn, hoping to replicate the tone the Order of the Beast used to call dragons to receive their offerings. When the dragon showed up, it would see a pair of dummies dressed to look like people on the pedestal. It wouldn't take long for the monster to realize the dummies were nothing more than stuffed rags, but by that time the plan would have succeeded or failed.

Trenton clenched and unclenched his gloved fists. “So your father fires the hooks up with the catapult, somehow manages to catch the dragon’s wings, and we get shot like a rocket out of these doors. Do you realize how little chance there is of all that coming together the way we’ve planned?”

The line started to form in Kallista’s forehead. “My father is a better engineer than either of us. If the approach isn’t right, he’ll call it off, and we can try again later. But it shouldn’t be that hard. You saw for yourself how straight that black dragon has to fly, and the huge ridge of armor on its neck is the perfect spot to hook it.”

“Let’s say everything works perfectly and we do get up in the air,” he said. “What then?”

“That’s what the winches are for. By pulling and releasing the cables, along with adjusting the drag, we get ourselves steady, then we’ll release the cables and fly away.”

“And get eaten by that monster.”

Kallista shook her head. “What are you looking for? Some kind of guarantee of safety? I don’t know what will happen. Maybe we’ll get killed. In fact, we probably will. Our chances of failure are incredibly high. But you know what will make us fail for sure? Not trying.”

She spun around in her seat to face him. “I once asked my father for the best piece of advice he could give me. Do you know what he said?”

“To put a bell around his neck so you’d stop losing him?”

Kallista wrinkled her nose. “He said to give yourself permission to fail.”

“That’s real encouraging.”

“It actually is,” she said, ignoring his sarcasm. “Because if you only try the things you believe you can do, you’ll only accomplish the things you already knew you could do. But if you give yourself permission to fail, you're free to try the things that seem completely beyond your reach. And that's when magic happens."

It was so insane it was brilliant. Back when he'd been assigned to food production, he never thought he'd enjoy it. But once he gave himself permission to try, it turned out he'd actually been pretty good at it. In fact, if the people of Seattle had given him a chance, he could have taught them a few things about setting up their own gardens.

Still, he'd feel a lot more comfortable if he had something stronger than cables to influence the dragon's directional choices. Something like a nice cannon or a . . .

"Hang on," he said, unstrapping his harness and climbing out of his seat.

"Where are you going?" Kallista said. "My father's going to blow the horn any minute."

"I'll be right back," Trenton said. "I want to see if I can give us permission *not* to fail."

Leaping from rung to rung, Trenton hurried down the ladder and ran to the airship. He raced up the makeshift ramp and ran to the far end of the burned-out gondola, being careful to avoid any parts of the deck which looked ready to collapse.

The cannons were gone, which meant the Whipjacks had taken everything else of value to them in an attack, but maybe in their hurry . . .

He ran to the spot where the explosives had been. The box was gone.

Disappointment burned in his chest. He looked around to see if it might have slid down the deck. It would have been so much easier to steer the dragon if he could simply light a fuse, toss a ball, and watch the dragon go exactly where he wanted it to.

Turning back toward Ladon, he noticed a small round shape under the edge of the collapsed envelope. Pulling back the fabric, he found a single explosive. He yanked away more of the fabric and discovered two more. And there, hidden beneath a pile of rope and silver material, was the whole box. It must have flipped across the deck during the crash and tipped.

"Ready to go?" Leo called out.

"Trenton," Kallista shouted.

"On my way!" He scooped up as many of the spheres as he could carry, ducked into the cabin, which smelled sour and acrid, and found a lantern hanging on the wall. "I give myself permission to fail," he said to himself, running back to the ladder. "But I also give myself permission to blow things up while I'm doing it."

"Where did you go?" Kallista asked as he climbed back into his seat.

Trenton jammed the explosives under his seat, in his coat pockets, and anywhere else he thought he could readily grab them.

Overhead, Leo blew the horn once, then twice. It sounded like a goose choking on its own tongue.

Strapped into his harness, Trenton pulled down his goggles and waited. Beneath his feet the turbines rumbled smoothly. The tail was extended upward to try to counterbalance the upward force of takeoff. The wings were spread, angled for maximum lift. The winches had enough slack to—

"It's coming!" Leo shouted. He peeked over the side of the opening. "Good luck!"

Facing straight up, bracing themselves against the backs of their seats, Trenton and Kallista waited.

Nothing.

Nothing.

Then a dark shape passed over the doors.

Trenton heard the twang of the catapult firing.

He watched the cables.

Nothing.

Had Leo missed?

Suddenly both lines whizzed through the air, and Trenton flew backward so hard his eyeballs felt like they were being pushed into his head. His cheeks pulled away from his teeth.

His hands slipped from the controls as the bay doors rushed toward him. Ladon's front right leg caught on one of the doors. Wood and metal screeched and exploded. The dragon flipped right, then left. An outraged roar filled the air, and they were flung left, right, and left again.

Trenton's head banged against something hard, and lights flashed in front of his eyes. He looked up and saw the ground above him. How could that be unless—

"We're upside down!" he screamed. "Roll us over!"

"I'm trying," Kallista yelled. Straining to lean forward, she grabbed at the controls. Ladon swung left, back to the right, then spun all the way around.

Finally able to see where they were going, Trenton realized the black dragon was taking them straight toward a grove of tall trees.

Kallista pulled back on the winch, but it was like trying to steer an elephant with a shoelace.

"Release the cables!" Trenton screamed.

Kallista pulled the release levers, and the cables snapped free, slicing through the air with a screaming twang of metal.

Trenton pulled back on the flight stick, and branches smashed around them. They barely cleared the tops of the trees. At the same time, Kallista turned sharply left.

Realizing it was free, the black monster snarled and circled back toward them.

Without any additional propulsion, Ladon's speed was nothing compared to the black horror closing in on them.

Trenton lit the lantern, grabbed three explosives from his pocket, and waited as the monster came nearer. Staring into its glowing green eyes was like looking into the eyes of an ancient demon. He felt the muscles in his stomach go loose.

He waited until the dragon was nearly in range to blast them out of the air, then lit the fuses of all three explosives at once. He knew he had no chance of hitting the dragon dead-on, but he didn't need to. All he had to do was distract it enough for them to get away. The flame touched the fuses, and they hissed to life.

Three, two . . .

He flung the spheres, and fire immediately lit up the night. He'd actually waited too long. Bits of shrapnel pinged off Ladon's metal frame, and Trenton's ears rang.

But it worked. The dragon veered left at the same moment Trenton and Kallista dove right, angling above the thin strip of land between forest and water. Using the trees as cover, they put as much distance as they could between themselves and the city.

Trenton kept watching over his shoulder, waiting for the terrifying eyes to appear, but they never did. After several minutes had passed with no sign of being followed, Kallista looked back and gave him a nervous grin. "I think we did it."

Trenton tried to smile back, but his face muscles couldn't seem to form anything more than a terrified grimace. "Please tell me it rained back there."

"No," Kallista said. "Why?"

"Because if it didn't," Trenton said, still clutching the controls in a death grip, "I think I wet myself."

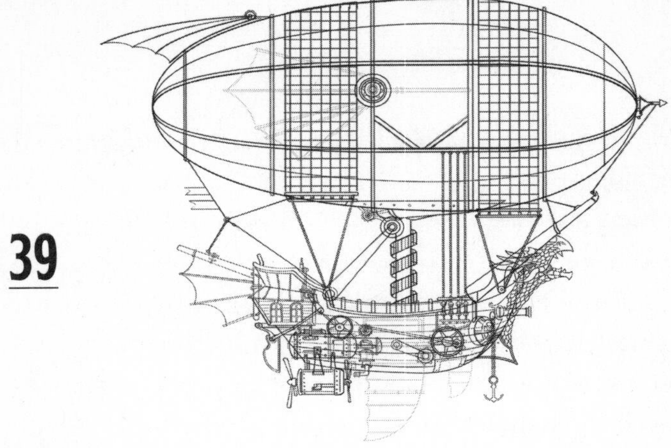

39

The closer they got to Discovery, the more nervous Trenton became. They hadn't seen a single sign of Cochrane's army. Trenton tried to tell himself it was because the Whipjacks had taken a wrong turn. Traveling on the ground would be much different than flying point-to-point. Whatever directions Plucky had been able to provide Cochrane would have been rough at best.

There were so many things that could have gone wrong with the dimber damber's plans. They could have had breakdowns. They could have been attacked by dragons. They could be completely off course and lost.

But another part of him realized Cochrane and his army could already be inside the city. For all their efforts, Trenton and Kallista might be too late. If the Whipjacks were already inside Discovery, a badly disabled Ladon would be too little, too late to save them.

Kallista glanced over her shoulder. "Have you noticed we haven't seen any dragons since the black one flew away?"

Trenton had been so focused on reaching Discovery that he hadn't noticed. But now that she mentioned it, it was odd. More than odd. True, they'd been keeping close to the tops of the trees using whatever cover they could to stay out of sight. With their limited power, an encounter with even a small dragon could prove disastrous.

But the sun had been up for several hours now. Dragons were most active in the morning, soaring through the skies looking for breakfast. They should have spotted at least two or three by now.

"Maybe we've been lucky?" he suggested.

Kallista frowned. "Something's not right. I don't like it."

Trenton craned his neck, searching the skies. She was right. The lack of dragons felt more than unusual. It seemed . . . ominous.

The closer they got to Discovery, the more his heart told him they were too late. They would arrive only to find their homes in ashes and their loved ones dead. He was so convinced that a catastrophe had occurred that when the mountain finally came into view, he was shocked to discover plumes of dark smoke weren't rising into the air.

"Down there," Kallista shouted, pointing to a spot ahead and to the left.

Trenton leaned over the side of Ladon, pushed his goggles up on his forehead, and saw what his gut had convinced him he never would. Traveling in a single-file line, still several miles from the base of the snow-covered slope leading up to the entrance to Discovery, was Cochrane's army of war machines.

The Whipjacks hadn't reached the city yet.

"Yes!" Trenton threw his hands in the air. He looked toward Discovery's closed gate. "Let's get down there and warn them."

Kallista chewed her lower lip. "We can't do that."

"Why not?" Trenton asked.

"Warning them isn't going to do any good."

Of course it would. Once the people of Discovery understood that the Whipjacks weren't there to help them, they'd refuse to let the army inside. They'd lock the gate and—

Trenton looked down at the machines, cannons, explosives, armored vehicles, and horsecycles he'd built. How long would even the best gate hold up against what Cochrane's army could throw at it? Even if the alloy bars didn't break, the rock they were set into would.

Warning the city might delay the Whipjacks getting inside for a day, even two. But with no defensive weapons to protect themselves, the ultimate result for the people of Discovery would be the same. Cochrane would get inside, and when he did, he'd take out his anger on the people who had tried to deny him what he wanted.

Trenton looked at Kallista, and a silent agreement passed between them. They knew what they had to do. He quickly counted the remaining explosives. He'd gathered twelve from the airship. They'd used three to escape the black dragon. That left nine. "Do we still have fire?"

"A little," Kallista said. "But it's not going to be as powerful, and it won't shoot as far. Also, our maneuverability is going to be extremely limited."

Looking down at the army crawling toward the mountain, Trenton did some quick calculations in his head. The Whipjacks hadn't spotted them yet. But once they did, the battle would be extremely one-sided. Those machines had been designed to offset exactly the kind of attack Trenton and Kallista were planning. How long could they survive a barrage of cannons shooting at them?

With Ladon fully functional, it would have been difficult. Now?

"We'll be lucky to damage a quarter of their weapons before they take us down."

Kallista looked grim but not afraid. "We'll fight as long as we can. Once we're too damaged to battle any longer, let's try to crash close enough to the mountain to warn Discovery of what's coming."

Trenton sat up straight, raising his chin. "Permission to fail?"

Kallista nodded. "Permission to fail."

• • •

They came in low and quiet. Trenton cut the engine speed until the turbines were barely spinning, gliding silently up behind the army convoy.

Kallista pointed at an armored vehicle loaded with boxes of explosives. If they could light it on fire, the explosion would damage several of the vehicles around it.

Hand poised above the fire button, Trenton timed his attack. *Almost, almost—*

Then one of the horsecycle riders looked up and screamed, "Dragon!"

Trenton revved the engine to give them as much power as possible and slammed his hand on the fire button. A ball of flame shot from Ladon's mouth. Kallista's aim was perfect, but the fireball wasn't as big as it should have been, and the vehicle's driver jigged the wheel at the last second.

Flames blackened the car, and the crew dove over the sides before the vehicle slammed into a tree. The explosion Trenton had been hoping for never occurred. Quickly, he lit the fuse of an explosive and tossed it over the side. The blast of white fire sent a horsecycle crashing to the ground with a satisfying crunch. The operator hit the ground and didn't move.

The Whipjacks' response was much quicker than Trenton had hoped for. Vehicles immediately broke from the line, turning to get a better position. Cannons swiveled upward. It was clear they'd become proficient at fighting dragons on their journey.

Trenton pulled back on the flight stick, hoping to get out of range, and Kallista banked right. But their climb was slower than it should have been. A boom sounded below them, and Trenton saw a puff of smoke before a cannonball crashed against Ladon's ribs.

"Take us around again," he called.

Keeping their altitude high enough to avoid cannon fire, they dropped one bomb after another on the army, but the Whipjacks had moved to a more scattered formation. At most, the explosives could take out one vehicle at a time. And from the height Trenton and Kallista were forced to fly at, it was difficult to be even that accurate with the small metal spheres.

All too soon, the explosives were gone. In order to use Ladon's flames, they'd need to get within cannon range. They wouldn't last long.

Down below, the Whipjack army was waiting.

"Ready?" Kallista asked.

Trenton nodded. "Let's do this."

Moving Ladon's controls together, they soared down on the Whipjacks.

"There," Trenton said, pointing to an all-too-familiar face staring up at him. Cochrane and Martin sat side-by-side in a heavily armored vehicle, with Weasel manning a cannon in the back. Stopping the three of them would make whatever happened after that worth it.

Before they could get within firing range, though, the cannons began blasting at them. Metal spheres soared through the air. One ripped through the metal fabric of their left wing. Another snapped Ladon's front right leg. A third came so close that Trenton felt it brush by his head.

The barrage knocked them left, right, and left again.

Kallista adjusted the wings, trying to keep them on course

while Trenton hit the fire button. Flames took out another horse-cycle and forced a Whipjack shooting one of the cannons to dive for cover. But the dimber damber was untouched.

Explosions sounded all about them, smoke filling the air. A cannonball the size of a fist smashed the side of Ladon's neck, knocking the dragon's head askew.

Cochrane skidded the armored vehicle to a halt, and Martin leaped out of the passenger side, running toward something a group of Whipjacks had wheeled out from under the trees. It took Trenton a moment to realize what it was. When he did, he yanked back on the flight stick.

"Catapult," he screamed.

It was one of the weapons he'd built for the airship. Only this one wasn't armed with hooks or nets. The large wooden bucket at the end of the arm was packed with small metal balls—fifty or more explosives, their fuses braided together.

Kallista turned right, trying to take evasive action, but the left wing wasn't responding.

A Whipjack lit the fuses on the bombs as a second one swiveled the catapult to follow their flight path.

Martin pointed a finger directly at Trenton, his face flush with excitement. "Fire!"

Trenton hunched his shoulders, knowing they were about to be blown to pieces.

Then a burst of flames shot from the other direction, engulfing the wooden catapult in a bright orange ball. A second later, the pile of bombs exploded in the bucket, flipping a nearby armored vehicle and blasting a crater in the ground.

Trenton saw a figure fly through the air, red robes bright with flames, then everything disappeared behind a curtain of black smoke.

Trenton spun left, trying to locate the source of the attack.

Sunlight flashed off metal. His mouth dropped open, and he stared dumbstruck as a second metal dragon soared above the ground a hundred yards away.

"Ladon?" he asked, wondering how their dragon could be in two places at once.

"No," Kallista shouted. "It's not Ladon; it's a copy of him!"

A cannon fired, and the second dragon wobbled away. Whoever was at the controls obviously didn't have a lot of flying experience. They turned with unsure, choppy movements. But they *were* flying.

A shadow crossed the ground to the right, and a second blast of fire nailed a pair of horsecycles. Trenton turned. A third dragon—a second copy of Ladon.

Kallista whooped, a wide grin on her face. "We've got help."

Two copies of Ladon? How had this happened? Who'd built them? And when? Trenton rubbed soot from his goggles. He recognized the people at the controls of the first dragon. "It's Simoni," he said. "And Angus."

He couldn't have been more surprised if someone had told him his mother had become an inventor. The two dragons circled overhead, and Trenton craned his neck to get a better view. "Clyde!" he shouted. "That's Clyde in the backseat of the other dragon." The sun blinded Trenton for a moment, and he couldn't see who was driving.

The second dragon circled around, laying down a stream of fire that sent Cochrane and Martin's vehicle racing for cover, and Trenton got a clear view of the person in the front seat.

Kallista clapped a hand to her mouth. "It's Plucky!"

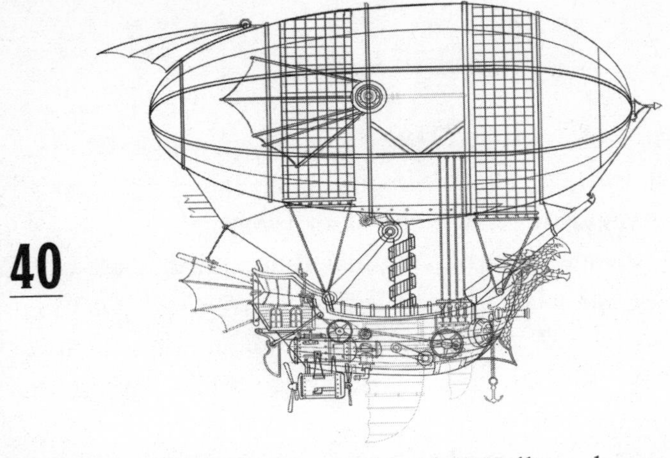

40

Since when is Plucky on our side?" Kallista shouted.

Trenton had no idea, but it was clear she was fighting *with* them.

The metal dragons, though . . . That wasn't something someone could throw together in a few hours or even a few days. With a finished set of plans and a full crew, it would take a month or more to build two dragons from the ground up. They would have had to have started around the time Trenton and Kallista left to look for her father. The only smelting factory capable of making the alloy was on the second level. The level where—

"Dad," he whispered. That's what his father was talking about when he said he might have something up his sleeve.

Simoni and Angus circled around for another attack when an explosion rocked them sideways. Their dragon spun in the air, clipped a pine tree, and nearly went down.

Above the range of the cannons, Kallista circled as Trenton searched for the source of the explosion.

Something moved in the branches of a nearby tree, and he spotted the bald Whipjack woman wearing a heavy backpack. "She's throwing bombs," Trenton said, pointing.

Kallista nodded and headed that way. Trenton saw the woman light one of her explosives, and he hit the fire button. A gout of orange leaked from the side of Ladon's injured neck, but enough hit the trees to cloak the nearby branches in a wreath of dancing flames. The woman screamed, and her bomb dropped to the ground, exploding near the base of the tree.

"Nice shot, yeah, yeah!" a familiar voice called.

As Plucky soared by on their left, Clyde waggled their dragon's tail. "I'm a dragon pilot!" he shouted. "Flaming destruction."

"Go destroy something!" Kallista yelled back, shooing him away.

Trenton had no idea why Plucky was there or how any of the other three knew how to fly a dragon. But with three Ladons in the air, their odds suddenly looked a lot better.

He signaled to Plucky, forming an X with his arms, and shouted, "Crossing pattern."

She must have understood, because she circled to the right, while Kallista banked left.

"Cannons can't turn from side to side quickly," he called to Kallista.

Attacking from the east, Plucky aimed at one ground-based weapon after another while Clyde strafed them with flames. As the Whipjacks turned their weapons to track them, Kallista soared in from the other direction, and Trenton used what fire he had left to blast them from the back.

Simoni quickly picked up on the plan. No longer able to focus on a single target, the Whipjacks found themselves trying to attack while simultaneously watching over their shoulders for approaching dragons.

Confused, the army began to lose its focus. Cochrane screamed instructions, but nobody was listening to him. One by one, the Whipjacks abandoned their weapons and ran for the trees.

Soaring above them, Simoni, Angus, Plucky, Clyde, Kallista, and Trenton blasted the abandoned vehicles.

"They're retreating," Simoni shouted, her face beaming.

"Don't even think about messing with my city!" Angus shouted, shaking his fist.

They'd done it. They'd fought off the Whipjacks!

"Great job!" Trenton shouted, his face breaking into a delighted grin.

There were a few Whipjacks remaining, but most of their weapons were flaming hulks, and even if they managed to regroup, the knowledge of what was waiting for them if they tried to attack again would surely send them running home.

He couldn't wait to get into the city and find out when and how his friends had turned into dragon riders. He was still smiling when a cloud of yellow gas came out of nowhere, and they flew straight into it.

• • •

Trenton instinctively ducked, covering his face with the sleeve of his jacket. The stink of burning leather filled the air, and his head felt like it was on fire. He yanked off his helmet. It was covered with bubbling acid that had nearly worked its way through the heavy material. His jacket was smoking as well. Trying to brush the acid off with his heavy gloves, he heard a scream.

Kallista turned around, batting at her face. Trenton's stomach lurched. Her eyes were gone, lost beneath a mass of steaming yellow goo.

"Help!" she cried, flailing her hands in the air.

No, he realized. It wasn't her eyes; it was her goggles. Quickly, Trenton unsnapped his harness and leaned forward. He grabbed Kallista's flight helmet in both hands, ripped it—and the goggles—from her head, and flung everything over the side.

Kallista coughed. Tiny red burn marks speckled her cheeks and chin. He prayed she hadn't inhaled any of the fumes.

"What was that?" Kallista wheezed.

"I don't—" Trenton began before looking past her. The side of the mountain raced toward them. He pointed forward. "Watch out!"

Kallista turned, saw the mountain, and cut hard left. Ladon's damaged wing groaned. The metal fabric snapped back and forth. Trenton yanked the flight stick toward him, trying to avoid the rocks and snow. The dragon's back foot brushed against the ground. An icy white cloud exploded around them. The controls shuddered in Trenton's hands, and he fought to keep his grip.

They hit the ground again, bounced, and then they were back in the air.

"Are you okay?" Trenton yelled. The front of his jacket was still bubbling, dark holes burned through in several spots. He ripped the ruined jacket off, and the wind tore it out of his hands.

"I think so." Kallista coughed. "What happened?"

Trenton searched the sky, his eyes stopping on the same scarred, acid-breathing red dragon they had fought the day they'd found the compass. It was coming in for another attack.

"Simoni!" he shouted. "Plucky!" Where were the others? Why hadn't they come to help?

He spotted a flash of metal to the right. Simoni and Angus were flying away from the mountain at high speed. He couldn't understand why until he saw a blur of gold zipping up behind them. It shot a small fireball that they narrowly avoided but only by flying straight into the path of another yellow creature ahead of them.

Two gold dragons? Where had they come from?

A roar sounded from the other side of the valley. Trenton's

head snapped around, and he saw Plucky and Clyde locked in battle with the green dragon.

Trenton blinked. That was impossible. The green dragon was dead. This one was slightly smaller. A younger sibling or a child, maybe?

The green dragon shot a fireball that caught the edge of the metal dragon's wing. Plucky jerked them into a sharp bank, coming around for a better angle.

Clyde shouted and pointed. Something huge and blue rose out of the trees. It was another dragon, but its wings were three times as long as its body, billowing in the air like sails. Its stomach stuck out so far it was almost comical.

But there was nothing comical about the way it screeched and flew straight toward Plucky and Clyde. Realizing the danger, Plucky turned toward the blue dragon. When they were aimed straight at it, Clyde hit the fire button.

A blast of flames raced toward the blue dragon. Trenton expected it to veer away from the attack. Instead, it opened its mouth and shot out a gush of steaming water that not only extinguished the fireball coming toward it but also soaked Plucky and Clyde in boiling liquid.

"Shoot it!" Kallista yelled, and Trenton turned to see the red dragon coming directly at them, its jaws wide. He slammed his fist down on the fire button. The resulting fireball was small, but it was enough to drive the creature away. At least for a moment.

Trenton took a quick count—one, two, three, four, five. Five dragons appearing at once? That *couldn't* have been an accident.

"They're working together," Kallista said, circling to keep the red dragon from their flank.

Yes. That's exactly what they were doing. They had

appeared together, and they were working in teams, the same way Trenton and his friends had worked together to attack the Whipjacks. The gold dragons had taken on Simoni and Angus, using their speed and agility. The blue and green dragons were teaming up on Plucky and Angus.

The only dragon attacking by itself was—

Trenton got a sick feeling in his stomach.

A blast of fire caught Ladon directly in the chest. Metal shrieked, and all the gauges on Trenton's control panel spun into the red.

A massive creature rammed into their side, knocking them up and to the left. With his harness still unsnapped, Trenton clutched at his seat to keep from falling out. He turned his head and stared directly into the face of the black dragon. In a second of perfect clarity, he saw the way its eyes lit up, as though powered by an inner fire. Its jagged teeth were yellow with age. A small, perfectly round scar marked the gleaming black scales on the side of its head.

Then they were falling.

Ladon spun through the air as the ground raced toward them. Kallista tugged on her controls, trying to pull them out of the dive. With one hand gripping the side of his seat, Trenton fought to pull back on the flight stick.

Ladon's wings shuddered and squealed. The dragon hadn't been built for this kind of attack. It was falling apart. Gears and brackets clattered and dropped away. With only seconds to spare, they pulled out of the spinning dive. But it wasn't going to matter.

Kallista pointed toward the ledge outside the gate to the city. It was their only chance.

Trenton nodded and tried to get enough elevation to make it that far. The engine was still running, but barely. He threw the fuel feeder control all the way forward, closing the steam release valve to build up pressure. Inside the turbine, the remaining fans screamed. He pushed the throttle all the way forward and pulled the altitude control back.

With no time to think about what was chasing them, Trenton focused on the opening at the back of the ledge. Wind sheered them to the right, and Kallista corrected. The needle in the pressure gauge snapped to the far side of the red. They dropped below the jutting rock of the ledge. Pulled up. Dropped down.

Trenton yanked back on the stick with all his strength. The engines howled. They were over, just barely.

Kallista was screaming something, but he hadn't been able to make out her words. Now he realized what she was saying: "Get down! Get down! It's shut!"

Trenton looked ahead, and his heart stopped.

They were flying straight toward the opening at full speed, and the gate was closed.

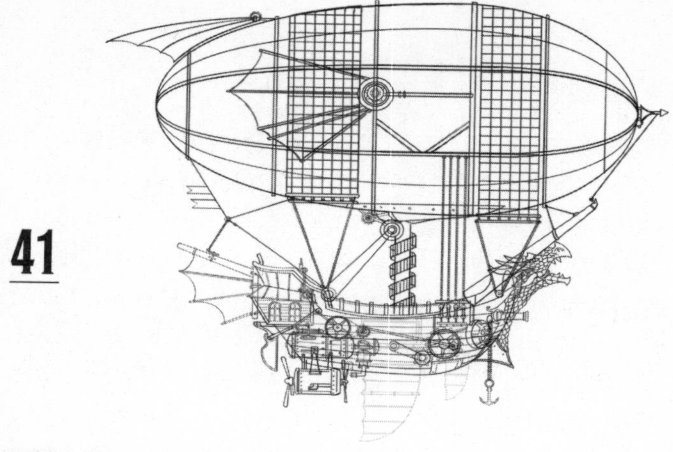

41

Two guards stared out through the bars in complete terror.

"Open the gate!" Kallista screamed.

Trenton tried to land them on the ledge, but they were coming in too fast. One leg snapped off, then another. He tilted the wings all the way forward, trying to use them as brakes, but it wasn't going to be enough.

They hit the ground hard, and Kallista's head slammed into the back of Ladon's neck. They bounced again, slid, but miraculously the gate was rising. Trenton ducked and saw sparks as Ladon's head hit the bars. Then they were inside, spinning and bouncing across the rough stone floor of the first level.

Eventually, they scraped to a halt several hundred feet inside the entrance.

Trenton sat up painfully. "Are you okay?"

"Fine," Kallista murmured. She pulled open her harness and rubbed her head. "Dragons," she said, sounding dazed. "How many?"

"Six." Trenton got out of his seat. "There's no way the others can hold them off. We have to get back out there."

Footsteps clanged on Ladon's ladder, and Trenton's father appeared. "You aren't going anywhere on this."

"Dad!" Trenton lunged forward and hugged his father. "I'm so glad to see you. Outside," he gasped. "Dragons."

"I know," his father said. "We've been up here watching since

Plucky arrived last night and warned us about the Whipjacks' plans."

"*Plucky* warned you?" Kallista asked, leaning across the back of her seat.

"She snuck out of their camp and climbed the mountain all night to warn us. She said she'd made one mistake and couldn't stand to make another."

Trenton shook his head. He had no idea what made that girl tick. He didn't have time to worry about that now, though.

"The metal dragons, were they—"

"—the project I've been working on?" his father finished. He nodded. "We had the plans and the materials. With the increasing number of dragons outside, it only made sense to build up some defenses. We've had several of the city's children training on them. Simoni, Angus, and Clyde have been practicing especially hard. I think it's because they wanted to help the two of you."

"Get another one ready," Trenton said, climbing past his father. "Kallista and I have to get back out there and help them."

His father's face fell. "We don't have any more. I'm sorry. We only had time to build two."

Outside, the sound of dragons roaring was punctuated by explosions.

Trenton jumped the rest of the way down Ladon's broken frame to the floor and ran to the gate. It was closed again. Several guards were watching what was going on outside. Trenton yanked on the bars. "Open this up! We have to help them. They're outnumbered, and they don't have enough flying experience."

"There's nothing you can do," his father said. "We don't have anything else to fight with, and your dragon isn't getting up in the air anytime soon."

Trenton spun around, looking from one person to another. "You're just going to leave them out there?" He slammed his fist against the bars. The black and red dragons had returned to the battle. Now it was six against two.

Plucky, Simoni, and the others had given up on offense, dodging and dipping in a desperate attempt to avoid the overwhelming numbers, but it was only a matter of time before the dragons closed in on them.

Kallista had jumped down from Ladon. She ran her fingers through her hair, looking more like her normal self. "The secret weapon."

"The secret what?" Trenton's father asked.

"When the founders first built Discovery, they were working on a secret weapon to fight the dragons." Kallista's eyes gleamed. "We have to find it and use it."

Trenton ground his teeth. Why were they wasting time on this? "We have no idea what it was or if it actually existed. Even if it did, that was over a hundred years ago. It's long gone by now. Maybe we can flag down Clyde and take control of his dragon."

Kallista took a step forward and grabbed his arm. "Listen to me. My father researched the inventors who founded our city. He's positive they were working on a weapon. Something powerful. Something no one but the top minds in the world could have imagined back when they were building it. He's sure the men and women who designed it would have saved it, even if they decided never to attack the dragons again. Just in case."

Trenton shoved her hand away. "Don't you think someone would have found it by now if it was here?"

"Not if they hid it. My father thinks they locked it away somewhere safe. Or buried it, maybe. Before we left Seattle, he told me to search for it when we got here."

"Great, so we just start digging everywhere—" Trenton stopped. *Buried.* If the founders did keep whatever they had been working on, and if no one had discovered it in over a hundred years, it almost had to be on one of the two levels that had been off-limits until recently. Buried on one of the top two levels—

He turned to his father. "The tunnel on level two. Have you dug through the rocks piled at the end?"

"Not yet," his father said. His eyes snapped wide. "You think the founders hid something there?"

"It makes sense. You said yourself it looked like the rocks had been placed there on purpose."

"What are you talking about?" Kallista asked. "What tunnel?"

"The mine shaft where we found the material for Ladon's wings. When Plucky and I came to meet with the city council, my father took me into the abandoned mine shaft on the second level. Come on," he cried. "We have to hurry!"

They took the freight elevator to the second level, raced to the mine, and hurried to the back of the shaft.

"There it is," Trenton said, pointing to the pile of rock. "But how do we get past it?" He wished he still had some of his explosives.

"Leave that to me," his father said. He ran back out the tunnel. A few minutes later, the sound of a steam engine filled the air, and his father drove in, seated behind the controls of a piece of heavy mining equipment. "We brought one of the diggers up here to start mining the coal seams," his father yelled over the noise of the engine. "Stand back."

Trenton and Kallista moved away from the pile of rocks. Grabbing each other's hands, they watched as Trenton's father used the large claw on the front of the machine to rip away at the pile.

"What if he accidentally damages the weapon?" Trenton shouted.

"Then we better hope there are a couple of good mechanics nearby," Kallista called back.

The machine clawed out an especially large boulder, and suddenly the entire pile came down with a roar. Rocks bounded down the tunnel, and the billowing dust made it impossible to see.

"Dad!" Trenton screamed, running forward.

A figure stumbled out of the gray cloud, waving a hand in front of his face. "I'm fine."

"Look," Kallista said, pointing through the haze of smoke.

There was an opening behind what remained of the pile. A door.

Quickly, they clambered over the rocks and through the door. A short passage led to a small circular room. Graffiti was scratched into the walls, including a heart with the initials KS+RB, as though whoever had last been there were wishing them luck.

In the center of the room was something covered by a large sheet.

The cloth was so old that it disintegrated in their hands when they tried to lift it off. Kallista brushed away the remaining strands to reveal a long metal barrel mounted on a tripod. A series of metal rings encircled the barrel. As Trenton moved around the back, he saw a handle with a trigger.

"It's a gun," he said. "I think. Or a cannon."

A large box was attached to all three legs under the barrel. A series of copper wires connected the box and the gun. The metal should have corroded years ago, but the rocks had protected it from any outside air.

Kallista opened a hatch on the back of the box and sniffed. "Coal dust. This is like a miniature steam engine. I think it powers the gun."

"Let's start it up," Trenton's father said. He ran into the mine and brought back some small pieces of coal, which he placed into the box.

"This looks like the ignition," Kallista said. She pressed the button, but nothing happened.

Trenton shook his head. "Broken. Maybe that's why they couldn't defeat the dragons with it."

"Hold on." Kallista looked under the box. "What's this?" She started turning a small crank. Something whirred inside the box. Steam puffed out from a small vent on the side.

"It's doing something!" Trenton cried.

Lights began turning on around the box. The rings around the barrel of the cannon started vibrating, creating a strange harmonic sound.

The three of them stepped away.

When nothing else happened, Kallista and Trenton looked at each other. "Should we try it?" she asked.

"We need to be careful," Trenton's father said. "We have no idea what might happen. The whole thing could explode."

"We don't have time to be careful," Trenton said. "The others are in trouble out there."

He started forward, but Kallista beat him to it. She walked around to the back of the gun, leaned down, and put her eye to the gun sight. "Stand back." Putting her shoulder to the stock of the gun, she rested her finger on the trigger, took a deep breath, and pulled.

The rings around the barrel changed pitch. The harmonics shifted to a loud whine. The box vibrated.

A soft red circle appeared on the wall, then went out.

"That's it?" Trenton asked.

"I guess it doesn't work," his father said.

Trenton couldn't believe it. How could it build up to all of that, then do nothing? "Why would they have bothered hiding it if it didn't work?"

He walked around to where the light had come out of the barrel, and, being careful not to stand directly in front of it, examined the opening. "Does this look like something's missing?"

Kallista joined him. She examined the end of the barrel and nodded. "It's like a piece should slide right here. A lens or something."

That's what he'd thought too. Only the spot where the lens should go looked like something else. "What does that shape remind you of?" he asked.

"It looks kind of like a dragon," Kallista said. "At least the head of one."

"A lens shaped like a dragon's head," he murmured. He'd never seen this weapon before, so why should that seem so familiar?

An image appeared in his head, and he knew what it was.

He turned to his father and Kallista. "I know where the missing piece is. See if you can move this. Take it outside the gate where we can get a clear shot at the dragons. I'll meet you there."

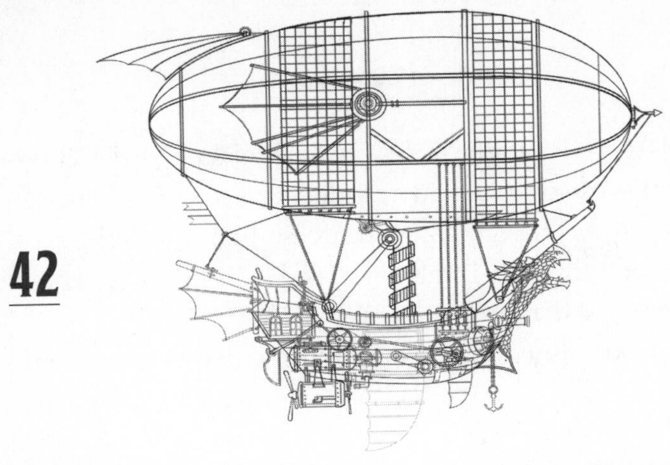

42

On the main level of the city, people were preparing for an attack. Citizens were barring windows and stacking bags of rocks and dirt around their doors. Heavy mining equipment had been parked at strategic intersections. Trenton wasn't sure what that would do against dragons, but maybe they weren't aware of what had happened. Maybe they still thought they were preparing for the Whipjacks to invade.

Racing toward the center of the city, he tried not to think about what would happen if he and Kallista failed. One dragon had nearly devastated the city. What would happen if six got inside? Barred windows and bags of rocks wouldn't stop fire, or acid, or boiling water.

How had things gotten so bad so quickly? Maybe Ander had been right. Maybe dragons could talk to each other. Clearly they were coordinating their attacks to create the greatest advantage. Did that mean Ander had been right about everything else as well? Could dragons understand humans?

As he ran up the steps to City Hall, another thought occurred to him. The dragons had shown up right after the Whipjacks' weapons had been eliminated. Was that a coincidence? Or were the dragons actually cunning enough to hold off their attack until the ground weapons were destroyed? And if they were smart enough to do that, what else might they be smart enough to plan?

Inside, the building was deserted. He assumed the council members were all occupied outside. He entered the council chambers, and there, right where he'd last seen it, was the head to Chancellor Lusk's silver walking stick. He picked it up, knowing at once it was the missing piece.

It only made sense that the lens to the secret weapon should be there. The walking stick had been passed from chancellor to chancellor since . . . Well, apparently since the founders hid their weapon. What better way to make sure no one used the weapon again without the government's approval? Trenton shuddered at the thought of how close the lens had come to being lost forever.

Holding up the silver dragon's head, he peered through the glass lens in its jaws. If it was more than a hundred years old, would it even work? It could easily have been chipped or cracked during its years of use. He had no way of knowing how that might affect the weapon.

There was only one way to find out for sure. Clutching the lens, he hurried out the door. Mr. Darrow, Angus's father, was standing in the hall.

"What are you doing in here?" the big man demanded. "Thought you could break into the offices while everyone is preparing for the attack *you* caused?"

Trenton stared up at him. "I didn't cause anything."

"You showed the outsiders where we live," Mr. Darrow growled. "Led them right to our doorstep. I heard you even built the weapons they brought to attack us."

"I don't have time—" Trenton said, trying to push past him.

Mr. Darrow grabbed Trenton's wrist. "What's this? Stealing from us as well? You're a traitor and a thief." He tried to grab the lens away, but Trenton twisted out of his grip.

"Right now your son is outside the city fighting six dragons."

Trenton held up the lens. "This may be the only thing that can save him. Get out of my way or I swear I'll do whatever I have to, to get past you."

Mr. Darrow must have seen something in Trenton's eyes, or maybe it was the tone of his voice. He blinked, then stepped away.

"You're a coward and a fool," Trenton yelled as he ran past. "And one day, your son is going to realize it."

Back at the elevator, he waited impatiently for the creaking car to make its way to the top level, all the while wondering if his friends were still alive.

At last the elevator clanged to a stop, and Trenton ran out. The gate was raised just enough to squeeze under, and Kallista and Trenton's father were outside on the ledge. They had mounted the weapon on a wheeled metal cart.

Trenton looked out to where Simoni and the others circled and dived. It was clear the two metal dragons had taken heavy damage, but his friends were still alive. He breathed a deep sigh of relief.

"Did you find the lens?" Kallista asked.

Trenton ran to the front of the weapon and held up the silver dragon's head.

Kallista gave a start. "Isn't that from . . . ?"

"Chancellor Lusk's walking stick," Trenton's father said.

Trenton slid the lens into the slot. It fit perfectly. "It's all that was left after the dragon ate him."

Suddenly, in the middle of a war, with dragons roaring all around them, Kallista grinned. She giggled.

"What's so funny?" Trenton asked. He wondered if the stress had finally gotten to her.

Kallista wiped her eyes. "Can you imagine what Chancellor Lusk, the man who hated creativity and new ideas more than anyone, would have done if he'd discovered he was carrying around the most creative, new idea the city had ever seen?"

Trenton's father chuckled. "I'm sure he would have destroyed it immediately."

"Let's be glad he didn't," Trenton said. He hurried to stand behind the gun. He pressed his cheek to the side of the barrel, his finger on the trigger.

Kallista pressed the button on top of the box and cranked the handle.

The rings around the barrel rose to a high-pitched squeal.

"Shoot!" Kallista yelled.

Trenton swung the gun to the right where the pair of gold dragons were trying to drive Simoni and Angus toward the acid-breathing red dragon. He locked the closest of the two dragons in his sights and pressed the trigger.

A flash of light shot out from the cannon. This time, though, instead of a weak red circle, the line of light was so intense it seemed to burn his retina. Instantly a circle of flame rose from the gold dragon's wing. Screaming in pain, the dragon peeled away from the fight.

Shrieking, the second gold dragon followed, giving Simoni and Angus enough room to maneuver away from the red monster in front of them.

"Plucky and Clyde need help," Kallista said, pointing left.

Trenton swung the cannon to see the two of them desperately trying to evade the red, green, and blue dragons. It was clear they'd taken a lot of damage, and their flying was growing more erratic as the two of them panicked.

The green dragon turned to attack. Trenton trained his sights on it and pulled the trigger. Nothing happened.

"What's wrong?" he yelled, pulling the trigger over and over.

"I think it needs to cool down and power up again," his father said. "The lights on the rings are starting to glow again."

Trenton waited until the rings were fully lit, then centered his aim on the blue dragon's belly and fired. Smoke hissed from the blue scales, and water steamed out.

"We have to bring them closer," Kallista said. She waved her arms in the air. "Plucky, over here!"

Trenton turned to his father. "You better go back inside. It could get dangerous out here fast."

His father put a hand on Trenton's shoulder. "I'm not going anywhere."

Plucky and Clyde broke away from the fight and flew toward them, but the green dragon was close on their heels.

The black dragon circled warily, watching from a distance. Trenton remembered the small circular scar he'd seen on the side of its head. Could that have come from this weapon? Was it one of the dragons that originally attacked the city?

Trenton waited until Plucky and Clyde were almost right on top of him.

The green dragon swooped low, opening its mouth to attack. Trenton aimed at its head and pulled the trigger. Red light shot out, but the dragon swerved and the beam only singed one leg.

"What is that thing?" Clyde yelled as they flew by.

"A light cannon," Trenton shouted back.

The green dragon circled. This time, recognizing the real danger, it flew straight at Trenton and Kallista.

Trenton turned the cannon on it, but the power hadn't cycled up enough yet, and when he pulled the trigger, nothing happened.

"Shoot it," Kallista said.

Trenton pulled the trigger over and over. "I can't. It won't fire."

As the dragon spread its jaws, a pair of fireballs hit it in rapid succession. It spiraled down and away, wings fluttering.

"Take that!" Angus yelled, pounding the side of his mechanical dragon.

"You want more?" Simoni screamed. "Because we've got a lot more."

The cannon lights came back on, and Trenton fired at the approaching red dragon, searing the base of its tail. The acid-breather yowled and wheeled away from both the metal dragons and the cannon.

By now, the uninjured gold dragon had returned. It zipped toward Simoni and Angus, but Plucky and Clyde came up from under it and nailed it with a fireball.

Between the two dragons and the light cannon, they were able to whittle the number of dragons down to four, then three, then two.

Focused on trying to hit the green dragon attacking Plucky and Clyde, Trenton didn't notice the sound of an engine approaching until it came up over the rise.

"Look out!" Kallista yelled.

Cochrane was behind the wheel of an armored vehicle just over fifty yards away. Standing behind him, Weasel had a cannon aimed directly at them. He held an open flame inches from the fuse.

Trenton started to turn his weapon, but the dimber damber raised a hand. "One move and Weasel'll kill the three of you. Isn't that right, my boy?"

"Sure is." Weasel grinned.

Trenton would have liked nothing more than to punch him in the face. He eyed the Whipjacks. He knew his weapon was more powerful and could fire faster than theirs, but the rings were still warming up.

"Step away from your gun," Cochrane said.

Slowly Trenton raised his hands and moved back.

Kallista looked toward the metal dragons, both engaged in battling the green dragon, but Cochrane shook his head. "Tell 'em to keep their distance or I blow you all up."

Trenton wanted to think the dimber damber was bluffing, but he knew better than that.

"Stay back," Kallista shouted, waving their friends away.

"What do you want?" Trenton's father asked.

Cochrane gave a high-pitched laugh. His eyes had always looked a little wild, but now they looked completely crazy. "Everything. 'At's what we wants, ain't it, Weasel?"

"Right ya are," Weasel agreed.

"You might be able to kill us," Trenton said, "but as soon as you do, our friends will kill you."

"That's not how this's going to work," the dimber damber said. "See, you're going to tell the guards to open up the gate and let us in. Once we're inside, the gate closes and the city is mine. We'll see how well your friends hold up once the dragons realize there's no one shooting at them."

"We won't do it," Kallista said. "We won't let you take the city."

"You will, luv, and you'll do it right now," Cochrane snarled. "I'll give you to three. One . . . two . . ."

Trenton's father suddenly looked up. "Watch out!"

Trenton knew it was a trick. A desperate ploy to draw the Whipjacks' attention. He kept his gaze on Cochrane and Weasel, hoping they'd look away so he could fire the light cannon.

The Whipjacks must have suspected a trap too, because they didn't even flinch. "Three," Cochrane said. "Kill them."

At that moment, an earth-shattering roar filled the air.

Trenton looked up and saw the black dragon diving toward him. It must have been watching, waiting until it knew no one could shoot it with the light gun. Then it attacked. Talons spread, mouth wide, it plunged toward him.

While everyone else was in shock, Kallista darted forward, swung the light cannon up, and pulled the trigger, all in one smooth motion.

It was a direct hit. The heavy armor on the black giant's neck glowed red and exploded. Out of control, the dragon spun toward the ground. It tried to recover, but it was going too fast. Screaming in agony, it shot a blast of flame as it smashed directly into Cochrane's armored vehicle.

Hundreds of pounds of explosives went off in a ball of fire that sheared the edge of the ridge completely away.

For a moment, everything seemed to freeze in place. Then dragon, vehicle, and hundreds of tons of rock crashed down the side of the mountain in a thundering avalanche.

With the alpha dragon gone, the last remaining dragon screeched and fled back toward the woods.

Kallista wiped a hand across her sweat-covered face, stepped back from the light cannon, and said, "Don't call me 'luv'!"

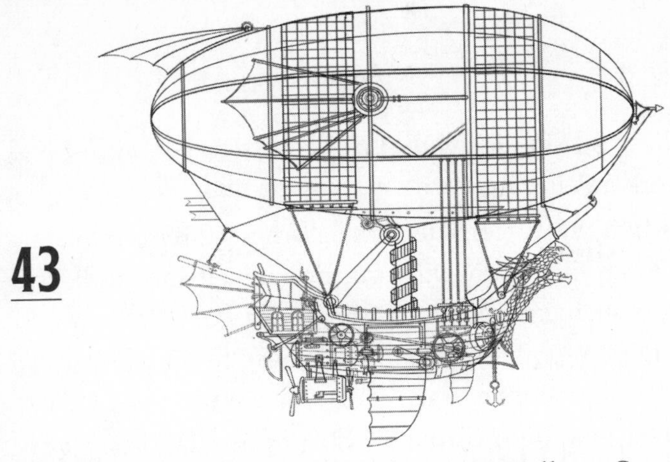

43

Standing outside City Hall, Trenton, Kallista, Simoni, Clyde, and Angus talked quietly among themselves. A few feet away, Plucky wound her leg braces, although Trenton suspected they were already plenty tight. He could tell she was no longer comfortable in the city.

When the door finally opened and he saw his father and Chancellor Huber step out, he knew what the decision was by the expressions on their faces.

"You're going to seal the entrance again."

The chancellor frowned. "We have no choice. Three more dragons have appeared in the last forty-eight hours alone. That makes ten sightings in the week since the black dragon died. I don't think there's any question they know what happened here. We can only assume more are on the way."

Kallista tugged on her gloves and tucked a telescope into the pack slung over her shoulder. "It's only a matter of time before there are too many for the light cannon to hold off."

"We think that's what happened to the city's founders," Trenton's father said. "They thought they had created the perfect weapon. They didn't count on the dragons bringing in reinforcements. Eventually they were overwhelmed."

Simoni folded her arms across her chest, cupping her elbows with her hands. "How soon?"

"We'll set off the first round of explosives as soon as you leave," the chancellor said.

"And when the dragons dig through that?" Trenton asked.

"We've salvaged enough gunpowder from what the Whipjacks brought to take down the entire side of the mountain if we need to," Trenton's father said. "And we can use the mining equipment to brace things up from inside. I don't see them ever making it through." He gripped Trenton's arm. "There's no need for you to go out there again. With all the new dragons . . ."

"I can't live trapped inside a mountain anymore," Trenton said. Until he'd seen the outside world, his city had seemed perfect. Well, maybe not perfect, but livable. Now that he knew what he was missing, he could barely stand being locked away from the sun, fresh air, and forests. "I want to see the ocean at least once in my life."

"We're going to find where the dragons are coming from," Kallista said. "My father thinks it's a place called San Francisco. Once we locate them, we'll do our best to stop them at the source."

The chancellor nodded. "If anyone can, it's the two of you."

Trenton turned to the others. "You don't have to come. You heard my father. You'll be safe if you stay." He chewed the inside of his cheek. "It might even be better if you didn't come. Kallista and I will be okay on our own."

"You're a terrible liar," Simoni said.

Plucky nodded. "What a great clanker, yeah, yeah."

"Besides," Simoni added, "now that I've discovered what a good flier I am, I'm not letting anyone else take my dragon. I'm going."

"I'm an artist, not a fighter," Clyde said. "But I want to see the outside world so I can paint it and share it with everyone here. I'm going too."

Trenton's father turned to Plucky. "You know you're perfectly welcome to stay here. If it wasn't for you, the Whipjacks might be running the city right now."

Plucky shook her head. "Wouldn't know what to do here, yeah, yeah. Likely end up snatchin' an' grabbin' everything in sight and find meself up on the three-legged stool."

"We don't hang people here," Trenton said. "No necktie parties."

Plucky shrugged. "Wouldn't feel right to stay. I'm going."

Trenton looked at Angus. Honestly, he was surprised the boy was there at all. "Why do you want to go? You've always said you don't care about anyone outside the city."

Angus cracked his knuckles. "I'm not going for anyone outside the city. I'm going for me. I've got a taste for hunting dragons."

Trenton wondered if that was true or if Angus was still trying to impress Simoni. Either way, Angus had proved himself to be a capable flier. And despite what he'd said, Trenton thought it would be a lot easier to stay safe with three dragons to protect each other.

The six of them gathered their supplies and took the elevators to the top level, where all three metal dragons had been repaired and outfitted. Things went much faster when you had plenty of trained mechanics and all the right equipment on hand.

"Take a minute to say good-bye to your families," Chancellor Huber said.

"Your mother wants to talk to you," Trenton's father said.

Trenton knew there wasn't much time before they had to leave, so he hurried to his mother's side, kneeling by her wheelchair. She took his face between her hands. "I still don't like these contraptions of yours."

"I know," he said.

"But I'm proud of you. You've saved the city twice now." She glanced toward the city entrance, where a dozen guards stood poised with telescopes, cannons, and explosives. "I hope you find a way to stop those dragons. I'm tired of being trapped in this hole."

"I could take you up for a flight," Trenton said with a mischievous grin.

She glared at him. "That's not funny." She kissed Trenton on the top of the head, then looked over his shoulder. "Plucky, come here and give me a hug."

Plucky hung back, but Trenton's mother and father urged her to come forward.

"Trenton told us about what happened to your family," Trenton's mother said.

Plucky glared at Trenton, her face red.

Trenton's mother turned Plucky's chin back so they were looking at each other. "When you get done out there, I want you to know that you have a home to come back to."

Plucky looked shocked. "You'd want me back? After everything I done?"

Trenton's father patted her shoulder. "You mean how you left your own people to warn us of the attack? Or how you courageously fought in the face of dragons and cannon fire to save our city?"

Plucky nervously tapped at her mechanical leg braces, eyes cast downward. "Them wasn't *my* people. My people never would'a done what Cochrane and his crew done, yeah, yeah. Don't figure I rightly gots no people now."

"Yes, you do," Trenton's mother said, pulling her into a hug. "*We're* your people."

Plucky's eyes filled with tears, which she quickly tried to brush away. "Thank you. When I get back, I swears I'm making you a rum pair'a these mechanical braces for yer legs, ain't I? Get you plum out that chair o'yours."

Trenton's mother blinked and forced a smile. "That would be very . . . nice."

"Everyone on your dragons," the chancellor called. "It's almost dark. Time to go."

As Trenton and Plucky walked toward the dragons, he asked, "What made you change your mind? Why did you turn against Cochrane?"

Plucky shuffled her crooked legs. "You and your folks treated me like I was a real person, didn't they? Ya took me in, yeah, yeah? I done for my family once. Didn't wanna do it again."

Trenton nodded. He felt like there might be more to her story, but he'd let her tell the rest of it when she was ready. He and Kallista climbed onto Ladon while the others climbed onto their dragons. In unison they started their engines with a roar.

Trenton had been trying for the last week to come up with a great exit line, but he hadn't been able to come up with anything special. Instead, he turned back to the chancellor. "We've saved the city twice now. I think we deserve a reward."

The chancellor tilted her head. "What did you have in mind?"

"After you blast the entrance, you'll still need to keep the vents open to get fresh air."

She nodded. "And?"

Trenton and Kallista looked at each other. They'd been discussing this for a while. Kallista cleared her throat. "The vents are too small for even a gold dragon to get through, but a person could. We're going to tell the people of Seattle that if they come here seeking safety, you've agreed to let them in. All of them. The same goes for anyone else we might find. It's about time the citizens of Discovery started looking out for someone besides themselves."

The chancellor and Trenton's father glanced toward each other.

"Raymond Coleman!" Trenton's mother snapped. "Do you really have to *think* about that? If you don't want to find a locked door when you come home tonight, you will answer yes, right now!"

Trenton's father rubbed the back of his neck and smiled. "I guess the answer is yes, then. We'll figure out a way to help anyone who needs our help."

Trenton and Kallista shared a grin.

The six friends lowered their goggles and, one by one, raced their dragons out of the mountain entrance and into the cold night air.

Epilogue

The sun was rising when Trenton signaled to the others. "Down there!" he called, pointing to where the city of Seattle lay hidden underground. Behind him, the two dragons circled slowly in the air. After just one full day of flying outside, his friends already looked more steady.

Clyde and Plucky made a great team. She kept a constant eye on everything, never missing a chance to get the most out of their turbines, and he kept everything relaxed, cracking jokes and talking nonstop. Trenton thought Plucky would have gotten sick of it by now, but she seemed to enjoy his constant banter.

Simoni and Angus argued almost constantly, but they'd also turned out to be a pretty good team. She was an amazing navigator, and his aggressive approach to flying and attacking had proved to be quite effective. Already he'd played a big role in fighting off two dragon attacks.

Kallista lined them up for a landing.

"We need to get in and out—quick," Trenton said. "More and more dragons are showing up."

"I know," Kallista said. "But I need to make sure my father is all right, and we promised we'd tell the people of Seattle they can go to Discovery. They might not have treated us very well, but everyone deserves a chance for peace."

Before they could land, Trenton realized something was

wrong. The entire landscape was different. As they neared the double doors to the bay, his heart leaped into his throat. It looked like a war had taken place. Huge holes had been ripped in the ground. The smell of charred wood, and worse, filled the air with a dank stench.

Dropping lower, he could see the blackened wreckage of homes and storefronts sticking out of the holes like skeletal fingers. Clothing, furniture, and tools were spread in a wide circle—all burned black.

"What happened?" Simoni cried, placing her hand over her mouth.

Trenton saw a flash of white in one of the deep pits and realized it was the remains of the stone steps in front of the Order of the Beast's headquarters. The dragons had been here. They had dug up every home, store, passage, and tunnel and had scorched them all, destroying whatever remained.

He searched the ground for some sign of movement, listened for cries for help. Surely the dragons couldn't have killed everyone in the city.

But there was no movement. No sound. Nothing.

"We have to go," he said, pulling back up.

Kallista spun around and grabbed his arm. "No, take us down."

Trenton shook his head. "Don't you see? Your father . . ." He couldn't bring himself to say the words. Tears burned his eyes. This was their fault. The dragons had taken revenge for the battle outside Discovery by murdering every defenseless man, woman, and child in Seattle.

They should have come sooner. They should have forced Leo to come with them back to Discovery. He put his head over the side of the dragon, gagging until he was hoarse.

"Take us down," Kallista repeated, her face resolute.

Trenton nodded and led the three metal dragons to the blackened opening where the bay doors had once been.

As soon as Ladon touched the ground, Kallista was over the side. She climbed partway down the ladder, jumped the rest of the way, and ran screaming, "Father! Father!"

Trenton wiped his mouth and climbed down after her.

He looked up at Plucky, whose eyes were dark and unreadable. "Do you want to . . ."

Plucky shook her head, mouth set in a straight line. "Ain't nuffin for me to lay me peeps on here, right? What I wants is to get outta this place and kill me some dragons, yeah, yeah?"

Trenton nodded. "The rest of you stay here. Keep an eye on the skies. If anything shows up, take off immediately. Don't wait for us."

"Don't worry," Angus said. "If any of the dragons that did this show up, they're all mine."

Clyde ran a hand over his eyes. "Would you like me to talk to Kallista?"

"No," Trenton said.

Reaching the floor of the bay, he considered going after her himself, but even in ruins, the city was a big place. And honestly, he didn't know what he'd say if he found her.

Instead, he waited for her to come back. He couldn't imagine how hard it was for her—finally finding her father, only to lose him again.

At last he heard footsteps coming down the hall. Kallista walked through the door, face and hands stained black with soot. She walked toward him. "They're all . . ." She stopped, unable to go on, and began to sob.

"I'm sorry," Trenton said, putting his arms around her and pulling her toward him. She buried her face in his chest. Standing in the center of the burned-out bay, they cried together. He felt the warmth of her tears soaking through his shirt, and he let his tears drip onto her shoulder.

When they were both cried out, he swallowed hard. "Did you find . . . ?"

Kallista shook her head. "There aren't any bodies. The dragons must have . . ."

She didn't have to finish. He knew what she meant.

Kallista clenched her fists and stared into his eyes. When they'd first met, he'd been the shorter of the two, but now their eyes were on the same level. "We're going to find them," she said, her voice soft but deadly serious. "We're going to make them pay."

Trenton nodded. If he'd ever needed proof that dragons were monsters, here it was.

"Come on," he said. "Let's get out of here."

He began to walk toward the ladder that would lead them out of the bay, then froze. Kallista, who had already begun climbing, stopped and looked down. "What is it?"

"I'm not sure," Trenton said. "It's just . . ."

He glanced around the bay. Something looked different. Well, everything looked different. The walls and floor were charred. The forge was melted into a pile of slag and rock. Even the cell where they had been locked up was dug out and savaged.

All of that made sense. Something was wrong, though. Something was . . . *missing*.

All at once he turned around and stared. His heart began to race.

"Trenton?" Kallista climbed slowly down the ladder. "What's wrong? What are you looking at?"

"It's not what I'm looking at. It's what I'm *not* looking at." He pointed across the bay, his finger trembling. "The remains of the airship. They're gone."

ACKNOWLEDGMENTS

As always, this book wouldn't be what it is without the incredible staff at Shadow Mountain publishing. Chris, Lisa, Richard, Rachael, Heidi, Sarah, Julia, and Ilise—you rock!

Brandon Dorman, your art inspires and delights. Thanks for taking what is in my head and bringing it to life.

Thanks to my BETA readers Jackson Porter and Cori Bailie. Your insights were inspired.

Thanks to Ander and Mikey for letting me put you in my book.

A special thanks to my agent, Michael Bourret, for inspiring, encouraging, and giving me the best advice—whether I wanted to hear it or not. I'm amazed they haven't given you your own Super Agent movie yet.

Finally, a heartfelt thanks to my family. My incredibly supportive and amazing wife, Jennifer. Your name should be on the cover above mine because I could never do what I do without you. My kids—Scott and Natalie Savage, Erica and Nick Thurman, Jacob, and Nicholas—thanks for giving me the time and encouragement (and Diet Coke) I need to make stories. And lastly to my five awe-inspiring grandkids: Graysen, Lizzy, Jack Jack, Asher, and Cameron. None of this would matter without my family to share this with.

Activities

1. *Gears of Revolution* fits into a genre called steampunk, which often focuses on technology. List all of the machines you can remember from this book. Then list machines from other books you've read recently. If you were writing a steampunk book, what machines would you include?
2. To save Ladon, Trenton and Kallista enter a jousting contest riding machines that are part mechanical horse and part motorcycle. If you could design a machine that was part animal and part metal, what would it look like? Make a poster of the machine you would ride.
3. Leo Babbage leaves a compass for Trenton and Kallista. Did you know you can make your own compass? All you need are a few supplies.

    - A needle, pin, or a straightened paper clip
    - A magnet
    - A piece of cork, wood, or anything that floats
    - A bowl or cup of water

    Stroke the needle, pin, or paper clip across the magnet fifty times to magnetize it. If you don't have a magnet, you can use a piece of fur or even your own hair. Poke the needle through the cork until it sticks out evenly on both sides.

Float the cork in a bowl or cup of water. The needle should align itself with the Earth's magnetic fields and point north.

4. When J. Scott Savage was researching the city of Seattle for *Gears of Revolution*, he discovered that there was a great fire just as Dimber Damber Cochrane describes in the book and that the people really did build their new city on top of the old one. Search the Internet or your library for "Seattle Underground," and read about the tunnels that still exist today. If you were writing a fictional story that took place in your city, what real places might you include?

Discussion Questions

1. Leo Babbage repeats a quote from Benjamin Franklin: "An investment in knowledge pays the best interest." Look up the definitions of *investment*, *knowledge*, and *interest*, and discuss whether or not you believe this quote is true.
2. The Whipjacks use different words than the members of the Order of the Beast. Depending on where you live, you might use any of the following words for a carbonated drink: *soda*, *pop*, *soda pop*, or *coke*. You might call a deli sandwich a *hero*, a *sub sandwich*, a *grinder*, or maybe even something else. Can you think of other things that are called by different names in different places? Why do you think different people use different words for the same thing?
3. The Order of the Beast believes the best way to get along with the dragons is to feed them. The Whipjacks believe the dragons should be attacked. If you lived nearby dragons, would you fight them, feed them, or do something else?
4. Kallista says that what she learns while trying to find her father is more important than whether she succeeds or fails. Do you agree? Describe a time when what you learned from a game was more important than whether you won or lost.
5. Trenton notices that the city of Discovery is organized and safe, but everything looks the same. Seattle is disorganized,

but people can build their houses to look like whatever they want. Which type of city would you rather live in? Why?

6. When the librarians of Seattle realize that dragons are going to burn down their city, they protect as many books as they can by putting them in the basement. If you could only protect five books, which books would you choose? Why?
7. Ander thinks that dragons and humans can talk to each other. Leo and Kallista aren't so sure. What do you think? Do you ever talk to your pets? Do you think they understand you? Do you understand them?